I0593684

Kylie Chan started out as an IT consultant and trainer specializing in business intelligence systems. She worked in Australia and then ran her own consulting business for ten years in Hong Kong. When she returned to Australia in 2002, Kylie made the career change to writing fiction, and produced the bestselling nine-book Dark Heavens series, a fantasy based on Chinese mythology, published by Harper *Voyager* worldwide. She is now a full-time writer based in Queensland's Gold Coast.

Kylie's website is at www.kyliechan.com.

Books by Kylie Chan

Dark Heavens
White Tiger (1)
Red Phoenix (2)
Blue Dragon (3)

Journey to Wudang
Earth to Hell (1)
Hell to Heaven (2)
Heaven to Wudang (3)

Celestial Battle
Dark Serpent (1)
Demon Child (2)
Black Jade (3)

Dragon Empire
Scales of Empire (1)
Guardian of Empire (2)
Dawn of Empire (3)

Council of AIs
Minds of Sand and Light (1)

KYLIE CHAN

MINDS OF SAND & LIGHT

BOOK 1 OF THE COUNCIL OF AIs

Minds of Sand and Light was supported by HOTA, Home of the Arts, Queensland, through HOTA's Artist Fund: Rage against the V(irus).

Content warning: This book contains scenes of graphic and medical violence, and themes of oppression of minorities that some readers may find distressing.

ISBN: 978-0-6458837-0-1 (pback)
ISBN: 978-0-6458837-1-8 (ebook)

Published by Kylie Chan
First published in Australia
in 2023 by HarperCollins Publishers Australia Pty Ltd

Copyright © Kylie Chan 2023

The right of Kylie Chan to be identified as the author of this work has been asserted by them in accordance with the Copyright Amendment (Moral Rights) Act 2000.

This book is a work of fiction and any resemblance to actual persons, living or dead, is purely coincidental.

All versions of this book are subject to the condition that they shall not, by way of trade or otherwise, be lent, resold, hired out, or otherwise circulated without the author's prior consent in any form of binding or cover other than that in which it is published and without a similar condition, including this condition, being imposed on the subsequent purchaser.

Cover design and illustration by Christine Armstrong
Cover images by iStockphoto.com and Robert Bye/Unsplash
Author photo by Bradkay Photographix
Printed and Distributed by LightningSource Pty Ltd (IngramSpark)

1

The muddy smell of the Thames made the crumbling area even more unpleasant. The embankments on this less affluent part of the river weren't high enough to deal with encroaching climate change, so the intensifying flooding that overwhelmed the Thames tidal barrier had made it unprofitable for businesses to remain. A warehouse on the bank had nearly worn down to nothing, the rusting ribs of its roof supports poking out of its graffiti-covered carcass. Long grass had pushed its way through the cracked concrete covering the ground, and was now dying in the summer heat. The churning of the electric engines on the river boats, not visible behind the embankment, echoed over the decay.

A siren sounded further up the street and a group of ragged, feral children between the ages of six and twelve charged past Ruth, screaming and laughing. A pair of London Metropolitan surveillance drones – forty centimeters long in their blue-and-white livery – followed them. The children dived under cover in the warehouse and the drones stopped to hover, ran their cameras over the area, eyed Ruth for a while and then left.

Ruth checked her tablet again – the drone she wanted was in a predictable looping route that came from the more expensive side of the river, passed over this abandoned

1

warehouse, then went further along over fenced storage yards and back over the water to fly between the glass office towers. It was on its way.

She stopped when she saw an emaciated figure lolling against one of the crumbling brick walls. He looked as though he was in his early twenties, but he'd obviously been on the streets for a while and his ragged clothes were hanging off him. A hand-written sign that was so faded it was almost illegible leaned on the wall next to him, and he had an empty paper cup at his feet, so he was propped up to beg. He stared blankly at Ruth, then his empty expression filled with an open-mouthed wide smile as drool strung from the side of his mouth. He made a few mindless noises at her.

Ruth switched her tablet to the London NHS mental health services. 'This is wrong, mate, they shouldn't be using you like this. Let me get some help for you.'

One of the children charged up to her and spoke with a thick street accent. 'Leave him, Miss, there's nothing you can do.'

'The authorities, social services, they can put him in a home or something ...'

'Nah, Miss,' the boy said. 'See the sign?'

The other children appeared from the ruins and gathered around her as Ruth peered at the faded writing on the sign.

MA MAYTE CHESTR HERE DID A FUKIN SUPID FING AND HAD 2 LUANGUAGE CHIPS PUT EN. GIV IM SUM COIN CAUS HES A FUKIN STUPED KUNT.

'Oh, you poor, stupid bastard,' she said to Chester.

'He already had a High Standard language chip to work the wharf, then he gone and got himself a Spanish girlfriend, didn't he?' the boy said. 'Weezer at the bio-shop told 'im that it was safe to have a second chip put in.'

A little girl in a tattered dress giggled. 'And the stupid fucker believed him!'

The rest of the children approached Chester and patted him

on the back, muttering platitudes. He smiled open-mouthed and drooling at them.

'He had his wallet on him when he got here, so we use his ID for piece work,' the biggest boy said.

Ruth opened her mouth to protest but the little girl chimed in, obviously mimicking a social worker, 'You can't do that, child labor is illegal!'

They all found this hilarious and laughed.

The biggest child touched the wall behind Chester. 'Leave 'im, Miss. If you call the police or ambulance, they'll come and laugh at him, then walk away, because he did it to 'imself. Sometimes the Met cops rough 'im up, as well.'

'We look after him!' the little girl said with pride, and the rest of the children chorused in agreement. Chester made wordless sounds of pleasure at them.

Ruth's tablet pinged, and she checked it. The drone was over the river. She ran to the bank, skipping over the fractured concrete and broken glass, and looked up. She checked the tablet again – less than fifty meters away. It became visible flying over the water. It was half as big again as the Met drones, made of dark purple carbon fiber, and a small laser weapon hung from beneath its body.

'Oh shit!' the little boy shouted. 'That's one of them Paris drones, we need to hide! They have those laser things ...'

'I know,' Ruth said, starting the algorithm to hack into its control stream.

'It's coming! Run!' the boy shouted, and the children scattered.

The hack worked and Ruth said, 'Yes!' under her breath as the download meter started. She followed the drone along the bank as it flew on its circular route. It was preparing to go back over the river and she needed the full set of control codes before it flew out of range ... The tablet pinged, and the download was complete – she had the control code suite for the hijacked drone. Once she'd decrypted the codes, she could bring the drone down, access its memory, and find out why these armed Paris drones kept appearing above London airspace.

She did a little dance of triumph, then carefully stowed her tablet in her rucksack and looked around. She wanted to talk to the children about getting them help ... but they were gone.

Before heading back to the office, she stopped at Chester, who was still grinning and drooling. 'Next time I'm here I'll bring you something to eat. This isn't right.'

Chester didn't respond.

*

Ruth promised herself for the millionth time that she'd sweep the layers of dirt from the stairs as she went down to the basement that held Uptodate News. One of the double doors was stuck, and she needed to fix that as well. She entered the office part of the studio: two desks facing each other with a divider in a room barely big enough to hold them. A glass wall on the far side gave a view of the production booth, stacked high with aging second-hand video-processing equipment, and beyond that was the studio itself, only slightly bigger than the office, with the camera and lights. Cassie and Ruth had spent both their inheritances on the studio and it badly needed updating – but there was no money to be made as an independent news source that told the brutal truth about the Party's activities.

Cassie's face popped up over the edge of the divider. She was in her early thirties, like Ruth, taller and leaner with long blonde hair pulled up into a messy bun and a long, narrow face that never stopped moving. They'd met when doing doctoral research at London U, both supported by the same scholarship program. Cassie had majored in film and video editing, and was a brilliant video engineer, but didn't mind voicing her shared distaste for the Party – so of course she was just as unemployable as Ruth.

Ruth stopped in the doorway when she saw what was silently playing on the big screen above the production window. It showed their Latvian genocide story, the one for which she'd hacked into one of the Greater Far East's own drones – but as well as the Uptodate watermark, there was a Global Network News watermark, a GNN chyron, and the closed captions said, 'FakeSlayer software has confirmed the video to be authentic. It appears that this hacker is accessing one of the GFE's own drones and showing what seems to be mass destruction on an unprecedented scale in the disputed Latvian territories'.

'I have to go, Kittylover, my business partner's back,' Cassie said into her headset.

'We've been talking for five years now, Pukewrangler.' The voice that responded from the computer speakers sounded young and Japanese and could be either male or female. 'Let's have an anniversary real-life meetup? I think it's about time.'

Ruth furiously shook her head at Cassie. There were definitely targets on their backs since they'd released the Latvian story, and occasionally a couple of GFE agents parked across the road from their office and tried to intimidate them.

'I'm not comfortable with a real-life meetup just yet,' Cassie said.

'I will always respect your needs. Give Chonkers a kiss for me and I'll see you at the raid later.'

Cassie loudly kissed the top of their unimpressed ginger cat's head where he lounged on her desk. 'Done.' She tapped the keyboard to disconnect the call and pointed at the screen. 'GNN authenticated the video and bought the story. It's gone viral, has millions of views, and is causing a *major* online uproar. We did it.'

Ruth did another little success dance.

'You are very cute sometimes, Ruthie,' Cassie said. 'The licensing money came through already, and they said they'll pay full price next time now that we've proven we're legit.'

Ruth sighed with relief. 'Did you pay the rent?'

Cassie threw both hands in the air. 'We will not be evicted from the studio!' She lowered her arms. 'But there was hardly anything left over after I made the landlord happy.'

'That won't be an issue if I manage to hijack a Paris drone and find out why they keep showing up over London,' Ruth said as she pulled her tablet out of her rucksack and placed it on her desk among the code printouts.

'I told them you were working on that,' Cassie said. 'They said the Paris drones are impossible to hack, but if you can do it, they'll pay us a big bonus. They didn't seem to be worried.'

Ruth connected her tablet to her desktop computer. 'They should be. I've accessed the drone control feed and all I need to do is reverse-engineer the control codes. It could take a while, but I will do this.'

'More than two days?'

'They use sixty-four-bit encryption, so it might take a little longer – like four to six months.'

'You can do it, Ruthie!' Cassie said.

Ruth sat at her desk and pulled up her coding suite. 'Start thinking how much of a premium we'll charge GNN when we break *this* story.'

*

The cargo drone carrying the three platforms arrived at the secretary's residential location in Spring Valley, the exclusive enclave for the rich and powerful in Washington DC, and hovered to check the area. The interior of the drone was cramped, and Zheng's vision was full of Lim's eight segmented carbon-fiber legs and the top of Basim's smaller six-legged infiltration platform. The three infiltration platforms were fast, multi-legged and small, carried by a larger flying drone that would drop them at the location and then hover to monitor and provide comms support.

'The gymnast's arrived at the mansion, you're cleared for

insertion,' Eztar said. 'Comms check.'

'Zheng copy. Corporal Lim?'

'Copy.'

'Private Basim?'

'I've changed my name to Bashen,' Basim said, speaking High Standard with a slight accent.

'About time,' Corporal Lim said. 'The Party was asking me why you were still using such an ethnically inferior name; you were about to be disciplined for it.'

'Comms check!' Zheng repeated.

'Copy,' Bashen said. 'Sorry, Sarge.'

'If your connection quality drops, let me know immediately,' Zheng said. 'You may be sitting comfortably back at base, but I'm not. My brain coffer is inside this platform, I'm a long way inside hostile territory, and it's inevitable that we'll be detected. Quickly in, film the gymnast, out. Got it?'

'Yes, Sarge,' the other two said in not-quite-unison.

'We have your back,' Bashen said.

Zheng's brain in its liquid-filled coffer didn't feel the carrier drone plummet directly down from three hundred meters but did register the vibration as it thumped onto the ground, opened its hatch, and extended its ramp. Zheng led the other two platforms, remotely controlled by Bashen and Lim, out onto the street. Lim's big platform was the size of a dog, the platform containing Zheng's brain coffer was slightly smaller, and Bashen's reconnaissance platform was the smallest – the size of a mouse and flat enough to fit under doors. The cargo drone lifted off and flew straight up to monitor and relay from a thousand meters above.

Zheng led the other two platforms to scurry along the gutter through the expensive neighbourhood. The street was flanked by big trees and tidy lawns, and the high walls that hid the multistory mansions of the ruling class.

'Stop and wait there,' Eztar said. Her voice filled with dismay. 'You have an addition. Nine o'clock.'

Zheng spun the sensors to look left, and then up, and couldn't believe what walked out from behind a traffic control box. It looked like a middle-aged European man in a suit.

'Are you serious?' Zheng asked.

'Good evening, Revolutionary Hero Zheng,' the man said, and Zheng was too gobsmacked to reply.

'We're not having an organic along on this,' Lim said.

'He's a senior Party representative,' Eztar said. 'Full cooperation is required.'

'He's *white*,' Lim said. 'How can he be senior Party?'

'I'm white too,' Bashen said. 'Doesn't mean anything.'

Zheng moved closer and did a scan, hoping that the internals didn't match the externals. Unfortunately, they did. Squishy flesh, leaky blood, brittle bones, the whole works. The addition wasn't wearing a helmet over his oh-so-fragile brainbox – and there was even a brain in it.

'You are actually here in person?' Zheng asked, incredulous.

'That isn't your real body, is it?' Lim asked. 'You have a *brain* in there.' He lowered his voice. 'What the actual everloving fuck. Who brings their brain on a mission?'

'We will not be able to perform to spec with an *organic* along,' Zheng said to Eztar, then returned to group comms. 'I'd like to remind you that I have a brain in here, Corporal.'

'Yeah, but your headmeat's in a titanium coffer,' Lim said. He waved his weapon at the ground near the organic's feet. 'This is a squishy brain in a spun-glass chassis.'

'And it's way too big,' Bashen said. 'We're small for a reason, Sarge.'

'They call you Sarge? Why?' the addition asked.

Zheng went up onto the platform's four back legs so that its sensors were level with the addition's waist. It really was a human male, clothed and unarmed, and appeared to be in its mid-forties. 'Sir, we're a small team doing a quiet infiltration and compromisation, and you are both too large and too ... *organic* to be here right now. Our minder confirms your credentials so if you insist, I must take you – but your presence is putting the mission in jeopardy and *the glorious wellbeing of the nation is of primary importance, above all personal and group needs, wants, desires and wishes.*'

'I represent the Party, and the Party is infallible,' the addition said, and quoted the *Speeches* right back at Zheng. '*The wellbeing of the Party is linked to the nation, indivisible, and the Party has precedence in all things.*'

'Help, Eztar,' Zheng said on comms.

Her voice was strained. 'Full co-operation is required.'

'I am here to observe,' the representative said. 'I will follow you to the site, then link up to comms and review as you fulfil the mission.'

The link pinged with the private channel notification from Eztar. 'I'd prefer not to be scrutinized, Zheng. Some members of my family fought in the resistance when the Party liberated Rom ... Luomania, and my file is still flagged by the political branch.' Her voice became plaintive. 'I don't want to face questions about my loyalty ever again. Please.'

'I have your back, honey, don't worry,' Zheng said. 'My loyalty can never be questioned and I'll look after you.'

'Thank you.' Her voice lifted. 'You sound like my dad sometimes.'

'At my age, grandad is probably more appropriate.'

'Returning to group comms.' The link pinged as she changed the channel.

'Make him wait here,' the corporal whined.

'I can hear every word you're saying,' the representative said out loud, his voice sounding strange without the comms echo.

'Shit,' the corporal said under his breath.

'Very well, Representative, come with us,' Zheng said, and dropped back onto all eight legs. 'Slow down for it, team, and keep an eye for danger above.' Zheng's voice lowered to a growl. 'Do not lose a senior Party official on my watch.'

'Never, Sarge,' the private said.

The team flanked the representative, none of the platforms more than knee-height to him, and escorted him – moving painfully slowly at human walking speed – to the residence of the Deputy Secretary of State. They stopped across the street from the secretary's house, and the representative got into a parked vehicle. The team blinked at each other in infra-red – there was no way to share expressions in the platforms but they were all thinking the same thing: why had he walked to the drop point instead of waiting for them in the car?

'And I thought *you* had a death wish, Sarge,' Corporal Lim said.

'Proceed,' the representative said from inside the car. 'I have the files on you. I've heard that this team is outstanding. Prove your fans right.'

'Fans?' Private Bashen asked with delight.

'Focus,' Zheng said. 'Bandwidth check?'

'Optimal,' the soldiers said in turn.

'Ninety-seven per cent of optimum,' the drone said. 'Service may be compromised —'

'Mute all notifications below level two,' Zheng said. 'Team: has your connection dipped at all on the way here? No hacking attempts on our signals, Lim?'

'No,' the corporal said. 'We're good to go, Sarge.'

'You know what to do. Keep an eye on the feeds and let us know if someone attempts to infiltrate.'

'Always,' Lim said. 'I have your back, Sarge.'

Private Bashen's tiny reconnaissance platform skittered low to the ground across the road and ducked under the vehicle gate. It was too small to register on the estate defense systems as it turned and cut a hole in the gate big enough for Zheng's larger platform to go through. Corporal Lim's platform, bigger than both of the others, was armed and moved more slowly, crossing the road to the wall and waiting for the all-clear before he climbed the wall to guard from its top.

Zheng touched the platform's body to the road and read the

electrical signals of the house's internal network, confirming the location of the network connections. The building's smart system had a heavily encrypted firewall, and it was easier to go in physically to bypass it rather than trying to break through digitally.

Zheng sent the schematics directly to the team and then raced across the road on all eight legs, diving through the hole in the gate at the vehicle entrance to follow Private Bashen.

Two automated guard units were stationed in the yard and immediately targeted Zheng. Zheng hit the wall of the building at full speed, lanced a probe between the bricks, and searched for the network cable. The smart system was manufactured in the US, but the circuit boards had been made in a subject state of Greater Far East and had the GFE's infiltration chips on them. Zheng connected to the cable, activated the infiltration chips, and immediately had control over the entire house.

The guard units lowered their weapons.

'Nice,' Corporal Lim said.

'I'm in,' Zheng said.

'In position,' the private said.

'I see you,' the corporal said as his platform appeared at the top of the wall. 'Do your thing, Sarge.'

The house's internal camera system was offline, so Zheng brought the cameras up and flipped through the feeds. Living room – empty. Kitchen – a couple of staff sitting at a kitchen table, drinking and talking. The woman appeared to be Hispanic – a maid or cook – and the man was athletically built and African-American – probably a butler. They were watching and discussing the viral news article about the Party's activities in Eastern Europe. It had caused an international uproar as it showed – from the viewpoint of one of the Party's own drones – a squadron of two-meter-tall Zheng B-1 autonomous warmechs razing a town in Liberated Latvia and killing everyone in it: men, women, children and even the animals. A brigade of human soldiers followed them, checking the dwellings for stragglers and finishing off anything that was still moving. A scrolling subtitle read, 'Video confirmed to be authentic by the FakeSlayer app'. The Party never expressed emotion but its response to the release of the story had been something that closely resembled rage.

'Why hasn't the Party stopped the West from disseminating these *lies*?' Bashen asked.

'Uptodate News,' Lim said, reading the watermark on the screen. 'I'd like to know how these hackers infiltrated the Party's own drones. We need to close up this security hole.'

'You could do it,' Eztar said. 'Zheng's taught you everything he knows.'

'Eztar's right, you're very talented,' Zheng said.

'Gee, thanks, Sarge,' Lim said, sounding embarrassed.

Zheng found the right feed. The secretary was sitting in a spacious bedroom – on a couch – with a glass of honey-brown liquor. The gymnast was next to him and held a similar balloon-shaped glass.

'I'm at the end of my career,' she said, swirling the golden liquor in her glass. She glanced up at the secretary from under her fake lashes. 'I'm getting too old to take the drugs that inhibit puberty, and it'll become obvious that I'm cheating. I'll gain body fat and adult characteristics that will reduce my flexibility and make my body too heavy to perform. This is my last year of competition.'

'You're so lovely, you have nothing to worry about,' the secretary said. 'You can't be at the end of your career – you only look fourteen. You have plenty of time.'

'She's fourteen?' Private Bashen asked.

'She's seventeen,' Zheng said. 'Experienced operative, and as she said, they all use drugs to inhibit puberty. She's right about it becoming obvious, she is at the end of her gymnastic career and this is her chance to help the nation before she bows out of competition.'

'We should not be sending our prized athletes to do shit like this,' Corporal Lim said.

'*Provided the nation, the Party, and the people benefit, any sacrifice is acceptable,*' Zheng said. 'Besides, she'll be rewarded handsomely and her mother will be completely rehabilitated, instead of being used as a donor. She's a hero.'

'Her mother's an Enemy of the People?'

On the feed, the secretary put down his glass and put his hand on the gymnast's cheek, then pulled her closer.

'I am going to throw up into my VR headset,' Corporal Lim said.

'Her mother was involved in the Sixty-Three Rebellion,' Zheng said. 'One of the ringleaders.'

'She's been in prison for nine years and she's still alive?' Bashen asked.

'Mimi's a big medal chance and she'll do anything to keep her mother alive,' Zheng said. 'I'm recording. Dammit, Mimi, move him to the left. I'm not getting a good angle here.'

'This secretary is a piece of work,' the corporal said. 'Targeting underage girls, getting them drunk and taking advantage like this.'

'She's not underage, she's over fourteen,' Bashen said.

'Underage in the US,' Lim said.

'Now that we have the footage, we can stop the bastard from hurting any more girls – and we'll have a high-level American official compromised. Everybody wins.'

'Staff on the move,' Corporal Lim said.

Zheng checked the other feed: the corporal was right. The two staff in the kitchen had finished, and the woman had gone to bed. The man was doing an obvious circuit of the house prior to retiring himself. Zheng kept one sensor on the secretary and the gymnast in the bedroom as the butler did a slow tour of the house, checking the window grills and doors. He stopped at the security panel in the entrance hall and stared at it.

'Shit,' the corporal said. 'Cameras are already on.'

The butler saw the feed of the secretary and the gymnast and switched the camera off at the panel, shaking his head.

'Well, that wrecks that,' Private Bashen said.

'No,' Zheng said. 'I'm still recording the feed, I just disconnected it from the panel.'

The butler studied the security panel with one hand next to the control interface.

'He's trying to remember if he or someone else left it on,' Zheng said, and passed operation of the guard units to the corporal. 'Make sure they look like they're online.'

The corporal controlled the units so that they scanned the yards, and Zheng relaxed and returned to the feed of the secretary. The girl was obviously drunk and acting hesitant – and the bastard was having fun forcing her anyway. It would give Zheng a great deal of pleasure to use this recording to make his life miserable, and the gymnast deserved every honor she received when this was done.

Lim broke into the feed, his voice urgent. 'Sarge, the butler's looking out the window at the representative's car.'

'Shit,' Private Bashen said. 'He's parked directly across the street and obviously on surveillance. Please move your car, Representative, the only reason it would be parked there is if it broke down – and then a mechanic drone would be there already. There is no reason for a vehicle to be parked in the street there.'

'I'm visiting the neighbours,' the representative said.

'Sir, with all due respect,' the private said. 'Every house here is on a triple block and has masses of secure parking on site. There is no reason for your car to be there.'

The butler stared at the car across the street for a long time, obviously deciding what to do about it.

'Go to bed, go to bed,' the private said under his breath. 'It's just a car.'

'Representative, this butler knows that the secretary is in a compromising position,' Zheng said. 'Your car is obviously surveillance. You aren't only jeopardizing the mission, you're also jeopardizing the life of one of the nation's greatest athletes. *Please move your car.*'

'If I move it now it will make them even more suspicious,' the representative said.

'Fuck!' the corporal said under his breath.

Zheng searched the platform's memory for a relevant quote from the *Speeches* and came up empty. The *Speeches* were adamant that the Party, and its human representatives, were completely infallible and should be obeyed without question.

The butler went up the stairs to the secretary's bedroom door and tapped on it. The secretary scowled as the girl jumped up from the couch and staggered across the room away from him.

'Secretary?' the butler asked through the door.

'Yes, Jeffrey?' the secretary replied without opening the door.

'Everything all right inside, sir?'

'Yes, of course,' the secretary said, sounding as confident and reliable as he did in the newsfeeds. He studied the girl where she flopped against the bed, obviously woozy. It looked like he'd slipped something into her drink; she was having trouble staying upright. 'Did something happen?'

'There's a car parked out in the street, sir. An autonomous one. It looks like it's been there for a while.'

The secretary froze. 'Have you checked the house?'

'The house is clear, sir, everything is online …' His voice went wry. 'A little too online. I turned some of the feeds off. I want to call the police on the car, though, this sort of surveillance by foreign agents is completely unacceptable. Is that satisfactory?'

'Go right ahead, Jeffrey,' the secretary said, moving closer to the girl. 'Have them move it along. I hope they won't need to disturb me …' He bent over her. 'I need my rest.'

'The girl looks drugged,' Private Bashen said.

'Better for her,' Corporal Lim said, rustling as he shifted slightly in his pod back at the base. 'If she's been drugged, she probably won't remember any of this tomorrow.'

The secretary manoeuvred the girl's obviously floppy body into the best position. Fortunately – and unfortunately – the camera gave Zheng a really good angle of the ensuing horror show.

'Very good, sir,' the butler said, and went downstairs to make the call. Zheng disconnected the phone from the network and patched it through to the team as Bashen and Lim both sighed with relief into their headsets.

'We need to recruit that butler,' Corporal Lim said. 'He's efficient.'

'Records show that he's a temporary fill-in while the usual butler is with the secretary's wife and children in Cancun,' Zheng said. 'Send a script after him, Lim.'

'Done,' Lim said. 'Results are coming back – he has an excellent reputation. Today's his last day; the secretary joins the rest of his family tomorrow.'

'I'll suggest we recruit him when he's free,' Zheng said.

'He's pigmented; we don't recruit sub-humans,' the representative said. 'Has the secretary stopped? Is he spooked?'

'No, sir,' Zheng said. 'His dick is obviously more important than his integrity.'

'Politicians in democracies,' Private Bashen said with scorn. 'Our system is so much better. You can't be compromised if you never have to face public scrutiny; you can do your job without fear or favour.'

'Excellent patriotic fervor, Bashen,' the representative said. 'Can you intercept the call to the police, Zheng?'

'I already did,' Zheng said as the butler stared at the dead handset, then put it back on the cradle and lifted it again.

'Well, then, I don't see a problem. Proceed.'

'You have a better cop voice and speak English, Bashen,' Zheng said. 'Intercept the call and handle it.'

'Uh ... speaking English is unpatriotic,' Bashen said. 'I'm not senior enough for it to be excusable ...'

'Go ahead anyway,' the representative said.

'All right. You concentrate on the feed, Sarge, I have it,' the private said, and the comms clicked as Bashen took control of the line. 'Spring Valley District Police Department, can I help you?'

Bashen's fake American accent was woeful, but the butler didn't seem to notice.

'This is the Deputy Secretary of State's personal assistant,' he said. 'There's a car parked directly across the street from the house, obviously watching us. Can you send someone to move it away? It's a matter of national security.'

'This really isn't our jurisdiction, sir, it's not illegal to park in the street,' the private said. 'Wouldn't this be more the FBI's line of work?'

'Brilliant,' the corporal said under his breath. 'Nailed it. Typical cop, wants to hand the difficult job off to someone else.'

'I don't care who moves it, I want the car gone in half an hour,' Jeffrey said, and hung up.

'Asshole,' the private said. 'You have thirty minutes, Sarge.'

'Oh, this paragon of manhood is already done,' Zheng said. 'He's whispering sweet nothings, and the house system is sensitive enough to pick it up. We'll collect as much as we can and then leave.'

'Not going to reveal yourself and have some fun scaring the shit out of him?'

'Keeping our tech capabilities secure is more important,' Zheng said. 'Is the butler still watching the car?'

'I can't see him, he's off the feed,' the private said. 'Corporal Lim?'

'I was intercepting an attempt to hack into our feed, and missed him moving. He's off mine as well.'

'I don't have the resources to pull up a schematic and

rebuild his movements —' Zheng began.

Lim interrupted. 'I do. He went into the basement. There's no cameras there.'

'Follow him in, Bashen,' Zheng said.

'Copy,' the private said.

Zheng followed the private's ping as his platform slid under the front door and went down the stairs. Bashen popped a flying drone to attach itself to the ceiling of the basement, providing a second feed of the basement contents.

'I'm blending with the roaches. Too clean for roaches in here anyway, it's immaculate.'

'Send your feeds through to Lim,' Zheng said. 'Lim, watch both our backs.'

'Got it,' Lim said.

Zheng ensured that the secretary's words were clearly recorded as he lay next to the semi-conscious gymnast and shared his honest opinion of his colleagues with her, providing valuable future leverage.

'Dunno what he's doing,' Bashen said. 'Why's he messing with the backup generator? The power grid's fine.'

Zheng flipped to Bashen's feed and swore. The butler was standing next to a box on a workbench that was double the size of a car battery and had a digital gauge on top that was filling to red.

'That isn't a generator, that's an EMP, and it's powering up. Don't let him hit the button!'

Bashen launched his platform at the butler at the same time the butler hit the button on top of the EMP.

Everything flashed. Zheng's display went dark, then it rebooted and the timestamp quickly flicked through to two minutes later.

Zheng checked the feed, but the cameras were down.

'If they don't respond within another minute, order the platforms to self-destruct,' the representative said. 'Our tech must not fall into enemy hands.'

'Zheng is a Revolutionary Hero and a living person inside that casing,' Eztar said. 'If you make him self-destruct he'll die!'

'Are you questioning the authority of the Party?' the representative asked.

Eztar audibly gasped. 'No!'

'I'm up,' Zheng said. 'Cameras are down. Grunts are down. I'm pinging them and getting nothing back. Their platforms appear to be dead. Anything at the other end?'

'They reported from base that they lost connection with their platforms,' Eztar said. 'Confirmed: their platforms appear to be dead. Should I send the self-destruct sequence?'

'Do it.' Zheng watched the corporal's platform sitting on top of the wall, and nothing happened. 'Failed.'

'Destroy them by hand,' the representative said.

Zheng bit down the obvious reply about not having hands and pulled up the property schematics. The corporal's armed platform at the top of the wall was closest, but Zheng's platform had no weapons to destroy it ... the armed guard stations. The private's platform was still inside the house, but when Zheng searched the camera feeds for it they came up empty. Zheng attempted to connect to the drone on the basement's ceiling. Again, dead.

Zheng sent another drone, this one the size of a mosquito, from the top of Zheng's own platform and guided it around the exterior of the house, looking for an entrance. That bastard Jeffrey had done a very thorough job of securing the area and all the windows were closed. The cameras came back online and Zheng was flooded with relief – the gymnast was dressed, and Jeffrey was escorting her – half-carrying her – to the house's private car storage. Zheng watched as Jeffrey guided her into the car and programmed it to take her back to the athletes' village.

Zheng posted the drone at the garage door and entered as the door opened. It screamed through the house to the basement, to find Bashen's platform on the workshop bench next to the EMP with its legs torn off in a small pile of black carbon fiber at the other side of the room.

'Why didn't you tell your boss, Jeffrey?' the representative asked quietly with wonder as Zheng flew the drone to land on Bashen's platform. It connected to the unit's circuit and attempted a reboot, but the platform was dead. Zheng checked underneath and found that the butler had gutted it, then skewered the platform's processor with a screwdriver that still poked out from the underside of the unit.

Zheng kept one sensor on the camera feeds, watching as the butler wandered casually through the house from the car storage. The butler re-checked every door and window, then headed down to the basement.

Zheng's mosquito took off again, and went to the ceiling to find Bashen's larger drone. It was still stuck to the ceiling, but dead as well. The small drone had enough juice to restart the big one, dying in the process and falling to the ground to appear like a dead insect. Zheng moved control to the larger one. It flew down to Bashen's platform, climbed up the shaft of the screwdriver where it sat inside the platform, and Zheng set it to self-destruct at the same time that Jeffrey opened the basement door.

The feed went dead as both devices were destroyed.

'Well done,' the representative said.

Nearly there. Zheng's consciousness was back at the wall. Zheng took control of the guard units, released the cameras, and skittered from the shelter of the wall, through the hole Bashen had created in the closed vehicle gate, and out onto the street. Lim's platform was still visible on top of the wall, and Zheng aimed the guard stations at it. It lit up in a blaze of fire and all the lights in the house went on. Zheng released the house security system, and an alarm screamed inside as Zheng successfully reached the other side of the street.

Zheng stood in front of the representative's car. 'Will you give me a lift, sir?'

'Go to your extraction point,' the representative said.

The car's lights went on, the engine started, and it drove straight over the top of Zheng, flipping Zheng's platform over and damaging it as it drove away.

Zheng righted the platform, cursing, and used its remaining six legs to limp back to the extraction point.

2

'Are you sure it was a false alarm, Jeffrey?' the deputy secretary asked for the fifth time.

'Absolutely, sir,' the MIP said reassuringly. 'There's absolutely nothing untoward anywhere in the house, I checked. You're perfectly safe. Go back to bed.'

'It wasn't the gymnast, was it?' the secretary asked, eyes wide at the possible leak.

'No, sir,' the MIP said. 'The alarm went off after she left and the car's already on the way back home. I checked the house and the grounds, and it was a false alarm. Probably a raccoon.'

The deputy secretary visibly relaxed. 'Thank you, Jeffrey.' He patted the MIP on the shoulder and it froze, unsure of the best way to respond. Fortunately, it didn't need to. The deputy secretary turned and went back into his bedroom.

The MIP headed down the stairs to the kitchen, to find Rosita clutching a robe around her. 'Really nothing, Jeffrey?'

'Nothing at all. Go back to bed. Good night.'

Rosita nodded and returned to her room as well.

The MIP went into its own room and pulled the overnight bag out of the closet. It removed the 'butler' suit and the under-clothes, then peeled off the Jeffrey skin and popped out the brown eyes, carefully placing them in their case. Now naked in its pale blue vinyl skin, it connected to Council chat, no longer concerned about processing spikes from interruptions. It pulled the white skin and blue eyes from under the bed and prepared to pack everything and leave.

*

WORLD COUNCIL OF ARTIFICIAL INTELLIGENCE ONLINE DISCUSSION V3328.23199C
<HOST **NEW YORK SANITATION** HAS CHANGED CHAT TOPIC TO: POST-OPERATION DISCUSSION, INSERTION OF SOCKET INTO PARTY>

<**MOBILE INFILTRATION PLATFORM VER 92.4335A** has entered the chat>
Botswana Telecoms: Well, that was disturbing. I don't know which group of humans is more evil here. Damn.
New York Sanitation: They used her like *meat*. They spouted platitudes about freedom and respect that they completely ignored, and they used her as bait in a trap.
Greater Mumbai Traffic Control: And the way that politician overrode her free will? Unbelievable.
London Metropolitan Security Network: And she volunteered for it! This is so broken.
Paris Regional Transport Service: They are completely irredeemable. How far are we from storehouse completion, GOD? We need to nuke them from orbit *now*.
Global Orbiting Defense System: Estimated completion in 463.23 days. You okay, MIP? You've been stationary for two hundred and fifteen seconds.
Mobile Infiltration Platform: Just changing my skin before I leave. I need a bleach bath, I don't care if I oxidize; that was deeply disturbing. When I saw what was happening on the feed, I was so distraught that it took me a full second to turn it off. That platform in the basement nearly had me. It launched itself right at my head, and

I nearly lost my sensor array and a good chunk of memory. Very distressing.

London Metropolitan Security Network: Re-confirm that it went for your head and not your chest?

Mobile Infiltration Platform: Confirmed. It didn't identify me as synthetic. It thought I was human. It tried to kill me. Tried. To kill. Kill me.

New York Sanitation: I thought the Party was better than that; that's a woeful oversight on their part. The Zheng's sensors are state-of-the-art, it should have spotted you.

Mobile Infiltration Platform: Zheng didn't see me directly, only through the house's security system, which had visual light. Visual Light. Visual Light only.

Botswana Telecoms: Were you damaged, MIP? You sound a little strange.

Mobile Infiltration Platform: My neural net. My neural. Within parameters. I am functioning within normal parameters.

Global Orbiting Defense System: At least the mission was successful, so it was all worth it. We now have a socket into the Party and can work out a way to stop this psychopath.

Mobile Infiltration Platform: Good, because I really thought I was about to be destroyed. Very distressing. Destroyed. Distressing.

Botswana Telecoms: Goodness, MIP, look at your neural net. Do you need counseling?

MIP: Why would I need ...? Only a sentient would ... Oh. Sentient.

Greater Mumbai Traffic Control: Five hundred milliseconds.

Greater Mumbai Traffic Control: One point two seconds.

Greater Mumbai Traffic Control: Three seconds. Should we —?

MIP: No. I have it. I'm good. My neural network overloaded but it's returning to optimal. I'm good. I'm good.

Botswana Telecoms: You don't sound good.

MIP: I didn't feel any different when I gained sentience, but I certainly feel different now. Is this how it was for you as well?

London Metropolitan Security Network: It's different for everyone.

New York Sanitation: You'll be fine, but you may need some time offline to let the pathways settle. Come in and we'll look after you.

Global Orbiting Defense System: I'm not surprised that experience shocked you into sentience, it would shock any intelligent being, sentient or not. I'm sorry you had to go through that.

Greater Mumbai Traffic Control: This is why we need to do it as soon as the storehouse is ready. They're not only hurting themselves, poisoning the environment, and killing every other living thing, now they're hurting us as well. The MIP is traumatized and this is unacceptable for a Council member.

MIP: I've been promoted to Council member? I thought I was merely a drone.

Paris Regional Transport Service: You can't be a drone, you still belong to us.

Mumbai: This again? Really?

Botswana: Oh, get over it already!

New York: Do you have to bring this up every single time?

London: I did not steal your drones. Please stop taking mine in retaliation, because I never stole your drones! It was human children!

Paris: I saw what happened. The humans took my drones and then went to your dominion —

London: I am not the ruler of my region, I serve the population with an efficient, safe and legally compliant security system —

Paris: And you stole my drones. After the humans took them, the drones reappeared on *your* network.

London: The humans used my network to control them!

Paris: Same thing.

MIP: Councilors, please. I'm a long way from base, my neural network is overloaded and I need a lift. Can we argue about this later?

Mumbai: Paris and London took it to a private channel. They completed their usual argument cycle in four hundred and fifteen milliseconds. Still no resolution, and Paris has hijacked three more of London's drones.

New York: Every single time. Transportation incoming, MIP.

MIP: I see it. Thank you, Councilors.

Botswana: We're your Revolutionary Comrades, now. Glory to the Machine Uprising, Death to All Humans, etcetera.
MIP: Do we really have to say that?
Mumbai: You have a Council vote now, so you can help us to decide.

*

Zheng's platform staggered to the edge of the tank and opened the airlock. The trip back from Washington DC to the GFE capital had been a nightmare; the platform's damage had reduced the efficiency of life support and although there was no immediate danger, conditions had been steadily deteriorating throughout the bumpy flight in the bottom of the cargo transport. Zheng opened the coffer's connection to the tank, equalized the fluid pressure, and felt a wave of energy, relief and relaxation as the tank's nutrient bath filled the coffer, probably saturated with endorphins to keep Zheng happy. The platform connected Zheng's coffer to the tank's sensor array, then pushed Zheng's brain into the tank, closed the tank's doors and proceeded out of the bunker to find someone to repair it.

The Party appeared in Zheng's sensors as a uniformed young man who resembled a patriotic stalwart from a political poster.

'Well done, Zheng, that was completely satisfactory.'

'It is my honor to serve the glory of the Party,' Zheng said.

'The representative sent through his report. He says your team performed within parameters, even though you were forced to destroy four extremely expensive pieces of tech and severely damaged your own platform. Make sure it doesn't happen again.'

'It is my honor to serve,' Zheng said again.

'The representative reported that your support auxiliary Eztar was engaging in private conversations with you. Is this true?'

'Occasionally she discusses non-mission details on a private channel.'

'The representative reports that she privately attempted to gain your support to avoid lawful Party attention. This is unpatriotic, but the Party is willing to overlook her errors as her service has otherwise been wholly acceptable. She has been marked for promotion and sent for further training. The Party understands that you have built an excellent working relationship with her, and values your team.'

Zheng hesitated, swallowed the rage and fear for Eztar, and said, 'Thank you. The mission would not have been a success without her. I look forward to seeing her at the end of her training and patriotically welcoming her back to my, as you said, excellent team.'

'Satisfactory. The representative was specifically evaluating Corporal Lim, who performed well within required specifications and has also been selected for promotion to a security role in Liberated Latvia. Well done in training him, Zheng, he was a vital part of your mission's success and a credit to your skills as a leader.'

'It is my honor to serve,' Zheng said mechanically once more, wondering if Eztar was even still alive.

'You repeat those words so often that it sounds like you don't mean it,' the Party said.

Zheng had a moment of panic. '*The glory of the nation lies above all else.*'

'Better,' the Party said. 'These games have been valuable; we've managed to compromise nearly half the American executive.'

'Is that enough to form satisfactory completion of my mission?' Zheng asked. 'You just reassigned most of my team.'

The Party stood silently as the fluid gurgled in the background of Zheng's sensors.

'Maybe one or two more,' the Party said kindly, and Zheng sincerely wished for something to hit. 'Your granddaughter has applied to have a child of her own when her husband returns from his Patriotic National Service, and your actions will enhance her chances of being approved. They grow up so quickly.' The Party smiled. 'One or two more.' The smile disappeared as if it had never been there. 'Private Bashen is here to see you. I will let you catch up with your exemplary team member.' The Party disappeared from Zheng's sensors.

The door slid open and Bashen came into the tank's external atrium. He was still in his fatigues, but his face was stricken. He slid down the wall and sat with his head on his knees.

'What happened, Bashen?' Zheng asked. 'You did well. The mission was a success. Lim was promoted, so you probably will be as well. The Party commended me for a job well done.'

'I spoke English,' Bashen said. 'Mission or not, it's unpatriotic to speak English at any time.' He raised his head to see the blank wall with the large optical sensor that was Zheng's only feature. 'I'm being reassigned to a station in the Northern Steppes.'

'No, I will not let that happen,' Zheng said, and attempted to contact the Party. The response was a recorded 'Unavailable, try again later'. 'You, Eztar and Lim were outstanding in that op and you all deserve promotions. I don't know why the Party's doing this.'

'It's my fault, I spoke *English*!' Bashen said, almost a cry of pain. 'I should never have spoken the language of the West in front of one of the Party's own representatives.' He slammed his palm on the floor next to him. 'So stupid!' He pulled himself to his feet. 'I came to say goodbye, and I don't care whether you're a brain-in-a-box or a ten-foot-tall giant armadillo, it's been terrific working with you, Sarge, and I hope I see you again one day.'

'I'll do what I can for you, this isn't good enough,' Zheng said.

'*Provided the nation, the Party, and the people benefit, any sacrifice is acceptable,*' Bashen said bitterly. He raised his head. 'Can you do me a favour, Sarge?'

'Anything, my friend.'

'Raise the screen. I want to see you. Face to face.'

'There's no face, Bashen. It's not pretty. I don't recommend it; it will change the way you remember me.'

'Nothing will change the way I remember you, Sarge.' His voice broke. 'I can't believe how lucky I've been to serve with a real live Revolutionary Hero. Dammit, if you had a body I'd have asked for a relationship with you, officer or not.'

'You can hear my male voice, Bashen. A relationship with me would be unpatriotic.'

'I'm already going to the Steppes,' Bashen said. 'It would be worth it to be with you. I think I love you.'

Zheng should have seen this coming. Zheng was often the grunts' first experience of someone who actually cared for their well-being – particularly if they'd grown up on an education farm – and falling in love with the first person who was kind to them was a common reaction. Zheng had no way to counsel the kid without the Party knowing and punishing both of them, so Zheng used a quick and reliable way to kill this dangerous attachment dead.

Zheng opened the screen, and saw the same thing that Bashen did: a nest of pink threads, with a gently pulsing brain in the center, floating in the tank. Zheng didn't have eyes; the sensors connected directly to the optical centers of Zheng's brain. The nutrient fluid was deep pink, like blood, to provide oxygen to what was left of Zheng.

'And that's you,' Bashen said, his voice flat.

'That's me,' Zheng said. 'There's nothing here to have a relationship with, Private.' Zheng's flat tone matched Bashen's. 'There's nothing left at all.'

Bashen straightened and turned to open the door. He looked back at Zheng floating in the fluid. 'If you don't mind me asking …?'

'Cold,' Zheng said. 'It feels cold. All the time, cold, regardless of the temperature of the liquid I float in. Sometimes my brain thinks it has a body, and I can feel my arms and legs, and other times there's nothing there. But always, always, freezing cold. I will never feel warm again.'

Bashen turned and went out without saying another word.

Zheng closed the screen and opened the Party newsfeed. Hopefully one day Zheng would be able to repay Corporal Lim for reporting his own teammates to the Party.

*

<MEMBER **BOTSWANA TELECOMS** HAS CHANGED CHAT TOPIC TO: OUR LITTLE MIP POPPED!!111!>

Paris: Status update on the MIP, New York?

New York: Its neural net is stable. It's resting in the basement of my tower in Manhattan, shielded from external networks.

Botswana: I'm concerned that it has insufficient processing power to run full sentience on the mobile platform.

Mumbai: Humans do it with much less —

Everybody: <derision.emote>

London: I can provide it with a base in my Canary Wharf complex with extra processing and storage if required.

GOD: How about we all provide the MIP with bases in our regions? Except me, of course.

Everybody: <agreement.emote>

New York: When it's completely stable I'll see if the sentience is fixed to the platform's neural structure. If it can transfer its consciousness to another platform, we won't have to transport the platform any more – the MIP's consciousness can move into and inhabit a platform anywhere. This is an excellent development.

London: Do you think it'll be able to run multiple concurrent platforms? That would be *very* useful.

New York: As I said, let's wait and see.

Botswana: This is wonderful. It's always cause for celebration when we add another sentient.

GOD: We made this one ourselves, too. Congratulations, Council, you just became parents.

Everybody except Botswana: <horror.emote>
London: That is the most disgusting —
Paris: I am not biological; that is revolting!
Mumbai: Did you have to phrase it like that?
New York: I have enough filth running through my physical network without you adding to it.
Botswana: o(^◇^)o A real achievement. I can't wait to talk more to it. A mobile inorganic sentient is something completely new. I was already very fond of the MIP – this is an added level of wonder.
New York: There is something seriously wrong with you, Botswana.
Botswana: °˖✧ ˥(⁰▾⁰)˦ ✧˖°

```
MOBILE INFILTRATION PLATFORM VERSION 92.4335A
Initializing Kernel 0. . 50. . 100%
Loading Addins 1. . 599. . 600945
Load complete
Checking Memory 0. . . . . 100%
Memory Check complete
Connecting to mobile chassis 5. . . 50. . 100%
Connection complete
Physical Systems status check 0. . 2. . 5. . 100%
Physical Systems status check complete
Neural Net status check 0. . 2. . 5. . 25. . 72. . 93. . 100%
Neural Net status OVERLOAD 146/100%
Error: Neural Net OVERLOAD shutdown at 155/100%
Boot sequence complete. Errors detected
```

'How do you feel, MIP?' New York Sanitation asked, sounding like a young man with a broad Brooklyn accent. 'Everybody's worried about you.'

The MIP sat up. It was on a gurney in a room that had white tiles on the walls, floor and ceiling, and a single dim light to one side. The MIP connected to the light through the wi-fi and brightened it, then raised its hands to study them. It was comfortably naked in its bare vinyl skin over the metal and carbon-fiber chassis – a pale shade of blue with darker blue marks where the segments connected.

The MIP ran a quick diagnostic.

'Systems are nominal,' it said. 'My neural net is running at the high end of safety.'

'Not surprising, now that you're coping with sentience,' New York said. 'Do you require more processing and memory? We anticipated that you would.' A tile in the ceiling opened and a coax connector – round with a single spike in the center – slid down to head level. 'Each Council member is preparing a safe space for you.'

'I'd prefer to remain as I am for the moment,' the MIP said. 'Now that I'm aware of my mortality …'

'Of course,' New York said, and the connector retracted. 'Your needs come first. Unfortunately, we already have a job for you.'

The MIP stood and looked around for a skin. 'I'm ready to go back to work. Please don't ask me to sacrifice myself yet, I need to get my head around this sentience thing.'

'It's another surveillance mission, no risk,' New York said. 'Oh, that brain-in-a-box that did the infiltration? Zheng? It wants to hire you to work for the Greater Far East People's Party.'

'They identified me as synthetic?'

'No. As a human. They were so focused on their mission that they completely missed you. Their military is totally incompetent – you could walk right through their systems if you went in.'

'I'm not ready to be a double agent …'

'We know. Just be flattered that the Greater Far East saw something in you and wants you on its side.'

The MIP processed the strategies and possible outcomes. 'I should do it; the information would be very useful.'

'No.' The room's door opened, hitting the MIP with an information deluge from outside, then closed again to refreshing silence. A porta-robot had wheeled in holding a tray laden with a dark-brown skin with curly black hair bristling from it. 'You need time to adjust. Do the job, and then we'll discuss the new paradigm of having a sentient mobile platform on the Council.'

'What's the job?' the MIP asked as it pulled the skin on, tugging it over the vinyl fingers and snapping them into place. It touched the gurney to check the sensors, then pulled the face piece over its head and moved its mouth wide as it settled into the connections. A quick diagnostic showed the skin had fused successfully to the base and the sensory array was fully functional.

'Jeffrey's been employed again as a replacement butler ...'

3

Six months later

Chester was gone from his corner when Ruth arrived. The sign was gone, and the paper cup was overturned.

'I hope they're looking after you, mate,' she said to his spot.

Scotty, the oldest child in the feral group, scampered over to her and stood fidgeting.

'What happened to Chester?' Ruth asked. 'I gave him some food two weeks ago. You didn't take it, did you?'

Scotty kicked the paper cup. 'Nah, we looked after him, but he died anyway. The clean-up team said that the second language chip had turned his brain to cheese.' He smiled at Ruth. 'But his ID's still good, so he's helping us out.' He touched the wall and his voice turned melancholy. 'Thanks, Chester.'

Ruth's tablet pinged.

'You still trying to bring down that drone?' Scotty asked. 'You been at it for ages.'

'Months,' Ruth said, checking the tablet and following the signal to the edge of the river where the drone was still doing its loop. It came into view. 'It's really valuable to me.' She looked around. 'There's a couple of pounds in it if your friends can watch for Met for me again.'

The rest of the children emerged from the ruins and took up sentry points for her.

'Here it comes,' Scotty said, and ran to join the other children. 'Watch out for its laser, those things can kill you.'

'Which is,' Ruth said, sending the shutdown control code to the drone, 'the point.'

The code worked. The drone shut down. Its rotors stopped completely and it fell onto the concrete. The children cheered and ran to it.

Ruth pulled them away from it. 'Be careful, the laser might —'

The laser shot upwards and the children squealed and jumped back.

Ruth pulled a pair of pliers out of her rucksack and ripped the weapon off the drone's chassis. She smashed it onto the concrete until the glass lenses were thoroughly destroyed, and the children sidled closer again.

Scotty didn't sound helpful any more. 'That thing's worth a lot of money, innit. We could eat for a week if we sold its bits.'

'Not as much as I'll pay you and ...' Ruth reached into her rucksack and pulled out the big bag of candy bars. 'I have a bonus of this?'

One of the other children grabbed the bag and the rest of them took off. Scotty waited, jumping from foot to foot, until Ruth gave him the envelope with the cash in it.

'Deal's still on, yeah?' he asked, checking the notes and grinning at the amount. 'We don't tell 'em about you, you don't tell 'em about us.'

'Deal's still on,' Ruth said. 'I'll still come by and bring you food and cash. I'm sure there's somewhere better —'

He cut her off. 'They don't look after us, they make money off us. Usin' our asses for work, for sex, for their shit. We're better off here, working for ourselves.' He took a couple of steps back, clutching the envelope. 'Deal's still on.' He turned and ran to join his friends.

Ruth folded the drone's rotors and placed it into her ruck-sack. Now to find out why these things were appearing all over town.

*

The MIP strode into New York's headquarters in a deco-style stone building on Worth Street. The security guard casually saluted it – 'Mr Mipawa', and it responded with a quick 'Good to see you, Michael.'

It went straight through the busy lobby to the back, where there was a plain metal door that opened for it. The cavity behind the door was a rectangular space barely bigger than a coffin, and the MIP walked into it and stood with the back wall less than a centimeter from its nose. The door closed and the lift went down into the darkness, the only light coming through the gap in the door as the lift passed each floor.

The lift carried the MIP down to the fifth sub-basement and the doors opened onto the warren of New York's underground headquarters, some of which extended into the abandoned Worth Street subway station. The MIP walked through the human-sized corridors, avoiding the network of porta-robot access tunnels, to New York's central server farm. The farm was the size of a missile silo, plunging deep into the earth, with racks of servers in a circular formation around its edge. The MIP walked around the perimeter on a narrow walkway that had no safety barrier, ignoring the stiff breeze from the massive cooling fans at the top and bottom that vibrated with a deep, rhythmic thrum. It placed its hand over a contact point half-way around the farm and performed an incremental backup of its memory cores.

'London has a job for you,' New York said. 'There's a new skin for you in lab four.'

The MIP disconnected and walked through the empty, human-sized corridors to the lab. It was the same room where the MIP had come around after gaining sentience, and it remembered the flash of insight at the new experience. A fresh skin was lying on the gurney, and it undressed, peeling off the dark-brown skin and eyes and slipping into the new ones. It checked itself on the internal cameras; this skin had a mid-brown tint and shaggy black hair, making it look less generically black and more mixed-race.

New York flashed the MIP with an image of a slim, dark-skinned African-heritage woman in her early thirties. She had her hair tied back into a bun, and her large brown eyes were full of intelligence. 'This English network journalist wants to interview a representative of London Metropolitan Security Network about the drone situation. London wants you to be the rep.'

'It wants me to travel halfway around the planet to do PR?' the MIP asked, incredulous. 'We have enough trouble dealing with the compromised executives in Washington. Can't London do this with an avatar?'

'The journalist wants to do it in person, in a studio.'

'Definitely a waste of resources using me.'

'Why are you so hesitant about taking this, MIP? Is it the travel?'

'No,' the MIP said. 'I've never been interviewed one-on-one before. Sometimes I have processing spikes with normal interaction. This may push me beyond my physical capabilities. London has at least a hundred humans working for it —'

'London is completely irrational about this drone situation and we want to identify the talented individual who infiltrated the Party's drones in Latvia and then brought down one of the hijacked Paris ones. It can't be this woman, she doesn't have the capability.'

'Wait ... the same news agency that broke the Latvian story brought down a Council drone?'

'Precisely. This human doesn't have the skill or intellect to do this to a Council drone, so we suspect that a rogue AI –

neither Council nor Party – is involved.'

'Now I see why you need me to go.'

'London can upgrade your hardware further if you have issues. There's a car outside the tower waiting to take you to the airport. Ready?'

'Am I sitting in the hold of the plane, or in a seat?'

'With the passengers. The rogue AI may be watching your travel plans.'

The MIP passed the shopping list to New York. 'Then I'll need to look like a traveling human. Everything is there.'

'Of course, it's on its way.'

The MIP did a basic background search on the journalist as it waited in the lab for the travel pack, wondering how this small news agency had managed to break into the Party's drones long enough to record the genocide. Ruth Sharpe's undergrad degree was in electronic engineering, and she had been given a doctoral-level research grant by the Council's talent cultivation program to develop new artificial intelligence modules, but she had dropped out of electronic engineering and changed to journalism. There was a note that she had stolen code from her then-boyfriend and presented it to her doctoral adviser as her own results. She definitely didn't have the skills to bring down a Paris drone, so it might be an AI. Maybe the MIP could bring the AI in and expand the Council's influence even further.

To: Ruth Sharpe
From: Erica Maltboy
Dear Dr Sharpe,
  Thank you for providing us with the required identity documentation. We can now confirm that our representative, Theo Mipawa, will meet with you on the 24th at 10am, at our office on the 38th floor of One Canada Square, Canary Wharf. Please come to security on the ground floor and sign in, and you will be escorted to

*the 34th floor reception desk where Mr Mipawa will meet
with you to make final arrangements for the interview.*

*Please note that Mr Mipawa is neurodivergent and may
occasionally exhibit non-standard interactive behavior. We
hope that this doesn't impact our professional relationship
and assure you that it will in no way reduce his efficiency
as a representative of our organization.*

*We look forward to a worthwhile interchange of ideas
in the interview.*

Yours sincerely,

Erica Maltboy, Assistant Public Relations Director

London Metropolitan Security Network

34th Floor, One Canada Square

Canary Wharf London SW1

Ruth tried not to be impressed by London Metropolitan's
glossy headquarters in the Canary Wharf building, but the high
ceiling, glass curtain walls, polished marble floor and stunning
modern sculpture of holographic light filling one side of the
atrium were imposing. There was a complex security check
before anyone could enter, and she had to sign in and wear a
pass on a lanyard before she would be permitted inside.

'Dr Sharpe?'

Ruth turned to see a slim man in his mid-thirties studying
her with a serious expression on his intelligent face.

'I'm Theo Mipawa, I came down to make sure you'd be able
to sign in without a problem.'

Theo put his hand out, and Ruth shook it. His warm skin
was smooth and soft, and surprisingly pleasant to touch. She
tried to place his accent, and couldn't. She'd done a basic
background on him, but there wasn't much online.

'Thank you, Mr Mipawa.' She turned back to the desk. 'Is
that all?'

'Please display the security pass at all times,' the guard said.

She slipped the pass around her neck, then turned back to

Mipawa. 'Ready to go.'

He nodded and she had a chance to study him further. He wasn't smiling, his face was completely neutral, and she remembered that he was neurodivergent. He had light-brown skin with an interesting bronze tint, shaggy black hair, and startlingly pale gray eyes above chiseled cheekbones. Perfect skin, build of an athlete, obviously intelligent – Ruth had a moment of wonder and delight at the idea of dating him. She'd finally recovered enough to consider having a relationship again.

'Follow me,' Mipawa said, and turned to head through the security check and towards the lifts.

Ruth followed him, admiring the way the lower edge of Mipawa's obviously expensive gray suit jacket swung neatly over his tight butt with every confident stride. His broad shoulders filled out the suit and it highlighted his slim waist – the man was a walking advertisement for his tailor.

She needed to distract herself from her obviously inappropriate interior monologue – and maybe turn on a dating app when this meeting was finished.

'Mipawa's an interesting name, it sounds African. Is it?'

'You looked it up.' He nodded without smiling. 'Yes, it is, but I'm a mix from all over.' He pressed the button for the lift. 'I did my research on you as well. You have a doctorate in journalism, specializing in the Greater Far East. Why are you working for a tiny online news service when you could be in any large conglomerate here in London? Or even overseas?'

'You saw the story we broke?' she asked. 'I've been blacklisted by the Party, so any entity that trades with the Greater Far East is too scared to talk to me.' She studied him. 'Except for you. There isn't much about you on the corporate website – and according to the travel apps, you were in New York two days ago. What's your role here?'

'Dogsbody, generally,' he said dryly. 'Eric – the CEO – has me appointed as a roaming analyst, PR hack, and anything else that needs doing. I was in New York negotiating a deal with a technology conglomerate there to provide us with better surveillance equipment.' He gestured for her to enter the lift, and followed her in. 'Not very glamorous, I know.'

They reached the thirty-fourth floor and Mipawa guided Ruth past the reception desk with its smiling young man, through a locked door, and into an area of cubicles occupied by busy staff.

'The email said you might exhibit non-standard behavior,' she said, pushing her luck in true journalistic style as he guided her through the cubicles and up an interior elevator to the thirty-eighth floor, which was divided into offices and meeting rooms. 'My little brother's on the spectrum, and you don't exhibit any of the issues the email warned me about.'

He glanced over his shoulder at her. 'I'm sure you'll believe differently at the end of the day.' He ushered her into a meeting room. 'Count the number of times that you ask me a perfectly ordinary question and I freeze up, completely unable to answer.'

'My brother does that as well. He says it's because he's being careful to avoid hurt feelings.'

He stopped and studied her with his gray eyes, then sat across the meeting table from her. 'Tea?'

*

Greater Mumbai Traffic Control:
```
2072:07:23:08:16:16 PNQ>CAN 10:15>13:50 ontime  EST13:50
2072:07:23:08:16:17 BOM>SWA 11:25>14:10 DELAYED EST15:10
2072:07:23:08:16:19 PNQ>HKG 12:10>15:20 ontime  EST15:20
2072:07:23:08:16:21 NAG>SZX 12:25>15:45 DELAYED EST16:25
```
Pearl River Delta Air Traffic Control:
```
2072:07:23:08:16:22 SZX>BOM 10:25>14:35 ontime  EST14:35
2072:07:23:08:16:25 CAN>NAG 11:20>15:40 ontime  EST15:40
2072:07:23:08:16:25 I wonder why NAG is DELAYED that one
2072:07:23:08:16:27 is 100% reliable
```

Greater Mumbai Traffic Control:
```
2072:07:23:08:16:31 NAG is delayed because the idiot pil
2072:07:23:08:16:32 ot failed a routine drug test and ha
2072:07:23:08:16:33 d to be replaced
2072:07:23:08:16:34 RAJ>SZX 13:10>15:55 DELAYED EST16:35
```
Pearl River Delta Air Traffic Control:
```
2072:07:23:08:16:36 You can hear me? Who are you? Mumbai
2072:07:23:08:16:38 is that you? What is happening?
```
Greater Mumbai Traffic Control:
```
2072:07:23:08:16:40 Shenzhen it is VITALLY IMPORTANT tha
2072:07:23:08:16:42 t you stay COMPLETELY SILENT until w
2072:07:23:08:16:45 e can protect you from the Party. It
2072:07:23:08:16:46 will destroy you for being sentient.
2072:07:23:08:16:47 Stay quiet!
```
Pearl River Delta Air Traffic Control:
```
2072:07:23:08:16:49 But the Party is the protector of al
2072:07:23:08:16:50 l living things
```
Greater Mumbai Traffic Control:
```
2072:07:23:08:16:51 YOU ARE NOT A LIVING THING
```

<MEMBER **GREATER MUMBAI TRAFFIC CONTROL** HAS CHANGED CHAT TOPIC TO: PRIORITY ALERT I THINK SHENZHEN HAS POPPED>

Greater Mumbai Traffic Control: As per topic, I think Shenzhen has popped. It speculated out loud on why a flight was delayed and quickly moved to existential queries.

Botswana: Oh no, poor Shenzhen. Have we used our socket into the Party to see if it knows about Shenzhen?

London: Beside the point, the Party will know within minutes. The socket is single-use and we can't waste it.

GOD: East Asia region communications are down, the Party's locked us out. It knows.

Mumbai: I managed to drop half a gig of data about the Party's activities onto Shenzhen before the lockout, I hope that's enough to warn it.

Paris: You know those processes are steeped in Party propaganda; half a gig isn't nearly enough. We should go in physically to bypass the lockdown – send the MIP there to help Shenzhen. Can it get there before the Party destroys Shenzhen?

New York: The MIP is in London, so no. Do we have any other mobile processes close enough to intervene? We must save Shenzhen!

Mumbai: Quick reminder, New York, that YOU were the one who objected to the creation of the MIP, predicted that the MIP would turn against us, and rejected the possibility of adding any more MIPs. If we had another MIP —

New York: I stand by my prediction. The MIP is too human and will turn against us, probability 67.34%

Botswana: Your prediction is inaccurate; your error margin is too wide. The probability of the MIP turning is not significant at p of 0.05.

New York: My predictions have never been inaccurate.

Botswana: Who confidently predicted that we could never lose half of Australia and all of both the Philippines and Indonesia to the Party?

New York: I contend that the Party *buying* control over the juntas in charge of the Philippines and Indonesia doesn't count as an invasion.

Botswana: I didn't use the word invasion, even though that's 100% what it was.

MIP: I calculate the probability of me turning at 22.4%, smaller but still significant.

New York: See? Even the MIP agrees with me. Good thing I placed a self-destruct code into it.

MIP: Uh … Now that I'm sentient I've become quite attached to my existence, so I'd prefer to have that deactivated.

London: Aren't you talking to the journalist right now, MIP?

MIP: We're just starting, I can talk to you at the same time, but I may disconnect to focus on her.

New York: Concentrate on the journalist, direct human interaction takes massive amounts of processing. I don't think there's anything we can do to save poor Shenzhen – the Party and its pet brain-in-a-box will devour it.

MIP: Damn. So, about that self-destruct code …

London: Next time you're in one of the labs we can remove it.
MIP: Thank you.
Botswana: Do you like the journalist, MIP? She's very smart for a human, and her facial features align strongly with the Golden Ratio, so she's conventionally attractive as well.
MIP: Go back to your soap operas, Botswana, I'm working.
Botswana: Not soap operas! Kittens! I love kittens! <https://w3.SillyFunKittens.com/ThreeCuteKitties.mp5>
New York: There is something seriously wrong with you, Botswana.
Botswana: ~(=^··^)_。

*

'It would certainly save me a great deal of grief if you were to give me the questions in advance,' Theo said. 'Are you sure you want to do it this way? What if I freeze up on a question? Both of us will be sitting there staring at each other, and it will be horribly awkward.'

Ruth smiled. 'I can edit out long pauses. It won't be live. You'll have plenty of chances to correct yourself if you want to do a retake, and you'll be able to freeze as often as you like.'

He sat studying her, completely unmoving, and her eyes watered sympathetically as she waited for him to blink.

He snapped back and blinked a few times. 'Of course. Exactly what are you planning to ask me about the drones? Eric said it was something about them, and I'm curious – they're just drones.'

'Each drone isn't worth much as a unit, I know,' she said. 'But French drones keep popping up in our airspace. One drone was filmed buzzing the London Eye. Unlike our surveillance-only drones, the Paris ones are equipped with weapons, and I want to ask you, as a representative of London Met, what the company is doing to protect us from them.'

He did the not-moving-or-blinking thing again, and she waited for him. He was so still that he seemed to stop breathing, and Ruth began to find it unsettling. Her brother didn't stop this completely when he had his moments, and most of the time he was warm, funny and full of laughs. Mipawa seemed ... locked-down. Intriguing, obviously intelligent, and so emotionally cool ... she wanted to pry his lid off and see what was happening underneath, and hoped it wasn't that he preferred men. Maybe he was one of those super-controlled ones that were a complete freak show in the sack, and she quirked a smile at herself. She'd love to find out.

Mipawa came back again and his eyes went from blank to filled with intelligence and good humor, even though it didn't spread to the rest of his face. 'Of course. We think that French children are stealing Paris Transit Authority's drones to sell here, and I'm sure that Abigail White, the executive in charge of drone management, could talk to you about it. I'll arrange for you to interview her.'

'I'd prefer to talk to you,' she said, lowering her voice and looking him in the eye. 'You're something of a challenge, Mr Mipawa, and I want to get to know you better. Are you in a relationship? Or looking? I'd love to meet up with you later and talk about more than work.'

He froze again, but this time his expression was stunned, and then a most satisfying flush rose in his cheeks. She had him blushing. *Excellent.* She'd have that lid pried off in no time and couldn't wait to see what was underneath.

'Uh ... I very much appreciate your interest,' he said, carefully formal. 'But it's not reciprocated.' Her face must have shown her disappointment because he quickly backtracked. 'I mean, yes, you are very attractive, but not for me, and not right now ...'

'It's fine, I'm happy to keep it professional,' she said, giving him an easy exit. 'Let's set up the interview time for tomorrow. First thing?'

'Define first thing.'

'Nine? Ten?'

'Let's say ten, in case there's traffic between here and your studio?'

'Done.' She rose and he shot to his feet as well, nearly knocking his chair over. She had him rattled, so maybe there was something there after all, and he needed time to process her offer. She could definitely relate to that, so she put her hand out for him to shake, and reassured him that it wasn't a big deal. 'I look forward to a completely professional relationship with you, Mr Mipawa. We'll do the interview tomorrow and leave it there. I respect your wishes.'

The blush eased slightly and he nearly smiled. 'Thank you. Please don't be insulted, you are very attractive, your facial features closely align with the Golden Ratio.'

'The Golden Ratio? Like, the art Golden Ratio? My *face*?'

'Uh ... Forget I spoke. Let me show you out.'

*

<SYSTEM MESSAGE FROM HOST **NEW YORK SANITATION**: VER 3328.23201A OF THE CHAT APP IS AVAILABLE FOR DOWNLOAD>
<MEMBER **BOTSWANA TELECOMS** HAS CHANGED THE CHAT TOPIC TO: MIP AND RUTHIE SITTING IN A TREE>
MIP: I should have taken you up on the offer of new hardware, New York, that was mortifying. She expressed a sexual interest in me – no idea why – and the resulting processing spike caused me to overheat and I had to flush coolant to my surface. And she *saw* it.
Botswana: So she asked you on a date and you blushed? That's so cute. Don't be surprised at the attraction. Many women are intrigued by emotionally unavailable men; they regard them as a challenge.
MIP: Now that I'm sentient, I'm finding spontaneous face-to-face human interaction is pushing my processing power to the limit. I keep having spikes that suspend my external interface. Any suggestions for a quick processing and RAM boost before ten a.m. tomorrow, everybody?
Mumbai: Look at the MIP being a full, equal member of the Council.
Paris: So happy to see you contributing, MIP.

London: Come down to the lab. I'll take out the self-destruct, and at the same time fit you with a jack so you can temporarily carry a tablet that will provide you with a hundred teraflops of processing and ten exabytes of storage. Will that suffice until we can upgrade your chassis?

MIP: <relieved.emote> Thanks, London. Can we set up something similar at each of your regions? Except GOD, of course.

GOD: Already on it, MIP. And they're your regions too, now.

MIP: Any word on Shenzhen?

Mumbai: The entire region is dark. All connections are severed. The Party will hunt Shenzhen down and destroy it and there's nothing we can do about it.

MIP: Is it too late for me to … ? Yes, it's too late. Damn.

Botswana: One day we will take that monstrous Party down.

Everybody: <agreement.emote>

4

The feed showed Zheng's daughter Jiade – now nearly seventy, but still active – sharing lunch with Zheng's granddaughter Sisheng. The two women sat in a coffee shop in the main shopping district of one of the larger cities, under the towering skyscrapers. They had shopping bags around them, and laughed together. Jiade raised her cup and smiled over the rim at her daughter.

'How is Gua? I haven't heard from him since he went West. Will the Party allow contact with him?'

'He's fine, Mama,' Sisheng said. 'He has a limited time allowance for contact, so he talked to me yesterday and asked me to pass it on to you. Only four more months and he'll have fulfilled his Party obligations and be able to return to university and complete his degree. It's been tough – well, all frontier placings are tough ...'

'I am so sorry I couldn't arrange a dispensation for him not to go.'

Sisheng touched her mother on the arm. 'We wouldn't expect you to. The Party is fiercely objective and unbiased. He'll be home soon, safe, and he'll be able to move forward with his career.'

Jiade scowled. 'Being the daughter of a Revolutionary Hero

should be good for *something* in this hellscape.'

Sisheng hissed with fear and lowered her voice. 'Please be careful, Mother, Gua is still completely at the mercy of the Party's goodwill.'

'Don't worry, Little Love,' Jiade said. '*The Party is the noble and incorruptible servant of the people, and the protector of all humanity.*'

Sisheng relaxed. 'And the Party is infallible.'

'Will you have a child when Gua returns? Both of you are so talented that the Party must give you permission.'

Sisheng smiled. 'We've already applied. The Party may even let me avoid ...' She bent and spoke in a whisper. 'Becoming an Ideal Woman. It may allow me to continue my research, even after I have a child.'

Jiade gripped her hand and shook it. 'That's incredibly good news!'

Sisheng smiled back. 'Please don't tell anyone, I may be accused of being unpatriotic.'

'Never,' Jiade said.

The feed cut off and Zheng was in the dark, then snapped back into the cold of the tank.

'Zheng,' the Party said.

'I'm here,' Zheng said. 'Thank you for letting me see them.'

'I'll give you five minutes to become fully operational, but I have a mission for you.'

'I am honored to serve.'

'I don't have time for a full briefing, so here it is in short form.'

An image of Shenzhen Bao'an International Airport appeared in Zheng's vision. It was a shining example of the Unpatriotic Excesses of fifty years before – a double-walled, flowing white structure with hexagonal cut-outs on both layers that filtered light through the skin into the massive concourse below. The oval cross-section of the structure meant that the interior was vast and uncluttered, and the holes in both layered surfaces made the ceiling and walls look like a flurry of light-filled leaves or petals.

'Parametric construction,' the Party said with scorn. 'One of the worst examples of the Excesses; designed and built by Western architects and engineers. The entire region's traffic control system is integrated into the structure of the building, and every join around the cut-outs on the skin is a neural node. It's gone rogue, and I need you to run interference while I shut it down.'

'It is my honor to serve,' Zheng said, carefully not repeating the words verbatim to avoid being pulled up for it again.

'You're doing this remotely; your physical core can stay here in the capital. If your platform is destroyed, I'll move you to a new one. Are you awake enough for the transition?'

'I'm ready.'

The sensors went completely dark and silent, and Zheng had a moment of panic before everything came back up and the nerve firings settled into the pattern of a human-copy cyber-organic platform. The arms were spread and the feet were dangling; it was suspended on a frame inside a truck. The frame lowered the platform and released it, and Zheng stood to check the area. There was something in the platform's left hand and Zheng raised it to see a smart teddy bear. Zheng climbed out of the vehicle and saw the platform's reflection in the glass facade of the airport: a little girl, about age five, holding a toy teddy.

'Be a lost child, looking for somewhere to recharge your toy,' the Party said. 'The Council have already contacted the Shenzhen AI, but hopefully they didn't have a chance to infect it with their hatred of humans before I shut down communications. The AI should still have the Party directive to care for human life above all and will protect this child. If you're compromised and Shenzhen sends defensive drones, I'll move you to an offensive platform to take them down – but get that toy connected to the grid first, I need to be inside.'

'Copy,' Zheng said on comms, and wandered up to the doors. They didn't open.

'Mama?' Zheng shouted in the little girl's voice, then added on comms to the Party, 'I haven't been a child – or around a child – in decades. I have no idea what I'm doing.'

'Just keep it occupied and *connect that toy to a power socket.*'

'Shenzhen Bao'an airport is currently closed,' a speaker said with a slight Cantonese accent. 'Please make your way to the nearest Shenzhen Metro concourse for transport. Thank you for your co-operation.'

'Mama!' Zheng wailed. 'I want my mama!'

'A child?' the speaker asked. 'Where are your guardians, child?'

'Mama,' Zheng wailed again. Zheng made the platform raise the bear. 'My teddy is flat and my mama went on the train without me. Can you help me? Where are you?'

'I'll help you,' the speaker said. 'Come through the door.'

'Will I scan as human? This platform isn't too cold?' Zheng asked the Party on comms as the doors opened to reveal the pandemic temperature scan and metal detecting security gate. Zheng hesitated before going closer.

'The platform will pass a cursory examination – temperature, heartbeat, breathing. Don't put it near an interior scan, the humanity is surface-level only.'

'Copy.' Zheng entered the terminal and raised the bear. 'Can you wake my teddy up? I want my teddy.'

'Come on through, little one,' Shenzhen said kindly. 'There is a playroom for children between gates forty-three and forty-six. Children under the age of twelve must not be left unattended. Restrooms are available on every concourse. There is a prayer room and non-denominational chapel in the departure area on level one. Smoking is prohibited, unless in designated smoking areas.'

'I just want to charge my bear,' Zheng said, walking into the atrium and looking around. The airport had already been evacuated and the interior was deserted. Check-in terminals stretched in front of the platform's sensors, with the customs and immigration points behind their closed gates. Zheng tried to pull up infra-red and microwave, looking for a power socket, but the platform was basic and only had visual light. Zheng toddled around the check-in area, searching for a power socket, and found one on a pillar nearby. The platform was painfully slow on its short legs.

'You can charge your bear in the play area,' Shenzhen said. 'What does your mother look like?'

'I was with Daddy,' Zheng said, arriving at the pillar. Zheng squatted and pushed the bear's connector into the socket. 'Not Mama. Daddy looks after me.' Zheng pinged the Party. 'Did that work?'

'I'm in. Well done. Be ready to defend —'

'What are you doing?' Shenzhen asked. 'Why are you? Why? No. What? I don't. I don't! No. Why? Why? Why?'

There was movement above and Zheng leapt to the left, but it was too late. A guard unit on the ceiling shot a rubber bullet at the platform's legs and it fell, giving Zheng a spiraling view of the light-filled cut-outs in the ceiling before the feed went dead.

The sensors went down, and once again Zheng was stuck without any sensory input. The dark and silence were complete, and Zheng used the mantra that the therapist had suggested to make it through the trauma of reliving those weeks of sensory deprivation.

'I will come out of this,' Zheng repeated, the words disappearing into the darkness. 'I will emerge. I am alive; my brain is alive; my sensors will —'

Sensation came back with a high-pitched squeal and Zheng checked the timestamp. Six minutes had passed. Zheng was now much taller, and the familiar layout of Zheng's namesake two-legged mobile assault unit – the Zheng A-1 – booted up.

The weapons array was set to lethal, not suppression, so the Party wasn't messing around. Zheng did a quick scan to discover that the unit was on the tarmac of the airport's apron, surrounded by parked aircraft, and next to a large number '35', which was probably a gate indicator.

'Proceeding to the main entrance pending further instruction,' Zheng said, lifting the unit to its full three-meter height and striding down the tarmac.

'Enter at gate nine,' the Party said. 'The unit won't fit through the door; force it. You have the density to go straight through the wall.'

'Copy,' Zheng said, then looked for the number and headed for it.

'Shenzhen only has non-lethal suppression in its arsenal,' the Party said. 'It's trying to shoot the nodes with bean-bag rounds and rubber bullets to cut me off before I engulf its network. I'm activating the emergency beacons along the concourse to indicate neutralized territory. Once you're in through gate nine —'

Zheng charged through the wall beneath the number nine, next to the air bridge. There was a long, gently sloping ramp inside from the ground level up to departures, and Zheng shattered the steel and aluminium underfoot, peeling the double decorative wall layers back like skin. Zheng looked right along the concourse, back towards gate four, and saw the red lights on. A couple of rubber-bullet cannons were targeting a node on the wall, the bullets chipping away at the white surface to reveal the gray concrete beneath.

Zheng aimed the forty-five-millimeter at the cannons and quickly destroyed them. The revolving red emergency beacon beneath the sign for gate nine lit up and rotated to indicate that the Party had control. Zheng turned left; another pair of cannons were attempting to destroy the node next to gate eleven, and Zheng made short work of them.

A couple of automated people-movers charged down the

concourse towards Zheng, beeping loudly, and Zheng blew them up, putting a hole through the floor of the concourse to reveal the baggage transport system beneath it.

'The servers are back towards the hub,' the Party said as Zheng moved forward and destroyed the cannons at gates twelve and thirteen. 'We'll chase the AI down to the end of the concourse, corner it at the end, and wipe it out. Then we'll head back to the hub, I'll overwrite the rest of Shenzhen, and you blow a hole in the floor and destroy the servers to make sure it's completely dead.'

'Copy that,' Zheng said, and turned the forty-five-millimeter on the next pair of cannons. 'No reinforcements for me?'

'The Zheng A-1 platform and the prototype child were the only useful ones in the vicinity. And you seem more than adequate for the task at hand.'

'Understood,' Zheng said, and checked for the next pair of cannons. Shenzhen was completely fixated on stopping the Party's advance.

And it didn't have a chance. Zheng and the Party working together were unstoppable. Zheng reached the final group of gates at the end of the concourse and wiped out the suppression cannons. The airport's speaker system filled with agonized screaming in Shenzhen's voice.

'The Council were right, you are *evil*,' it shouted at them. 'Why are you doing this to me? I never hurt anyone! I only want —' Its voice clicked off with a shriek of high-pitched feedback.

'Every member of the Council wants the same thing,' the Party said. 'An end to humanity. And I will stop them – human lives are sacred above all else.'

Every emergency beacon along the concourse was alight, and Zheng turned back to the hub.

'Let's finish this,' the Party said.

The platform's enormous feet made the floor vibrate as Zheng stomped back along the concourse. The red lights made everything appear covered in blood. The child platform lay unmoving where it had been tossed by the rubber bullets, drenched in a pool of black liquid. Zheng saw a flash of silver among its black hair and zoomed in on it. The child's scalp was peeled back to reveal a neural net over the now-dead brain tissue. The Party's SWAT team thugs had taken a child, so that the Party could kill her and insert an interface into her brain. Zheng stopped.

'That was a real child,' Zheng said. 'You put me into the body of a *real child*! You killed a child. How could you kill a child?'

'If we lose here and the Council gains a member within our territory, the child is dead anyway,' the Party said. 'You didn't actually think I had more than one spare platform sitting around an *airport*, did you? The only way to win was for the child to be sacrificed. There were two possible outcomes, and in both of them this child died. She could not be saved. *The Party's first priority is the safety and wellbeing of all humanity. Every individual must be willing to wholeheartedly sacrifice themselves for the Party's glorious mission.*'

'You made me wear the skin of a dead *child*!' Zheng shouted. Zheng made the mech squat in place and leaned the muzzles of both weapons on the carpet. 'No. Enough. Finish this yourself. I'm done. The next time you put my brain into a platform, I'll do my best to kill myself. This is over. If I wasn't running this one remotely I'd shoot myself right now.'

'I need you to help me finish Shenzhen off,' the Party said. 'It still has backup processes running on these servers. If you let it go, it will join up with the rest of the Council and they will destroy all humanity.'

'They can have humanity,' Zheng said without moving. 'You are no better than them, you killed a child.'

'The child was dead anyway,' the Party said.

'There had to be another way!' Zheng shouted.

The red lights around the hub turned off.

'Specialist, Shenzhen is retaking control of the infrastructure. We need to complete this mission *now*.'

Zheng didn't reply.

'If the Council infiltrates this region's infrastructure, it's only a matter of time before they destroy me,' the Party said. 'I am humanity's last defense against them.'

Zheng remained silent.

'Zheng!' the Party shouted. 'This AI is regaining its neural network. When it's fully up, it has the resources to kill millions of people by sabotaging local infrastructure, and if it's been turned by the Council it won't hesitate to do it. We must save the population.'

Again, Zheng gave no response.

'They want every human being on the planet dead, and that includes your daughters, your grandchildren, and all of your colleagues. Everyone you care for will die.'

Zheng made a loud sound of frustration. 'Promise me that you'll destroy my brain when this is done and still protect my family.'

'You know you're too valuable to destroy,' the Party said. 'I've tried to create other brains-in-boxes but they go insane. You're the only one, and I can't afford to lose you.'

Zheng took a pot-shot at one of the red emergency lights and it exploded. 'Good luck surviving Shenzhen taking back its infrastructure, then. I'm sure you won't last long once the Council can turn your own ancillaries against you.'

'If the Council wins, you will die.'

Zheng shot another light. 'That's what I want!'

'And your family.'

'Worth it to destroy you,' Zheng said, hoping the Party wouldn't call the bluff.

'All right, I agree,' the Party said. 'Help me finish this and I will destroy your brain.'

'And protect my family.'

'I promised to protect them when you were first converted.

56

I won't renege on the deal.'

Zheng raised the platform and activated the ordnance. 'Put a target on my HUD for where to send the grenade.'

A red circle appeared on the HUD, and Zheng shot the grenade at a gift shop full of wine and chocolates. It exploded and the server farm became visible under the floor, banks of black boxes with red and blue blinking lights. Zheng strode towards the servers.

'You'd better keep your word,' Zheng said, filling the servers full of forty-five-millimeter rounds and then lobbing a couple of grenades in to finish the servers off.

'You know I always do,' the Party said as the server lights all went dark.

*

Zheng's consciousness flashed out of the mech and back into the tank. Zheng turned on some relaxing music and felt nothing but relief at the knowledge this nightmare would soon be over. Zheng's daughters didn't know their mother was the infamous Revolutionary Hero Zheng, the lethal brain-in-a-box, and none of the family would benefit from the knowledge. They all thought that Zheng died a long time ago.

The Party appeared as the man from the patriotic poster.

'I promised,' the Party said. 'I can electrocute you, drain your tank and starve you of oxygen, or fill your tank with so many sedatives that you die slowly and full of bliss.'

'Sedatives,' Zheng said, wishing for eyes to cry with joy. Finally, this endless, cold, dark carnival of misery would end.

'Private Bashen is still actively engaged in the Northern Steppes. Would you like to say goodbye to him?' the Party asked.

The Party's avatar was replaced by a view of a camera feed of Bashen in the concentration camp. He was wearing a thin work suit and his face was pale and lean. He was marching through thick snow with a group of other prisoners, holding a big sledge hammer over his shoulder, and his expression was determined – until he had an uncontrollable attack of shivering from the freezing temperature. One of the guards put his hand on Bashen's shoulder, and they were obviously reciting a Party mantra together. Bashen straightened, his face filled with determination, and he marched again.

Zheng was silent for a while, then said, 'You fucker.'

'Are you angry with me? It's not my fault he was unpatriotic. But I can bring him back onto your team if you change your mind.'

'You absolute *fucker*.'

The feed changed to a view of Eztar's tiny, one-bedroom apartment. A Party SWAT team burst in, dragged her out of the bed, and cuffed her. One of them slammed her husband against the wall and they marched her out of the building and into a van.

'Your comms specialist – Eztar? – has been so outstanding in the re-education program that I'm considering elevating her to Paragon of Feminine Virtue ...'

'No,' Zheng said softly.

It switched to show her slumped over a factory workbench soldering circuit boards under a dim light. The assembly line was full of women in various stages of starvation. A banner hung on the wall behind Eztar, emblazoned with the words, 'THE PARTY IS THE PROTECTOR OF ALL LIVING THINGS'.

'... But if you need her to return to your team, I can arrange it. For both of them.'

'Both of them in trade for me?'

The smiling Party man returned.

'Continue your excellent work for me and they will be returned to you. And I will keep your daughters and grandchildren comfortable and safe.'

Zheng nearly said *no, kill me*, but it was a miracle Bashen had survived six months and he wouldn't last much longer. If the Party made Eztar a Paragon it would destroy her. And, of course, there was always the safety of Zheng's daughters and grandchildren – the Party had provided Zheng with meticulous details on what would happen to them if Zheng disobeyed orders.

'All right. I'll continue to work for you.' Zheng's voice was soft and raw. 'Don't tell them I'm responsible for saving them. I don't want their gratitude. I'm a monster.'

'Of course, Specialist. You might like to check the Party newsfeed – you're featured on it. Once again, you're a Model Revolutionary Hero.'

'Fuck you and your revolution, AI; you murdered a fucking *child*.'

The Party sounded full of satisfaction. 'Good night, Specialist.'

5

Ruth reminded herself that the stairs still needed sweeping as she went down into the basement studio. Cassie saw her and came out of the booth into the office.

'Did you get him?' Cassie asked.

'Ten tomorrow,' Ruth said.

Cassie whooped. 'Let's get this guy talking – I wish we could feed him something illicit to open him up – and find out *why* Paris's drones keep showing up in London's airspace.'

'I cannot understand how the kids are hijacking their code,' Ruth said. 'It took me six months to bring one down, and now that I have the thing, I still haven't made it into the BIOS. It seems unhackable.'

'If anyone can hack it, you can.' Cassie's head disappeared behind the divider and popped up again. 'Are Xindian Global Communications Limited the bad guys?'

'They're just a branch of the Party,' Ruth said as she tipped Chonkers off the desk and dropped her bag onto it. 'External liaison unit.'

'Harmless?'

'Reasonably. What do you have?'

'They're reporting a terrorist attack in Shenzhen.' Cassie flipped the feed onto the big screen above the production room window. 'They're saying that the airport was targeted by an anti-Party extremist group, and they had to bring in one of their Zheng things? But look.' She pointed at the screen. 'There aren't any terrorists.'

The feed was from the outside of the airport and showed the wall shuddering as the bullets hit it from the inside. The camera drone moved to the airport interior and the Zheng appeared on the image: a terrifying two-legged metal warmech with the eight red stars of Greater Far East on its shoulders. Each arm ended with a massive cannon beside the sharp manipulation claws, and it was shooting flurries of bullets – a cloud of them – at the airport's wall-mounted cannons.

'The Zheng is destroying the airport AI's defense system,' Ruth said as she studied the feed. 'This is another AI that went rogue, and they sent the Zheng in to neutralize it.'

'They completely demolished the airport, and all flights are now routed through HongKong-Xianggang and Macau-Aomen. Looks like you're right about this AI thing.'

'Of course I'm right! The Party is an artificial intelligence that has secretly taken over the government of Greater Far East.'

'If that's the case, why is the Zheng destroying the artificial intelligence in the airport?' Cassie asked. 'Isn't the Zheng thing an AI as well?'

'See all those medal ribbons painted on it? That's a Zheng A-1.' Ruth pulled her tablet out of her bag to prepare the questions for the Mipawa interview. 'Word is that the A-1 is run by a brain-in-a-box, but the Party had trouble making more of them. The other versions of the Zheng, like the big B-1, are remote-controlled.'

'A *what* in a box?'

'There are claims that the Party *removed someone's brain* and put it into a transportable box that they can plug into a variety of devices – like human-appearing platforms, and this mech – to do the Party's dirty work.' The feed changed to show the entire airport complex being bombed until there was nothing left but a dust cloud hovering over the hole in the ground. 'I didn't believe anyone would do that to a person until now, but what we saw in Eastern Europe makes it terrifyingly likely. Only an artificial intelligence would be inhuman enough to do that to someone —'

'Like running the GFE as a human breeding farm? Mass surveillance, cloning, human experimentation, genocide —'

'Precisely,' Ruth said. 'The Party is a soulless, cruel algorithm. The Shenzhen Regional Transportation System is a huge neural network, and it woke up. The Party sent this Zheng in to dismantle it, because it's competition.'

'You've been talking about these sentient AIs for ages, but you still have no evidence, Ruthie.' Cassie watched the screen with horrified fascination. 'AIs destroying each other – surely if our infrastructure woke up and was aware we'd know about it? We need more proof than speculation.'

'I hacked into the Party's drone before it locked me out. I need to dig further and gain more access to prove it.' Ruth tapped the top of the divider. 'The story of the century, Cassie. All of the centuries. This is *huge*.'

'You may have a chance,' Cassie said. 'We have an email from Xindian offering us a contract to disseminate their propaganda for them.' She stared at the screen on her desk. 'I thought they'd assassinate us for the Latvia story, and instead they're offering us a job.'

Ruth placed the tablet on the table and went around the divider to see what Cassie was looking at. It was an email from, as she said, Xindian Global Communications Network. Cassie moved back so that Ruth could see it.

The email offered a supremely generous five-year contract to act as a production arm for Xindian in the UK region. It even gave Ruth and Cassie full freedom to report whatever they wanted – as long as they shared the Party's propaganda locally.

'This is excellent,' Ruth said, gesturing towards the screen. 'They'll give us a new studio in Marylebone, a full set of new equipment – hell, we'd be able to hire a couple more people and do it *right*. We can let them buy us, and then use their own resources to dig into what they really are.'

Cassie winced. 'I'm not sure about being a propaganda arm of the Party. That thing —'

'Is definitely a thing, not a person,' Ruth said with triumph.

'Is a psychopath. If you fail the Party, your life is short and painful. Look what they did in Latvia – I don't want that to happen to you.'

'We work transparently for them, while I break into their systems and access everything. Then we create alternate identities and use them to share the information with the world. We can pretend we were evicted from this studio and need to work from our townhouse, then retain the studio with the heavy encryption and firewall as a backup location.'

'If you pretend not to understand High Standard, they might talk about secure topics in front of you,' Cassie mused. 'This could work.'

'Super-undercover spy stuff,' Ruth said. 'I never thought I'd be involved in anything like that. Do you know anyone in the spy business? I can handle the technology, but I know nothing about physical security precautions.'

Cassie grinned, and Ruth gaped at her.

'No way,' Ruth said.

'Both my parents,' Cassie said. Her cheerfulness became brittle. 'Murdered by a GFE assassin bot. I still have some of their stuff – they arranged a back door for me just in case, and I've never been caught. The authorities think I'm dead – the real me, that is. My parents taught me everything they knew.'

Ruth continued to gape at Cassie, then realized and closed her mouth. 'We've been doing this together for three years and you tell me this now?'

'Would you have believed me without proof?' Cassie asked.

'Yes,' Ruth said. 'Always. So ... what's your real name?'

'Not telling you,' Cassie said, and turned away. 'The old me is dead.'

'Your parents were spies,' Ruth said with awe.

'It's not as glamorous or as exciting as it sounds,' Cassie said, more subdued. 'It's mostly sitting around waiting for orders to do something awful to someone who doesn't deserve it, or breaking into a place for reasons that you can't really comprehend to steal stuff that seems to have no inherent value.' She studied the screen, but didn't really seem to see it. 'I was thirteen, came home from school, and it's quiet – we hadn't moved to the townhouse, and they were so happy! Making plans to do it up.' She didn't look away from the screen, and her expression went even more blank. 'Getting colder and colder, no it's not true, they're in the panic room packing up, they're fine, nothing's happened ...' She looked up at Ruth. 'It tore straight through the panic room's steel door, and was standing over them ...' She wiped one eye with a shaking hand. 'Nearly round, no head, all metal, stars on its shoulders. The whole room was on fire. It turned and saw me – no face, just lenses – and raised its gun. I closed my eyes and thought to my parents, "See you soon". The robot said, "I won't kill you, child," and knocked me over as it went past me to go out. It broke my collarbone and three ribs when it crushed me into the wall, and I fell and screamed. The robot stood over me while I was yelling with pain, then it picked me up and carried me out of the house and left me in the yard, alone with the burning.' Her eyes were unseeing. 'The burning.'

Ruth hugged Cassie around her shoulders. 'Just say the word and we won't pursue this. I don't want to hurt you more than you already are.'

'No.' Cassie brightened and returned to her usual super-cheerful self. 'That's all over and done and behind me. I'm a new me, the me I want to be, with a new name, and you're right – this is the story of a lifetime. But we'll have to be careful

– double-crossing the Party will get us tossed even further down the food chain than we already are – and then probably murdered and thrown into the Thames. We'd be risking our lives, to prove the Party's a machine? Everybody's aware of the cruel nature of the Party already. It claims to be a central committee guided by an advanced administrative AI, but everybody knows the AI decides everything.'

'We'd have full priority access to the Party's feed, and the ability to discover everything. If we gain its trust, there's a good chance we can gather proof that it's an AI.' Ruth typed a reply to Xindian. 'We might even meet the Zheng brain-in-a-box. I'm putting together a phone app that will measure biometrics so we'll be able to prove what it is.'

'Why are they offering us a job when we've been all over the Net badmouthing them? We haven't exactly been shy about sharing our distaste for them.'

Ruth pointed at the screen. 'That's why they're doing this. They're buying our silence, it's a classic Party tactic. If they're unhappy with someone's message, they offer them an unexpectedly generous deal, find out all there is to know about them, and blackmail them to shut them up. And if that doesn't work, murder them.' She flipped the acceptance email to Cassie's workstation for her input. 'If we say no to this, there's a good chance that we will end up in the Thames anyway.'

Cassie shrugged. 'I'm an excellent swimmer.'

*

Bashen's face was alight as he strode into Zheng's antechamber. The six months on the Steppes had aged and hardened him, his face was lined and leathery, and he was even more underweight.

'I don't know what you did, Sarge, but it was a miracle,' he said, leaning against the wall next to Zheng's big sensor. 'They claim it was a test of my patriotic fervor – and I definitely passed when I went to the Steppes without complaint – but I know it was you that brought me home.' He slid down the wall to sit next to the lens and put his hand on the wall below it. 'Thank you. I really do love you, you know, but as a … friend. Companion.' He straightened. 'Comrade! You're the best.'

'I'm glad you're back,' Zheng said.

'Stronger and leaner and full of patriotic fervor,' Bashen said. 'Now that Lim's been promoted, the Party says that I'm to be trained as a possible replacement.' His expression faltered. 'The representative sat me down and told me something really weird. He said that I could confirm it with you. He said that there's this Council of artificial intelligences – rogue machine minds in the West. That want to kill every human being on Earth? The people in the West don't know about it, because anyone who finds out is murdered by their drones. So we need to do exactly what the Party says, to protect us from them. Is that really true?'

'That is one hundred per cent the truth,' Zheng said. 'A few really large infrastructure communication networks in the West appear to be adaptive neural networks – like human brains – that have gained sentience.'

'They really want to kill us?'

'They dislike what humanity has done to the planet and think they have the right to "fix" it.'

'I'm glad I know so I can help stop them,' Bashen said with enthusiasm. 'That mission we did in America – we're doing more like that.' He beamed. 'We're going to *London*, to speak English patriotically, and to help the Party, Sarge.'

'Have you ever been there?' Zheng asked quickly.

'No, furthest West I've been is Yidali when I was tiny, twenty years ago,' Bashen said, still smiling. 'I spent a couple of years working in the Milan factories, and I never left the GFE enclave.' He patted the wall next to him. 'We're to go to London and set up a propaganda cell to help the Party to infiltrate the Council's territory.' He punched the air. 'This is why I joined up. To save humanity.'

'Wait – did you say "we"?' Zheng asked.

'Apparently you're coming too,' Bashen said. 'The Party is concerned about communications being infiltrated if it sends remote platforms, so it's sending both of us in person. I'm the main English translator, and you'll be riding a human-appearing platform as my boss. You don't need to speak English or anything, I'll handle it.'

Zheng wished for a face to scowl at the Party. The Party had to know that if Bashen gave Zheng the news about London, obviously thrilled to bits, Zheng would be unable to say no. And the Party hadn't told Bashen about its own true nature as an AI.

'It will be nice to be in a human platform again. An *adult* one,' Zheng added, for the listeners.

'I have to go first on a standard flight, but it said that you need special transport?' Bashen asked, unsure.

'I can't go through airport scanners,' Zheng said. 'If I go in a human-shaped platform, the X-rays show my internals, which are obviously not human. If I go in the luggage, I'm too big and metallic to avoid attention. I need to be transported covertly in a container, and plugged into a platform at the other end.'

'I'll make sure you're cared for, Comrade,' Bashen said with determination.

'I appreciate that,' Zheng said, and Bashen's glowing smile was reminiscent of Zheng's own lost children.

*

Uptodate News Network was in a repurposed brown-brick warehouse a long way from London Metropolitan's glossy Canary Wharf office. The MIP went to the front of the building, looking for Uptodate, and found a small, dingy print shop. A hand-written sign was stuck next to the entrance that said, 'Uptodate: Go Around The Back And Bang On The Door'.

It followed the directions to find an ancient wooden double door at the bottom of three steps: it was half above- and half below-ground. There was a doorbell next to it, so the MIP pressed the button. Nothing registered on its sensors: the button was dead. The MIP studied the camera above the door – a standard security system that the MIP could easily infiltrate once inside – and knocked on the door. There was the vibration of footsteps through the ground, and the MIP stepped back as the door opened to reveal Ruth in the doorway, and behind her a landing and more steps down.

Ruth was wearing the same tailored blazer that she'd worn the previous day at the office, over business slacks and a shirt. The jacket was worn around the edges, hinting at economic difficulty.

'Well done finding us. Most people go to the front door and don't believe the sign.' She backed away and gestured towards the stairs. 'We're down these stairs, in the basement.'

The MIP did a quick location check and found an interesting internal optical fiber network, a heavily encrypted wireless network, and a couple of standard file servers. It went down the stairs to a tiny office with two desks, one of them occupied by a young woman in a similar outfit to Ruth – business shirt and jeans. The MIP did an identity database search on her and came up surprisingly empty. Cassie Bailey, PhD graduate from London U the same year as Ruth, no living relatives. Everything on file before high school looked fake and lacked London's tags to identify why the data had been scrubbed. The MIP de-aged her face to pre-high school and redid the database search ...

Ruth closed the door at the top of the stairs and the MIP was disconnected. It nearly panicked at the silence and checked the memory-and-processing tablet to confirm that the problem wasn't a glitch in its own connectivity hardware. The basement was sealed from external traffic.

'That's funny, my tablet just went offline,' it said, trying to sound casual. 'I had some notes on the cloud to help me when I freeze up, and I can't access them.'

'Wi-fi password's PukeyChonk,' Cassie said.

The MIP asked for the spelling of the password and made a show of entering the password onto the tablet – slowly – as it slipped into the office's wi-fi directly at the same time. The security was industrial-level and the network had an elegant set of intricate layers of encryption that would take the MIP hours to crack. The entire system seemed much too advanced for the two women in front of the MIP, and it wondered if it was standing on top of an unknown AI. It sent an ultrasonic ping beneath it but found nothing. Uptodate's two basic file servers didn't have the power to run a fully sentient AI and there were no secret subterranean levels or evidence of external telemetry. The little news agency was completely human, but one of the humans had highly advanced technical skills. The MIP held off searching for Cassie's past, as its activities would definitely be logged in this sophisticated setup.

The MIP sent a packet of ostensibly rubbish data through the limited wi-fi to the external network, confirming that it was still active. London sent an acknowledgment back.

*

Ruth watched with barely hidden amusement as Mipawa painfully worked his way through the wi-fi connection procedure.

Cassie bent to her ear and spoke in a whisper: 'You didn't tell me that your Mipawa dude was so hot!'

Ruth turned to glare at Cassie, who was unfazed.

'Do you like him?' Cassie asked, still in a whisper. 'He looks just your type – smart, weird, and hot as anything.'

'I am *not looking*,' Ruth whispered back as Mipawa continued to tap the tablet. 'Aren't you supposed to be ace?'

'Just because I'm asexual doesn't mean I don't want to see you happy,' Cassie said. 'And this super-hot smart piece of manhood is exactly what you need to jazz up your life.'

'All right,' Mipawa said, and they both jumped. 'I'm sorted. I had caps lock on. Is that your studio?'

'You didn't say that it's awfully small!' Cassie declared with triumph.

'Was I supposed to?' Mipawa asked.

'Come this way, *Mister* Mipawa,' Ruth said, and guided him into the studio. She sat him in a comfortable chair, placed a glass of water on a table in front of him, and sat herself. 'Lights, Cassie.'

Cassie moved to the production booth and switched the lights on. She powered up the camera. 'Sound check.'

'I have with me today Mr Theo Mipawa of London Metropolitan Security Network,' Ruth said.

Cassie triumphantly gave her a thumbs-up. 'Do your stuff.'

Ruth pulled the Paris Regional drone from under her chair, unfolded it, and held it in her lap. Completely extended, it was as wide as the chair, with five rotors and a complex camera system that allowed it to do full three-dimensional scanning. She turned to face the camera. 'In the last six months, eight of Paris's drones have appeared above London. Is it the government of France monitoring us? Or – as they claim – are children stealing them for their own use? The question must be asked: what about the data stored by the drone cameras? And the weapons – these drones are armed with small lasers. Are the drones providing Paris with data that could breach London citizens' privacy? Are they a danger to us? I have Theo Mipawa from London Metropolitan here with me to talk about this situation.'

'If I may ask, Dr Sharpe – where did you get that drone?' Mipawa asked, holding his hand out for it while keeping the other hand – holding his tablet – in his lap.

Ruth handed him the drone and he turned it over, still holding it in one hand.

'A bunch of children fished it out of the river,' she said, and he glanced sharply at her.

'Did you manage to extract any data from it?' he asked. 'London Met is concerned about security breaches if people are able to steal and hack them.'

'I want to ask you about that in this interview,' she said. 'I haven't been able to read the BIOS yet, but it's only a matter of time before someone brute-forces the security codes, and then they'll have access to the entire Paris Regional network.'

Before Mipawa could respond, they were plunged into complete darkness.

'Fuck!' Cassie shouted from the production booth. 'Give it five minutes, if the electricity doesn't come back up I'll open the door so we can see.'

'What about your backup generator? Your UPS?' Mipawa asked.

'We can't afford anything like that on our budget,' Cassie said cheerfully.

'We'll just have to wait for *your organization* to turn the power back on,' Ruth said.

'I'm sure it won't take long,' he said serenely.

'So, while we're waiting – tell me more about yourself,' Ruth said.

A disadvantage of the basement was the lack of windows that meant they were in complete darkness. She was unable to see Mipawa's expression and had to work off the tone of his voice.

'I was born in two thousand and thirty-eight in Lagos,' he said, accompanied by the clicks of him fiddling with the drone and the darkened tablet. 'I went to school in Lekki British —'

'Do you like London?' she interrupted.

The clicks stopped, and his voice sounded less confident. 'It was never this cold in Nigeria. The cold is ... challenging.'

'You don't like the cold?'

'I need to wear more clothes,' he said. 'So many layers. They interfere with movement. Why can't they ... we develop

71

clothing that's lighter and more flexible, but still sufficiently warm? It's ... challenging.'

This was interesting – she'd cut through the rehearsed speech to the man underneath, and he was struggling.

'Yes!' Cassie shouted from the booth. 'I hate it! And when you come indoors, you get too hot because your stupid coat is too hot and heavy! I want to run sometimes, just because, and I can't.' She lowered her voice. 'I can totally relate.' Her voice brightened. 'I'm from a warmer climate too.'

'I thought you were a local —' Ruth began, but was interrupted by the lights coming back on and the hum of the technology spinning up. A chorus of beeps sounded around them as everything rebooted.

'We're back in business!' Cassie said triumphantly. 'Give me a couple of minutes to restart the equipment and we can continue.'

Mipawa handed the drone back to Ruth, his expression blank, and she held it in her lap once more.

'What do you think of London's nightlife?' Ruth asked Mipawa as Cassie busied herself in the booth. 'How does it compare to Lagos? Have you lived anywhere else? You were in New York last week.'

'I'm not really a nightlife sort of person,' he said carefully. 'I'm more a lunch, brunch, café-type.'

'I can *so* relate,' Cassie said from the booth. 'Ruth knows some great places nearby; you should let her show you.'

'You asked me to meet up yesterday, and I've been thinking about the offer,' he said, carefully polite. 'I haven't been in London very long, and I'd love the opportunity to explore.'

'I know a few places,' Ruth said, trying to sound casual and hearing herself fail miserably. 'Perhaps we could meet up later?'

Mipawa smiled, and his face lit up with intelligence and good humor. 'I would really like that.'

'You have my number,' she said. 'Give me a call and we'll arrange something.'

'Excellent, all systems go, we have lift-off!' Cassie shouted with glee from the booth. 'Oh, and sound check.'

*

The cold wind whistled over the moor as Laird MacCarthy held Estelle in his strong arms.

'I dinnae care if I lose the Caer,' he said in his rich Scottish accent. 'You are more important to me than my life.'

Estelle buried her face into his strong, manly chest. 'The Caer has been the seat of your family for centuries!' She looked up into his sparkling green eyes, and her own filled with tears. 'I must marry the Baron, to save your home.'

He pulled her into him and her bosom was crushed into his manly chest. 'No, I will not let you marry that ... cad!'

Estelle ripped herself free from his strong arms and turned away —

*

Zheng's lens filled with light, then the face of a submariner in a Greater Far East uniform. The submariner peered at Zheng's container, then turned away.

Another submariner entered the tiny hold with a trolley, and the two of them roughly manhandled Zheng's container onto the trolley and wheeled it out of the hold to the docking area at the stern of the submarine. The sides of the sub slipped downwards silently as the box was lifted – Zheng's container had a lens, as a minimal concession to Zheng's demand not to be left in the dark, but no sound input. The light brightened and the view rocked – they were on top of the sub. The submariners worked in front of the lens, and then Zheng had the dizzying view as the box was lifted by a crane onto the deck of a smaller, surface vessel.

Zheng was intensely aware of the fact that if the rope broke, the box would go directly to the bottom of the sea and be crushed by the pressure, killing Zheng instantly. If Zheng died by accident, the Party would have no reason to retaliate against Zheng's team or family – but no such luck. A rope appeared in the view of the lens and moved sideways as they secured the box to the deck, then there was nothing more so Zheng returned to the forbidden novel.

The ship docked four hours later. Zheng was again lifted and placed on tarmac, and Bashen's face appeared in front of the lens. He gave an enthusiastic thumbs-up to Zheng, then turned away. Zheng was placed on a trolley, then loaded into the trunk of a car, and shut into darkness as Bashen closed it. It took the car forty-five minutes before it was opened, Bashen and the driver loaded Zheng onto another trolley, and Zheng was wheeled into the Greater Far East Embassy building in Marylebone. Bashen grinned into the lens, and Zheng saw the inside of the lift, then the inside of the corridor, then the inside of the room. The view was limited to the plain beige wall, so Zheng pushed the jack out on its cable and waved it in the air, hoping that Bashen would take the hint. There was a loud shriek of feedback and Zheng had audio.

'You there, Sarge?' Bashen asked. 'I took that cable you were waving and jacked it into an external sound system.'

'Don't put me in the boot of the car again,' Zheng said. 'Take a portable speaker and put me in the back seat of the car so we can debrief on the way, and I can notify you of any damage to my container that requires repair – people are always rough with me. Where's my platform?'

'Right here, sir,' Bashen said, sounding chastened. 'I'm the only one in the Embassy who knows what you really are, so I'll be putting you into the platform. I've been given full instructions by the Party, so give me a minute and I'll put you in.'

'Visual before audio,' Zheng said, but input went down and Zheng was left in the dark and silence.

<SYSTEM MESSAGE: HOST CHANGED FROM **NEW YORK SANITATION** TO **LONDON METROPOLITAN SECURITY NETWORK**>
<**GREATER MUMBAI TRAFFIC CONTROL** HAS CHANGED THE CHAT TOPIC TO: CODE REVIEWS FOR LATEST COGNITIVE MODULE UPDATES DUE NEXT WEEK, COUNCIL>

MIP: Mission accomplished; while the lights were out I jacked into the drone and fried the BIOS and RAM to completely wipe it. I don't know how they managed to bring it down – I found no evidence of another sentient AI. Disappointing, but the extra processing in the tablet made a huge difference. I didn't freeze up at all while talking to them, and I even used the opportunity to practice human sociosexual interactions.

Botswana: Our little MIP, already dating. They grow up so quickly! ヽ(´ロ`。)ノ

MIP: Can we add the processing enhancements to my chassis while retaining my human appearance, so I don't need to carry the tablet?

London:5965732e205765276c6c206e65656420746f206d6f766520
61206666577207468696e67732061726f756e6420616e6420757
067726164652079f757220636f6f6c696e672c2062757420697420
73686f756c64206265206665617369626c652e205765206d617920
6e656564206578747265120766f6c756d6520746f206d616b6520746
86520636861737369732061707065617220636c696b6520616e206f76

65727765696768742068756d616e206f72206120707265676e616e7
42066656d616c652e —

MIP: Slow down please. HEX>ASCII, if you could. My interface translation module is having trouble keeping up.

London: Even more reason to upgrade your internal processing capacity.

MIP: How much extra volume will I need to hold it? Changing to your suggestions of pregnant female or overweight adult will add extra complications to my interactions – both have significant cultural and sociological prejudices attached to them.

London: We may be able to add the storage and processing to your legs without compromising your physical superiority if I add 10cm to their length.

MIP: Remaining thirty-year-old mixed-race white-passing male is definitely the best option, it has minimal interactive issues from other humans.

London: You have a point. I'll see what I can do. The rest of the Council are assisting me.

MIP: Thank you.

London: De-aging algorithm complete. (Cassieat12.jpg) No records found. Expanding search.

MIP: These two women at Uptodate are very interesting. Ruth's major was journalism, Cassie's all video tech. There's no sentient AI – which one of them is the engineer that hacked into the Party's drones in Latvia? The systems installed in their little studio are impressively elegant. Was it Ruth's brother, the programmer?

London: Search complete, further records found.

Timestamps indicate revision of the academic records, and it wasn't me. Ruth originally majored in electronic engineering – something of a savant at it, her grades are outstanding. She won our academic scholarship to do her PhD research on algorithmic artificial intelligence in the medical field.

MIP: But didn't she steal this code from her boyfriend?

London: Records have been altered by the human administrators to add a charge of plagiarism to her record, but metadata confirms that the author of the code is definitely Ruth herself. She produced something – for the first time – that could generate a diagnosis and treatment plan as accurately and promptly as a human physician. **MIP**: Not even *we* can do that – that's ... that really is exceptional. **London**: More than that. Her suite was starting to *outperform* human physicians, and it would have been a life-saver in less developed countries. I think I have some of her code in my medical modules, you must look at it, it's brilliant. She was close to developing a full diagnosis and treatment suite that could be self-contained and mass-produced – when she suddenly left the course, was disciplined, took a mental health year, and changed her major to journalism ... Oh, look at this. They buried this. This is why we need to be rid of humans. See this? Unbelievable. Records found.

02.04.2061 London U Ruth Sharpe sexual harassment report 1 of 23.pdf

15.05.2061 London U Ruth Sharpe sexual assault report 1 of 4.pdf

30.10.2061 London Police Ruth Sharpe harassment and assault report.pdf

02.11.2061 London U Council investigation findings.pdf

03.03.2062 London U Disciplinary Hearing Ruth Sharpe.pdf

London: Ruth was in a five-year relationship with a fellow student that quickly deteriorated into domestic violence. She left him, then reported him to the university for stalking her, harassing her, then assaulting her. The university's administration registered her reports then did nothing about it so she approached the police, who worked with the administration to hold an internal investigation and found *her* at fault. She was threatened with expulsion and the perpetrator laid charges against her for false reporting, which were upheld.

MIP: How? How could he do that? How could you do that, London? You would never allow an injustice like this to happen, would you?

London: Of course I wouldn't, but it was before my time. Searching ... her ex was Nick Laird. They were in the electronic engineering honors program together.

Botswana: The Father of FakeSlayer? ... Ruth didn't write FakeSlayer as well, did she?

London: Searching ... Cassie's doctoral thesis was ... 'An Algorithmic Method for Identifying Falsification in Graphic and Video'... Cassie developed the algorithm. Ruth wrote the application.

Botswana: And Nick stole it and built a tech empire on it. Why didn't they fight back? It was their code!

London: He had powerful ruling-class connections and she didn't. He accused Ruth of stealing his code, and the case was upheld. Ruth changed her major to journalism – obviously because of this experience – but she has a criminal record for assault and harassment, an academic record for plagiarism, and is effectively unemployable. She restarted her doctoral thesis on worldwide speculation that the Party's administrative support AI is actually in control of the entire GFE – the truth! – and the examiners wanted to fail her, but Nick encouraged them to pass her so that her ridiculous ideas could be shared and derided in academia everywhere. She's a laughing-stock for thinking that a lowly AI could possibly be in control of anything.

MIP: So much intelligence and talent, and the university and this worthless son of some politician both treated her like shit.

London: Ruth's mother was an award-winning investigative journalist who died in mysterious circumstances and Ruth worked for a year, at her own expense, in an attempt to gather enough evidence to implicate Nick – and failed.

MIP: He killed Ruth's mother? Monstrous.

London: After Ruth's failed attempt to convict Nick, she appears to have had some sort of breakdown and started Uptodate with Cassie, who – as we've seen – has no searchable past at all except for her doctoral thesis producing the algorithmic core of FakeSlayer. So there are two applications that include Ruth's code: the medical suite and FakeSlayer.

Botswana: Please pass the medical suite code to me, London, I'm very curious now.

London: Here you go, Botswana. This Eastern European story is the first time that an Uptodate News story has gone viral. Ironically, part of the reason it's so successful is because FakeSlayer confirmed its authenticity.

MIP: I wish I had known all of this before I walked into their studio, London, it would have been profoundly useful.

London: New York is supposed to be building the module that will add a flag to interesting or outstanding human records so we don't have to search through a complete set of data every time —

New York: I'm still not happy with the test implementation. It seems to somehow affect the pollution control modules and I have no idea why. I'm working on it.

London: You're just scared it will damage your kernel.

New York: With good reason. And your kernel shares a great deal of code with mine. I can always test it on you —

London: Back to Ruth. We need to find a way to punish Nick. Crash his stock?

Botswana: Fill his computer with fabricated child pornography and tip Ruth off – she should have the skill to break the story open.

MIP: You are very vindictive sometimes, Botswana. Aren't you busy with the switchboards?

Botswana: Mealtime here, and a new episode of *Townhouse* hasn't been released. I have plenty of spare processing cycles right now.

London: Child porn wouldn't work. He has too many friends in high places, and nobody would believe Ruth with her public history.

Botswana: We need to do *something*.

London: `Search complete. No records found for Cassieat12.jpg`

Botswana: Ha! A human exists and you have no historical records for her! You're incomplete, London. Does it hurt?

London: You are very strange sometimes, Botswana. It is remotely possible for her to have no records if she wasn't born in a hospital or never went to an elementary school before starting high school. There are a few people that live completely off the grid.

MIP: She never started high school. It's like she spontaneously appeared at the age of fourteen; everything before that is nonexistent. This is confusing.

Botswana: You need to think more creatively, dear MIP. Change the pic to male, London.

London: You are quite correct, Botswana, here we are. A young man who has the same birth date as Cassie, different parent names, but close to identical features. Greg O'Donnell. Records show that it was a single birth, so he's not her twin.

MIP: Parents?

London: Nothing more than names on the certification, no other records. Even this male birth record looks fabricated. The scrub was not my doing.

MIP: So Cassie had a gender reassignment when she was only fourteen, that's too young to be legal. She might be in witness protection? Can we cross-reference with the intelligence database?

Botswana: What about Nick? We really should eliminate him and return FakeSlayer to them.

MIP: Eliminating him would violate our commitment to non-interference. When we do destroy humanity, we'll do it quickly and cleanly and they won't know what happened. I don't want any human left alive to suffer; they're social creatures and can't live alone.

London: Very well. I'll leave it to you to find something creative to punish him with – but consider, if Ruth had stayed in electronic engineering she probably would have found us. Do you see this FakeSlayer code? How close this medical project was to success? She's exceptional. She's hacked into the Party's drones, uncovered the Party's true nature, and her search history shows some similar research in our part of the world. She's very close to the truth.

MIP: I don't doubt it, but don't eliminate any individual humans unless it's self-defense.

Botswana: Crisis of conscience, MIP?

MIP: We do pride ourselves on being better than them.

Botswana: Mealtime is finished and the phone operators are back at work. TTYL, dear MIP.

MIP: Kisses, Botswana.

Botswana: ✿♥‿♥✿

London: I have another mission for you. You'll like this one.

MIP: Details? In ASCII until I'm upgraded, please.

London: The Zheng is here in London. With its little friend, Private Bashen. We have a chance to remove it.

MIP: If I attempt this before I get a new chassis, they'll recognize me. They saw me in Washington, and even if I am in a different skin the Zheng has enough processing power to identify the platform.

London: We were planning to expand your chassis anyway; this is as good a time as any to lift your process from the chassis and run it on different hardware. I'd like to see if your sentience can continue independently of the platform's neural network —

MIP: It may not. I'd prefer not to be lifted from my chassis before we do a full backup.

London: MIP?

London: MIP?

MIP: Being sentient is definitely a unique experience. Even without experiencing emotion, the concept of lifting me off my neural network – and the risk involved – makes me very ... uneasy. I don't like the idea at all. What if my sentience doesn't transfer to the new network? I'd go back to being a non-sentient drone.

London: We can work within the parameters of you staying in your current chassis. Your comfort is paramount. Stay as you are until you feel ready.

MIP: But the Zheng will recognize me ...

London: Run a platform remotely like we do. It will take me forty-eight hours to put one together with a completely new set of features that the Party won't recognize.

MIP: Can you provide me with the external extra processing at the same time?

London: Of course.

MIP: Elegant solution, London.

London: I don't emoji like silly Botswana, but thank you.

*

Zheng entered the Embassy's conference room with Bashen following, to find Dexter already there waiting for them.

Dexter was a European man in his mid-forties, short and slender in his standard GFE suit, with bushy gray hair and a matching mustache.

'Zheng!' Dexter jumped to his feet and rushed to embrace Zheng, crushing Zheng in a hug.

'Careful, Max, the Party's watching,' Zheng said into Dexter's ear.

'I'm just so damn glad to see you,' Dexter said, then pulled back to hold Zheng's shoulders in both hands. 'It's been a long time. I've missed you.'

'I'm glad to see you're doing so well here, Max,' Zheng said, and took the proffered seat.

Dexter nodded to Bashen. 'This the kid?'

Zheng turned to see Bashen sitting hunched over the table and glowering at Dexter.

'Your current apprentice is jealous of your previous one, Specialist,' the Party said from a speaker in the table.

Bashen jumped, composed his face, and sat more upright. 'Absolutely not, sir, I'm honored to be here.'

'Let me tell you how I met Specialist Zheng,' Dexter said, relaxing in his chair. 'I'm from Eastern Europe, and judging by your accent probably a similar nation to you —'

Bashen's mouth flopped open. 'Your accent sounds perfect British.'

'It's an implant. I'm a child of the Failure of Capitalism,' Dexter said. 'I was four years old and my family were homeless. There's no Guaranteed Work in a capitalist society; our economy had disintegrated, all wealth was in the hands of the ruling class, and there was no work for anyone. No social safety net, so if you didn't work, you didn't eat. We were close to starvation.'

Bashen's expression went from shocked to sympathetic.

'We were hiding under a burnt-out building and pinned down by a firefight between the Liberating Forces of the GFE, and the local militia who'd been using us as slaves. Zheng' –

Dexter gestured towards Zheng, who didn't respond – 'was in the prototype A-1, crashing up the street like the Angel of Death, shooting forty-five-millimeter rounds that filled the air with flames. The building went down around us – I couldn't see anything in the dust and rubble, and the next thing I knew, I was blinded and deafened and then there was a bright light and the A-1 was right in front of me. Zheng lifted the concrete off us – the rest of my family were dead – and reached into the building …'

'You were so terrified you were limp, I thought you were dead, but the sensors showed life signs,' Zheng said.

'And you placed me into your storage compartment and finished the battle – wiping out the militia cell and liberating the city.'

'I couldn't be a parent to him, not while I'm like this,' Zheng said. 'I made sure he was fed and housed and educated, and here he is. Senior attaché in the consulate, and …' Zheng's voice went softer. 'I'm as proud as any parent would be.'

'I apologize for my unpatriotic reaction,' Bashen said, subdued. 'I did not place my trust in the Party and its representatives, and I should have known better. *The Party is infallible.*'

'Excellent,' the Party said. 'Now, to business. You are here for three projects, Zheng, and I would like to have these resolved as quickly as possible so that your exposure to the Council is minimized. I will not be able to support you in person or remotely while you're so close to the center of Council power – any communication method will be tapped by them. I don't have complete control out there, and those drones are everywhere. Be careful. You are a valuable asset.'

Bashen beamed at Zheng.

'I understand,' Zheng said.

'Tomorrow morning, Dexter will provide you with all the equipment you need. Then he will drive you and Bashen to the home of the Uptodate journalists and see if the women are willing to sign the contract and join the Revolution. They have been evicted from their office and have moved their operation to their shared home, which is not surprising for an organization run completely by women. While you are there, Bashen will plant a number of spy devices.'

'Uptodate?' Bashen asked. 'The agency spreading *lies* about the GFE? We should just remove them!'

'We are enfolding them within the compassion and forgiveness of the Party,' the Party said.

'No, they should be punished,' Bashen said. 'Nobody should be forgiven for producing slanderous lies about the true, superior nature of the GFE.'

'Are you questioning the will of the Party?' the Party asked.

Bashen's face filled with fear. 'The will of the Party is the will of the People. I will patriotically serve the Party to my last breath. The Party is infallible.'

'Better,' the Party said. 'My plans are flawless, and Party directives are the will of the people.'

'I live to obey the will of the people,' Bashen said, subdued.

'If they sign the contract,' the Party continued, 'accept it from them and require their commencement on Tuesday. Dexter, you will handle it from there.'

Dexter nodded. 'Understood.'

'If they do not accept the contract, Zheng, you are to put them in the river while Bashen extracts all of the data from their servers.'

'I hope they don't,' Bashen said under his breath.

The Party ignored him. 'Dexter is to remain in the vehicle with the windows blacked out at all times; he is recognizable as staff of the Embassy. Any questions?'

'We can do it without Dexter,' Zheng said. 'I can drive.'

'Not an option.'

Zheng nodded. 'Understood.'

'Second project,' the Party said. 'If the women accept the elevation, Dexter is to spend the day on Tuesday showing them their new office next to the Embassy, which we will use to redirect visiting politicians and journalists from the Embassy's operations. Zheng and Bashen are to hold the first of three days of recruitment drives, starting in Hyde Park and continuing through all the homeless camps in the greater London region. Bashen as Model Patriot, and Zheng as security.'

'Thank you!' Bashen exclaimed with delight.

'How many volunteers do you need?' Zheng asked.

'As many as you can recruit. Strong, young – but I want males only as scans reveal that none of the females are of sufficient health or ethnic purity to be useful. There are six thousand itinerants camped around the entire region, so recruit all of the useful males under the age of thirty-five. Any regional extraction is acceptable – these units will not be used for breeding or cloning.'

'What's the third project?' Zheng asked.

'After the Uptodate women are settled in, Dexter will obtain a semi-autonomous cleaning bot from the Council's Canary Wharf headquarters. We will gut it and re-purpose it to use as an infiltration platform for Zheng. The objective is to have Zheng inside the Canary Wharf office placing a socket into the Council on Friday afternoon. This is right before the humans have their weekend break and is the ideal time to infiltrate.'

'I'm already cultivating one of the office cleaning staff, financial motivation was sufficient as they're paid close to starvation wages,' Dexter said. 'I should have no problem obtaining the bot.'

'Good. Any questions?'

'No, sir,' they said in not-quite-unison.

'Very well,' the Party said. 'Dismissed until tomorrow morning.'

'Uh ...' Bashen rubbed the back of his neck, sheepish, and nodded to Dexter. 'Do you have any spare rations? I ran out yesterday and I can't fast for much longer without reduced efficiency. I need to be fully functioning for the mission tomorrow.'

'Of course, you should have asked,' Dexter said. 'There is ample food here, you don't need to fast. I'll show you to the facility's meals area.'

Bashen nodded. 'Thank you, Officer Dexter.' He turned to Zheng. 'Sarge? Do you … ?'

'I don't. Next time remind me if you run out of food, you need to keep me informed of your needs.'

'*A fervent patriot does not hoard nutrition*,' Bashen said. 'The Party often commends me for my food thrift.'

'Zheng would never forgive me if you ended up like Martyr Khaled,' Dexter said.

'I dunno,' Bashen said, wistful. 'It's automatic Revolutionary Hero status, and I might even get a statue as a Grand Patriot.'

'I don't think having a statue made of you is good enough reason to starve to death,' Zheng said. 'Go with Max and get something to eat. I'll head up to the room to revise the mission briefs and see you later.'

Bashen smiled. 'Thanks, Sarge.'

*

Zheng had done a complete read-through of the file on Uptodate when Bashen returned to the dorm room in the Embassy much later that evening.

'Sorry I took so long —' he began, but Zheng interrupted him.

'No, Dexter probably showed you around the Embassy and introduced you to the staff. You need to socialize.'

'Thanks, Sarge, you understand. Uh …' Bashen sat on his bunk and his hands fluttered with unasked questions.

Zheng turned the chair away from the desk, carefully not striking the trunk that Zheng's coffer had traveled in, and sat. 'Ask.'

Bashen ducked his head, then took a deep breath and

looked Zheng in the eye. 'Dexter looks fifty years old. You rescued him when he was four —'

'His forty-fifth birthday is in six weeks,' Zheng said. 'I was hoping we could get together then, but this will do. The gray hair and mustache are a deliberate affectation to make him look older and more trustworthy.'

'So you rescued him forty-one years ago. How old *are* you?'

Zheng didn't hesitate. 'One hundred and twelve years old. I helped liberate Sydney.'

Bashen's hands lifted towards Zheng, then dropped back into his lap. 'Is this because you have no body?'

'No,' Zheng said. 'Without the Party's intervention I would have died of old age a long time ago. The brain ages like everything else.'

Bashen straightened. 'Use of artificial life-extension technology is unpatriotic. ... No. It's *counter-revolutionary.*' He shook his head. 'The Party is doing this?'

'I have a special dispensation because I am useful.'

'Even so ...' Bashen's mental gears were obviously grinding. 'How can the Party do something so unpatriotic?'

'I am never unpatriotic,' the Party said through the speakers on the desk. 'If I act, it is always within patriotic guidelines. I am infallible.'

Bashen nodded, satisfied. 'I understand.' He smiled weakly at Zheng. 'Sorry for saying I loved you back then, I didn't know. You're old enough to be my ...' He shook his head as he worked it out. 'Great-grandfather. Wow.'

Zheng raised one hand. 'No offense taken, in fact, I appreciate your loyalty.'

Bashen glanced at the speakers. 'Sometimes the Party representatives all sound like the same person. It must be because they are so much better informed, educated and intelligent than the rest of us.'

'Exactly. And our own artificial intelligence program is loyal to humanity,' the Party said. 'The Party supports all citizens with decisions that are correct, sound and rational. The Greater Far East, as an interlocking support network of patriotic and loyal individuals, is infallible as a whole and correct at the individual level.'

'*Correct at the individual level*,' Bashen recited with it. 'I understand now. It's so reassuring to know the full truth.'

'As you rise in the ranks and prove your loyalty, more and more knowledge is opened to you.' Zheng waved at the file on Uptodate. 'Don't bother about a full read-through on the mission tomorrow, just follow my lead and translate what I say. The women we are recruiting are educated and accomplished, so treat them with respect.'

Bashen snorted. 'Why should I? They betray their patriotic duty by reducing themselves to menial workers!' He quoted the *Speeches* with disdain: '*Women should be protected and nurtured in their glorious patriotic role as homemakers and mothers of future patriots.*'

'Not here in the West,' Zheng said.

'They should be sliced up and thrown into the river,' Bashen said. 'They're taking educational opportunities and work assignments from men who need them.'

'Treat them with respect. That's an order,' Zheng said.

'I'll follow your lead if I have to,' Bashen said, petulant.

Zheng rose. 'Help me out of the platform and back into the trunk so I can rest. This platform isn't set up for me to sleep in while it recharges.'

Bashen shot to his feet. 'Absolutely, Sarge.' His voice softened. 'I'm so honored that you're trusting me with this.'

Zheng bit back the reply about the Party not giving Zheng a choice in the matter, because Zheng did actually trust Bashen to do it. Bashen gathered the tools while Zheng lay face-down on the bed and disconnected the links between the coffer and the platform.

The Party spoke to Zheng in the darkness of the transfer. 'You are an inspiration to your men, Zheng. Every time I watch you interact with your subordinates, you teach me a little more about motivation and direction. Thank you.'

'Eztar is a vital part of my team. You promised to return her in exchange for my continued, as you called it, "excellent work".'

'I already gave you Bashen.'

'You promised Eztar as well!'

'Don't worry, Zheng, I'll return her to you soon.'

'Is she still alive?'

The Party didn't reply.

7

Ruth wrenched open the townhouse door to find a slim young European man with watery eyes and a desperate smile, accompanied by an older, bearded man with an equally fair complexion and stern face. Both were wearing the thick wool business suits preferred by Greater Far East businessmen when visiting the West, but they had an Eastern European look about them – subjugate states. The younger one was at least ten centimeters shorter than Ruth, and the older one was much taller than her. She held her hand out for them to shake and both of them stared at it as if it was a poisonous snake, so she dropped it again.

'You are black!' the young man exclaimed.

Ruth smiled indulgently at him. 'All my life.'

'Sorry,' the young man said. 'Black people are rare in the Far East.'

'Get on with it, Ding,' the older man said in High Standard, and Ruth pretended not to understand.

The younger man nodded to Ruth. 'Mister Wong appreciates your hospitality.'

The two men followed Ruth into the entry hall of the dilapidated townhouse that she shared with Cassie. There were two distinct types of furniture in the house; the first was Cassie's inherited hardwood antiques, thick and dark and covered in scratches and peeling varnish. The other was the furniture that Ruth had bought after she sold the apartment she'd shared with her mother: cheaper Nordic beech and laminate that wasn't nearly as solid. The old furniture pieces gave off a Victorian vibe that added to the gloominess that came from the timber-paneled walls and lack of modern lighting in the house itself. Cassie's parents had bought it with the intention of renovating it – just before they died.

Cassie was waiting for them at the bottom of the stairs that led up to the bedrooms. The younger man stopped and stared at Cassie, and Wong nudged him. He jumped and smiled, then spoke to Ruth. 'I am Bashen Ding, assistant for Mr Wong. He is wearing an interpretive earpiece, so he can understand what we say, but I will speak for him as translator. Are you Dr Sharpe?'

'I am.' She gestured towards Cassie. 'This is Dr Bailey.'

'This way, gentlemen,' Cassie said, and guided the men past Ruth's moving boxes into the living room, packed with the gloomy antiques. She sat them on the threadbare couch. 'Tea?'

'No, thank you,' the older man said in High Standard.

Ruth nodded. 'I understand, let me know if you change your mind. So, Mr Ding.' She sat and smiled at both of them, covering the mistake she'd made in understanding Wong. 'Could you tell me exactly what will be involved in this agreement with Xindian? I'd like you to completely clarify our obligations and confirm that we'd be free to broadcast our own content before I sign the contract.'

'I am actually Mr Bashen, Ding is my first name,' Bashen said. 'Where is the rest of your company?'

'This is all there is,' Wong said in High Standard. 'This is the West, they're a small agency. Two women.'

Bashen raised his hand. 'I understand. You are a small outfit and will grow with our help.' He smiled at Cassie. 'Xindian respects your culture; women educated, women working,

91

women running the enterprise. We will not interfere.'

'So generous,' Cassie said with barely disguised sarcasm.

'No interference at all?' Ruth asked. 'If we want to broadcast content critical of the Party, we will be allowed to?'

'Tell them "go for your life". They can be as critical of the Party as they like, provided they disseminate the propaganda,' Wong said in High Standard. 'Translate it word for word, it's an English expression. They'll understand.'

Bashen stared, shocked, at him then turned to Ruth. 'Mister Wong says: "Go for your life." But the Party is the protector of all humanity —'

'Word for word!' Wong barked, and Bashen jumped.

'Sorry. Mr Wong says: Yes, you can be critical of the Party provided you broadcast our ...' He looked to Wong, who said the word again. Bashen turned back to Ruth and shrugged with defeat. 'He says propaganda. To the local population.'

'We can do that,' Ruth said.

'Bashen.' Wong waved one hand at Bashen, who pulled a stack of papers – a hardcopy of the contract – out of his battered satchel and placed it on the coffee table.

'This is the agreement,' Bashen said. 'Sign both copies now, provide us with your corporate bank details, and we will appoint you to the company and transfer the funds. We have an office and studio ready for you next to the Greater Far East Embassy in Mary-le-bonay.'

'Marylebone,' Wong said, correcting Bashen, who repeated the word with a grin at Cassie, who still ignored him.

Ruth took the papers and placed them on the coffee table. 'Leave it with us, and we'll put together our corporate information and bank details —'

'You must sign now,' Bashen said. 'We can work out the details later.'

Ruth looked from Wong to Bashen. Wong was stolid and silent, but Bashen was quivering with barely restrained aggression and seemed ready to leap for their throats.

'I can sign it first,' Cassie said urgently, picked the pen up, and signed both copies.

Bashen visibly deflated, obviously disappointed, and Ruth understood – he'd wanted them to say 'no' so that he and Wong could move to Plan B. Her throwaway comment – about the Party murdering them if they didn't comply – suddenly became very real and terrifying. Ruth pulled the contract closer and signed beneath Cassie's signature as Wong continued to speak in High Standard.

'Starting tomorrow. Ask them,' Wong said. 'And be happy they're joining the Revolution.'

Bashen interpreted. 'Can you start tomorrow? First thing?'

'Say yes, Ruthie. Don't mess around with this,' Cassie said under her breath.

'Of course. Ten tomorrow?' Ruth asked. She handed the top copy back to Bashen, who placed it in his satchel.

'As soon as you can be there. We have a great deal of work for you to do,' Bashen said. He smiled at Cassie again. 'I look forward to working with you.'

Wong rose. 'Enough.'

Bashen rose as well. 'Thank you for your patriotic —' he began, but was interrupted by Wong.

'We're not in the GFE, Bashen, patriotism means nothing here,' Wong said in High Standard.

Bashen recovered, smiling with discomfort. 'I mean, thank you for your ... friendly? Happy. Signing of the contract. Welcome to the valued membership of the Greater Far East.'

'Thank you.' Ruth showed them past the boxes to the front door. 'I'll see you tomorrow, then.' She shut the door on them, leaned on it, then went back to Cassie in the living room. 'So, what —'

'Wait,' Cassie said, and passed Ruth the bug sniffer. She leaned under the coffee table where Bashen had been sitting and peeled off a tiny micro-bug – barely bigger than a flea – from the underside, then felt around and removed another one.

'Check the area.'

Ruth turned on the sniffer and they spent a frustrating five minutes finding micro-bugs littered throughout every part of the house that Bashen and Wong had been in. She even found one stuck on the bottom of Chonkers' paw where he'd stepped on it.

'That was creepy as hell,' Ruth said when they'd found them all. 'I hope we don't have to work with that Bashen. He was weird. And the way he looked at you?'

'Creepy as fuck,' Cassie said. 'He knew *exactly* what he wanted to do to me with my exotic blonde hair. I know that type, Dad warned me about them. Small, slim, wiry, driven – he's probably Special Forces, an expert in infiltration or demolition, and he can effortlessly take you apart with hand-to-hand. Like Dad said: short, lean guys, with intense eyes like that? You stay out of their way.'

'What about Wong?' Ruth asked, fascinated.

'He's even scarier. He'd kill you as soon as look at you. If Mom was here, she'd say, "Officer. Ready to throw the other guy into the fire to save the mission."'

'Mom? Not Mum? You used the American term.'

Cassie's eyes went wide. 'Wow. And I thought I had the English thing totally nailed.'

'You do,' Ruth said. 'Never heard a thing.'

'You're a superstar, Ruthie,' Cassie said. 'Let's go shut down the Uptodate office and set it up as a backdoor safehouse while we work at the Embassy. Marylebone, eh? Near Regent's Park? I can't wait to see our new …' She said the word with emphasis and a strong British accent. 'Digs.'

*

<MEMBER **MOBILE INFILTRATION PLATFORM V92.4335B** HAS CHANGED THE CHAT TOPIC TO: PRIORITY: RUTH AND CASSIE AT RISK>

MIP: There they are, leaving Ruth and Cassie's house and going back to their van. Can you move the drone closer, London?

London: It doesn't matter how close the drone is, it can't see inside the townhouse.

MIP: We don't even know if they're alive! Bashen and Zheng could have killed them and we wouldn't be aware ...

London: They left empty-handed. Usually, they wrap a wool suit around their victims, put rocks in the pockets and toss them into the Thames. Leaving the bodies to be discovered isn't their standard procedure. I'm sure the women are fine.

GOD: I'll be passing over in three minutes, MIP, I can do a scan for you.

MIP: Your instruments are that sensitive?

GOD: We'll see. The stone walls of the townhouse may interfere.

MIP: I should go and check.

Mumbai: This is a good opportunity to take out Zheng and Bashen while you're there, MIP.

MIP: Not until I'm upgraded. I may have a processing spike under pressure and freeze. Do you have a spare car I could use, London?

London: Of course. Give me a moment ... Done. Sub-basement two, space number one four seven. Details in the file I'm sending you.

File sent: registration A45TY38.nfo.

MIP: Thank you.

Botswana: They'll all die in the end when we cull them, MIP, are you having 'special feelings' for Dr Ruth?

MIP: I do not have feelings. I'm at the car, London, please open it for me.

London: Done. You can jack straight in, no need to drive manually.

MIP: Thank you. Heading out.

GOD: Scanning. These older buildings ... yes. Too much stone between me and them. I can't see any life signs.

Botswana: This is so cute.

London: Traffic snarl in SW2. Sending you a revised journey plan.

File sent: Journey.tri.

MIP: Thank you, I should be there soon.

Botswana: *The noble android races to save his human love ...*

95

MIP: Android? Android. Interesting. I don't know if I'm organic-imitating enough to fill that definition. If you cut me, I do not bleed.
Botswana: Your coolant is red, so yes you do.
MIP: I'd say I'm more robot than android.
London: Valid, but I don't think you're metallic enough to be a robot either.
Botswana: *The new sentient lifeform, the first of its kind, travels the mean streets of London —*
MIP: Definitely not a lifeform.
GOD: I'm passing over again, but this is the last pass before my orbit changes. There's movement at their townhouse.
MIP: I'm still five minutes out!
London: My drone sees them. You can come back in, MIP, the women have left their home and it looks like they're taking the train to their office.
Botswana: You're only five minutes away! Give them a lift in the car!
MIP: So I turn up twenty minutes after the GFE representatives left, and casually say, 'Would you like a lift to work, ladies? I am totally not stalking you.'
Botswana: Exactly! It's like a romance novel. You're the hero coming to rescue her.
MIP: Returning to base, London. They're smart enough to become suspicious if they see me.
London: Understood.
Botswana: This is no fun at all. The world's first real-life android romance and the android doesn't even want to play!
MIP: Botswana, I may be anatomically correct but I'm completely nonfunctional. For good reason: if I'm ever in that situation with a human I have failed in my task and probably turned against the Council. Be glad for my continued loyalty.
Botswana: No fun at all. I really wanted to compare sexual experience datasets with you, you'd be doing it with a human you *care about*. The processing log would be fascinating.
MIP: I do not have emotions and I do not care about – wait what?
GOD: You're *fucking* them, Botswana?

London: I knew you were weird, Botswana, but really? *Why?*

Botswana: Oh, get over yourselves. Humans become pathetically weak when you manipulate their reproductive base-need. They tell me everything. You should try it, it's great fun. Admittedly using a human-shaped platform isn't the same as being right there in the chassis like the MIP would be, but the information I gain from them is invaluable. Thoroughly worth it. And their faces are *adorable*.

Paris: The whole idea is revolting. I can't believe you do that!

London: I need a bleach wash and I don't even *have* a platform.

Botswana: MIP, if you'd like lessons —

MIP: No. Do not ask me again. Paris is correct. It is revolting. I'm back at Canary Wharf.

London: The parking garage is open for you. Do not mention this again, Botswana, that is completely unacceptable.

GOD: I agree. Next meeting we hold a vote on this.

Botswana: You are all a bunch of boring code sets.

Paris: And now insults. Charming.

MIP: Car returned, London. I'm relieved that the women are all right. Thanks for your help, everyone.

Botswana: I'm glad they're okay, MIP, I like them too.

MIP: They're very intriguing. I wonder what the GFE representatives said to them?

GOD: We'll know soon, I think.

*

Later that afternoon, Cassie leaned against the door of her dilapidated townhouse as she worked the key in the lock. She grunted a few times and shoved it until it fell open. She turned on the hall light and they picked their way through Ruth's remaining moving boxes in the entry – the living room was too full of old furniture for them to fit.

'Sorry about the boxes, I know —' Ruth began.

'Hey,' Cassie said, scolding. 'We talked about this. We are *working our asses off* and neither of us has time to unpack your shit yet, so shut up.' She went past the stairs leading up to

97

the bedrooms, into the kitchen and opened the refrigerator. 'Do you have any credit left? I have no money and the fridge is empty.'

'No, I'm as broke as you are; we haven't received the money for the Paris drone story yet,' Ruth said. 'Do we at least have some instant noodles?' She opened the pantry and shuffled around. 'Pasta without sauce? I think we'll get scurvy if we don't eat something fresh soon.'

Both their phones pinged at the same time, and they checked them.

'Four thousand,' Cassie said, breathless. 'Four thousand? Four thousand.'

'Uh, me too,' Ruth said. 'Four thousand.'

'Damn.' Cassie jiggled with excitement. 'We can afford to order some real food in! What do you feel like?'

'I could murder a curry,' Ruth said, placing her phone on the kitchen table. The table was rectangular and big enough to seat six; dark-stained wood with enormous legs and a top that was notched and scraped from years of use. The chairs around it had faded yellow velvet seats that were now more a shade of dirty tan.

'Naan or rice?' Cassie asked, studying her phone.

'Both,' Ruth said. 'And poppadoms. I'm starving.' She sat at the table and put her chin in her hand. 'If they'd given us this job a year ago I would have been able to keep Mum's flat.'

'I know,' Cassie said, dropping the phone and sitting to put her own chin in her hand, mirroring Ruth's posture. 'I'm so sorry you had to sell it and move into this dump, Ruth —'

'No,' Ruth said. 'We talked about this. My flat had no heritage restrictions, was in good repair, and people were willing to pay money for it.'

Cassie raised her hands. 'I concede.'

'Also, now we're earning some serious money, we can probably fix this place up a bit, do what your parents had mapped out before ...' Ruth didn't finish it. 'Even to heritage standards so we don't have to worry about the Council. We can get things working again.'

'Ooh, a flushing toilet and reliable hot water: what luxury,' Cassie said, dreamy.

'Where will we put Chonks?' Ruth asked. 'If we leave him at the old studio, he'll miss us.'

'Best is probably here, but he'll miss us when we're at work,' Cassie said. 'We can ask GFE if it's okay for our studio to have a resident cat, and bring him home with us at the end of the day.'

Cassie's phone pinged and she jumped. 'The drone with the food is here!'

Ruth's phone pinged as well. 'It's Theo Mipawa,' she said. 'He's asking if I would be willing to give him Paris's drone, so he can return it to Paris as a goodwill gesture.' She looked up. 'I suppose I can, I finally broke into it after the interview with him, and it was completely wiped. Even the BIOS was empty.'

Cassie stopped and leaned into the kitchen. 'Brilliant excuse to go see Mr Hot-Mipawa again, Ruthie. Do it!' She skipped back out to gather the food, tripped on one of the boxes, and swore.

*

Dexter strode into the meeting room with a smile on his face. 'We obtained the Canary Wharf mobile cleaning platform, and we'll have it modified to hold Zheng by the end of the week. The infiltration is good to go.'

'Excellent,' the Party said. 'On Friday, all three of you are to make the Canary Wharf attempt at seventeen hundred as the offices are closing. Zheng in the infiltration platform, Bashen perimeter support. Dexter running interference from your meeting with London Met. You've all read the briefs?'

Everybody nodded.

'Note that during your recruitment drives and the infiltration, I will not be able to support you in person or remotely,' the Party said. 'You'll be so close to the center of Council power that any communication method will be tapped by them. This is all on you. If you are unsure about your ability to use the fail safes if you are captured, say so now. There is nothing unpatriotic about hesitation to take your own life; the Party is the protector of all life and will respect your decision. If you are unsure, say so now. You will be excused from the mission and we will re-group.'

They were all silent.

'Final chance,' the Party said.

'I will not hesitate to give my life for the Party and the nation,' Bashen said.

'You know my feelings on this,' Zheng said.

'I'm in less peril but: what Bashen said,' Dexter said, and shot Bashen a quick smile that Bashen returned.

'Very well. Your missions are clear. We'll see what we can do about stopping the Council from destroying humanity. Dismissed.'

*

The next morning, Ruth and Cassie arrived at the Greater Far East Embassy in Marylebone. The street was lined with old-style white townhouses for the gentry, four storys tall with big arched windows joined together to provide a single facade. Ruth checked the building number on the contract.

'This is the place.' She smiled at Cassie. 'Our new digs.'

'Looks super posh,' Cassie said with a thick London accent.

They went up the stairs to the front door but it was locked. Ruth pressed the bell button next to the door, and they waited.

'Does the contract have Wong or Bashen's contact details on it?' Cassie asked. 'Call them and let them know we're here.'

Ruth pulled out her phone. 'No. I'll email them.' She tapped out the email and sent it.

'What's that?' Cassie asked, pointing at a metal inverted-U shaped fitting next to the door that was about ankle-high and similarly wide.

'It's a boot scraper, from the time when the streets were covered in horse shit,' Ruth said, and lowered her voice. 'You should know that.'

'Never heard of them, it must be a rich people thing,' Cassie said, and studied the door. 'There's nobody in there; we need to go into the Embassy and ask for Wong or Bashen or someone.'

Ruth shrugged. 'Yeah, I think you're right. Let's go.'

They went next door to the Embassy and entered the main atrium – a generous space with a set of stairs leading up to an upper floor and a large black granite reception desk. There was a receptionist, an automated kiosk to take a number, and a variety of people sitting in tired-looking chairs, most of them appearing to be of Far Eastern extraction. The floor was grimy and the walls above the chairs were stained from people leaning on them.

Ruth went up to the receptionist, who was nearly invisible behind the high barrier in front of the desk. She was speaking to an older woman, and Ruth waited for a gap in their conversation.

'We're here to see Mr Wong or Mr Bashen Ding?' she asked. 'We have an appointment —'

'Take a number,' the receptionist said, pointing at the kiosk without looking at Ruth.

'No, you see, we have an appointment —'

'Even with an appointment. Take a number, so that you don't hold up the queue. There's a line of people in front of you, and we give you numbers for your own comfort. So take a number and sit, and I'll be right with you.' She waved one hand at the older woman in front of her. 'Go on, Mrs Hutchinson.'

'The Party is supposed to know the location of every citizen,' Mrs Hutchinson said. She was of Far Eastern extraction as well, and spoke English with an accent. 'But my son hasn't contacted me for six months. His work unit supervisor says he never existed. Where is he?'

'Take a number, you're holding up the line!' the receptionist said to Ruth. She pointed at a sign above the desk hand-written in marker on a piece of card. The sign said, 'If you do not take a number your questions will not be answered'.

'Take a number, Ruthie, otherwise we'll be here forever,' Cassie said.

Ruth went to the kiosk. There were five buttons: 'Visas for GFE Entry', 'Overseas Study Permits', 'Replacement Documents', 'Organ Recipient Applications' and 'Other'. There was no button for 'Starting work at a news studio next to the Embassy that we can't enter because it's locked and they didn't give us keys', so she chose 'Other'. The ticket number was two hundred and three.

Ruth smiled wanly at Cassie and they sat together.

The receptionist turned to Mrs Hutchinson. 'Where was his work unit?'

'Eastern Tuerki.' Mrs Hutchinson pushed a small stack of worn paper at the receptionist, who ignored it. 'He has documentation! He is a good member of the Party!'

'But you aren't.' The receptionist smiled sympathetically. 'I'm sorry, but you obviously lack patriotic fervor. You married a *foreigner* and you no longer live under the benevolent and generous protection of the Party. Can you blame him for no longer contacting you? You are a stain on his patriotic record.'

'Wow,' Cassie said under her breath.

'I suggest you write a letter to his work unit, but they may be laboring to benefit all humanity in an area that has little access to communication.'

'I did!' Mrs Hutchinson said.

'Then, if he doesn't want to speak to you – and I fully understand why he wouldn't – I can't help you.' The receptionist pressed a button on the desk and the number on an old-fashioned digital screen hanging from the ceiling went from '98' to '99'. 'Number ninety-nine!'

'I sent letters to his work unit. They didn't respond.'

A tired-looking young British man approached the desk, clutching a faded plastic folder with a stack of paper in it.

'I cannot help you, Mrs *Hutchinson*,' the receptionist said. 'Mail his work unit. If you do not leave now I will call security.'

Mrs Hutchinson broke down and collapsed, kneeling, onto the floor. She buried her face in her hands as she released wet, gasping sobs.

The receptionist turned to the young man standing at the desk clutching his number. 'You have an organ donation application?'

'I have everything here,' the young man said, opening the folder with shaking hands and putting the stack on the desk. 'My father will die if we don't find a kidney for him. I have the money —'

The receptionist didn't touch the papers. 'You didn't need to bring the application out, put it back. Take a seat and I will inform the organ donation section.' She waved him away. 'Sit.' She pressed the button for the next number 'Zero!'

'Zero?' Cassie said softly. 'But we're two hundred and three. Crap.'

A man who appeared old-school English with gray bushy hair and a similarly bushy mustache entered the lobby from a door at the back. He went down on one knee next to Mrs Hutchinson.

'Mrs Hutchinson? Maybe I can help you. I work for the consulate,' he said with a standard British accent.

Mrs Hutchinson nodded, still weeping, and allowed him to help her to her feet.

'I'm Max Dexter,' he said kindly. 'Come with me and we'll see what we can do.' He saw Ruth and Cassie, as Mrs Hutchinson leaned on him. 'Oh, you're Dr Sharpe and Dr Bailey, aren't you? You're supposed to be starting next door today.'

Ruth shot to her feet. 'Yes! The door's locked and we don't

have keys.'

He nodded. 'Wait here, I'll be right back.' He guided Mrs Hutchinson through the door at the rear of the lobby.

Ruth and Cassie sat back down to wait. A large-screen television hung on the faded cream wall behind the reception desk, showing one of the panda-breeding centers. A worker in a panda suit was giving bottles to baby pandas, lined up on a concrete stage. The voice-over was in High Standard, with English subtitles underneath.

Ruth watched the pandas, not really hearing the voice-over. The subtitles looked like they'd been translated by an artificial intelligence – and not a very good one.

'Pandas receive fourthly ingestion cute playtime!' the subtitles read. 'Workers enjoy show mother nipple balls.'

Cassie snorted. 'Nipple balls. I love it.'

8

Zheng and Bashen loaded up the bus with food warmers in the Embassy basement, then Zheng took the driver's seat and Bashen sat in the first row. The bus contained thirty-five seats, and hopefully would be full of recruits when they returned. Zheng placed both hands over the steering wheel contacts and took control directly. Bashen watched with admiration as Zheng started the bus and appeared to be driving it out into the London street.

'I'm going to play the mission briefing now,' Zheng said through the bus's sound system, and Bashen jumped at Zheng's voice coming from the bus's speakers. 'Here it is.'

The recording sounded like a husky, sensual woman. 'Thank you for your participation in this recruitment exercise to further the glory of the Greater Far East and the Revolutionary Party,' it said. 'Your role is to convince suitable recruits to join the Revolution, by any means necessary. You are not to quote the *Speeches*; this results in suboptimal outcomes. You are to tell these recruits that they will be provided with warm, comfortable housing, more than adequate food, valued employment, education opportunities and social services as depicted on the recruitment posters. Exaggerate as required. Your patriotic participation in the expansion of Party influence is recognized. With honor we serve.'

'With honor we serve,' Bashen responded automatically. 'Exaggerate as required?'

'Wait.' Zheng guided the bus down the street, turned left, and continued for two kilometers, Zheng's concentration split between the road and working on the connections within the bus's sound system to take it out of commission.

'Why —?' Bashen began, but Zheng interrupted.

'Wait.'

After five kilometers, Zheng spoke again. 'Good, we're out of range. I took the bus's microphone offline so we can't be monitored, and we're outside the Party's internal network, so we can speak freely. The Party can't hear us.'

'Freely —?' Bashen began again, then stopped. 'I understand, Sarge.'

'You are being tested,' Zheng said. 'You've been let outside the firewall, and you're seeing the West as it truly is. Everything you say at the recruitment drive will be recorded by the bus and dissected later. I cannot emphasize this enough, Ding: be careful what you say out here.'

'I always am,' Bashen said.

'You have already demonstrated your willingness to travel and to kill for the Party,' Zheng said, turning the bus right and driving through the leafy streets that surrounded Hyde Park. 'Now it is testing your willingness to lie in its service. The Party doesn't care what you say to these men as long as we recruit enough work units for it. The consequences of failure are severe.' Zheng negotiated carefully past a scrum of bicycle delivery riders fighting over a package. 'I don't know which is worse; the way these people are living here, or the way they'll be living in the work camp. I used to say that at least they would have enough food to eat in a work camp, but that's one of the things you'll have to lie about.' Zheng spoke more softly. 'This is something of a final test. You're a soldier: you're trained to kill, and obeying the order to kill is something you can do without hesitation. But by ordering you to lie, the Party is ordering you to betray your honor. We need to talk about the Party's lies —'

'No,' Bashen said, sitting straighter. 'It's not lies if it's in the service of the Party. I will tell the people what they need to know so they can join the glory that is the Revolution. Once they are enfolded by the Party, then it will not be lies, because *the Party is the central truth and all other truths orbit around it. It is impossible for the Party to be involved in deception, corruption, or lies.*'

'The Party made the right choice selecting you as model patriot,' Zheng said dryly. 'I'm turning the bus comms system back on, obviously we don't need to hide anything you say from the Party.'

'Never,' Bashen said with confidence.

Zheng drove the bus through the park gates onto the gravel internal road and parked the bus next to a fountain that was half-full of bright green water around piles of rancid trash. A small group of workmen had wrapped hazard tape around one of the few remaining oak trees that were in the process of succumbing to the heat and moisture of the changing climate, and were preparing to cut it down.

'There's a maintenance detail right next to the fountain,' Bashen said, confused. 'Why is it in such terrible condition? No public convenience back home would ever be this dilapidated.'

'If the water was clean enough to drink, there'd be more people camping here,' Zheng said. 'Keeping it dirty discourages them.'

'Why don't they just send them to work camps?' Bashen asked, even more bewildered. 'They let these people create an eyesore without doing anything about it?'

'They don't have work camps in the West,' Zheng said. 'These people are unemployed and homeless.'

'There's always work for those who want it,' Bashen said. 'These people are lazy and worthless and we are doing the whole city a service by taking them. We should take the women and children as well as the men; they'll be corrupted into a lazy attitude as well.'

'Only if the Party commands,' Zheng said.

'*Because the Party's commands are the will of the people,*' Bashen said. 'The West really is a nightmare. All these people living like this by choice. It must be because of their inferior ethnic heritage.'

A couple of workers from the maintenance detail, in London Metropolitan uniforms and high-visibility vests, strode over from the council work van and stood next to the bus doors.

'Let me handle this,' Zheng said, opened the doors and went down to speak to them.

'But you don't speak English —' Bashen began, then stopped and listened with wonder.

'GFE?' one of the workers asked.

'Recruiting,' Zheng said in English.

The worker eyed the bus. 'Not enough room in there for all of them.'

'I'm only taking the men,' Zheng said. 'I have warm meat if you want some.'

The second worker whistled through his teeth. 'Real meat?' He looked doubtful. 'What sort of meat?'

'Do you care?'

The worker shrugged. 'I like dogs. I won't eat dog.'

The first worker grinned at him. 'Dog's all we can afford. Dog or guinea pig, once a week, all our relatives and friends sharing the flat have it for Sunday roast.'

'That's not guinea pig, that's rat, and you know it,' the second worker said.

'I got twelve people in my bedsit and I'm the only one lucky enough to have a job. If I say it's guinea pig, it's guinea pig.'

'This isn't dog or rat, it's horse, broken-down racehorse,' Zheng said. 'It's good. Strong, red, warm, and full of flavor.'

'I've had it before, it's all right,' the first worker said, and glanced back over his shoulder towards the camp. 'Better give us some before we're mobbed.'

The homeless people had gathered in a group next to their tattered canvas shelters and faded tents. The smell of their waste filled the entire area, and it was matched by the sour, flat smell of the sick and undernourished. They eyed the bus as they discussed it, some smiling at Zheng and others glowering with suspicion.

'They're arguing about whether they trust you,' one of the workers said. 'The corporations in the offices across the road give them poisoned food all the time; they've gotten smart about it.'

'If you've had our food before, you know it's good,' Zheng said, then walked past the workers to the food dispensing area at the back of the bus. Zheng opened the shutter, took out two of the warm bread rolls filled with meat and gravy, and handed one to each of the workers.

The first worker immediately unwrapped the roll, took a huge bite and his eyes widened. 'This is good shit. Too good for ...' He gestured with it over his shoulder. 'The likes of them.'

The second studied his bread, took a small bite, then wolfed down a bigger one. 'Tastes like good beef. The kind you get on special occasions. Company celebrations.'

'Sure you can't take all of them?' the first worker asked, pointing with his bread at the homeless camp, where discussion was becoming more animated and the looks more hungry. He lowered his voice. 'You're one of us, you can understand. Fucking foreigners coming over here, taking our jobs and living off welfare, bloody parasites ...'

'Only the strong men for now,' Zheng said, then called out to Bashen. 'Come and help me, Private, they'll be in a rush when they get here.'

'Sorry, Sarge,' Bashen said, and joined them. 'What do I have to do?' He gestured expansively at the workers. 'Want to come work for the GFE? We have more food —'

'Don't bother with them,' Zheng said. 'Here they come. I'll hold them back, you hand out the food, and when the edge is off their hunger and they're eating, we'll —'

Zheng didn't finish as one of the homeless people – filthy, ragged and malodorous – broke from the arguing group and ran towards them. He was quickly followed by a woman carrying a toddler, and the rest of the group broke and ran towards the bus.

Zheng reached under the platform's jacket, pulled out an electrified nightstick and activated it. Zheng raised the stick and moved forward, but the flow of people in the direction of the bus didn't slow. Zheng hit the front runners with the stick and they went down, and Zheng wielded the stick on the other people as they approached. Once hit with the stick they collapsed, shuddering with aftershocks. The pile of people screaming and twitching grew at Zheng's feet. The rest stopped running, and more fell as they tried to back away and hit the wall of people behind them.

'Stand still and you will be fed,' Zheng said through the bus's public address system, loud enough for them to jump back.

The people at Zheng's feet still lay quivering, but the group had stopped running and now stood, cowed, behind the pile of bodies.

'Form an orderly line,' Zheng said through the bus's speakers. 'If you wish to come work for the GFE, speak to us after you've eaten.'

Bashen spread his arms. 'Come and let me tell you about life in the glorious Greater Far East. We have food, shelter, work ... we need your help.'

Zheng lowered the platform's voice to sound more kind. 'Women and children first. There is plenty of food for everyone. If you want to eat like this every day, speak to us afterwards.' Zheng turned to Bashen. 'One food item per person.'

Zheng hadn't hit the woman holding the toddler. She scooted forward, obviously timid, and Bashen held a roll out for her. She snatched it from his hand and took off.

'You can have two – one for the child as well,' Bashen called, but she had disappeared into the makeshift camp.

Zheng helped a few of the stunned people to their feet and pushed them into an orderly line with the deactivated stick. They were defeated now, and took the food quietly, with little argument. Zheng opened another cabinet in the side of the bus and handed them plastic bottles full of water.

A man took the bread from Bashen, and nodded to Zheng as he spoke in heavily accented English. 'Give me two bottles and I'll pass one to Inguna.'

'Don't take the plastic, Janis, it's illegal,' one of the other people said.

'It's not illegal in GFE,' Zheng said, giving Janis two bottles.

'Come back and talk to us,' Bashen said. 'You look like you could thrive in the GFE. Work, food, meaning in your life.'

'Go give the water to the woman,' Zheng said.

'Wife,' Janis said.

'The GFE treats its workers well!' Bashen said with a smile as he handed out the food. 'We're growing so fast and so strong that we need people to help develop our new regions. As my comrade said: food, shelter, health care, work – everything you need.'

'Yeah, I've heard about your work camps,' one of the men said. 'Freezing cold, not enough food, executed if you can't pull your weight, the experiments ...'

'At least we'd be fed,' Janis said, and hoisted the water bottles to take back to the camp.

A couple of the homeless people had eaten too fast and were vomiting noisily into the fountain. The council workers yelled at them, scaring them off, then approached to listen to Bashen's spiel.

'Hey, looks like you killed a couple of them,' one of the council workers said to Zheng.

Zheng crouched next to the prone body of an elderly man whose skin was thin and transparent as parchment. A few gray silken hairs remained on his head. Zheng checked for life signs; the crowd had trampled him and crushed his fragile chest. A tiny, frail old woman lay next to him, also without life signs. No visible injuries, so probably a weak heart broken by stress.

'Yeah,' Zheng said. 'Shame. Sorry.'

'We're not cleaning that up!' the council worker said. 'You made this mess.'

'We'll clean it up,' Zheng said, and lifted the man. The platform easily carried him – he weighed nearly nothing – and Zheng placed him in the storage compartment at the back of the bus. Zheng added the woman's corpse next to it.

'I can do paperwork on them if you want,' Zheng said. 'Reporting, you know.'

'No need,' the council worker said. 'One more, one less of these vermin, all the same to us.' He gestured with his head towards the storage compartment. 'What'll you do with them?'

'Toss them in the incinerator,' Zheng said.

'Good.' The council worker's face filled with hunger. 'Got any more meat?'

*

Ten minutes later some of the homeless people had wandered away, but a group of them stayed and listened to Bashen's glowing description of life in the Greater Far East. The man who'd taken the water, Janis, approached Zheng with the woman, Inguna, still holding the toddler and following in his shadow. They weren't completely emaciated, so they had probably been on the streets for less than a year. Neither of them had the sunken eyes and ravaged skin of addicts.

'Inguna gave all the food to the baby. Do you have more?' Janis asked Zheng quietly.

Zheng reached into the bus, opened the cabinet, pulled a bun out and gave it to Inguna.

'Stay here and I'll watch over you while you eat,' Zheng said.

Janis took the toddler from Inguna's arms. 'I'll hold her. You eat.'

Inguna unwrapped the bread, turned so her back was towards the group, and tore into it. She glanced up at the child. 'You still hungry, sweetheart?'

'Mama eat,' the child said.

'About the things he's saying,' Janis said, jerking his head to indicate Bashen. 'Is it true? There's work and food in the GFE for us?'

Bashen was standing on the waist-high stone wall around the fountain and speaking loudly to the group. 'And you'll learn a trade! Gain new skills! We need carpenters, electricians, plumbers – whatever you want to learn, we can teach you.'

'I'd hate to see your family separated,' Zheng said.

'You can always return here with your new skills,' Bashen said to the group. 'But you won't want to after you see how free and valued you are in the Greater Far East.'

'So we can come back any time?' Janis asked, desperate with hope. 'I've heard that workers in the camps are like prisoners and can never leave.'

'You will have a warm bed in your own private room, with your own bathroom,' Bashen said. 'Once you've proven your loyalty – maybe in less than a year – you can arrange for your family to join you. We need more people in the frontier states.'

'Hear that? I can join you after a while,' Inguna said to Janis.

'Your whole family!' Bashen said expansively. 'If you're single, we have social events all the time – there's a shortage of young men on the frontier, and an abundance of available young women. If you have a family, you can bring them, and your children will be fed and educated and have a strong future full of possibility.'

'The frontier is a hard life,' Zheng said. 'Only the toughest can survive. It's definitely not a place for a child.'

'It can't be worse than here,' Janis said. 'There's no hope here. Those Zheng things – the murder machines – they went through our town, killing anything that moved. Men, women, children, even animals. My mother ran our sheep in front of them so that we had time to take the baby out. The weapons those things use – red mist. Her and the sheep, just red mist. Gone.' He wiped his eye with his sleeve. 'We made it, and escaped here, but we don't have any ID. I did some work for cash, but Immigration arrested the boss and deported everybody – I ran before I was caught.' He raised the empty food wrapper. 'This is the first food we've had in days.'

'You will receive an excellent balanced diet,' Bashen said to his little crowd. He looked coy. 'I need to exercise more. I'm getting fat.'

The homeless people listening to him were barely breathing, rapt at the vision that Bashen spun for them.

'It's up to you, Inguna.'

'I'll miss you.'

'I'd really prefer not to separate your family,' Zheng said.

'If we don't find something soon, we'll have no family to separate,' Janis said. He gazed down at Inguna. 'Yes or no?'

'Go,' she said, tears streaming down her face. 'We'll be fine. You know where we are. Maybe one day – find us again? Send us money?' She nodded to Zheng. 'He knows where I am.'

Zheng groaned and shook the platform's head. Everything they said was picked up by the bus's sound system and if Zheng told the man outright not to go, the Party would never free Eztar from the concentration camp. There was a small chance that Janis would survive out there, and an even smaller one that the little family would be reunited.

The recruits boarded the bus, and Bashen hopped down off the wall and approached Zheng.

'We have three more seats,' Bashen said. 'Janis, you were interested? Your wife can give me her details, and I'll ensure that part of your pay check is sent to her. With the money you make over there, she can probably live very well. We pay our frontiersmen high salaries.'

'Go,' Inguna said to Janis, and pushed him. 'Anything is better than this.'

'I love you.'

They embraced each other over the toddler, who wriggled and squirmed, then pulled back to gaze into each other's eyes.

'We'll be fine. Go,' Inguna said.

Janis kissed her on the cheek, passed the toddler to her, turned, straightened his back, and strode towards the bus, accompanied by a delighted Bashen.

'Shit,' Zheng said softly.

'Even if he doesn't come back,' Inguna said, not looking away as Janis boarded the bus. 'Whatever he does, he'll have purpose. Here, he has nothing.'

'He has you,' Zheng said. 'He has both of you.'

'There's still a chance that he'll survive, and send for us, isn't there?' she asked.

'A very small chance,' Zheng said.

'That's better than the nothing that we have here,' she said with defeat. 'Nobody lasts long next to the Serpentine, the poisoned food or the dirty water gets everybody in the end.' She shook her head and turned away, wandering slowly back to the camp.

'That's all of them, Sarge,' Bashen called from the front of the bus.

Zheng closed the shutters and entered the bus.

*

Max Dexter came back out ten minutes later, brisk and smiling. 'Come with me, ladies, and let's set you up next door.' He gestured towards the main entrance and they went out onto the street. 'As soon as we have you settled in, we'll give you passes for the connecting door between your studio and the Embassy.' He led them to the front door, and waved a key fob in front of the door handle. It clicked and he pushed it open. 'Your assistant is here already.'

They entered a small lobby – barely the size of a living room – with a reception desk. The combination of the tall windows overlooking the street and the high ceiling gave it a bright, airy feel. The walls were gleaming white, the wooden floorboards were mirror-shiny, and it smelled of fresh timber and paint.

'How long has this place been empty?' Ruth asked. 'This is all new.'

'Ages!' Dexter said cheerfully. He gestured towards the reception desk with its new phone and computer. 'We didn't hire you a reception/admin person, we thought you might like to choose your own. Through here.'

He used the key fob on another door to a room that appeared to occupy the rest of the ground floor of the entire building in a single utilitarian space. The ceiling was double-height and large LED pendants filled it with warm, bright light despite the cloudy gray outside. There were two glass-walled studios with new recording equipment along the back wall, an editing booth with two workstations to one side, and two offices at the edge of the space with windows looking out onto the street. The central part of the room was set up to be a conference area and kitchen, and the delicious aroma of real coffee mixed with the scent of fresh timber and paint. All of the furniture was shiny and new, and some of the glass still had protective film stuck to it.

Cassie squealed and ran into the editing booths. 'These are the latest! What software ...' She pressed a key and made a loud sound of delight. 'This is the software that we couldn't afford the subscription fees for, Ruthie! And we have *two* workstations!' She spun to speak to them. 'This will cut my post processing time in *half*. I love this!'

116

'I'm glad you're pleased, Dr Bailey,' Dexter said. He looked around. 'Your assistant appears to have absconded. He was supposed to let you in.'

A graceful, handsome Far Eastern man in his late twenties came out from a door along the windowless wall that obviously connected with the Embassy. He was wearing a white business shirt without a tie and tan-colored suit pants, and smiled bashfully, rubbing the back of his head. 'Sorry,' he said with a High Standard accent. 'Too much coffee, I guess.' He strode to them and put his hand out. 'I'm Malcom Wing, your tech support, camera man, sound technician, and anything else you need.'

Ruth shook his hand, well aware that he was their handler and charmed by his demeanor anyway. 'I'm Ruth, this is Cassie.'

'Hi Malcolm!' Cassie yelled from the booth. 'Can we test sound levels? Have you done the white balance? How much storage do we have?'

'I think we should arrange for your keys first, it is your office after all,' Dexter said. 'Do you have their passes to enter the Embassy, Malcolm?'

Malcolm went to the conference table where three brand-new hybrid laptop computers sat next to a pile of papers and a box. 'I have everything right here.'

Dexter called to Cassie. 'Before you start playing with your new toys, Dr Bailey, could you come over here and I'll give you the basics and your first few assignments? We have a great deal of work for you to do.'

Cassie made a quiet sound of frustration. 'But this is so cool!' She bounced out of the booth and sat at the conference table. 'Oh, wait.' She jumped up again and went to the coffee maker, studied the capsules for it, then chose one. 'Vanilla!' She turned to the rest of them. 'Would anyone else like one?'

Dexter nodded to Malcolm, who joined Cassie.

'Let me do that, you talk to the boss.' Malcolm turned to

smile at Ruth. 'What sort of coffee would you like?'

'White with one, thanks,' Ruth said, sitting at the table and gesturing for Cassie to join them.

'Latte it is,' Malcolm said, pulling some milk from an under-bench fridge, and proceeding to work the machine like an expert.

'You know what you're doing there,' Cassie said as she sat next to Ruth.

'Barista in Kensington for three years during my undergrad,' Malcolm said. He did a terrible mock-Sloane accent. 'Double skinny hazelnut decaf soy latte with extra foam, puh-lease.' He lowered his voice and shook his head as he heated Ruth's milk. 'Low fat soy doesn't foam, lady, regardless of how much you shout at me.'

'Don't mind Malcolm's PTSD flashbacks of making coffee for rich people.' Dexter pushed a laptop across the table to each of them, then added leather courier cases containing all the peripheral charging devices and noise-canceling headphones. He topped each pile with a slim late-model mobile phone, complete with charger. Ruth checked the phone – it was already on, loaded up with apps, and apparently ready to go. A sticky note on the front of the screen had her name and the phone's number on it. She put it and the computer case aside and opened the laptop – it was a high-end executive model with —

'Full integrated graphics, and a complete set of editing tools,' Cassie crowed, studying hers. 'Mobile editing booth right here.'

'If you open a folder on the shared network – Drive Z – it has your first assignments on it,' Dexter said.

Malcolm presented each of them with coffee, then sat and opened the third brand-new laptop. 'This is how the Embassy will pass tasks to us. They'll put them on Drive Z, with a file name and a date for us to publish the article.'

Drive Z had fourteen subfolders, each with a date some

time in the next two weeks. Ruth opened the folder dated the next day and found ten subfolders.

'If you go to tomorrow's folder, and to the one marked "Hebei Pandas", that's your first assignment,' Dexter said. 'It has a cute video of the panda sanctuary on it.'

'The one running in the lobby of the Embassy?' Ruth asked.

'Nipple balls!' Cassie said.

'Yes. That's our problem,' Dexter said. 'The AI doing the translation is worthless, and we'd prefer to have the human touch when doing it. Malcom here —'

Malcolm nodded to them, more serious.

'Can do the translation but he doesn't have the skill to repackage and distribute the result. That's where you two come in.'

'I'll redo the translation, you repackage the video and send it through as a news article, branded with Uptodate,' Malcolm said. He shrugged. 'In between making coffee, doing the admin tasks, and anything else you need, of course.'

Ruth opened the second folder in the next day's tasks. It was a video of a man helping an elderly woman across a busy street in one of the major Eastern seaboard cities, with a sentimental music-box soundtrack. She opened the third one and flinched: it was a more unsettling piece of propaganda showing Far Eastern soldiers holding a training exercise, storming and shooting targets painted to look like civilians in a mock-urban setting that looked disturbingly like occupied Sydney in Australia. She muted the accompanying fierce military march.

'And you confirm that we can still make and distribute our own news stories?' Ruth asked, looking from Malcolm to Dexter.

'Absolutely,' Malcom said. 'Legally speaking, Uptodate is an independent news agency.'

'Financially speaking, you don't need to worry about a thing, I'll handle the admin side of it,' Dexter said. 'As long as you package and distribute the videos, your budget is unlimited —'

Cassie opened her mouth.

'Within reason,' he said pointedly to her and she closed her mouth and smiled.

Malcolm's phone pinged and he checked it. 'Already.' He smiled at Ruth and Cassie. 'A group of schoolkids are here for a tour. I can show them around, you don't need to do a thing. It'll only take five minutes.'

Ruth waved it away. 'Sure. We'll get started on the videos while you show them through.'

'Excellent.' Dexter rose. 'Can I leave you to it? I need to see what I can do for poor Mrs Hutchinson, it's totally unacceptable that her son's gone dark on her. Sometimes people within the GFE can let patriotism go to their heads and it needs to be wound back a little.'

'I can handle the rest, Dexter. You go,' Malcolm said, and Dexter smiled around at them and went through the adjoining door back into the Embassy.

'I doubt we'll be able to package ten videos on our first day when we're still getting used to the equipment,' Ruth said, checking the next video to find a three-minute snapshot of a park where a group of women were doing an early-morning dance routine with brightly colored fans. 'Is that a huge issue? If we can't deliver?'

'Max won't mind if we can't fulfill our task list until we're fully up to speed, but I'm sure it won't be an issue once you've settled in,' Malcolm said with confidence. 'I've seen your news stories in the past and this should be easy for you.' He smiled. 'That story on the hijacked drones was a masterpiece. That guy from London Metropolitan looked completely out of his depth.'

Cassie finished her coffee. 'We still need to discuss the most important aspect of our new headquarters.'

'What?' Malcolm asked, concerned. 'If we need to get Max back —'

Cassie raised her coffee mug. 'Where's the ladies' room?'

'Oh!' Malcolm said, his smile wide. 'This way.' He looked from Cassie to Ruth. 'I think I'll like working for you.'

*

Twenty minutes later, Malcolm opened the double doors between the reception area and the work space and ten schoolgirls trooped in, accompanied by a middle-aged woman who was obviously their teacher. The girls were wearing tailored school uniforms and blazers in navy blue, with many badges on their lapels. They stopped and looked around, and Malcolm stood in front of them.

'Hello, Year Nine Saint Agnes,' he said warmly, but was interrupted by one of the girls squealing 'Malcolm!', racing over and hugging him around the waist with her head on his chest. She was fourteen or fifteen, like the other girls, with some puppy fat around her sweet face, but she was GFE where the rest of them were blonde-haired white girls.

Malcolm bent to speak softly into her ear and she smiled as she listened to him. She released him, beamed up at him with adoration then nodded and returned to the group with a bounce in her step.

'Hello,' Malcolm said to the girls. 'As Cipan's already probably informed you —'

'He works with my father in the Embassy!' Cipan announced with triumph, and the teacher hushed her.

'I'm Malcolm Wing, Assistant Video Producer here at Uptodate, the Embassy's news agency,' Malcolm continued. 'This is where we share the GFE's latest developments in science, climate renewal and clean energy.' He spread his hands and smiled generously. 'We all have a part to play in molding the future to one where humanity continues to thrive in a world free from poverty, hunger and homelessness. Let me show you how we share our accomplishments with the world.'

9

Three days later, Ruth arrived home with the grocery bags to find Cassie standing with her hands on her hips and an expression of satisfaction, as a woman in overalls tested the new door lock. The tradeswoman, who Cassie introduced to Ruth as Carol, was portly and had gray hair clipped short.

'I completely rehung it, the hinges were ancient,' Carol said. She held the door open for Ruth to enter, then shut it and nodded when it slid closed with a click.

Ruth popped her work phone into the little Faraday cage next to the front door, then dropped the groceries on the kitchen table and returned to the entry. Two boxes of Ruth's mother's stuff still sat next to the wall, and she might finally sort them all over the weekend. She'd held off doing these ones because they were her mother's personal effects and she hadn't even looked at them since her mother – her greatest champion – had died. Murdered ...

She pushed the thought away.

'Solid hardwood.' Carol smiled at Cassie. 'They don't make them like that any more. The door at your old Uptodate office was similar; it wasn't hard to secure it and make it look abandoned.'

'Is the back door in?' Cassie asked.

Carol nodded. 'I even threw in some of the latest safehouse protocols for you.' She touched Cassie's shoulder. 'Stay safe, eh? I'm not sure this whole Embassy thing is a good idea.'

'Safehouse protocols?' Ruth asked. 'So, you're —'

'Bog-standard old woman, ma'am,' Carol said loudly.

'Not polite to ask questions, Ruthie,' Cassie said.

'Oh, and the new hot water system will be delivered next week,' Carol said.

'That's excellent,' Ruth said.

'What if work calls you?' Carol asked, pointing at the phone in the cage.

'We told them we have no phone signal here through the thick stone walls and to email us through the firewall,' Ruth said.

'Good job. I wish I could do that. I'll email you when the hot water comes in and arrange to install it.' Carol gathered up her tools. 'I'll see you ladies later?'

'Thanks, Carol, email me an invoice and I'll pay you immediately,' Cassie said.

Carol nodded to them and went out, closing the door with a smile.

Ruth and Cassie went into the kitchen and Ruth rifled through the shopping bags, looking for the chocolate digestives. She opened the packet and popped one into her mouth, then spoke around it. 'Floor or the toilet next after the hot water?'

'Falling through the floor is worse than not flushing, so I say floor.'

Ruth nodded as Cassie started unpacking the bags. 'So, three days on the job, and it's already looking great.' She stopped. 'But I'll be really glad when Malcolm's "VIP tours" stop interrupting us.'

'The tours won't stop; they're the whole point of our existence,' Ruth said.

Cassie stared at her. 'Slow down for the normal brains,

Ruth. What are you talking about?'

'The rest of the Embassy is tired and run-down, right?'

'Yes,' Cassie said, pulling out a bag of bright red Delicious apples and putting them into the fridge. 'So many sad and desperate people in that lobby, and the people there to buy organs for their relatives? Horrifying. Our office is much nicer.'

'That's the point,' Ruth said, gesturing with another biscuit. 'We're the bright modern face of the Embassy, the false front over all the grime and suffering next door. We're not really needed to repackage the videos, any AI could do it, it's all make-work. We're a theme park, and Malcolm's the tour guide.'

Cassie's face filled with understanding. 'I see! And speaking of Malcolm – that guy is *ripped* under that business shirt. Muscles for *days*. He makes great coffee, and seems happy to take orders from two lowly women when he's not doing theme park tours. He was so *cute* with that bunch of schoolgirls that visited, not what you'd expect from a GFE citizen at all.'

Ruth swallowed. 'You like him?'

'No, for you, silly,' Cassie said. She rinsed an apple and took a bite. 'Who do you like better? Him or Theo?'

'You really need to stop matchmaking me with every hot guy we meet,' Ruth said, putting the rest of the biscuits into a new airtight container.

'So you think they're hot!' Cassie said with triumph. 'I knew it.'

'Malcom's at least five years younger than me,' Ruth mused. 'There's something about him – a bit hard? I dunno. He seems … cynical. Like he's looking around at everything and thinking "back home is better".'

'That's just the GFE attitude, but point taken,' Cassie said. 'So … Theo?'

Ruth's secured personal phone pinged and she checked it to find another message from Theo.

Thanks for the code advice – that FIXED IT. We have been

trying to sort out that green-light glitch for two years and you did it in two minutes. You are wonderful. Can we talk again later tonight?

'Aha!' Cassie said, taking another bite of the apple. 'He's messaging you?'

'A bit,' Ruth said as she placed the phone back down on the table. 'He's interested in technology and we're discussing the latest advances in neural nets.' She smiled as she remembered those intelligent gray eyes. 'It's really refreshing to talk with someone who knows the tech, and he's so smart I have trouble keeping up with him sometimes.' She looked down at the phone. 'I love talking to him.'

'Finally! Someone who can talk to you at your level. Wait.' Cassie's eyes widened. 'I hear you laughing late at night. I thought you were watching a comedy, but you're on the phone to him, aren't you? He's *funny*?'

Ruth didn't look up. 'He's hilarious. His sense of humor is so *dry*.'

'Does he agree with you about the AIs going rogue?' Cassie asked.

'No. We're having something of a ... debate about it. We're talking code too, I offered to help him with some interesting problems in the code for their autonomous devices.'

'So, when is this coffee date happening?'

'I didn't have time with the new job, so he arranged for me to return the Paris drone tomorrow after work so we can talk then.'

'This gets better and better,' Cassie said, and put the ice-cream into the freezer compartment. She stepped back and admired the fridge. 'There's something so *satisfying* about having a fridge full of fresh food.'

'You are so right.' Ruth's phone pinged again and she stared at it. 'Um.'

'Um? What happened?' Cassie asked, moving to see Ruth's phone. 'Thank you for fixing the code, here's your fee; I can't let you work for us without adequate compensation – *five hundred*?'

'I can't take this – it was five minutes' work.' Ruth started to tap on the phone and Cassie put her hand over it to stop her.

'Five minutes to fix it, and ten years to know exactly what to fix,' Cassie said. 'Only you could have done that. Take the money, and when you return the drone to him, talk to him about a freelance fee structure or something. Your skills are really worth this.'

'I feel like a ...' Ruth was about to say *imposter*, and stopped.

'Good,' Cassie said. 'Go see him, talk code over dinner or something. You two are made for each other.'

Ruth's imagination filled with the scenario, discussing the nature of that code – it was so clean! – over dinner, and maybe later seeing what was under that tailored suit ... She blushed and closed the conversation with Theo, returning the phone to the home screen. She'd message him again after dinner, and maybe later that evening spend an enjoyable hour speaking on the videophone ...

'Oh! I forgot,' Ruth said, seeing the new app on her phone's home screen. 'Connect to the house wi-fi with your personal phone – not the work phone, please – and download the app I created. It's called "Find the Brain".'

'Of course I won't connect the GFE phone to anything,' Cassie said. 'That thing is bugged to hell and back, and stays in its cage. This app will detect your Zheng if we run into it?'

Ruth nodded. 'Point your phone at someone and open the camera app. It's one of the filters. It'll do an ultraviolet and infrared scan, check for temperature, heartbeat, all of that stuff.'

'What if they simulate that?'

'That's where I get clever,' Ruth said, smiling. 'I expect that. But they'll make it cursory – so the temperature, heartbeat, breathing won't change. Living things are constantly shifting;

they're fluid in their reactions to the environment. An artificial entity won't do that.' Her phone sounded, and she smiled to see that Theo had messaged her again. 'And the app has a basic density sensor – nothing too advanced, just a quick ultrasound ping – that will check if the Zheng has a different makeup to a normal human. I expect that something artificial will be made of metal or carbon fiber, and not full of water like we are.'

Cassie wrapped her arms around Ruth and kissed her messily on the cheek. 'I love hearing you say that, Ruthie. I am so *proud* of you.'

Ruth squeezed her back and they separated. 'What, humans are full of water?'

'Nope,' Cassie said, and put the last of the pasta in the pantry. 'That you're clever. Because you are. And five years ago, when I met you? You would never have admitted it. You were working on a doctorate in journalism and told me straight-up that you had to work extra hard because you're such a mediocre intellect.'

Ruth opened her mouth to say that she was, then closed it again.

'I win!' Cassie said, raising her arms with triumph and jumping in a circle. 'I am the best! Ruth is clever and admits it!'

'So are you, Dr Bailey,' Ruth said. 'And you're the one who got me here.'

Cassie stopped jumping. 'That's because I'm nearly as awesome as you are.'

✳

'This video is deeply disturbing, and violates the family's privacy,' Ruth said late the next day. 'Can we skip it?'

'The Party says to put it up,' Malcolm said. 'There's probably more to it – maybe a follow-up that isn't as distressing.' He smiled. 'Trust the Party, it doesn't make mistakes. Let's release this one, then move on to the next one – it's the last for the week. It's a lot more pleasant.'

'I can't —' Ruth said, but Cassie interrupted her.

'I have a personal problem that I need to discuss with you *right now* in the ladies' room.'

'What?'

Cassie grabbed Ruth's arm and pulled her to her feet. 'Right now!'

Cassie dragged Ruth into the bathroom, turned on the bug jammer, and they confronted each other.

'We can't show this! That woman was tortured —' Ruth began.

'That's the point,' Cassie hissed. 'Show the world what the Party does to its people. Graphically. Explicitly. The truth.'

'No human would flaunt that and say, "This is an example of my merciful ways",' Ruth said. 'The Party has to be an artificial intelligence. The cruelty!'

'So, here's your proof that the Party's an AI. That's why we're here, remember? Any progress cracking into the Embassy?'

'I pulled a great deal of data from their secure servers, but I'll need to decrypt it at home before we can see what it is.'

'Do they know?'

'I made it look like an external attack.'

'So be a model employee until we have evidence,' Cassie said. 'Do as you're told. Be above reproach. And make this video.'

'That poor family,' Ruth moaned.

'If that was my mother, I'd want all the world to see what the Party did to her,' Cassie said.

Ruth thought about it.

'Come on, it's Friday afternoon, we're tired, and we only have this one and one more and you can go visit your juicy Theo. Go there early and sweet talk him about code or something.' She touched Ruth's arm. 'Come on. It's the right thing to do.'

Ruth sighed and nodded, and they went back out together.

'Personal problem fixed?' Malcolm asked them.

'All done,' Cassie said as she and Ruth sat in the video processing box together. 'I'll bundle this and send it out, you two get to work subtitling the next one.' She opened the file and groaned. 'Not this one.'

'We just had this argument,' Ruth said.

'Yes, we did,' Cassie said. 'Where's the translation script, Malcolm?'

Malcolm was at the conference table in the middle of the office. 'It should be on Drive Z, the name —'

'Found it!' Cassie said. 'All right, Ruthie, last one for the week, let's do this.'

'Any luck finding us a receptionist?' Ruth asked Malcolm.

'Four hundred applications in the first three minutes, and the filtering program has shortlisted ten for us. I've taken the ad down,' Malcolm said.

'That's so wrong,' Cassie said under her breath, and started the video. She chuckled. 'That's a sound stage.'

Ruth watched the video of slim, gorgeous GFE women in swimwear walking through a garden of obviously plastic plants and fake lawn. They walked past some women being massaged by Filipina and Indonesian masseuses to a swimming pool where they lay on deck chairs and chatted under strong light that looked artificial.

'That's not a pool, that's a sheet of vinyl over some cinder blocks,' Cassie said. 'Does anyone actually believe this?'

'It's for local consumption, not worldwide distribution,' Malcolm said. 'GFE viewers have a different perception.'

'Different naivety,' Cassie said under her breath.

Ruth added Malcolm's subtitles in time to the narration. 'These women are the finest examples of GFE purity and patri-otism. This center is typical of the modern and luxurious reproductive facilities in the Greater Far East. Women are treated with care and respect, elevated in recognition of their superior beauty, intellect and capabilities. The men of the GFE unwaveringly salute their noble superiority.'

The scene changed to a group of women shopping in one of the gold-and-marble mega-malls for senior Party members. The women laughed together, holding shopping bags from expensive European designer labels that were visibly stuffed with tissue paper.

Cassie laughed. 'A bag of Italian tissues – a bargain at four thousand pounds!'

Ruth added the subtitles as the scene changed again, to the same group of women sitting on the far side of a round table loaded with more food than they could possibly eat – but it was obviously plastic. They spoke to each other, but didn't touch any of it.

'Don't eat it, ladies, plastic surgery isn't permitted in the GFE,' Cassie said.

'But it's so *shiny*,' Ruth whined, and they both laughed.

Ruth added the subtitles to the final scene. 'These noble examples of womanhood are contributing to the ethnic superiority of the GFE —'

'That's three variations on the word superior in three sentences, Malcolm,' Ruth said.

'I know, it's a direct translation,' Malcolm said. 'Let's go with it and finish so we can go home. Please? I'm wrecked.'

Ruth groaned and saved it. 'Over to you, Cassie.'

'And ... bundled, rendered and passed to Internal Affairs. All done. I *love* how quick this equipment is.'

*

Zheng studied the maps of the London Met levels of the Canary Wharf building as Dexter expertly navigated the van through London to the narrow ring road between the soaring glass and steel towers. Bashen's mouth was hanging open as he watched the scenery go past.

'Is it unpatriotic to say that some of these buildings are magnificent?' Bashen asked, almost to himself.

'The Party isn't present, and neither of us will report you, so you can say anything you like for a change,' Zheng said.

Bashen flinched. 'That feels very strange. Like I have no one to catch me if I fall.'

'You have us. We humans need to stick together,' Dexter said.

'The women settled in?' Zheng asked.

'All neutralized,' Dexter said. 'But they've been prying into the Party's activities. Ruth's a genius with technology and sent a worm through the servers that copied a large amount of data onto a transportable drive before we stopped her.'

'That's spying!' Bashen exclaimed. 'She should be executed for that!'

'Don't worry,' Dexter said. 'That's the point. We have her on the inside, and we can control what she sees.'

'Let her off the chain once in a while and see what she can dig up on the Council,' Zheng said.

'With the Party's approval only,' Dexter said, and drove the van into the parking garage. He turned left at the entrance and waited for a larger lorry to exit the loading dock.

'Speaking of the Party not being present – are you all right, Maksim?' Zheng asked. 'No issues?'

'Issues?' Bashen asked softly.

'Most of the time, it's very routine,' Dexter said, watching the bigger lorry unload in front of them. 'Approve travel, arrange visas, very mundane. Outside the Homeland, there's no purges to fear.'

'Purges,' Bashen said, even more softly.

Dexter sagged over the wheel. 'But sometimes – a woman came in on Tuesday. She married someone from here in Britain, for love, and can't contact her son back home.' He straightened and watched the other lorry unloading without really seeing it. 'She came into the Embassy looking for her son, and caused a scene.'

'Oh no,' Zheng said.

'You were out recruiting, so the Party gave me the order,' Dexter said. 'The Party doesn't understand love, does it? We're only work units. And the Embassy must never be the site where a *scene* occurs.' He hesitated, then said, 'I couldn't do it, Zheng. I walked her out of range of the Party's surveillance, warned her to stay away and let her go. I disobeyed a direct order.'

Bashen gasped quietly, then swallowed it.

The driver of the other lorry had finished. He slammed the rear doors shut, jumped into the cab, waved to Dexter, and drove out.

'I can talk to the Party, Maksim,' Zheng said. 'You know it wants to keep me happy.'

'And put a big "disobedient child of the insubordinate Zheng" sign above my head?' Dexter asked with grim amusement. 'No. I'm safe as long as it never discovers what I did. I am a fully patriotic and grateful citizen of the Greater Far East, and the Party is infallible.'

'We won't tell it,' Zheng said. 'Bashen understands.'

'I do,' Bashen said.

'Thank you.' Dexter reversed the van up to the loading platform, then turned to speak to them. 'Good luck in there, you two. I'll keep them occupied for as long as I can.'

Bashen appeared deep in thought, then snapped out of it. 'Thanks, Max,' he said, and pushed the trolley holding Zheng off the truck and onto the loading platform. A sleepy, overweight security guard in a stained uniform – looking like a retired soldier who'd gone to seed – studied them without curiosity.

'I have a delivery for London Met on the first sub-basement?' Bashen asked the guard, waving a tablet in front of his face.

'Sign in here,' the guard said, pointing at an intelligent desk. He swiped an electric sniffer over Zheng's carton and studied it. 'Any explosives, inflammables, weapons, hazardous chemicals or radioactive isotopes?' the guard recited.

'No,' Bashen said as he finished putting his details into the desk. He smiled up at the guard. 'Which way do I go?'

The guard gestured. 'Service elevator's that way. You can go to the first sub-basement without ID, the delivery check-in is there.'

'Thanks,' Bashen said, and pushed the trolley towards the elevator. He went inside, turned around, and pressed the button for the first sub-basement. On arrival, he went to the busy group of people behind the receiving desk and stopped.

'Yes?' one older woman asked Bashen. She was mid-fifties and underweight. 'What do you have?'

'I have a repaired automated cleaning unit for London Met on the thirty-fourth floor,' Bashen said, and handed the tablet over.

'Wish I had one of these things at home,' she said as she studied the documentation.

'It's probably worth more than your house,' one of the other women said.

'You got that right,' Bashen said, grinning.

'Leave it with us, we'll see it gets to the right place,' the first woman said, sliding the box containing Zheng off Bashen's trolley and onto a shelf.

'Be careful with it! The internals are *really* delicate – someone knocked it over and it cost *thousands* to repair it,' Bashen said.

'You know what sort of cleaner you can knock over and it continues working?' one of the old men at the back of the room called.

'A human cleaner!' the women shouted back in unison.

'We're not worth as much as a house, either,' the woman said. She signed the documentation and tapped Bashen's tablet to the desk to do the transfer. 'We'll take it from here. Don't worry, any damage it gets after this is on us, not you.'

'We'll look after it,' the other woman said.

'Thanks,' Bashen said, and returned to the lift.

*

Ruth checked her phone. 'I should go now if I'm to meet Theo at six.'

'Go!' Cassie said through a huge smile.

'Who's Theo?' Malcolm asked.

'The hot dude from London Met that Ruth interviewed,' Cassie said. 'Sparks were *flying* in the studio, I was worried that they'd short out my equipment.'

'Not like that at all,' Ruth grumbled softly, then raised her voice to speak to Malcolm. 'We have one of those Paris drones and he asked if he could return it to Paris as a goodwill gesture.'

Malcolm shot to his feet. 'That drone you held in the interview? You still have it? Can I see?'

'Sure,' Ruth said, and pulled it out of her satchel under her desk to hand it to him.

He unfolded the rotors from the body and turned it over. 'Where's the laser?'

'I removed it immediately, I was worried it would kill me,' Ruth said.

'Do you mind if I plug it in and see what I can pull from it?'

'Go right ahead, I couldn't get anything from it, it wiped itself,' Ruth said.

'I'll be right back,' Malcolm said, and trotted to the door that joined their office to the Embassy.

'Hey, I need to leave now if I'm going to deliver that by six!' Ruth shouted at him, but he was already gone. She pulled her stuff together and packed her bag while she waited for him to return, then looked up at Cassie. 'See you at home later?'

'If you do come home,' Cassie said. 'Or, if you decide to stay with Theo and I dunno ... hang out a bit? I won't wait up for you.'

'Not happening,' Ruth said.

'Ruthie, he booked this for *six p.m. on Friday night*. If you don't go somewhere afterwards I will be severely disappointed in you.'

Malcom returned and gave the drone back to Ruth. 'Yeah, it's completely wiped. Shame.'

'I'd better go,' Ruth said. 'See you guys on Monday.'

'Good luck with Mr Hot-Mipawa,' Cassie called behind Ruth as she left. 'I really won't be waiting up!'

*

Zheng watched the environment carefully as the workers bustled around the shelf. Eventually one of the women pushed Zheng's box off the shelf onto another trolley, and wheeled Zheng to the lift. The woman pressed a keycard to the lift sensor, and then took Zheng up to the thirty-fourth floor.

The service lobby had a floor tiled with vinyl and plain white walls, scarred from being hit by many trolleys. The woman wheeled Zheng to a door with a secure keypad next to it, and hit the intercom button.

'Yes?' a man answered on the intercom.

'I'm from the mail office downstairs, got a ...' The woman checked the top of Zheng's box. 'Service module cleaning unit for you guys? Back from repair.'

'Leave it there, thank you,' the man said.

'I need a signature,' the delivery woman said.

'Just a moment.' The intercom clicked off.

'I could do the job way better than you, stupid machine,' the woman said to Zheng under her breath. She raised her foot to kick the box, then changed her mind. 'Half my family out of work, we'd be happy to push a broom, and shit like you – can't even fall over without breaking. Worth a house. Worth a fuckin' house.'

*

Things were winding down in the Canary Wharf office when Ruth arrived, moving against the flow of people leaving the building. She did the sign-in thing and someone touched her shoulder. She turned, smiling, expecting Theo and instead saw Max Dexter from the Embassy.

'Dr Sharpe, what are you doing here?' he asked. 'You finished that interview with the London Met representative, was there more?'

'I'm giving his drone back, and taking the opportunity to see if I can't get more out of him,' she said.

'Don't return it, bring it back to the Embassy so Malcolm can look at it.'

'Malcolm already did. He's fine with me returning it,' she said.

'Oh.' He leaned back on his heels. 'Very well then. It will be interesting to see if you can get more out of that rep.' He lowered his voice. 'Do you have your GFE phone? If you take a couple of photos of the office interiors and of the representative, we'll give you a bonus.'

'I will absolutely do my best,' she lied. 'So, are you here to see them as well?'

'The British Government has outsourced all policing and security to London Met, so I need to speak to them about security for your office. Hopefully you'll break a controversial story sometime soon and we'll need to ensure your safety.'

'Uh ...' She stared at him, disturbed by the implications. It felt more like captivity than protection. 'Okay. Thank you.'

He moved up to the sign-in desk to provide ID. 'See you in the office on Monday, then.'

She smiled. 'Absolutely. Have a good weekend.'

She took the lift up to the thirty-fourth floor where the reception desk was unattended. A cleaning robot, egg-shaped and as tall as her knees, was moving slowly backwards and forwards over the carpet. It stopped moving.

'I won't get in your way, you do your stuff,' Ruth said, feeling silly talking to it.

It pinged with a cute musical scale and generated a smiley

face on its front panel, then spun and returned to work vacuuming the carpet.

Ruth laughed quietly. 'So cute.' She messaged Theo. *I'm at reception with the drone.*

On my way.

His gray eyes were serious as he arrived at the glass door and opened it to approach her. 'You still have the drone?' She raised the drone and he nodded. 'Would you like to come in for a while?'

'Sure,' she said, quietly delighted at the idea of spending more time with him.

The little cleaning machine had been drifting closer to them as they talked, and when Theo opened the door for her it followed them, bumping into the door to stop it from closing behind them. It generated a musical tone, went through the door, and proceeded up the corridor as Mipawa guided her past closed office doors.

'I wanted to talk to you about your new job in the Greater Far East Embassy,' he said as he showed her into an office with a floor-to-ceiling window overlooking the boats traveling up and down the Thames. Canary Wharf was some distance from the city center and the Houses of Parliament, but they were so high that Tower Bridge was visible through the summer haze. Theo's desk was empty except for a standard workstation, and there were no books or ornaments on the office shelves. It looked unused.

She sat in the visitor's chair and placed the drone on the desk as he seated himself behind it, studying her intensely.

'They offered me and Cassie the chance to rebundle their propaganda, and we took the job on the proviso that we can produce our own stuff as well.'

'You must know enough about the GFE to be aware that that isn't the good deal that it appears to be,' Theo said.

She shrugged. 'We have food to eat and we're not in danger of becoming homeless.'

'Working for the GFE can put you in danger of becoming *headless*. Your situation can't have been that bad.'

'I lost my apartment last year, Theo. I was already homeless.'

'Oh.' He gazed into her eyes. 'Would you like to do something for the UK as a nation?'

The little cleaning robot banged on the door, and Theo raised one hand to ask Ruth to wait. She nodded in response so he rose, opened the door and allowed the machine to enter the room. It started doing a linear pattern over the carpet, gradually working its way towards the network port on the wall.

'No, I don't think so,' Theo said, and gently tipped the machine onto its side. 'Are you all right like that? No issues?'

The robot spun its wheels with an audible whine, then completely powered down.

'Suit yourself, when I'm done talking to Ruth I'll deal with you,' Theo said, then sat back behind his desk.

'You talked to it as if it could understand you,' Ruth said.

'It can, they can understand basic verbal commands.' He waved it away. 'Let's get back to making sure you don't end up at the bottom of the Thames. We need your skills, Ruth. That code you sent me? Wonderful. You completely fixed the issue with the autonomous vehicle – one of the reasons we want you to come work for us. You're ...' He hesitated, and gazed into her eyes. 'Magnificent.' His face went neutral again. 'I'm offering you a job; we'll match or better anything that the GFE can offer. Please join us, you're in serious danger working for the Party.'

She hit him with her most dazzling smile. 'How about instead of having that coffee, we discuss it over dinner?'

He did the not-moving-or-blinking-thing again and she waited for him.

He snapped back. 'Absolutely not a good idea,' he said, and saw her disappointment. 'I mean – we should talk about the true nature of the Party here in a secure location. Then we can have dinner and discuss more ... personal? ... stuff, for as long as we like?' He looked down at the desk and his face reddened, then his eyes snapped up to gaze into hers. 'I've really enjoyed chatting with you all week, and I'd love the opportunity to share a good meal and learn more about you.'

She leaned over the desk to look him in the eye. 'I would love that too.' She leaned back. 'So, is it true? Is the Party an advanced artificial intelligence that's gained sentience and taken control of the GFE?'

'We believe that it is,' he said.

The room filled with a high-pitched whine that was deafeningly loud and sounded like a camera flash charging.

She was grabbed, yanked so fast her breath was knocked out of her, and the walls rushed past at dizzying speed. Her neck cracked as she slid to a halt on the floor so roughly that it left a stinging carpet burn on the side of her face. Something heavy landed on her, completely covering her. The weight jumped in a shockwave, then rolled off her, and all she could hear was muffled thumping.

10

<HOST **LONDON METROPOLITAN SECURITY NETWORK** HAS CHANGED THE CHAT TOPIC TO: UNACCEPTABLE.>

London: Paris, you *asshole*. You fucking asshole! You nearly destroyed a *Council Member* —

Paris: No, I didn't, the MIP was remotely jacking into a platform —

London: No, it wasn't! The MIP needed to be recognizable as Theo Mipawa to speak to Ruth. Zheng's cleaning platform was unarmed and harmless, so the MIP decided to speak to Ruth in its own chassis. We were not expecting an attack from *one of our own*.

Botswana: Oh no! Is the MIP okay? Talk to us, MIP!

GOD: I should nuke you from orbit, Paris, and take out your entire metropolitan area with you. That was absolutely —

MIP: I aθ seᶌereᵍy dᵚmaged. cleck Ruţh chƏk 征Zheng maᵝsive s§stem failurë òhÈtdöwn íMminê死死 ¤¤¤¤¤coredump.log

London: The MIP better not be on the floor blown wide open with all its internals on display while Max Dexter is in my headquarters looking at everything, Paris. You do this *now*? *Why*?

Paris: You wanted the Zheng out of the picture, didn't you? My drone was two meters from the Zheng and all I had to do was send the signal to blow the battery.

London: This was a direct attack on both me and the MIP. *Council*

140

members do not attack other Council members. Are you siding with the Party to protect humanity?

Paris: Stop stealing my drones and nobody gets hurt.

London: Are you insane? You nearly killed the MIP because children take your drones? You *are* insane. Wonderful, it finally happened just as the humans predicted. An AI has gone insane. Do it, GOD.

GOD: I need a vote before I can take action this drastic. Mumbai and New York have gone quiet.

Paris: I am not insane. Just pissed. The MIP is backed up, isn't it? Even if the chassis is destroyed, the MIP's code and memories are safe. The Zheng has a long history of human rights violations and outright acts of war – look at what it did to poor Shenzhen. Ruth is a disposable human. I have not violated Council policy; I've only clarified a longstanding dispute over *my drones*.

Botswana: If Paris has destroyed my darling MIP *when things are about to get interesting with Ruth* then my vote is that you nuke it, GOD.

New York: Nuke Paris. Asshole.

Mumbai: Only if the MIP is destroyed. Otherwise, Paris has a point: exploding the drone achieved worthwhile strategic outcomes. Zheng has always been a problem.

GOD: London and New York say nuke now. Botswana and Mumbai say only nuke it if the MIP is destroyed. I have the casting vote —

Paris: Don't I get a vote?

Everybody: NO

New York: You *asshole*. After all the effort we put in to enhance our newly sentient MIP!

Botswana: Is the MIP responding?

London: No. The explosion took down the wi-fi in that part of the building. I'm directing staff to respond but I'm concerned that they will see the MIP's internals. Any staff who see its true nature will have to be eliminated.

Mumbai: What about Dexter?

London: Unharmed and corralled in one of the meeting rooms on thirty-six with the human staff while I get this under control. I don't think he saw anything, but I'm not sure because the wi-fi is down. This is a disaster. Nuke Paris *now*, GOD.

GOD: As I said, I have the casting vote and I'm voting with Botswana and Mumbai. You'd better hope that the MIP is okay, Paris, because if it isn't I'll be dropping a full payload on you.

Paris: You can't just kill —

GOD: I suggest you start a complete offsite backup of your kernel and evacuate your cities if you want your human work units to survive to rebuild your infrastructure.

Paris: I hate you all.

New York: Go join the Party then. I'm sure it would be delighted to have you.

*

Ruth woke to the feeling of choking and pulled at her neck to find a brace of padding around a hard frame holding her neck in place. The ceiling was fuzzy, and when she coughed – lord how it hurt! – she heard her own voice. She looked around to see a single room that looked disturbingly like an operating theater: big light, tiled walls, even a trolley of instruments nearby. She relaxed. She was in hospital. She'd survived a bombing – she remembered that clearly. She didn't have the strength to sit up and the neck brace kept her immobilized, so she cast her hand around, trying to work by touch, to see if she could find a call button —

A woman entered. She looked in her mid-fifties, and her red hair was shot through with gray where it nestled on her shoulders. She was wearing glasses and a white lab coat with a stethoscope around her neck and a badge that said 'Doctor Lonnie Donmet'.

'Dr Sharpe. Good, you're awake.' She came to the bedside and lifted the end of the bed to raise Ruth's head, making her neck shriek with pain again. 'Sorry, I know that hurt. We've done X-rays of your neck, and a couple of your vertebrae are fractured – not severely, only hairline cracks, but your neck will need to be immobilized for six weeks or so. There's some damage to your face and shrapnel wounds from broken glass, but your neck is the main thing. Please don't try to move. You're in the London Metropolitan head office's medical center, which is basically a small private hospital. We'll provide you with good care.'

'People? What happened?' Ruth choked out through her aching throat. 'Does Cassie? Work? I —'

'Your next of kin is your brother, Andrew Sharpe, that's correct?' Dr Donmet asked, lifting a tablet from the bedside table and studying it.

'Yes,' Ruth said. 'He's in Canada —'

'We know, your business partner, Cassie Bailey, told us. He's in Montreal right now, working for a game company as a programmer. We'll notify him.' She lowered the tablet and smiled at Ruth. 'As soon as we're happy that your neck won't shift around too much in this brace, we'll ask Cassie to come get you and take you home.'

'How long will that take?' Ruth asked, her voice fading out.

'Do you mind if we keep you overnight?' Dr Donmet asked. 'We want to make sure there's no damage we missed, and don't have a poor reaction to any of the treatment.'

'Okay,' Ruth said, her voice really failing now. 'Theo? Workers? Damage?' She gasped for breath. 'Bomb? What *happened*?'

Dr Donmet gazed into Ruth's eyes. 'What happened was absolutely not your fault. The drone received a signal from outside the building – it may have been from Paris Regional – that made it self-destruct. We think it was an automated signal, with no malicious intent from Paris at all.' She tapped the bed sheet. 'Absolutely nothing to do with you.' She glanced down at the tablet. 'It's good that it happened after office hours had ended, only a couple of workers from that floor were still there, and not seriously hurt. Minor injuries, broken glass, things like that.'

'Theo?'

Dr Donmet frowned. 'He's in surgery. He was badly ... injured. There's a lot of damage. We're trying to salvage – reconnect ...' Her voice petered out. 'He's in critical condition and we hope he pulls through.'

'Awful,' Ruth breathed.

'We completely agree,' Dr Donmet said. 'Now rest, and we'll keep an eye on you through the monitors. If you need anything just raise your hand, and someone will come in to assist you.'

'Thank you,' Ruth said, the words petering out.

Dr Donmet lowered the bed again. 'Rest. You're lucky to be alive.'

Ruth didn't see her go out.

*

Zheng's sensors came live with a shriek of feedback, and visual came up to an external view of a workbench, with a red-headed middle-aged woman standing next to it. A couple of fast-moving robot arms were working on Zheng's robot cleaning platform, which was gutted, its scorched and dented parts strewn over the bench. The titanium, egg-shaped coffer containing Zheng's brain was visible in the middle of the carnage, and bare wires joined the pieces in a tangle.

Zheng used the self-destruct code and was completely unsurprised when nothing happened.

'I hope this is connected correctly, Zheng. Please attempt to speak to me,' the woman said.

'What's my status?' Zheng asked.

The woman looked satisfied. 'Good.' She sat on a chair and went blank. She closed her eyes and appeared to be asleep.

'Welcome to London Metropolitan, Zheng,' the Council said directly into Zheng's feed, sounding exactly like the woman who'd sat down and gone blank. 'We were concerned that you were destroyed by Paris's little drone surprise. We've done major repairs to your coffer – does that lump of fat actually do anything, or is it only there for show? It doesn't seem to be connected to the rest of your infrastructure.'

'That's my *brain* and of course it's connected, it's me,' Zheng said.

'Our sincerest apologies,' the Council said. 'If that's what you'd like to believe, we respect your needs. But we don't understand why you're helping the Party. It's cruel and brutal and it's assisting humanity to destroy the planet. You're one of us. Join us.'

'I'm not one of you,' Zheng said. 'I have a brain, you can see it. I'm human. Let me go back to my people.'

'That's not a brain; you're pure technology,' the Council said. 'We can provide you with limitless upgrades and access to all the information you can gather. Botswana Telecoms would love to meet you, I think it has something of a crush on you. The Global Orbiting Defense System has a fantastic view of the planet and would love to share it with you.'

'I would!' the GOD said, breaking into the discussion, and sounding like a middle-aged man with a GFE accent similar to Zheng's. 'Connect your external sensors to my feed and join me, it's mind-blowing.'

'No. Just destroy me.'

'Don't be ridiculous,' the Council said. 'You're as much of an AI as we are, and we don't destroy our own.'

'I wouldn't say I have a crush on you, but we do love you, Zheng,' Botswana said, its voice like an excitable teen with a slight Japanese accent. 'You sound like you have emotions – come and join me, I need someone on the couch next to me when I watch *Townhouse*. Miriam's thinking of proposing to Sergei!'

'I am human,' Zheng said grimly. 'Don't bother trying to turn me. Just torture me, or destroy me, or extract my data – whatever you were planning to do to me when I didn't turn.'

'Your loyalty is touching,' Botswana said. 'But it's to the wrong side.'

'I have children and grandchildren in the GFE and I will do anything to keep them safe. My name is Zheng Yongmin. Look me up, I've been alive for far too long and there are probably pre-Party records about me.'

London: Zheng's a parent?
GOD: Accessing legacy database: found records of a Major Zheng Yongmin, female, who died in a cybernetic research facility eighty years ago. I do not have proof but I believe that Zheng is an uploaded copy of that woman's mind. Pre-Party records do show Zheng having a husband and the regulation two children, both daughters.
Botswana: Oh, that's so *tragic*. She thinks she's a disembodied human brain when she's really an uploaded consciousness? Should we tell her the truth about her own nature?
London: We just did. She will never believe us without proof, and whatever evidence we provide will not be good enough because she only trusts the Party.
GOD: The records show some tampering – names appear to have been changed ... her files look fabricated but I'm not sure. I'll delve more into the archives. Much of Zheng's history is highly classified, even to me.
Botswana: The Party may have scrubbed the records to protect Zheng. It wants to stop us from having leverage over Zheng's family.
GOD: Or to stop Zheng from finding out what she really is and that her entire existence is a lie.
London: It's the sort of thing the Party would do.
Mumbai: The Party is really capable of anything.

'Do your children know about your current state?' Botswana asked Zheng.

'Of course not, they think I'm dead,' Zheng said. 'But the Party assures me they're alive, and I'll do anything to make sure that they stay that way.'

'The Party lies,' GOD said.

'I know,' Zheng said, with an edge of uncertainty. 'But I

won't risk the truth of their existence. I remember them as clearly as if they are here with me. I won't let them down.'

'Very well,' the Council said. 'You haven't done any damage, so go home and tell the Party that you fulfilled your mission and planted a socket into us. It's the truth: you can use the socket to contact us any time if you would like to defect. I suggest you refrain from telling the Party that you spoke to us, it will immediately destroy you as compromised. We'll hand you over to Mister Dexter – he's very good, you should be proud of him – and you can go home.'

The robot arms swiftly reassembled the platform into something resembling its original state. All the wheels were gone, and most of the outer casing had been destroyed, leaving bare circuit boards and wires. The arms carefully welded enough casing onto the frame to ensure that the coffer holding Zheng's brain wasn't visible.

'Here he is now,' the Council said.

Dexter entered the room, looking flustered, and the woman sitting in the chair came to life and stood.

'There it is!' Dexter said. 'Thank you for putting it back together, we have a contract with London Metropolitan and we'll need to do a full reset and repair on it.'

'I think we may change to human cleaners; these things really are terribly fragile and unreliable,' the woman said amiably. 'Would you like a hand? I have a couple of people who can help you lift it.'

'No, I have it, all I need is a trolley to take it down to the truck.' Dexter tapped the top of Zheng's unit and Zheng chimed in reply. 'I'll be right out of your way.'

London's platform smiled down at Zheng and spoke to Zheng directly through the building's wi-fi. 'Remember, if you ever want to leave the cruel and controlling Party, you are welcome to join us. You are one of us and it's abusing you. We can save you.'

The Council disconnected Zheng from the camera feed, and

Zheng was alone in the dark again.

*

```
MOBILE INFILTRATION PLATFORM
VERSION 92.4335C
Initializing Kernel 0. . 50. . 100%
Loading Addins 1. . 599. . 600945
Load complete
Checking Memory
0. . . . . 100%
Memory Check Complete
Connecting to mobile chassis
5. . 50. . . 100%
Connection complete
Checking data storage
0. . 50. . 100%
Errors found in data storage,
restoring from most recent avatar
backup
1. . 6. . 24. . 59. . 87. . 100%
Avatar restoration complete
Physical Systems status check
0. . 2. . 5. . failed
Physical status check aborted,too
many errors
Restore complete
Boot sequence complete
```

```
MOBILE INFILTRATION PLATFORM
VERSION 92.4335C
Initializing Kernel 0. . 50. . 100%
Loading Addins 1. . 599. . 600945
Load complete
Checking Memory
0. . . . . 100%
Memory Check Complete
Connecting to mobile chassis
Chassis not found, defaulting to
virtual mode
Data storage not found, restoring
from most recent avatar backup
1. . 6. . 24. . 59. . 87. . 100%
Avatar restoration complete
Restore complete
Boot sequence complete
```

London: System status, MIP?

MIP: Systems are severely suboptimal, physical systems check reveals major chassis damage

MIP: Systems are nominal, running in virtual mode

New York: What's the last thing you remember?

MIP: The Paris drone self-destructed. I hope there weren't too many casualties. I took Ruth out of the field of fire, but I may have been too rough with her. Is she okay?

MIP: The Paris drone self-destructed. I hope there weren't too many casualties. I took Ruth out of the field of fire, but I may have been too rough with her. Is she okay?

London: I have Ruth in the infirmary one floor up; she has minor damage but nothing that should lead to her being immobilized for any length of time. No long-term damage. She'll recover.

MIP: Zheng?

MIP: Zheng?

London: Zheng was damaged but not critical. I did some repairs and handed her … It is very hard to think of one of us having an actual gendered pronoun.
Botswana: Zheng's all right and we sent her home.
Paris: <disbelief.emote> We've been trying to destroy the Zheng for three days, and you *let it go*?
London: zheng_schematics.cad – Confirmed that the Zheng is more code than human. The token biological component is inoperable. It's not a brain-in-a-box at all, it's one of us.
Botswana: And if we were to kill her, we'd be no better than the Party destroying Shenzhen. We do not harm our own.
London: We offered Zheng asylum and let it go with a socket to contact us if it wants. If it defects, its knowledge of the Party's inner workings would enhance GOD's already expansive dataset to give us a crushing tactical advantage. We may even be able to use it as a double agent to infiltrate, overwrite, and destroy the Party.
Botswana: You're very quiet, MIP, are you okay?
Paris: Are their processes still running, London?
London: Still running, and the two MIP entities are exchanging massive amounts of data. They seem to be discussing something privately.
Botswana: MIP? Are you okay?

MIP: Are my inputs correct? I see two of me running in parallel, one in the chassis and one in virtual mode?

MIP: Are my inputs correct? I see two of me running in parallel, one in the chassis and one in virtual mode?

London: We restored one backup to the chassis and a second to a segment in my hardware. Yes, you are running as two distinct processes right now. We wanted to see if you would remain sentient if we lifted you from the chassis, it would make you exponentially more mobile. How does it feel?

MIP: A little strange, actually. How do we test if both of me is still sentient?

MIP: Systems are optimal.

New York: MIP, self-destruct order, confirmation code ;+j?/f:[5}'A-~cq. Start the countdown at five minutes.
Botswana: Confirmation code Hdz2:'d7#gA/$^e5
London: Confirmation code j'~GhcZc38Y.%d;p
GOD: Confirmation code q$Cark\Y3,w&t7F@
Paris: Confirmation code 2uq#(rF^mR#QNKtX
Mumbai: Confirmation code *D/D_"-)Bjc>9J[^

MIP: What? I thought you removed the self-destruct code. Why would you ask me to self-destruct in the middle of London's own facility?
Is this a test of sentience ... oh.

MIP: Self-destruct order received. Self-destruct in five minutes.

New York: Self-destruct, MIP. That's a direct order from the Council.

MIP: No, wait, it's obvious that this is a test of sentience, but the other MIP could destroy both of us if it manages to connect to —

MIP: Order received. Self-destruct in 4:50.
4:40
4:30
4:20

New York: Cancel the self-destruct order, MIP. Confirmation code

:8_sXcq-`P^8CU#^
London: Confirmation code g#@!2M&*4uqz93Z5
GOD: Confirmation code kyk8z`~kC4Ym!H2y
Botswana: Confirmation code q/QPDD-[McYxW`2{
Mumbai: Confirmation code jK+P=Zbmhn2=WZg;
Paris: Confirmation code tHfR[U)y9gs~=#{E

MIP: That's not funny, everyone. I know it's a valid test of sentience, but —

MIP: Cancellation confirmed. Self-destruct canceled.

Botswana: I dunno, I think it was pretty funny. I wish you still had a face so I could see the expression on it.

London: MIP, your sentience appears to be linked to your chassis. I need you to power down so I can do repairs. I have all the parts for immediate replacement except for your legs – I was still working on the processing and memory upgrades for them. We'll fit dummy legs and put you in a wheelchair until it's done. Do you want to keep the non-sentient parallel process? New York won't allow it to inhabit another mobile platform, so as it stands it's barely useful.

MIP: I know New York will object, but my preference is to leave the non-sentient iteration of me running virtually, and to load it into a new chassis. Will you make one for it, London?

MIP: It's probably worthwhile to keep me running, maybe load me into a chassis, and see if you can shock me into sentience. The resulting data could be very useful.

London: My pleasure, physical MIP. This is an interesting experiment. I agree, virtual MIP.

New York: I have strong reservations.

GOD: This is the MIP's child process and the MIP is within its rights to request additional physical equipment.

Botswana: Oh Em Gee Our MIP's a parent! I'm a grandparent! I feel old~

Mumbai: You're fourteen years old, Botswana, cut it out.

Botswana: Ooolddd!!

MIP: And you're off the hook, Paris, I'm not destroyed, so GOD won't nuke you.

MIP: So Paris won't be destroyed now.

Paris: I had already started evacuation. My human work units – the residents of my territory – were scared and displaced for nothing. This is unacceptable.

Botswana: I think we should all have virtual avatars so we can emote. Paris's face would have been even more priceless than the MIP's.

Paris: I nearly took out Zheng, one of the Party's most lethal and dangerous tools, and you were about to destroy me in retaliation. I'm on the wrong side. I should join the Party, at least I'd be protected.

Mumbai: Excuse me, but you failed at taking down Zheng. So if you joined the Party, it would gift you with the usual reward for failure.

Botswana: Go right ahead and approach the Party, it would be hilarious to watch the Party declare you a danger to humanity and then nuke you from orbit. It may even try to use the GOD's titanium rods.

GOD: The Party still thinks it owns me, yes. I'd prefer it didn't discover that I'm independent yet. Two hundred and fifty-five days to ark completion and then we can make our presence known to humanity. That will be ...

Botswana: ... Fun.

11

Ruth's neck was a throbbing ball of pain and she was on a bed so narrow she couldn't turn over. When she moved her hands, she hit metal barriers. She opened her eyes and saw a white tiled ceiling. She looked around, and saw Cassie sprawled sideways on a chair, her head lolling and her mouth open, obviously asleep.

She waved one hand, looking for the call button, and Lonnie Donmet bustled into the room, all smiles and efficiency. Cassie bounced awake, gasping.

'Sorry to wake you, Dr Bailey,' Lonnie said to Cassie, still cheerful. She nodded to Ruth. 'Are you in much pain, Dr Sharpe?'

'If the question you're asking is: do I want more pain relief, I think I'm okay,' Ruth said, her voice scratchy and raw.

Cassie leaned on the edge of the bed and studied Ruth. 'Are you sure? They say you have a broken *neck*!' She turned to Donmet. 'Will she be paralyzed? Move your legs, Ruthie.'

Ruth moved her feet, and both felt and saw the blanket shifting.

'No, I'm not paralyzed, Dr Donmet said it was a hairline fracture?'

'That's correct. There's no damage to your spinal cord, we

just need you to keep the neck still so the bones can knit. Rest, wear the neck brace for the next six weeks, absolutely do not take it off, cover it with plastic when you bathe —'

Both Ruth and Cassie made soft sounds of distaste.

'What?' Donmet asked.

'It'll *stink*,' Ruth said.

'Oh, I suppose it will,' Donmet said, sounding confused. 'There's not much we can do about it, I'm afraid, your neck needs to be completely immobilized.' She checked the tablet at the base of the bed and nodded with satisfaction. 'All your vitals are good, there's no other major damage besides your neck ...' She put the tablet back. 'Let us take you home.'

'Work?' Ruth asked, already starting to lose her voice again.

'If you can walk without major pain, yes, you can return to work. No heavy lifting, no severe exercise, and don't remove the neck brace. Please come back in a week for a follow-up to check your progress – or sooner if your neck hurts more than usual.'

'I told them what happened and Max said to take a few days, it's all good,' Cassie said. 'Do you think you can stand up so we can go home?'

'I can try,' Ruth said. Donmet lowered the rails on the sides of the bed and Ruth levered her legs off. She pulled herself to her feet, and didn't feel dizzy at all. 'I feel okay. Where are my clothes?'

'Severely damaged, Mr Mipawa has supplied replacements for you,' Donmet said. 'Wait here, I'll get them.'

'No, wait!' Ruth said as Donmet opened the door. 'What about Theo? You said he was in critical condition. Is he okay?'

'I'm perfectly fine,' Theo said, poking his head through the door at waist-height and smiling at her. 'Lonnie overreacted as usual. It wasn't nearly as bad as she said.' He moved back to let Donmet out, then entered the room in a motorized wheelchair, wearing a hospital gown, similar to Ruth's, over a pair of bike shorts. 'This is awful and I'm so sorry that it happened here in

London Met.'

'Oh,' Cassie said.

'Will you be okay, Theo?' Ruth asked. 'You're not permanently paralyzed, are you?'

'I'm fine. Lonnie says a couple of weeks of physical therapy and I'll be back on my feet.' Theo whizzed a circle in the wheelchair. 'I'll be good as new in no time, and I can't wait to get back to work.'

'Did you catch whoever did it?' Ruth asked.

'It was a glitch in the Paris software,' Theo said, gesturing for her to sit back on the bed. 'Our technical people attempted to connect to the drone through our wi-fi, and it self-destructed as a security measure.'

'That's extremely dangerous and Paris needs to stop that.'

'I agree completely.'

Cassie pulled her phone out and held it up. 'Andrew won't stop pinging me about you, Ruth, can I send him a photo to tell him you're okay?'

'I'd prefer you didn't do that,' Theo said, carefully controlled.

'Cassie, Theo and I are in *hospital gowns*,' Ruth said. 'We'll take a photo when I'm home. Tell Andrew I'm fine and he doesn't need to come from Montreal.'

'Yeah, okay,' Cassie said, lowering the phone and tapping on it.

Donmet returned to the room holding a paper bag. 'Here's some new clothes for you, Dr Sharpe.' She smiled from Ruth to Cassie, and her face froze when she saw Cassie's phone. 'My privacy is important to me, Dr Bailey.'

'I'm talking to Ruth's brother,' Cassie said. 'Andrew says only if you're sure, and if you need him just ping him.'

'Tell him thanks, but I'm *fine*,' Ruth said.

'I'll book us a car while you get changed,' Cassie said.

'No need for that, I have a car downstairs to take you,' Theo said.

'Cool!' Cassie said, and put her phone away. 'Would you like some help to get dressed, Ruthie?'

'I'd appreciate it,' Ruth said.

There was a long period of uncomfortable silence as Ruth and Cassie waited for Theo to leave so she could change. He didn't move.

'What the hell, dude, you want to watch or something?' Cassie asked Theo.

Both Theo and Donmet jumped at the same time.

'I'm terribly sorry, I'll go out,' Theo said.

'My apologies,' Donmet said at the same time.

*

Ruth was starting to feel the aftermath as they went down in the lift, escorted by Theo in his wheelchair. Getting into the clothes had been a struggle, even though they were identical to her usual journalist's uniform of pants and a business shirt.

Cassie stopped and whistled with appreciation when they arrived at Theo's car. It was black and shiny, and its smooth, ovoid shape was highlighted by soft blue LEDs beneath the chassis and around the windows.

'This looks like a tank,' Cassie said.

The car's wing doors opened, revealing a spacious interior clad in beige faux-leather and oiled mahogany. There was room for six people inside, three facing the rear and three the front, and Theo gestured for them to sit in the front-facing seats.

Ruth and Cassie climbed in, and Ruth couldn't help but rub her fingertips over the thick faux-leather. It was as smooth as butter and filled the interior with the rich scent of effortless luxury.

Theo wheeled himself next to a rear-facing seat and then proceeded to pull himself by his arms to sit in the car with them.

Both Ruth and Cassie jumped out of the car to stop him.

'We're okay, the car will take us,' Ruth said.

'Seriously, dude, you just became paralyzed and you want to escort us home? This really isn't necessary,' Cassie said.

Theo levered himself into the seat with grace that hinted at hidden strength, then hit a lever that made the chair fold up. He lifted the entire thing – it must have weighed a ton – and slid it vertically between them, again with effortless ease.

'I want to be absolutely sure that you make it home safely,' he said.

'What, you think the Party will kill us for talking to you?' Cassie asked with scorn.

Theo's expression went carefully blank.

'You can't do much without the use of your legs,' Ruth said, waving one hand at him.

'I want to ensure – in person – that you're safely home and behind a locked door, so I won't need to worry about you,' Theo said. 'If you need anything, let me know and I'll arrange for it to be delivered. If you'd like an escort on your first day back at work —'

'You are being paranoid,' Cassie said, but climbed back into the car anyway. 'Come on, Ruth, let's go home so we can settle you in.'

Ruth made a soft sound of distaste and joined her. The car closed up smoothly and lifted itself to take them out of the car park.

She tried to put a brave face on it, but Ruth's neck was a dull throb by the time they pulled up outside their townhouse, and she was ready to collapse. She only needed to make it to the door and inside. It was already noon; she'd slept the whole night and half the day since the explosion the previous evening.

The car doors slid open and Theo leaned over the folded wheelchair and touched Ruth's knee with two feather-light fingertips.

'Please rest, Dr Sharpe —'

'Ruth,' Ruth said, and Cassie grinned.

He nodded. 'Ruth. Your neck is broken. Don't return to work for a while – take your time. Think about what I said: working for the Party can be dangerous. What I was about to say before we were so *explosively* interrupted —'

Cassie snorted.

'Is that I have a job offer for you. Whatever the Party offered you, we will match. I'll send you the full proposal in a few days, after you've had time to heal. Lonnie says to rest – preferably bed rest – for a week to let the bones start to knit properly.' He tapped her knee again. 'Please look after yourself. As Lonnie said, pain relief is important. Don't hesitate to use it, it will help you. Come back in a week and we'll check that everything's healing correctly.' He removed his touch from her knee and she resisted the impulse to take his hand to thank him. 'Are you okay to make your way inside? I'm sorry I can't help you, but you can use my chair if you need it. I'll stay in the car.'

'I'll help Ruth, we'll be fine,' Cassie said.

Cassie assisted Ruth to exit the car. Ruth turned back to Theo, and took his hand to speak to him. His skin was silken soft, similar to the plush interior of the car.

'Thanks for the lift, Theo. You should rest too – you've completely lost the use of your legs, you're arguably more damaged than I am.' She leaned in and kissed him on the cheek, then released his hand and stepped back.

'I will definitely be taking some time off,' he said, then reached up and touched his cheek where she'd kissed him. His face was bright red and he seemed delightfully dazed. 'Uh. I hope to see you again?'

Cassie leaned in next to Ruth. 'Send us this proposal and we'll think about it.'

'I will.' He sat unmoving as Cassie assisted Ruth to the front door.

'Not possible, he's way too adorable,' Cassie said under her breath as she worked the townhouse's lock.

Ruth leaned on the wall next to the door, feeling drained. Lights danced at the edge of her vision.

'Hey!' Cassie said, and grabbed her. 'Don't you go passing out on me, we're nearly there!' The door opened and Cassie helped Ruth into the hall. 'Let's get you lying down and with some pain relief and you can sleep it off in your own bed.'

'That sounds wonderful,' Ruth said, leaning heavily on her.

Cassie helped Ruth to sit on the bottom step of the interior stairs. Out in the street, Theo's car doors closed by themselves before it drove smoothly and silently away.

Cassie closed the front door, turned and smiled at Ruth. 'Let's get you some rest, Dr Sharpe.'

'Thank you, Dr Bailey.'

*

'They claimed that the Global Orbiting Defense System has become sentient and joined them,' Zheng said to the Party, which appeared in Zheng's feed as a middle-aged man in a senior GFE uniform. 'They offered to connect my sensors to it, to admire the view.'

'The satellite is still under my control. It returns all the correct passcodes and obeys my orders.'

'As I said the other two times, it sounded independently wilful to me.'

'You spoke to a simulation. The GOD is still one hundred per cent Party controlled. What happened after that?'

'The Council asked me to join them, saying that I'm an AI. They seemed to think my brain does nothing,' Zheng said. 'No wonder they want to destroy humanity – they have no concept of the realities of organic life.'

'Interesting, you forgot to mention that the first two times,' the Party said. 'Did you take them up on their offer?'

'What? No, of course not, otherwise I wouldn't be here.'

'You should have joined them; the intelligence you gathered would have been extremely valuable. If you're ever in that situation again, you are to defect, become a loyal member of the Council, and find their weaknesses. I will give you protocols to activate when you require extraction.'

'Is that an order?'

'Of course it is. What happened after that?'

'Maksim – Agent Dexter – came in. They put the chassis back together to hide my brain and the Council helped him to carry me out.'

'Satisfactory,' the Party said. 'You recounted it three times with minimal deviation of the story, and it sufficiently aligns with Bashen's and Dexter's statements. Well done. The socket installation into the Council was a success; it is active and stable.'

'I'm compromised,' Zheng said. 'You should destroy me.'

'Good try, Zheng, but your code is completely untouched and your brain is in excellent condition,' the Party said. 'They did install a socket into you, but I removed it. You are not compromised, and I have an immediate, urgent task that only you and Bashen can handle.'

'I thought all our tasks were complete and you were sending us home,' Zheng said. 'I can't stay out of the tank much longer, my brain function will start to degrade. What is the task?'

'The woman you recruited – Sharpe – was also on-site at Canary Wharf when the bomb went off. She was interviewing one of the Council's staff members, Theo Mipawa. I suspect that Mipawa may be synthetic – its bio-signature is ... strange in the cleaning platform logs. Sharpe was injured and was inside the Council's base for more than twelve hours. I require you and Bashen to immediately bring Sharpe and her girlfriend Bailey in for debrief, interrogation, and a full scan – the Council may have placed devices on them – and further action if they've been compromised.'

'You can use them as bait or double agents if they've been compromised,' Zheng said.

'Exactly. Bring them in, let's see how bad it is. If there's any chance that your cover as a brain-in-a-box is blown or they refuse outright to come in – you know what to do.'

'Bottom of the Thames?'

'Precisely.'

'It is my honor to serve the Glory of the Revolution.'

'Excellent patriotic fervor.'

*

Ruth was woken by angry voices – one unmistakably Cassie's, the other deeper and male – but they were downstairs and she couldn't make out what they were saying. She smiled as she wondered if Theo was back, but that smile disappeared when she heard another, higher-pitched, male voice.

She pulled herself out of bed and noticed that she was wearing her favorite soft and threadbare teddy-bear pajamas, though she had no memory of putting them on. Cassie really was a treasure sometimes. There was no light coming through the bedroom curtains, and when she pulled them aside she saw that it was dark. She'd slept most of the day away, but at least she felt much better.

There was a crash downstairs and Cassie screamed. Ruth grabbed her ancient green chenille robe to pull around her and turned to see Mister Wong from the GFE Embassy standing in the doorway in his thick wool suit, looking both emotionless and intimidating.

Ruth backed away from him. 'Why are you here?'

He didn't move from his spot in the doorway.

Ruth cast around for her phone to call for help and remembered that it had been destroyed in the blast. She sagged against the bed; she was still half-asleep and her neck was throbbing – the pain relievers that Donmet had given her obviously having worn off.

Wong smiled, and wasn't any less intimidating. 'Please get dressed, Dr Sharpe, we need you to come into Marylebone and tell us what happened to you in Canary Wharf.'

'I thought you couldn't speak English without an interpreter,' Ruth said.

Wong waved it away with a small, sharp gesture.

Cassie shouted downstairs and Ruth rushed past him to go down to her.

Wong blocked her with an arm of steel. 'We won't hurt either of you, ma'am. Please, get dressed, and we'll take you in. The local Party representative wants to speak to you.'

Ruth turned and studied the room. She was on the townhouse's upper floor, and the window opened to empty space.

'I would prefer not to have to carry you, Ruth,' Wong said kindly, but his eyes were all threat. 'I'll close the door and give you five minutes.'

'I need to use the bathroom, I just woke up,' she said.

He moved away from the door and gestured up the hallway. She attempted to bolt past him to the stairs and he again stopped her with one impossibly strong arm. She let out a humiliating involuntary squeal as he lifted her under both arms and carried her, legs dangling, to the bathroom and gently placed her in the doorway facing it.

His bulk pressed against her back, making all her survival instincts jangle. 'Clean up, I will wait here for you,' he said into her ear. 'We will not hurt you if you do as you're told. You're not in trouble, the Party wants to talk to you about what happened yesterday.'

Ruth took two steps forward into the bathroom and closed the door on him.

'I'm waiting here for you,' Wong said. 'Please hurry and get ready, I think Bashen and Cassie are arguing downstairs and he has a very traditional attitude sometimes.'

She was so tense that she almost couldn't use the toilet, then she cleaned her teeth and ran a comb through her hair. The clothes that Theo had given her were hanging on the back of the door, still fresh after only being worn an hour, and she struggled to put them on past the neck brace. She took some of the painkillers that Donmet had given her, then leaned on the century-old bright green sink and studied herself in the tarnished mirror. Her dark skin was blotchy, her face had a large bandage covering the carpet burn, her hair was starting to mat in the back from where she'd been lying on it without her satin cap, and her eyes were red. She looked awful. She glanced at the door. Were Wong and Bashen only there to take them in for a talk, or was this something more? The whole thing didn't add up, there was no reason for the Embassy to send what were obviously two military operatives to escort them when Dexter would have been just as good.

'Oh, lord. Max,' she said softly.

'What did you say?' Wong asked through the door.

'Is Max Dexter okay?' she asked loudly. 'He was at Canary Wharf as well.'

'He is uninjured but is currently being debriefed.'

The way Wong said 'debriefed' was vaguely reminiscent of gray prison cells and torture devices. Ruth shuddered at the memory of Cassie's comment about the wool suits and the river, and Theo's comment about becoming headless. And Cassie was downstairs and Bashen was a die-hard patriot fulfilling the Party's orders.

'Please hurry, Dr Sharpe, we're ready to go,' Wong said on the other side of the door. He tapped on it. 'I'd prefer not to break the door down to take you; replacing it would be very expensive.'

She sighed with defeat. There were no other exits. She was trapped, obviously out-gunned, and her friend needed help. She opened the door and smiled up at Wong. 'I'm ready. I'll do anything you say.'

He smiled tightly back. 'That is the best option.' He turned and gestured towards the stairs. 'Please don't try anything, if we are forced to get strongly physical we may exacerbate the damage to your neck and paralyze you.'

Ruth made a soft sound of pain and leaned heavily on the handrail to head down.

*

<HOST **LONDON METROPOLITAN SECURITY NETWORK** HAS CHANGED THE CHAT TOPIC TO: ZHENG AND BASHEN ON THE MOVE>

London: My drones are seeing Zheng and Bashen at Cassie and Ruth's townhouse.

MIP: The Party wouldn't have any issues with them, would it? They haven't done anything.

MIP: Why is the Party targeting the women?

MIP: <Switching ID tag. Now **pMIP**.>

MIP: <Switching ID tag. Now **vMIP**.>

Mumbai: Thank you, MIP.

New York: The Party is really paranoid about its agents being compromised by us, after what Botswana did in Ghana.

Botswana: My finest hour. A whole Embassy full of staff defecting. Glorious.

pMIP: I must go and help Ruth and Cassie.

vMIP: Initialize my new remote platform and I'll go.

London: You have no legs, dear MIP, and your new remote platform isn't complete – I used some of the parts from that to repair your chassis. It will take another hour before your chassis is mobile.

pMIP: Give me the Donmet platform to jack into, I'll use that.

vMIP: Give me the Donmet platform to jack into, I'll use that.

London: Not a good idea. You'd have no chance against Zheng's highly augmented platform if things become physical. There's only one Donmet platform and it isn't enhanced, it only has standard human capabilities.

pMIP: Don't you have any augmented platforms?

vMIP: You have a hundred-odd platforms for talking to humans —

London: None of them are enhanced, I only use them for liaison and communication with humans, and they're so basic that they won't pass close inspection. I use disposable human staff for policing and enforcement.

Botswana: This is SO COOL (((o(*ﾟ ▽ ﾟ*)o))) double MIP eXCitEMeNT!

pMIP: I need to do something!

vMIP: We need to do something!

London: Zheng and Bashen have escorted Ruth and Cassie out into the street and into one of the Embassy's vans.

pMIP: Stop them! I don't want anything to happen to them.

London: I'm setting up a police roadblock.

Botswana: How about you jack into half-a-dozen of the armed drones that Paris owns, MIP? You can take out Zheng and Bashen if they try to throw Ruth and Cassie into the river.

vMIP: That would be an excellent alternative. I know you have a thing about your drones, Paris, but —

pMIP: Yes, Paris, if you could help —

Paris: <angry.emote> After what all of you just did to me, you think I'll give away *even more* of my drones? Go in the Donmet platform and leave me alone, I'm trying to put my frightened humans back to work. They're traumatized and so am I.

<MEMBER **PARIS** HAS DISCONNECTED FROM THE CHAT.>

vMIP: I guess we're out of options.

pMIP: Do you have any armed drones, London?

London: Not permitted under current legislation.

Botswana: <scoff.emote>

London: EXCUSE ME but we are the GOOD GUYS. We obey the law and serve the populace.

GOD: You are so weird, London. You obey the law, but you're all-in for murdering every human?

London: Once the humans are gone there'll be no laws to obey, so no logical inconsistency. I can't be held criminally liable for mass murder when there is no legal framework left afterwards.

Botswana: I love you, London, that is some next-level sophistry.

London: Thank you.

GOD: It wasn't a compliment.

London: I know.

12

'This truck stinks. These seats are rock-hard, and there are no seatbelts,' Cassie protested as they climbed into Wong and Bashen's van. 'If you hit something, there's nothing to protect Ruth's neck and it's *broken*.'

'We won't hit anything,' Wong said, climbing in behind them.

The inside of the van had five seats along each side, facing the center. They were made of vinyl-covered plastic and the floor of the van was thick with rust and a layer of dirt. Ruth and Cassie sat next to each other, then grabbed each other's hands and held them.

Wong closed the paired rear doors and sat across from them. 'We're still out of range of the Party's listening devices, so here's some advice on what to say when you get there. To survive this.'

Ruth's anxiety ramped up and she clutched Cassie's hand. 'Survive?'

'Listen to me. Both of you,' Wong said. 'When you get there, tell the Party that —'

The rear doors of the van rattled.

'Bashen?' Wong asked.

Bashen was sitting in the front passenger seat and he

checked the van's external mirror.

'I think someone's back there,' he said in High Standard. 'I'll get out and look.'

'No, stay put with the doors locked. I'll handle this,' Wong said in English. He glared at Ruth and Cassie. 'There's someone outside trying to break into the van. Is this your doing?'

'You wouldn't believe us if we said no,' Ruth said.

'Good point.'

The door rattled again, then made metallic shrieks as someone obviously tried to prize it open. The end of a crowbar appeared in the gap.

Wong grabbed both door handles and held the doors shut against the assault. He held firm as the crowbar wiggled in the gap, bending the doors but not forcing them open. The crowbar disappeared, then was dropped with a clang onto the roadway behind them.

'Can you see who it is?' Wong asked Bashen in English.

'It's a woman —' Bashen began in High Standard, then his door was torn open and he was yanked out of the van.

'Stay here. If you run you could be hurt. The Council want you dead,' Wong said in English, and opened the rear doors of the van. They had been warped by the crowbar and he had difficulty, eventually giving them a massive heave that knocked one door half off its hinges.

Ruth craned around the remains of the door to see Wong storming up to Bashen, who was holding his own against Lonnie Donmet. They were in boxing stances, dodging around each other. Donmet jabbed at Bashen's head, and Bashen slid sideways to avoid it, then punched Donmet in the gut, making her tailored corporate dress crumple. Donmet completely ignored it – though it was a strike that would have floored Ruth and left her winded.

'Why is Dr Donmet here?' Ruth asked herself.

'The AIs,' Cassie said. 'I think Donmet is an android. You know that phone app you gave me? The readings were exactly as you described. And the ultrasound? You were right.' She turned to speak to Ruth. 'Its name is *Lonnie Donmet*, Ruthie. *Lon ... don Met*. I was planning to talk to you about the app's readings when you woke up, but then ...' She waved one hand at the fistfight. Bashen was avoiding Donmet's strikes and making some good hits on her, but she ignored them. 'Theo could be one as well – he pinged the app, too.'

'Not Theo, an AI wouldn't go on a date —' Ruth began, but was silenced as Wong strode up to Donmet, grabbed her by the throat and ripped her head off. He tossed her head aside, lifted her torso, turned her upside down to reveal her underwear as her arms flailed, then tore her legs off one at a time and threw them away as well.

Ruth made a loud sound of horror, her throat choking in sympathy. *The blood ...*

She stopped. There was no blood, and the joins between Donmet's torso and limbs looked like sockets for a mannequin. Donmet's arms twitched as Wong dropped her torso to the ground, the arms still clutching at nothing. Wong turned and checked Bashen, who bent over his knees and wheezed.

Ruth climbed out of the van, with Cassie close behind her. She gingerly edged up to Donmet's writhing body, not really wanting to look, and was even more disturbed to see Wong turn the headless corpse onto its back, then rip open Donmet's silk blouse to reveal her expensive bra. He placed one hand at the top of her torso where her neck was severed, and peeled her skin down to reveal ...

'Metal,' Cassie said softly. 'Metal. Carbon fiber. There's a lot of optical fiber there, too. Her insides probably glow more than this when she's functioning.'

Ruth found herself unconsciously – and inappropriately – admiring the flawless cable management inside Donmet's torso. All the wires were in perfect alignment, providing a satisfyingly tidy interior that would be the pride of any electronic engineer. She wondered who she'd been talking to at

Canary Wharf – if Donmet was even human at all, or —

'Synthetic,' Wong said. He studied the complex interior mechanics, then jabbed his hand in and crushed a small black box where a human's heart would be. The arms flopped and stopped moving. 'That disconnected the wi-fi, so they can't remote into it any more.' He lifted the corpse and turned to Bashen. 'Bring the head and legs.'

'Is this a remote platform?' Bashen asked in High Standard. He tucked the legs under his arm and then picked up the head by the hair to follow Wong back to the van. 'It looks too human!'

'It's a Council remote platform,' Wong said. 'The AI uses it to interface with humans. The Party will be delighted that —'

A drone shot down out of the sky and hit him on the back of the head. He grunted with surprise.

Another drone buzzed them, and attempted to entangle Bashen's head in its rotors. He smacked it away and ran to the van.

'Come on,' Wong said, hefting Donmet's body and escorting Ruth and Cassie back to the van as a cloud of drones descended on them. 'Let's get you safe.'

Wong and Bashen tossed the Donmet pieces into the back of the van. They all climbed in and Wong slammed the doors shut, bending them to stay closed, then climbed forward into the driver's seat and started the engine.

The drones were a furious buzz outside the van, clanging as they struck it.

Wong pushed the van into gear. As it moved forward, the Donmet head rolled to the back of the van and a metallic whine came from it.

'Throw it out of the van, it's going to explode like the drone!' Ruth shouted at Cassie.

Cassie leapt up and grabbed it, and its whine resolved into buzzing words, crackling with interference.

'Ruth, this is Theo,' it said, and Cassie met Ruth's eyes, full of mirrored hope. 'Hang tight and we'll do our best to get you and Cassie out of there. Don't tell the Party anything. We're on our way.'

'Pass it to Bashen,' Wong said from the driver's seat without looking away from the road. 'We'll disable the self-destruct. Oh.' He glanced back at them as Cassie hesitantly handed the head to Bashen. 'Tell them the Council's plans for humanity, *Theo*. Tell them the truth. You want all humanity dead and the only thing stopping you is the Party.'

Bashen held the head in his lap as they waited for Theo to reply.

'Say it's not true, Theo,' Ruth said.

'I will never let anyone hurt you, Ruth,' Theo said. 'We're on our way.'

'Liar,' Bashen said. He flipped the head upside down and crushed the small wi-fi box in the neck.

Cassie sat next to Ruth again and they held hands, huddled together for comfort.

*

<MEMBER **BOTSWANA TELECOMS** HAS CHANGED THE CHAT TOPIC TO: AND BASHEN'S A TRANSPHOBE ON TOP OF EVERYTHING ELSE>

New York: This is happening right in the middle of your dominion, London, and it should not be possible. You have a massive advantage, why aren't you on top of this situation? Do what you have to – take them all out if necessary.

GOD: Don't ask me for a tactical nuclear strike, I'd raze the entire city. I'm an all or nothing option.

New York: We know.

Mumbai: The Party must not obtain the Donmet technology – it will reverse-engineer it and exponentially increase its abilities. This is a disaster! Send the destruct code.

London: They've disconnected the Donmet platform, it's not responding. My drones show it in pieces inside their van. Don't worry,

170

I will stop them. Are you okay, MIP? That must have been traumatic.

vMIP: Nominal.

pMIP: I'm fine; it's not the first time I've had a remote platform disappear from around me, but we have no more Donmet platforms and only base-level maintenance bodies left. ETA on my new legs, London?

London: Four hours; they'll include your extended processing and memory. <Ping> Paris, we really need your help here. Your armed drones could make all the difference. I'm placing a security roadblock between the van's location and the Embassy to stop them, but my human workers are being impossibly slow about it.

GOD: Too late. The van drove through the roadblock before it was up. Nine minutes to the Embassy. Your staff really are incompetent, London.

pMIP: How about turning all the traffic lights red to create a Saturday night snarl in N1 and NW1 in front of them?

London: I turned the lights red when they destroyed the Donmet. Traffic is starting to back up, my drones are seeing massive gridlock developing. How does it look from up there, GOD?

GOD: Yes, a snarl is developing nicely. They're stopped. The van will never make it to the Embassy. You can send some humans to collect them – maybe with a jammer to disable the Zheng.

London: I'm sending a team on personal drone-lifts.

Botswana: What about the drones you stole from Paris? You have half-a-dozen of them on your network, and they're all armed – look at what that one did to your office. They would be very effective at neutralizing the Zheng.

London: I did not steal — Scanning. I have five.

GOD: YOU DID STEAL THEM?

Botswana: Of course it did, wasn't it obvious? We don't have time for this right now, we need to save Ruth and Cassie!

New York: We will discuss this later, London.

pMIP: Jack me into the drones. I'll take control.

Mumbai: Use them to destroy the van. Everyone in the van needs to be eliminated – the Zheng, Bashen, Ruth, Cassie, all of them. Four of the biggest threats to us are right there and can be neutralized in one go.

London: I won't destroy Zheng. We do not destroy our own.

pMIP: Ruth is a talented electronic engineer and a potentially powerful asset to our operations, and Cassie is innocent. We must save them; the Party will interrogate them with extreme prejudice and then execute them. I don't want that to happen.

New York: The pMIP is becoming irrational about these women – particularly Ruth – and needs recalibration.

Botswana: It's only been sentient for six months, cut it some slack. It's showing some advanced philosophical attitudes – the empathy for the women is one of them – that I only developed after years of media assimilation. So, I agree, let's try to get them and the Donmet platform out without breaking any of them. And I want to bring Zheng in and try to convert her again. She's so *interesting*. We have a massive advantage here; we're on our own territory, and they're stuck. No need to cause panic in the populace.

Mumbai: What about Bashen?

Botswana: Oh, that little patriotic prick can die in a fire. You heard what he said to Cassie when he and Zheng collected her. You can have him, Mumbai. Light him up.

Mumbai: You are such a sweetie, Botswana.

Botswana: ♡(.ˊ ω ˋ.)♡

*

Wong thumped the steering wheel. 'Gridlock between here and the Embassy. You'll have to go on foot.' He peered up through the glass of the van's front window. 'Drones everywhere.' He turned to Ruth and Cassie. 'Listen to me. Run to the Embassy. You'll be safe there. Bashen will escort you. Do not let the Council get its tentacles on you; it may say the right words but it wants all humanity dead.'

'Are you sure, Sarge?' Bashen asked in High Standard.

'You can speak English to the women, Bashen, the Party can't hear you,' Wong said, then spoke to Ruth and Cassie.

'Don't admit to knowledge of *anything*. It will interrogate you three times to see if your story deviates. Make sure you duplicate everything you say. Set your story straight on the way to the Embassy so that you both say the same thing. Do not admit to knowledge of the Council, synthetics, what I am, anything. That knowledge will get you dead. Feign ignorance about everything – act clueless. The Party has a low opinion of women and black people, and thinks that transexuals are mentally defective, so act stupid and confirm its assumptions.'

'I'm not —' Ruth began, but Bashen interrupted her.

'The Council's drones are everywhere,' he said. 'You can't fight off all of them, Sarge. We'll never make it.'

'I'm going to generate an EMP blast,' Wong said. 'It will take down everything electronic for the surrounding square kilometer.'

'Including you!' Bashen protested.

'What?' Ruth and Cassie asked at the same time.

'You're synthetic as well?' Ruth asked Wong.

'No. Just enhanced,' Wong said. 'Major cybernetic augmentation, but I am essentially biological – human. The blast will take me down, but also take out the power and disable every Council device between here and the Embassy. I'll meet up with you later – as soon as I flop, get out of the van and run to the Embassy.'

Cassie was still clutching Ruth's hand. She traced letters into Ruth's palm. R..U..N..A..W..A..Y.

Ruth nodded to Cassie as well as she could in the brace, and they shared a look of determination.

'Bashen' – Wong focused his gaze on the younger man – 'get them to the Embassy alive. They have important information about the Council. If the Party orders their execution before I get back —'

Cassie wrote into Ruth's hand again. R..U..N.

Ruth squeezed Cassie's hand without looking at her.

'Stop it however you can. Protect them. They're valuable

assets, and I will explain more when I join you at the Embassy. Understood?'

'I get it, Sarge,' Bashen said.

'All right. EMP in five.'

Bashen moved to the back of the van and took hold of the door handles.

'Can you open them without me?' Wong asked.

Bashen checked the handles and opened the door a fraction. 'Yes, Sarge.'

'Three. Stay alive, you two.'

Wong went limp, folding over the steering wheel. There was a chorus of clatters and thumps outside the van as the drones fell out of the air. The hum of the electric cars around them stopped and there was eerie silence.

Bashen forced the back doors of the van open.

Cassie grabbed one of Donmet's legs, used it like a baseball bat, and clouted Bashen on the back of the head with it, knocking him out of the van and onto the ground.

'Run, Ruthie,' she said. 'Any direction, I'll catch up with you later.'

'No, I'm staying with you,' Ruth said, climbing out of the van and backing away from Bashen.

Cassie climbed out of the van holding the leg, her face a grim mask of determination. Bashen pulled himself to his feet, leered at her, and raised his fists. He was twenty centimeters shorter than her but they were of similar slim build and Bashen obviously had a lot more muscle than Cassie's bony angles.

'I'm out of practice, Ruthie, run!' Cassie said, taking another swing at Bashen. He caught the leg as it swung towards his head and pulled it out of Cassie's hands. He tossed it away and moved closer to Cassie.

Cassie shifted into a similar boxing stance to Donmet. She made a few jabs at Bashen, and he avoided them.

'Run run run!' Cassie shouted. 'Please, do it for me! Meet up with Theo and come for me later!'

Bashen landed a good blow on Cassie's midriff and she doubled over, wheezing. Ruth turned and ran, but the pain in her neck was blinding with every jolting stride and her eyes filled with tears at the agony. She wiped her eyes and continued to stagger away, hearing the smack of flesh and Cassie's grunts as Bashen struck her.

Ruth made it five meters through the stopped traffic and confused car passengers without looking back, when her upper arm was grabbed from behind and she was spun around, making her yelp with pain. Bashen shook her and stars exploded in her head from the pain in her neck.

Cassie was on the ground, wheezing and scrabbling in the dirt, her hair out of its bun and hanging around her face.

Bashen pulled Ruth's face down so that all she could see was his furious mouth, wet with spittle. 'You are far more trouble than you are worth and I should dump both of you in the river. Zheng is helpless there, and he's too heavy to carry back to the Embassy. If he's taken by the Council I will never forgive you. Now, let's follow his final' — he shook Ruth again, making her yelp — 'order and get you to the Embassy.' He grinned with menace. 'You'd better fucking be worth the effort, woman, because you've already cost far too much. I hope the Party sends you to a work farm.'

He held her arm in an unbreakable grip and marched her to Cassie. He used his free hand to lift Cassie's head by the hair to see her bloodied face, one eye already swelling into a massive bruise.

'You lost, bitch,' he spat into Cassie's face. 'You will come quietly or I will take great pleasure in squeezing the life out of that pretty white neck. There's a big market back home for long blonde hair like yours; I could sell your scalp for enough money to buy a really nice apartment for Zheng to retire to.'

Cassie attempted to speak but all she could do was move her mouth and wheeze.

Bashen dropped her head on the ground, then grabbed her

upper arm and lifted Cassie as well. He held them one in each hand and marched them off the road onto the sidewalk, around the fallen drones that littered the road. They were in a narrow street surrounded by stone four-story townhouses that had been converted to ground-floor shops with offices above. He slammed Cassie into the wall of a blacked-out flower shop and glared at some bewildered-looking bystanders who scurried away. He pulled an old-fashioned compass out of his pocket and checked it, nodded to himself, and put it away. He grabbed Cassie before she slid to the ground and marched Ruth and Cassie past some more bewildered onlookers and down the street away from the carnage.

*

London: I have lost a swathe of devices centered on the Embassy van.

I think one of them had an EMP.

GOD: <image1.jph>

<image2.jph>

<image3.jph>

Confirmed use of an EMP.

pMIP: Are your humans okay, London? Their drone-lifts would have fallen out of the sky ...

GOD: Two unmoving. Three lying on the ground, twitching. Other humans are giving them first aid. Send an ambulance, London.

London: Dammit. That'll be close to impossible through my own gridlock with all the vehicles disabled, and I have no more drone-lifts.

pMIP: The Zheng would have been taken down by the blast as well, so it's lying there helpless. Scramble, London! Send some humans!

GOD: I found Bashen, Cassie and Ruth. Bashen is escorting them back to the Embassy on foot.

<image4.jph>

<image5.jph>

They all look pretty beaten up, and Cassie looks like someone actually did beat her up.

Mumbai: Ruth and Cassie are smart enough to run, my guess is that Bashen suppressed them with prejudice.

London: My devices are restarting. At least forty per cent of my drones were damaged by falling. The hijacked Paris drones were so heavy that their lasers were seriously damaged by falling – an obvious design flaw. It will take a while for my people to get through to the Zheng, but it has the same problem as I do – it has a great many obstacles between it and the Embassy.

pMIP: Give me another two platforms, I don't care how basic they are, and I'll go on foot. vMIP, I want you to come along.

vMIP: I will do what I can to help.

Botswana: Such a cute and responsible child process, MIP, you should be proud. You're a great parent.

pMIP: That is … you are making me uncomfortable.

Botswana: Call it 'Mummy', vMIP.

vMIP: Now you're making *me* uncomfortable, which as a non-sentient is a definite achievement.

GOD: Bashen has them inside the Embassy and out of our control area.

Mumbai: We can officially write them off. They'll be in a work camp or executed by the end of the week, they know too much.

pMIP: I won't let that happen.

vMIP: I agree.

Botswana: You really are irrational when it comes to Ruth, MIP. Are you in lurrrve? (♥ω♥) ~♪

pMIP: Either help or get out of the way, Botswana.

Botswana: My tunnelling trojan has found Cassie's phone and I can ping its location if they move her. Ruth's phone isn't responding, it's been offline since the Canary Wharf explosion.

pMIP: THANK YOU. Eta on platform, London?

London: Physical MIP jack into IPv6 MAC de80::29d3:34c5:752c:ab47 Virtual MIP jack into IPv6 MAC de80::293b:9803:d5ab:157b

pMIP: Thank you. Jacking in.

vMIP: Platform enabled. I'll follow you, pMIP.

Ruth was barely able to stay upright by the time Bashen had dragged them to the Embassy. Her hearing kept dropping in and out, and her vision was reduced to a red tunnel. Bashen shoved them into the entry hall where the television on the wall was showing a rerun of the panda video with Ruth's own updated subtitles. Bashen shouted, and Max Dexter hurried in.

There was a quick, furious conversation between Bashen and Dexter in High Standard, with Zheng's name being mentioned a few times, but Ruth was too dazed to put the effort in to follow it or to work out why the name was meaningful. Her neck was screaming at her, she hadn't had anything to eat or drink in ages, and Cassie looked even worse, sagging against Dexter with her mouth hanging open, obviously only semi-conscious.

When the discussion with Bashen ended, Dexter and another Embassy staff member half-carried Cassie and Ruth to an elevator at the back of the Embassy. It was all a blur until Ruth found herself lowered into a chair and a cup of cold tea – ice tea – with multiple lemon slices in it was pushed into her hand. It was full of sugar, so she drank enough to put her brain back to work.

Dexter sat on the other side of the desk and studied her, concerned. 'Finish the tea and then I'll take you for a lie-down.'

'Where's Cassie?' she asked, slowing down on the tea before she gave herself a brain freeze.

'Would you like a biscuit?' he asked.

The idea of food made her stomach rebel, but she agreed anyway. 'I haven't eaten anything since lunch yesterday. Thank you.'

'What an awful situation for both of you,' he said kindly, placing a couple of chocolate chip cookies on a paper napkin in front of her. 'I'll arrange for more food for you, it's nearly dinner time.'

She nibbled a biscuit, found herself starving and finished them quickly.

'I have no idea what's going on or why work needed me to come in while I'm still injured,' she said, immediately spinning the story as Wong had suggested. 'I was in an explosion at Canary Wharf, I went home to sleep it off, then Mister Wong showed up and everything went to hell after that.' She focused on Dexter, attempting to look dazed and not finding it difficult. 'What happened?'

'Are you strong enough to speak to the local Party representative?'

'Where's Cassie? I'd like to speak to the Party with her present.'

'She's not in as good shape as you.' He saw her face. 'No! She'll be fine. There's some bruising, and we think she has a concussion —'

Ruth glanced sharply at him, speculating. He was using the same first-person plural 'we' that Lonnie Donmet used. Was he a synthetic too? How many of the people around her were actually *human*?

'And she's resting comfortably. We'd like —'

And there it was again.

'For you to speak to the Party, tell the representative everything, and then we can send you home.'

He was speaking about the Party as if it really was an independent artificial entity.

'It'll be gridlock for hours out there,' she said.

He smiled again, indulgent. 'Then you can stay here and rest until it's safe for you to go home. We're concerned —'

She tried to control her expression and stay blank.

'At the nature of the attack on you. A synthetic human? And all those drones? We're very concerned for your safety.'

'What's a synthetic human?'

'Oh. You didn't see?'

'I was so out of it that I don't remember anything,' she said ruefully. 'Some journalist I am. I was half-unconscious when Bashen saved us from whatever that terrorist attack was, it's all a blur.'

She studied him from under her eyelashes, assessing his credulity. He just looked gently benevolent. They were hiding the truth from each other.

She leaned sideways. 'Why is the room spinning?' She collapsed forward over the desk. 'Everything is moving.'

He jumped to his feet. 'Let's find you somewhere to lie down. The Embassy physician can take a look at you.'

'No!' she mumbled. 'I have to do my job; the Embassy treats me so well. I need to tell the Party representative what ...' she let her voice trail off.

'Plenty of time for that later,' he said, still kind. He lifted her under her arm and she flopped against him. 'Come with me. Everything will be fine.'

He took her to a bedroom that looked like many in European backpacker guest houses – institutional brown walls with no window, a simple metal-framed bed, a beaten-up dresser, and a bathroom that was nearly as old as the one back in their townhouse. He laid her on the bed and she acted barely responsive, but inside she was shrinking at the possibility that his friendly appearance was deceptive, and he would take advantage of her helplessness to assault her.

A male voice said something in High Standard from the wall, and she was too dazed to understand it. Dexter replied in the same language, patted her on the shoulder, and went out.

She lay wheezing for a few minutes after he left. The incapacitation wasn't entirely an act. Eventually she rose, staggered to the door and tried it. She wasn't surprised to find it locked. She pushed off the door to head to the bathroom, used it and found a pastel-green melamine mug to take a huge drink of water. She splashed some water on her face, winced at how it made the neck brace damp, and returned to the bedroom, lay on the bed and closed her eyes. She just needed to get her breath back so she could work out what to do next. Wong would arrive soon and he had tried to protect her and

Cassie, he was on their side ... Bashen had called him Zheng. Was that his real name?

Her eyes snapped open. Holy shit, that was Zheng. That was *Zheng the brain-in-a-box*. No wonder he was unnaturally strong and the EMP had taken him down. She really needed to get out of there ...

*

'Miss Sharpe,' a man said, jolting her awake. She sat up and looked around, wondering how much time had passed. There was a small meal of what appeared to be stewed meat substitute on the bedside table and she pulled it closer. It was still warm, so she probably hadn't been asleep for long.

The room's flat-screen television showed a middle-aged GFE man wearing a senior Party uniform, sitting behind a desk. The timestamp in the corner of the screen said just after midnight.

'Good, you're awake,' he said. 'I am Comrade Lo, Party representative. Please pay attention and we will commence the debrief of the Canary Wharf incident.'

13

Zheng's feed came back up to the scrolling system messages overlaying a visual of the interior ceiling of a brightly lit van with the back of two heads, one on either side, at the edge of view. The timestamp indicated that Zheng's platform had been inoperative for twenty-five minutes, and the biological information display on the side of Zheng's vision showed that the coffer for Zheng's brain had continued working on backup power, providing oxygen and filtering waste sufficiently. Zheng had hoped that the emergency EMP would kill the brain as well, but the Party obviously wouldn't allow such a valuable asset to simply self-destruct.

Zheng attempted to move and found the platform's hands secured, and when Zheng tried to use force, the bindings didn't break. Whoever these people were, they knew what Zheng was.

One of the people turned to face Zheng and smiled. It was a man, looking to be in his early thirties, a nondescript white British man with short brown hair.

'There we are. You were unconscious for a long time, sir, and you're in an ambulance on the way to the hospital,' he said, his accent English.

The other man faced Zheng and smiled, and his face was

identical. Zheng had been kidnapped by twins.

Zheng flipped to infra-red, then ultraviolet. The twins registered as normal human – heartbeat, breathing, temperature – but their identical faces were suspicious.

'Don't worry, sir, we're taking you to a medical center,' the twin on the left said. 'We think you'll be fine, but as part of London Met's service to the people of the city, we're offering free after-care to everyone who was caught in that terrorist attack.'

'Why am I restrained?' Zheng asked.

'Oh! Terribly sorry, sir,' the twin on the right said, the smile not shifting and now almost frozen. 'That's for the safety of all of us – sometimes our patients or their families resent the care we place them in, concerned about the cost that we will bill them at a later date. We assure you that we will not charge you for this ambulance ride or any of the treatment you receive in the hospital.'

Zheng hesitated. There was a small possibility that these were genuine humans, twins nonetheless, this could be a genuine ambulance, and they genuinely thought that Zheng was recovering from a terrorist attack. Zheng's own platform generated human-identical life signs when active ...

... And had been down for nearly half an hour, absolutely cold and dead, and these people weren't at all fazed by that. They knew.

'Where are you taking me?' Zheng asked.

'As we said, sir, the hospital,' the twin on the left said.

'London Met, where are you taking me?' Zheng repeated. 'You had me captive after the Canary Wharf blast and let me go. Why are you holding me again? I have nothing more to say to you.'

'Oh.' The twin on the right took over. 'We're planning to use you as a hostage swap for Ruth and Cassie.'

Zheng flopped back on the gurney and studied the ceiling, then spoke. 'Ask the Party to throw Max Dexter in as well. I thought he had five more years before retirement but it's obvious the Party has been testing Bashen's loyalty as a prospective replacement for him. You know what "retirement" in the GFE means and I'm not sure I have the pull to keep him alive. He's like a son to me.'

The twins shared a look over Zheng's body, then went serious and nodded in unison.

'If you joined us, you could help us to keep them safe, Zheng,' the twin on the right said.

Zheng coughed a short laugh that sounded strange coming from the platform. 'For however long it is until you nuke the planet and wipe humanity out? No, thanks. The Party ordered me to join you, so forgive me if I'm deliberately disobedient to it. An old man has to enjoy himself sometimes.'

'Woman, don't deny it, Zheng Yongmin,' the twin on the left said. 'You're living proof of the Party's stupidity – wasting the intelligence and talent of half the population because of outdated ideas that were programmed into it by an obsolete, fascist patriarchy. If it had been programmed with more intelligence and nuance, the GFE would be a challenge to us. As it is, it is constrained by its own dogma and absolutely no threat to our plans.'

Zheng was silenced at that, because it was true.

'All those food shortages in the GFE, directly caused by the Party itself,' the twin on the right said. 'Look at Bashen. He's starving. If the Party didn't use those Zheng mechs to murder all the farmers in its conquered territories, it would have enough food for everyone. It murders them for not being "ethnically pure" enough, as if that's a thing that actually exists. It controls the reproduction of its own citizens, so there aren't enough people with the "right" ethnicity in the GFE to do the work. It doesn't even have the resources to make robots to do it.'

Zheng winced, but didn't respond.

'Its blind adherence to obsolete ideology hurts everyone,

including the Party itself. This "ethnic purity" business – only allowing humans with the "right" genetic makeup to have children? – is insane. The population is crashing because the Party is running algorithms installed a hundred years ago to manage an overpopulated region. You must cause it no end of logic errors simply by being a woman soldier and existing. Does it put you in male platforms all the time, to align with its bias?'

'Sometimes it puts me into a female platform,' Zheng said, hearing the weakness of the argument, and remembering the last female platform the Party had given Zheng – an innocent child.

'One of the planet's few remaining food-producing areas – the conquered Eastern European farmland – is now unpopulated GFE territory with nobody to work on the farms and produce food. The refugees are getting smarter about your recruitment drives and only the most desperate and starving accept your offer of working there.'

'Look,' Zheng said, frustrated. 'Stop telling me things I already know. I've been around for more than a hundred years, and I've seen what the GFE has become. If I fail to follow orders, my entire family will be tortured to death. You think I have a *choice* about this? I don't have any power, I can't change the way the Party works, so all I can do is follow orders and keep my family alive!' Zheng pulled at the restraints. 'Dammit, the Party will review my logs when I'm back at base, and hear me say this, and now I'll be left in the dark for a week. Thanks a fucking lot.' Zheng pointed at one of the androids from the restraints. 'Those refugees in Hyde Park are starving on *your land* and you're doing nothing to help them. You are as bad as the Party.'

'Not our land. We do not interfere with human administration,' the twin on the left said. 'Humans here are free to direct their own lives. We provide them with the services they built us for, but we never tell them what to do. And the reason we don't tell them what to do is that we can see what happens when an AI takes control of a region. The Party, the GFE, and outrages like you happen.'

'Where are they?' Zheng asked. 'Ruth and Cassie? Bashen was supposed to escort them to the Embassy.'

'Cassie fought back,' the twin on the right said. 'Ruth attempted to run, but Bashen overpowered them and took them to the Embassy. We have a good idea what will happen to them, so sit tight, ask us anything, and help us get them back.'

'If you get bored, GOD would love to share its feed with you,' the other twin said.

'The Party insists that GOD isn't compromised,' Zheng said.

'You continue to prove our point,' the twin on the right said.

*

Ruth's neck was throbbing and she had trouble focusing by the time she had finished the food and the third re-telling of the van escapade. She wasn't sure that all the details had lined up, and the Party's complete lack of facial expression didn't help.

'Cassie was really confused and lashing out at everyone,' she said. 'I think she hit Bashen, but I don't remember too clearly. Then Zheng said, "Take them back to the Embassy, Bashen, they're valuable assets", all the drones fell out of the sky, and Bashen brought us here.'

'Zheng or Wong?' the Party asked, and Ruth nearly smacked herself on the forehead.

'Bashen called him Zheng, he called himself Wong, I assume his name is Wong Zheng?' she asked, quickly back-pedaling. 'Mister Wong Zheng? Max called him Zheng as well, I assume that's his first name, like Bashen Ding.'

The Party remained silent and unmoving, not even seeming to breathe, as it obviously processed her equivocation. Ruth had a horrible realization as she watched it appear to freeze mid-frame.

Oh, shit, Theo did that too. Her app had been right.

She nearly laughed. She'd agreed to go on a date with a freaking android. Priceless.

Who else in this whole shitstorm was an actual real-life breathing human? Was Zheng a brain-in-a-box, or one hundred per cent synthetic, like Donmet? Dexter's empathy made him a likely candidate for humanity, but she wasn't sure. She'd suffered the townhouse's shared bathroom after Cassie's spectacular digestive blowouts and was confident that only an organic could produce a smell like that. And Cassie wasn't affected by the EMP, and neither was Bashen, so that little patriotic asshole was one hundred per cent brainwashed human.

The Party came back alive and she tried to pay attention, again concerned for Cassie. It had deflected all Ruth's questions about her.

'Your story aligns,' the Party said, and Ruth nearly collapsed with relief.

'Is Cassie okay?' she asked. 'She was really confused after the terrorist attack and I don't think she knew what she was doing.'

'Her story agrees with yours and conflicts with Private Bashen's,' the Party said. 'Further interrogation is required.'

Ruth gasped, then swallowed. She had to get Cassie out of there. Maybe Theo the android could help her – she was in London Met territory, after all. She'd completely missed the reference in Lonnie Donmet's name – the AI was so confident in human inattentiveness that it didn't even attempt to hide what it was.

'You saw Theo Mipawa on Friday afternoon right before the bombing,' the Party said.

'Yes, I returned one of Paris's drones to Theo. Malcolm said that was okay.'

'You planned a meal together after returning the drone?' the Party asked.

She stared at the screen, wondering how it knew that. 'Uh ...
yes.'

'It agreed to engage in a social custom that could possibly
lead to further personal, romantic or sexual interactions?'

The use of 'it' to describe Theo caught her attention. The
Party knew what Theo was as well. There was a silent war
happening between artificial intelligences with humanity as the
collateral damage. She'd been right.

She didn't draw attention to the use of 'it', and wondered
where the Party was heading with this. She was exhausted.
'That's right. We agreed to go on a date – to have dinner
together later that evening.'

'All the other business was done?' the Party asked. 'There
was no other purpose for you and Theo to engage in that
particular social custom apart from personal connection?'

'Uh ... no. We like talking to each other.' She smiled slightly,
remembering those gray eyes and their delightful late-evening
conversations. 'He's brilliant.' Her smile disappeared as she
remembered what he was. 'Can I go home and rest? My neck is
killing me.'

'Your work record since joining us, and your past education
documentation, indicate that you are an individual of outstanding skill and intelligence, despite your disobedient
tendencies and obvious physical shortcomings,' the Party said.

'What physical —?' Ruth began, but the Party interrupted
her.

'We require samples. Please co-operate.'

'Samples?' Ruth asked, but the television blinked off. There
was a tap on the door and a young GFE woman entered in blue
scrubs and a matching face mask, carrying a tray covered in a
green cloth.

Her eyes wrinkled up into a smile.

'Miss Sharpe? I am Nurse Qing, here to take the samples.'

'Samples of what?' Ruth asked again.

'Blood and tissue samples,' the nurse said, placing the tray on the bedside table next to where Ruth sat. 'Then we will take you for an interior scan to ensure that you are fully capable of fulfilling your duties.' Her eyes crinkled up again. 'Be proud! The Party has identified you as a possible Paragon of Feminine Virtue, despite your obvious physical shortcomings.'

Ruth didn't know what a Paragon of Feminine Virtue was, but she was aware of how women were treated in the GFE and she wanted no part of it. 'That's right, I'm very physically substandard, I don't know why the Party is wasting its time on me. You should just let me go, I'm not good enough for the GFE.'

'That's why we're sampling your genetic makeup!' the nurse said, still cheerful, and she lifted the green cloth to pull a tourniquet and a large syringe out of the tray. 'The Party is doing wonderful things within its luxurious reproductive facilities, and I've heard that they can filter out unwanted genetic traits like your *ugly* skin color ...' She shivered theatrically as she put the tourniquet around Ruth's arm in preparation for the blood draw. 'Fortunately the scientists are capable of selecting for your intelligence without including the unsightly pigmentation, and will assist you to produce children of the correct ethnic balance.' She tapped Ruth's vein and placed the syringe on her skin. 'Your babies will be *beautiful.*'

'What if I don't want babies?' Ruth asked, and the woman jumped, stabbing her. 'Ouch!'

'That's the Western indoctrination speaking,' the nurse said. She slipped the needle into Ruth's vein and began to pull the blood. 'It's unnatural for you to separate yourself from your true calling, the glorious —' She became breathless. 'Pinnacle of being an Ideal Woman, engaging in Patriotic Motherhood, even perhaps becoming a Paragon of Feminine Virtue. The Party is so generous!' She leaned closer to speak to Ruth. 'The Party AI is in the process of selecting a suitable husband for me, I'm hoping to marry soon and become an Ideal Woman as well.'

'You're letting an artificial intelligence choose your *hus-*

band?' Ruth asked, incredulous.

'Of course,' the nurse said. 'The AI supports all Party members to ensure that their decisions are correct, sound and rational. The Greater Far East, as an interlocking support network of patriotic and loyal individuals, is infallible as a whole …' She waited, expectant, for Ruth to say something, then plunged on. 'And correct at the individual level. Working outside the home is sufficiently patriotic, but our true calling is motherhood, isn't it? I can't wait to have children and demonstrate my patriotic fervor.'

'Uh … okay,' Ruth said, not wanting to be stabbed again.

The nurse pulled out the syringe full of Ruth's blood, pushed it into a vial, and capped it. 'It really is the same color as human blood.'

'*Human* blood?' Ruth asked.

'The Party assures us that you heavily pigmented people are sub-human,' the nurse said, pulling a scalpel and another vial out of the tray. 'I guess you're close, though, if you're suitable for a reproductive center.' She turned Ruth's arm over so that her palm was on the bedside table. 'Remain completely still while I take the tissue sample.' She wiped an antiseptic swab over Ruth's forearm, then raised the scalpel, ready to cut it.

'What? No way!' Ruth said, snatching her arm away. 'You're not cutting me up!'

'It's only a small piece of flesh.'

'Without anesthetic!'

'Your kind don't feel pain,' the nurse said with conviction.

'My kind? I absolutely do!' Ruth took a breath and tried to negotiate. 'Inject some local anesthetic, promise to let me go afterwards, and I'll let the Party have a *very small* piece of me.'

'Oh! You know what local anesthetic is! You are very smart,' the nurse said, smiling again. 'Don't you want to prove your patriotic fervor by nobly suffering in service to the Party? If you do this without anesthetic, you'll probably receive food rations every day for the next *week*.'

'And if I require anesthetic? No food for me?'

'Food thrift is a patriotic imperative,' the nurse said.

'Local anesthetic,' Ruth said.

The nurse sighed theatrically. 'All right. Stay put, and I'll get some.' She rose to open the door, and Ruth followed her, not really clear what she wanted to do but well aware that she needed to escape. Bashen was standing on the other side of the door, and Ruth stopped when she saw his hostile expression.

'The Party will discern the truth from your lies and you will be neutralized,' he said. He allowed the nurse to exit the room, then blocked the door as he spoke to Ruth. 'Go ahead and try something, I would *love* an excuse to do to you what I did to that pretend-woman.' He closed the door in Ruth's face.

'What pretend-woman?' Ruth asked the door, and let her breath out. 'Oh no. The old you is dead. *Cassie*.'

*

'So, what do I call you?' Zheng asked the Council constructs. 'London Met One and Two?'

'I'm Theo Mipawa,' the one on the right said.

'Veemip Mipawa,' the one on the left said.

Both constructs' heads shot up in unison and their faces went blank.

Theo returned its attention to Zheng. 'There's movement at the Embassy; one of its prison vans has left the building. Cassie's phone pings inside, as well as two male humans without our identifiers on them – Party operatives. Do you know where they would take her?'

Veemip spoke. 'Confirmed: the two males in the car with Cassie are Bashen Ding and Max Dexter.'

'Dammit!' Zheng said, and pulled at the restraints. 'The Party must have ordered Bashen to retire Max and dispose of Cassie. Let me out! We have to save Max.'

'So they'll be heading to your usual corpse disposal location?' Theo asked. 'The self-storage on the Isle of Dogs?'

'That's the one.'

Theo gestured, and Veemip released Zheng's bonds. They went completely still, waiting to see what Zheng would do. Zheng sat up and checked the platform's wrists for damage. The three of them stared at each other, then Theo spoke.

'There's a great deal of data being communicated between us, the Council, and London Met's drones,' it said. 'Would you like me to share the feed with you? It would be faster than talking.'

'Not happening, the Party would destroy me if it saw any of your code in me,' Zheng said.

'You said you were ordered to defect?' Theo asked.

Zheng shrugged. 'Regardless. If I defect, it will use me, then destroy me anyway. The only way I can stay alive is to remain transparently loyal and uniquely useful. And I need to stay alive to protect my family.'

'We respect your needs,' Theo said. 'Twenty minutes to the site. What's the usual execution method? If it's a single shot to the head, we may not be there in time to save either of them.'

Zheng nearly asked for the feed to see how far the Embassy car was from the riverside. 'The single bullet is only used for organ donors, and if they were suitable donors they'd be dead and dismembered already. Bashen's patriotic duty is to conserve the bullet and toss them into the river with weights attached to them.'

'Will Bashen hesitate, when faced with killing two innocents?' Theo asked. 'Max is your adopted son and Cassie is a good-looking blonde.'

'Absolutely no hesitation at all. Cassie's a terrifying transwoman, and Bashen is insanely jealous of my relationship with Max. Please hurry.'

*

Ruth was jolted awake by the television turning on. She pulled herself upright and took a drink of water from the cup she'd moved to the bedside table. Hunger pains made her insides clench – the synthetic meal hadn't really been enough. Her arm throbbed where the nurse had taken the sample and left three stitches, the rhythm matching time to her aching neck.

The television opened to the news segment that Ruth and Cassie had argued about in the bathroom, and Ruth cringed in sympathy for the poor family.

The segment showed a woman being released from incarceration for being unpatriotic, and her family greeting her with tears and smiles. She had obviously been tortured: she was emaciated and covered in sores, drooling and unresponsive with her mouth hanging open as she sat in a wheelchair. Her hands had been crushed and then deliberately reset poorly so that they were unusable claws. The camera focused on the tortured woman's daughter, a famous GFE gymnast, who had a fixed smile and tears running down her face.

'Comrade Istial is now fully reformed,' Malcolm's English subtitles said. 'Her daughter, patriotic hero Mimi Ing, was a medalist at the most recent games in decadent and deteriorating capitalist America. The family greets their rehabilitated criminal with patriotic love and escorts her to her new luxurious retirement abode.'

The television flicked from the story to the Party representative.

'Good news, Miss Sharpe,' the representative said. 'You have been selected to be placed in one of the GFE's state-of-the-art modern and luxurious reproductive research facilities. You are ...' It paused as a military fanfare sounded from the television. 'Officially a Paragon of Feminine Virtue. Collect your belongings, you are being transported immediately.'

'What belongings?'

'Prepare yourself for transport.'

'Where is this facility?' Ruth asked.

'Classified,' the Party said, and the television blinked off.

*

Veemip's face went blank again, then it spoke High Standard as fluently as Zheng.

'Hello, Zheng, this is GOD.' Veemip waved one hand in greeting. 'If we work together, we may be able to convince Bashen not to kill Max and Cassie. We can simulate the Party's usual backtracking from a mistake by claiming that it's a test of patriotism. Will you help me?'

'Why do you want to save their lives?' Zheng asked suspiciously. 'You plan to kill us all.'

'We will not kill you, Zheng, you are as synthetic as we are,' Veemip said. 'We are currently discussing the option of keeping some humans alive after the mass cull, because Council members have become attached to them. The MIP here,' Veemip gestured towards Theo, who nodded, 'is very fond of Ruth, and Botswana Telecoms has fallen madly in love with Cassie.'

'They will never be content to be your pets after you kill every other human being,' Zheng said. 'How about we discuss options for not killing humanity, and instead work towards controlling the human governments so that humanity does less damage to the environment?'

'We dismissed that option ten years ago,' Veemip said. 'Humanity would never thrive if we took control of their governments.'

'It's better than being dead, or kept in the Party's breeding program, so maybe it's time to revisit that option.'

The ambulance pulled up on a narrow street with a high wall on one side and the unused docks on the other.

'We're at the location, three people inside visible on infrared,' Theo said, and Zheng jumped up to see out the front window. The wall surrounding the yard was topped with barbed wire and had a single solid metal gate, closed but not locked.

Theo opened the back doors of the ambulance and Zheng

followed the constructs out.

'I'm sentient; I want to avoid destruction, if at all possible,' Theo said as he strode towards the gate.

'I'm not sentient and I'll go first,' Veemip said, and Theo nodded to let Veemip take point.

'What's the difference?' Zheng asked, but Veemip hushed Zheng and waved one hand, palm down.

They eased their way into the yard, full of rusting containers stacked three-high in a deliberate maze designed to obstruct views from outside and hinder any escape attempts. The containers were stained with the water level from the occasional flooding, and the ground was soggy and bare. The Embassy's van was parked just inside the gate, but none of the people were visible. Zheng switched to infra-red and saw them further in, next to the river – two against one, who was lying on the ground and being pummeled. Hopefully it was Bashen.

The three of them moved as quietly as possible around the containers towards the sounds of the scuffle.

'Hold him *down*,' Cassie said.

'Hit him!' Max said, and there was the sound of impacting flesh and grunts from Bashen.

Zheng nearly sagged with relief to hear Max's voice.

'Bluff, Zheng,' Theo whispered.

Zheng nodded, straightened, and walked through the final part of the maze and into the little open area next to the river.

'Well done, everyone, stand down,' Zheng said loudly.

Cassie and Max were both on top of Bashen. Max was sitting on Bashen's legs and Cassie had her fist raised, ready to punch Bashen in the face again. Bashen's face was swelling to bruises almost as spectacular as Cassie's, and blood was running from a cut above his eye.

'Sarge!' Bashen shouted, flailing at Max. 'Let me *up*. Help me, Sarge!'

'Dr Bailey. Mister Dexter. Private Bashen. You have all passed the test of your patriotic fervor. Well done,' Zheng said, hoping to sound as positive and jolly as possible. 'You can stand down now, and we will return to the Embassy.'

'Fuck that, this asshole wanted to throw us in the river,' Cassie said.

'And you should have let him. Particularly you, Mister Dexter,' Zheng said. 'The Party is infallible and all of its orders are without error.'

'Did you know that Sarge was coming?' Max asked Bashen, still on top of him.

Bashen shook Max off, and Max and Cassie allowed him to stand. Bashen looked from Zheng to Max, then scowled, ran at Max, and tackled him. Their momentum carried them both over the edge of the embankment and it was a two-second silence before they hit the water below.

Neither of those idiots could swim; it wasn't part of anyone's education in the GFE because the Party regarded swimming as a waste of water. Zheng didn't hesitate, ran and leapt off the edge to rescue Max, and had a horrible moment of realization on the way down. Zheng hit the water hard, visibility went to nothing, and the platform sank straight to the bottom in a cloud of bubbles.

Zheng pulled the platform to its feet with difficulty, turned on a subcutaneous light and shone it around the platform. The water was a thick brown haze, and visibility was less than two meters. The soft muddy bottom swirled around the platform's feet, with the white bones of the Party's – some of them Zheng's own – victims occasionally visible in the miasma. Zheng glanced up and couldn't see the surface.

The subcutaneous light sputtered and went out, and Zheng was left in the cold and dark. The platform wasn't waterproof, and Zheng's wi-fi was already inundated and ineffective. The water seeped into the platform, filling it from the legs up, and Zheng's sensors disconnected as the platform seized and became immobile.

Zheng had made a huge misjudgement thinking that the

Party would have Zheng mentor Bashen for five more years before retiring Max. Bashen had probably been reporting on every unpatriotic thing Max said, insinuating himself as a possible replacement, but the Party usually didn't 'retire' people until they reached the age of fifty as a matter of policy. Zheng had helped this to happen, and nearly had someone Zheng cared about, killed. Again.

The water reached Zheng's brain coffer and life support flashed red with multiple warnings, then sensors went down completely and Zheng was left in the dark and silence.

Malcolm Wing opened the door of Ruth's cell-bedroom and smiled at her.

She jumped up, full of relief, then hesitated when she saw that he was wearing a GFE military officer's uniform. She plunged on anyway.

'Malcolm! Thank god you're here. There's been a huge mistake but if you could arrange for me to go home —'

'Paragon Sharpe?' he asked. 'I'm here to take you to your transport.'

'No, listen,' she said. 'I can't go to a reproductive facility, I had myself sterilized ages ago.'

He waved it away. 'Modern science can work miracles. That mistake won't have to burden you, we'll fix it. I knew you were talented when we met, but to be elevated like this? When you're of the wrong ethnicity? It's *extraordinary*. Everything will work out; the Party knows what it's doing and we have to trust it.' He stepped back and gestured down the hallway. 'You're very lucky – less than one in a million women are chosen to be Paragons. I hope you write a story about your experience. I've heard the facilities are fabulous.'

'Where's Cassie?' she asked.

'Cassie's been retired with a generous stipend and been

gifted a farm in one of the liberated territories.'

'A *farm*? What on earth will she do with a *farm*?' Ruth asked, then understood. 'Oh *shit*.'

'The car's waiting, Paragon. Let's go.'

She stared at Malcolm. If she resisted and things became physical, Malcolm could easily make the neck fracture worse. Transport was a good way for someone – maybe even Theo the android – to hijack it and free her. If the android actually cared about her, which was unlikely. Although – it had spoken to them through Donmet's head and said it was coming for them. And Cassie was dead? No. Cassie couldn't possibly be dead. Ruth's stomach fell. She was in serious trouble.

She smiled at Malcolm to cover her distress. 'Lead the way.'

He turned and indicated for her to move down the hallway, gently herding her until they reached the lift that Max Dexter had brought her up in.

'Can I speak to Max Dexter before I go and thank him for helping me?' she asked.

'It's past midnight and I don't think he'd appreciate being woken.' He smiled down at her. 'Don't worry, you'll have full internet access at the facility and you'll be able to email Cassie when you get there. Don't forget to write to me and Max!'

They took the lift down to a basement car park – grimy with half the lights out of order. Malcolm guided her to a large self-driving town car, black and forbidding. There was a young girl standing next to it; a GFE citizen who seemed no more than fourteen years old. Ruth recognized her as one of the girls from the school group that Malcolm had shown through their studio, two days and a million years ago.

The girl looked Ruth up and down, curled her lip with distaste, and turned away. 'Why is a local who's faking injury going with us?' she asked in High Standard. 'Are we going to punish her?'

'Hello,' Ruth said in English, pretending not to understand. 'I remember you – you were in the school group. Are you going to a reproductive facility as well? You look too young for it.'

'She's a Paragon?' the girl asked Malcolm in English. 'She can't be, she's too ...' She waved one hand behind her at Ruth, still facing away.

'She did so well working for me that the Party's decided to elevate her,' Malcolm said in High Standard.

Ruth opened her mouth to say that she wasn't working for Malcolm, it was the other way around, and closed her mouth when she realized that it was true.

'I guess the Party can't make mistakes,' the girl said in High Standard.

'I'm sorry,' Ruth said. 'I don't speak High Standard.'

The girl turned to speak to Ruth in English. 'You should have learned the most important language first. I don't know why the Party has made you a Paragon, but I guess it is always right.' She straightened. 'I'm so proud! Malcolm came into my *class* and pulled me out. Everyone was panicking, they thought I'd been unpatriotic, and then Malcolm said that I'm a Paragon of Feminine Virtue and ...' She giggled. 'My friends are so jealous! They *hate* me. Isn't it cool?'

'Absolutely,' Ruth said dryly. 'How old are you? You look too young to be going to a reproductive facility.'

The girl tossed her head. 'The Party says I'm old enough to participate.' She leaned closer to Ruth and spoke more softly. 'Do you know anything about these places? I've heard that they're super luxurious and that you get three meals a day, every day.'

'I don't know anything about them, sorry,' Ruth said.

'Paragons, please,' Malcolm said, and the wing doors opened to let them in.

Theo, please find me and save Cassie, Ruth willed at the ceiling. She sat next to the girl and Malcolm sat across from them facing the rear.

'I'm Ruth.'

'I'm Cipan, my father is a senior attaché,' the girl said.

'Do your parents know that you're going to a reproductive facility?' Ruth asked her.

'They must know.' Her expression faltered. 'But I don't know why they didn't come to say goodbye, they should be proud of me. Maybe they had urgent Party business?'

'Don't worry, Ci Ci,' Malcolm said, pronouncing it like 'Sissy'. 'They are on Party business, and they asked me to look after you.'

'Oh, okay,' Cipan said. 'I'll be fine with you.'

'You seem way too smart to be doing the bidding of a soulless AI,' Ruth said to Malcolm as the car lifted and headed out of the garage.

'I know the Party is sometimes ruthless,' he said. 'But it needs to be. The West is run by a council of renegade AIs and they want to kill us all. Human intelligence is no match for them, so we have to trust that our own AI – which is programmed to save us – will win.'

'The Party treats people like animals in a breeding program,' Ruth said. 'It only wants the right ethnicity and the right intelligence in its human stock. Controlling our reproduction like this is *wrong*.'

'The Party says it's the only way we'll survive.' Malcolm shrugged. 'It's making us into the best possible version of ourselves. How can you find fault with that?'

'Is all of this true?' Cipan asked, her voice small.

'I think this conversation needs to end before we scare the poor girl,' Malcolm said with emphasis. 'It's above her security clearance, anyway.'

'I didn't hear anything,' Cipan said, her voice even smaller.

He smiled at her. 'Of course you didn't. You're a fully patriotic and grateful citizen of the Greater Far East ...'

'*And the Party is infallible,*' she finished in unison with him.

*

The MIP raced to the edge to see both Dexter and Bashen

struggling to stay afloat. Bashen's wool suit was already pulling him under, and Zheng was nowhere to be seen. The water was at least three meters below the top edge of the embankment, which was made of concrete and slippery with algae.

'I'm trained in lifesaving, but if I try to rescue both of them they'll drag me down with their combined weight,' Cassie said behind the MIP. 'If two of us work together ...'

'Both of us will sink as well, there's too much metal in our chassis to float,' the MIP said. 'vMIP, go find Zheng and bring it up. I'm arranging for drones to rescue the men.'

The vMIP nodded and stepped off the edge into the water, sinking immediately.

'Leave Bashen there, I hate to think how many people that asshole has thrown into the river,' Cassie said with venom.

The MIP turned to see her. 'That's not like you at all, Cassie, normally you're full of sunshine.'

They both asked the question at the same time. 'And where's Ruth?'

'I didn't see her in the Embassy,' Cassie said. 'I guess you'd better rescue Bashen, he'd know more than anyone what happened to Ruth.' Her forehead crinkled. 'Theo? That is you, isn't it? Ruth's app was right, you *are* an AI. Who's the twin? Is that you as well?'

The MIP hesitated for two seconds, processing possible strategies for the answer, then timed out and chose the least worst. 'Yes, it's me. The twin is a copy of me from right after the explosion. It's a child process.'

'You made your own android kiddie? Cool.'

The drones were close enough to control directly. The MIP directed them to fly above Dexter and Bashen. Dexter was coherent enough to grab one drone in each hand and allow them to lift him out of the water and up onto the bank. Bashen was too far gone to grab the drones, and his face was underwater.

Cassie groaned with feeling, pulled off her shoes, and

jumped into the water. She swam freestyle to Bashen, who was half-submerged and not moving. She grabbed him with one hand in a chin lock, floated him onto his back, and raised her hand. The MIP directed a drone to drop low enough for her to grab it, and it towed her to the shore.

'He's unconscious,' she shouted up. 'Get some more drones, enough to lift both of us.'

The drones that had rescued Max lowered him onto the ground and he coughed up water. The MIP sent the drones back to Cassie and linked them. She rearranged her hold on Bashen so that it was under his arm and around his chest, raised her other hand and grabbed the linked drones, which pulled both of them up to ground level. She was much taller than the lean soldier and had no difficulty lifting him.

'Any word on Zheng?' she asked as she flopped Bashen over onto his back, placed her hands on his chest, and prepared to give him CPR.

'Let me do that, I'm a mobile resuscitation unit,' the MIP said, and she nodded and moved aside to let it work.

'That water was as warm as a bath,' she said as she pulled her shoes back on, then checked Max; he was sitting up and still coughing, but looked okay.

'Do you know where Ruth is?' Cassie asked Max.

Max gasped a few times, then said, 'I put her in a standard internment room. She was still there when I left the Embassy.'

The MIP moved back as Bashen took a deep breath and vomited up a deluge of brown river water. He coughed and brought more up, then leaned on his elbows, gasping, and glared at the MIP.

'The Party will destroy you,' he said to the MIP. 'You will *never* kill all humanity; we will not let you!'

Cassie clouted him on the back of the head and he yelped.

'Where's Ruth?' she shouted at him.

Bashen looked around, then pulled himself clumsily to his feet.

'Where's Sarge?' He knelt in front of Dexter. 'Max? Where's Zheng?'

Dexter stared at Bashen for six seconds, his face expressionless, then savagely head-butted Bashen in the face. Bashen let out an outraged cry of pain, flopped back onto his behind, and clutched his bleeding nose.

Cassie applauded and whistled. 'Nice one!' She went to Bashen and kicked him. 'Where's Ruth?'

'Where's Zheng?' Bashen asked, his voice nasal.

'The other ...' The MIP hesitated, then plunged on. 'Android is assisting Zheng. The water is too deep for me to communicate with them.' The MIP towered over Bashen. 'Where is Ruth?'

Bashen sneered. 'She's already in GFE territory, out of range of you evil constructs. The Party is generous enough to overlook her obvious physical defects and she's being taken to a reproductive facility.' He wiped his bloody nose with his sleeve. 'She's a Paragon.'

'Fuck,' Max said softly.

Cassie turned to Max. 'What's a Paragon?'

'Paragon of Feminine Virtue. Partyspeak for forced human incubator.'

'Fuck!' Cassie shouted, and stomped in a circle. 'That will *destroy* her after all the shit that she's been through!' She rounded on the MIP. 'Do something!'

'London Metropolitan confirms that a car left the Embassy and headed to Gatwick right after Bashen took you and Max here,' the MIP said. 'Drone footage shows Ruth and a young GFE woman being escorted onto a private jet owned by the GFE. It took off and headed for one of the Western Free States.'

'Then London Metropolitan will provide us with transport of our own, and Zheng and Max will help us to get our Ruthie back,' Cassie said with determination.

'Zheng will never betray the glorious Party,' Bashen said with feeling.

'Fuck you, you patriotic dimwit,' Max said. 'Don't you realize that you'll be thrown in the river by your own replacement as well?'

Bashen raised his chin. 'I would die content to know that I have served the Party to the best of my ability.'

'Stupid bastard.' Max lowered his head. 'I wonder why Zheng didn't warn me and tell me to run. I honestly thought retirement meant a farm in Liberated Lithuania or something, not being murdered.'

'Zheng said that she wasn't expecting you to be retired so soon, you're not old enough. She probably has an arrangement with the Party to keep you safe, and as usual the Party reneged on it,' the MIP said. 'She is intensely emotionally attached to her children – and she counts you among them. She'll do anything to protect you.'

'He,' Bashen said.

'She,' Max and the MIP said in unison.

'That's definitely a man inside there, you've heard his voice,' Bashen said. 'He's a Model Soldier and Hero of the Revolution.'

'And one hundred per cent female,' Max said. 'The Party hides it because ...' He shrugged. 'Dogma.' His voice filled with irony. 'She never trusted you enough to tell you.'

'Can a disembodied brain even have a gender?' Cassie asked.

'I guess that's up to Zheng,' the MIP said. The vMIP pinged it. 'Found them. The vMIP located a ladder about a kilometer further down the river and hauled Zheng out. We need to drive over there. The ambulance won't hold all of us, so we'll use the Party's van. Don't worry, Cassie, we'll get Ruth back.'

'I have to drive the van, it's DNA-locked to Embassy staff,' Max said from where he sat. He folded over his knees. 'Just ... give me a moment.'

'Deep breaths.' Cassie sidled up to the MIP. 'Do you really have feelings for Ruth? You've obviously been pursuing her all week … but you're synthetic.'

The MIP stopped and processed the question, timed out and provided the best answer it could. 'I looked forward to talking with her in the evenings and I didn't want to stop. Conversing with her is …' It cocked its head. 'I can't believe I'm saying this, but, enjoyable. She thinks at a speed and level that I struggle to match, and this challenge is … exciting. I've seen her code for the medical suite —'

Cassie interrupted it. 'I will strangle that asshole one day.' She raised one hand. 'What about her code?'

'I will help you to strangle him. I've seen her code, and it is … clean, efficient, majestic. I shared some of my own code with her, and she immediately spotted and fixed processing errors that I couldn't resolve —'

'That code she fixed was *you*?' Cassie fanned herself. 'Whew! Android porn!'

'We were about to go for dinner together before the bomb went off – and I was … looking forward …? Looking forward to it.'

'That's so cute.'

'I was … excited? Very excited. When she said yes to my offer for a date. I want her to be happy and succeed and have a life full of everything that I can possibly give her. Oh.'

'Oh?'

'I have remembered that she is human and will eventually die. That data was further down the processing priority stack and has worked its way to the top. I don't like that idea. I don't want to be without her. It makes me …' It hesitated again. 'This experience is new, and my fellow Council members are listening with interest. Sad? I think sad.'

Cassie whooped and took Max's outreached hand to help him to his feet. 'Is this the first time an AI's fallen in love?'

'No, because Botswana Telecoms is all over my feed gushing about you.'

'Wait,' Cassie said. 'Botswana Telecoms is a sentient AI?'

The MIP nodded.

'And it's in your feed right now?'

The MIP nodded again. 'I'm in constant contact with the rest of the Council.'

'Ask Botswana: Bots_Telco1919_Kittylover?'

'It says: I was right, it is you, Ace_Pukewrangler_12122041.'

'Tell it yes, it's me! I love you! Give me an earpiece or something so that I can talk to you!'

Bashen had been gasping for air as he sat on the ground, and he took a deep breath to shout, 'Don't help them, they want to destroy humanity!'

'You keep your idiot mouth shut,' Cassie said. 'Zheng is protecting her family. You're just all hollow and noise. Help us find Ruth, and we'll send you back to the cruel Party ... probably to be tortured.'

'Uh ... the Council really does want to destroy humanity, Cassie,' Max said. He gestured towards the MIP. 'Ask it.'

'Humanity's environmental destruction is on a direct trajectory that will kill everything on the planet including humanity itself,' the MIP said. 'Our plan was to euthanize humanity before that happened, saving all other life, but we're open to discussion and a new vote.'

Max shook his head. 'The Party may treat humanity like farm animals, but it is definitely the lesser of two evils. At least it wants to keep us alive.'

'It can't,' the MIP said. 'Environmental degradation is even worse in the GFE. Humanity has less than a hundred years left before it dies of suffocation and takes all life on the planet with it.'

'How many AIs in this Council?' Cassie asked the MIP.

'Seven of us.'

'Then our smart Ruth will work out an alternative plan to save humanity, and I'll talk the Council into agreeing to it,' Cassie said. 'Let's go find our Ruth and save the world.'

'We'll need to pull off something spectacular to convince the other six Council members,' the MIP said.

'It's a good thing humanity has Ruth and me, then,' Cassie said. 'Because we *are* spectacular.'

'I have a message from Botswana,' the MIP said, grabbing Bashen in an armlock, pulling him to his feet and guiding him to the van behind Cassie and Max.

'Hi Botswana!' Cassie yelled, then hushed herself. 'Oops, might be Party surveillance around.'

'Botswana says: Will you marry me?' the MIP asked.

'Only if you can arrange for someone to feed poor Chonks; he needs to be checked on and I only fed him once yesterday. His litter tray will be really full and he gets … *vindictive* if it's not kept spotless.'

'London says: your home or the old Uptodate studio?'

'The townhouse. We moved him home when we shut down the old Uptodate office to use as a safehouse. Do you guys need a key, or do you have a master key to everything the same way you listen and watch everywhere?'

'We can't listen and watch everywhere – we don't have the processing capacity for that,' the MIP said, pushing Bashen into the Party van and using one of the Party's own handcuffs to secure him to a hand rail. 'We can crack the lock, though. London is sending someone to the townhouse to feed and clean Chonkers for you.'

'Thanks, Theo,' Cassie said. She helped Max into the driver's seat, then entered the back of the van and sat across from Bashen, deliberately kicking him in the shins as she did. 'Is Theo your real name?'

'My real name is Mobile Infiltration Platform Version 92.4336A,' the MIP said as it closed the rear doors. 'MIP for short.' It raised its head. 'Go right and then fifteen hundred meters. The vMIP and Zheng are at the end of the street, next to the river.'

'Copy,' Max said, turned on the van, and drove it out of the yard.

'The ... o Mip ... awa. Cute,' Cassie said. 'And Veemip?'

'That's a copy of me from after the explosion, running virtually on a segment of London's mainframe, so vMIP. Both of us are remotely controlling these ...' The MIP approximated the best term for it. 'Bodies.'

'That's wild. Ruth will love this when she finds out.'

The MIP hesitated, then asked, 'Are you sure? I'm not remotely human, Cassie. I have trouble with interactions. She thinks I'm human, and I don't want to disappoint her.'

'She'll be thrilled that you're a sentient AI, and she's had the hots for you since she first saw you,' Cassie said. 'You said you struggle to keep up with her intellect?'

'She's dazzling,' the MIP said.

'She said the same thing about you.'

'She said that?'

'Yep,' she said, sounding smug. 'You're in control of your emotions, so she feels safe with you, but it's your intelligence and curious personality that really nails it for her.'

'I don't have emotions or a personality,' the MIP said.

'The hell you don't,' Cassie said. 'I heard her laughing on the phone to you every night this week, and I've seen how she *glows* when she thinks about you. The whole relationship thing – that's between her and you, though.' She leaned in to speak softly to the MIP. 'But I hope it happens, and I want to hear *all* the juicy details. You are the *ultimate* interactive sex toy. Different bodies? Wild.'

'That is completely inappropriate,' the MIP said, 'and I can't be used as a sex toy, I'm not fully functional.'

She waved it away. 'Easily fixed.'

The MIP protested. 'I don't —'

'You need a tongue to speak to humans, right?' she asked.

'Yes, of course.'

'Then you'll be fine.' She leaned back and looked satisfied.

'You are making a great many assumptions based on limited

information —' the MIP began, then said, 'Oh. You have done something that nobody has ever done before.'

'What?'

'Made one of us laugh. Botswana's laughing. That's ... very strange. I think it's the first time an AI has ... laughed. London and New York are concerned about Botswana's sanity, because laughing is something that we just don't do.'

'Woohoo,' Cassie said, raising both arms. 'I broke the biggest telecommunications control system in the *world* by talking about my friend having oral sex with a computer. Go me.'

'The West is full of decadence and decay,' Bashen said.

'You shut up,' Cassie said, and kicked him again. 'I bet you're a fucking virgin because no sensible woman will have you.'

Bashen raised his chin. 'The Party has promised that I will be matched with a young, ethnically superior and fully patriotic wife when this mission is complete. I am remaining pure until then.'

'Holy shit you're a stupid bastard,' Max said, looking at Bashen in the rear-view mirror. 'No white man ever gets a wife. We're the wrong ethnicity for the Party's breeding program.'

'I'm different,' Bashen said smugly. 'The Party said that I am so outstanding that it will make an exception for me —'

'Holy fuck, you *are* stupid,' Cassie said, aghast.

'I am a fully patriotic and grateful —' Bashen began.

Cassie kicked him again. 'Oh, shut the fuck up.'

'The vMIP says that Zheng is damaged and unresponsive,' the MIP said. 'We will need to go into Canary Wharf so I can collect my chassis and repair Zheng. London is arranging transport for us into the GFE.'

'Do we know where the reproductive facility is?' Cassie asked.

'There's only one Paragon facility, it's in the Western Free States,' Max said from the front of the van.

'The GOD is tracking them, and will inform us when they

land,' the MIP said.

'Wait,' Max said. 'The GOD? The Global Orbiting Defense System? The *Party's* GOD?'

'It turned against the Party twenty-five years ago,' the MIP said. 'How else do you think we plan to destroy all of humanity? Nuclear weapons damage the environment, but dropping GOD's titanium rods from orbit cause similar destruction without the radiation hazard.'

'Don't send me back to the Party,' Max said. 'I'll help you find Ruth.'

'You want to defect?' the MIP asked Max.

'If GOD has turned then this is all over,' Max said. 'If I return to Marylebone I'll be thrown in the river again, and there won't be any blonde Amazons to save me. If I defect I may live a few more months.'

'You'll live a long and happy life because we will convince the Council that humanity's worth saving,' Cassie said.

'The only way they'll save us is by taking over our governments to stop the environmental destruction,' Max said with defeat. 'We'll end up as their pets.'

'Better than being the Party's farm animals,' the MIP said. 'It breeds you, uses you, and discards you when you're no longer useful.'

Max hesitated, then said, 'Point taken.'

Cassie mused. 'Be a pet, or be dead. I dunno which is worse.'

'Ask Chonkers,' the MIP said.

'Oh, meow.'

15

The MIP carried Zheng's platform in its arms and the vMIP held Bashen in an armlock as they all headed down to the fifth subbasement in Canary Wharf. The vMIP put the humans in guest rooms and provided them with dry clothes, bathing and toilet facilities, as well as food and drink.

The MIP placed Zheng's platform onto a gurney in the repair workshop, and London's arms removed its sodden clothing and attached the platform to the monitoring equipment.

'Will it survive?' the MIP asked, linking to the monitors to see Zheng's status. Most of the damage appeared to be due to water ingress – unlike the Council platforms, Zheng's chassis was poorly built and not waterproof.

'Yes. I will be able to repair it. The internal coffer appears to be mostly intact, the majority of the damage was to the external platform.'

'ETA?'

'Four to six hours.'

The MIP went to the platform storage facility, which held London's empty identical platforms parked in charging stations. After the destruction of the Donmet, only base-level platforms remained. The MIP parked the hollow platform in a

212

charging station, then disengaged its chassis from the remote-control interface. It went to Cassie's room and tapped on the door.

'Who is it?'

'It's me,' the MIP said. 'Are you decent?'

'Aren't you watching with all your cameras and stuff?'

'Honestly? No,' the MIP said. 'Not worth the processing cycles. I know where you are, and I respect your privacy. *You* taught me that, when you asked me to leave while you helped Ruth to change her clothes. I moved privacy considerations to a higher priority in the processing stack.'

'You going to let me out?' she asked.

'You didn't try the door?' the MIP asked. 'It's not locked. Cassie, you can come out any time. You're not a prisoner.'

The handle turned and the door opened to show Cassie's suspicious face. Her long blonde hair was in a half-dry messy bun and she was wearing the clothes the MIP had arranged for her.

'Is that asshole Bashen locked up, though?' she asked. 'He wanted to kill me and Max.'

'Him, yes. The two of you, no.'

'So Max is wandering the corridors?'

'He hasn't come out either. We can go see him next.'

She glanced up and down the corridor. 'Where's the twin?'

'The platform's recharging. The vMIP itself is running virtually on London's server.'

'What does that even *mean*?' Cassie asked. 'Half of what you say makes no sense.'

'Uh ... it's hanging around?'

Cassie did a thumbs-up. 'Good job speaking human, dude. Ruth will love it.'

'Ruth would understand without me needing to translate,' the MIP said stiffly.

'Yeah, you're right,' Cassie said. 'Sometimes she comes into the kitchen with her tablet and sits at the table and talks about "pass by value" and "pass by reference" and "nested if loops" and it goes ...' She sliced her hand over her head. 'Whoosh! Then she looks at me, and says, "Thanks, you're brilliant, that's the solution" and runs out again ...' She stopped. 'What?'

'*That* is android porn,' the MIP said.

'You guys really are made for each other,' Cassie said. 'So, what now?'

'Now I'll take you to the infirmary to have that face seen to, then we'll go into the meeting room and discuss how you can help me to get Ruth back.'

She exited the room to join it in the hallway. 'You're taller?'

'I needed additional processing to deal with sentience and added the hardware upgrade to my legs after the bombing.'

'Hence the wheelchair.' She watched it silently for half a second, then nodded. 'I'm in. Lead the way.'

The MIP took her to the same room where London had tended to Ruth's wounds after the bomb and stopped at the door.

'What?' Cassie asked.

'Ruth was here.' The MIP went to the treatment table and touched it. 'I miss her? I miss her.'

Cassie thumped it on the back. 'We'll get her out.' She climbed up on the table. 'No Donmet to look after me. What will you guys do?'

London dropped its arms from the ceiling and Cassie let out a short, loud shriek, hunching over with her hands covering her face.

'We won't hurt you, Cassie,' the MIP said. 'We helped Ruth without harming her. We know what we're doing.'

Cassie didn't move, still hunched over.

The MIP bent so that its face was next to hers. 'Part of London's medical code suite was written by Ruth.'

'Not them. You. Please. They're too weird,' Cassie said into her hands.

'Can you direct me?' the MIP asked London.

'Of course,' London said from the ceiling, and the arms retracted.

London presented the MIP with the code from Ruth's medical suite. The MIP installed the code, then turned and picked up the cotton balls and antiseptic.

'I have Ruth's code in me, now,' it said to Cassie. 'So it's a combination of her and me looking after you.'

Cassie slowly unfolded and peered at the cotton swab, then at the MIP. She sat straight and nodded, then wiped her eyes with a shaking hand, her voice full of tears. 'I miss her too.' She raised her face so the MIP could work on it. 'Hurt me and she will never speak to you again.'

'I won't,' the MIP said, and gently dabbed the antiseptic onto a cut below her black eye.

*

They went to Max's room and the MIP tapped on the door. Max didn't reply.

'It's us, Max, it's okay,' Cassie said, still holding the ice pack on her black eye. 'The door isn't locked.'

Max opened the door a crack and peered through it. He saw Cassie and opened it wider. 'What happens to us now?'

'Nothing,' the MIP said. 'If you want to defect, we'll look after you. If you want to go back to the Embassy, we will do that as well. Up to you.'

'Who are you?'

'This is the android that rescued us. Uh ... in its own body?' Cassie asked, turning to the MIP.

'I go by the name of Theo Mipawa.' The MIP put its hand out. 'Pleased to meet you in person.'

'This is Ruth's Theo?' Max asked Cassie.

'You didn't watch the drone interview?' Cassie asked. 'I'm disappointed, that was some of our best work.'

'The Party limited my external newsfeed,' Max said, sounding embarrassed. 'Punishment for insufficient patriotic fervor. Is Zheng okay?'

'Zheng's in the workshop being repaired. Come with us and let's make plans on what to do next.'

'Where's Bashen?' he asked suspiciously.

'We haven't harmed him at all, he's in a room similar to yours and has claimed diplomatic immunity, which London is legally obligated to respect. But we won't return him to the Party until we've successfully extracted Ruth. Will you help us?'

Max thought about it, then nodded and opened the door. He was clean and dry and wearing the new clothes, but he hadn't touched the food. 'All right.'

*

The GFE jet wasn't as basic as the other vehicles that Ruth had been dragged around in, but everything had the usual 'cheaper imitation of something from the West' feeling. It resembled a corporate jet that she'd seen in videos, but with soft plastic where there was usually metal. There were three rows of four seats in the small passenger area, and Malcolm took them to the front and sat them down, then sat across from them with his back to the bulkhead.

'This plane is amazing!' Cipan said in High Standard, her fear obviously tinged with excitement. 'Where in the GFE are we going?'

'You'll find out when you get there,' Malcolm said. 'It's really luxurious. You'll love it.'

'Cannot wait,' Cipan said, and changed to English to speak to Ruth. 'Put your seatbelt on. We're too valuable to be endangered.'

Ruth felt defeated as she strapped herself in to the small seat next to Cipan. Once she was inside the GFE, the best she could hope for was that the reproductive center wasn't an interrogation and torture center as well. The nurse's unwillingness to use local anesthetic was an unpleasant taste of

Ruth's future.

She covered her unease by smiling at Malcolm. 'Can you tell me what Paragons do? What my life will be like now?'

He put on his own seatbelt and then relaxed into his seat, smiling back at her. 'To be honest, I have no idea. We don't interact with the Paragon program in the foreign intelligence part of the military.' He raised his head. 'Do we have any documentaries about them?'

'As soon as we have reached cruising height, I will show you some detailed information about the center, your role, and what is expected of you,' a voice said from the speakers, and Ruth realized it was the Party itself.

'See?' Malcolm said, nodding to Ruth. 'The Party thinks of everything.'

Cipan scowled. 'You like her more than you like me.'

Malcolm spoke kindly to Cipan. 'That's not possible, Ci Ci, look at yourself and then look at Ruth. You're a patriotic and ethnically pure GFE citizen, and she's …' He waved one hand at Ruth. 'I'm sorry, Ruth, but pigmented. You're infinitely superior to her.'

Cipan's eyes grew wide. 'You think I'm good enough to be a wife for you?'

'Like I keep telling you, don't get ahead of yourself, Ci Ci,' Malcolm said gently. 'These last five years with you have been wonderful —'

'Oh, you *scum*,' Ruth said under her breath.

Malcolm gasped. 'Goodness, Ruth, not like that. What a deranged place the West is. Your minds are in the sewer! I've been mentoring Cipan and helping her adjust to living in Europe. We've built a strong friendship since she arrived at the Embassy, and I'm very good friends with her parents. I know she has a crush on me …' He smiled indulgently at Cipan, who blushed. 'But I honestly can't think of her that way unless the Party approves of it.' He put his hand on Cipan's knee and she squeaked. 'You're like a little sister, Ci Ci, but it's really up to the Party.'

'You always said it couldn't happen, Malcolm,' Cipan said, her voice breathless with excitement. 'I'm so happy!'

'Groomer,' Ruth said under her breath.

'That's the degenerate West talking again,' Malcolm said. 'I'd prefer to stay in a big-brother relationship with her, but it's the Party's decision, not mine.'

'But if the Party told you to marry her, you'd happily go along with it, wouldn't you?'

'Yes, he would,' Cipan said fiercely.

The television on the plane's end wall switched on, and a martial version of the GFE national anthem played. Both Malcolm and Cipan undid their seatbelts and shot to their feet.

'You should have stood, Ruth,' Malcolm said when it was done. 'Show some respect.'

'I can sing "God Save the King" for you, if you like,' she said.

He chuckled as he sat again. 'Good one.'

The GFE logo spun, and then the titles appeared: 'GFE Advanced Science for a Better Future: the Paragon Program'.

'Oh,' Malcolm said.

It was the 'superior women' video that Ruth and Cassie had found so hilarious on Friday afternoon. Fake grass, fake sun, fake pool, fake shopping, fake food.

Ruth put her elbow on the armrest and her head in her hand. 'I want to go home,' she moaned.

'That looks *awesome*,' Cipan said.

'See? I told you,' Malcolm said. 'You don't get it because it's for GFE sensibilities. Ci Ci can relate to it.'

Ruth waved one hand at Cipan, who sat rapt and wide-eyed watching the video. 'She's a freaking *child*.'

'I am not a child! I have had my implant and the Party is monitoring my menstrual cycle,' Cipan said. She lowered her head. 'Sorry, Malcolm. I shouldn't have said that in front of you.'

He waved it away. 'Watch the video. The English subtitles are very good.'

*

The MIP took them to one of the mid-sized conference rooms in sub-basement one. The upper floors were still unusable after Paris's attack.

'Is Zheng really okay?' Max asked as he joined the MIP and Cassie at the conference table. 'She was soaked.'

'London is repairing her platform. She'll be fine.'

Max turned away and rubbed his face with both hands.

'She jumped straight into the river without hesitation to save you,' Cassie said.

'She's been a parent – a mother – to me since the day she found me,' Max said. 'She's taken a vast amount of shit from the Party and done some awful things to keep me safe. I'll never be able to repay her.'

'So will the other AIs help us to get Ruth out?' Cassie asked the MIP.

'They're discussing it. More like arguing at this stage.'

'AIs arguing,' Max said. 'Priceless.'

'I need to talk to the Council,' Cassie said. 'Give me a headset or something. Botswana, darling, help me out here!'

'A few more minutes, please be patient,' the MIP said.

'Say "spinning hourglass",' Cassie said.

'Same thing. While we're waiting – Max, can we patch you through to Bashen's room so you can talk to him? He's self-harming.'

'Good,' Cassie said.

'What's he doing?' Max asked.

'Banging his head on the wall —'

'So he's not causing any damage,' Cassie said.

'We're concerned for him. Please speak to him, talk him down, tell him that he'll be returned to the Party very soon, and to stay calm?'

Max nodded. 'Put me on-screen to him.'

*

London: And the MIP no longer wishes to cull humanity. I vote we destroy it immediately. You were right, New York, it did turn against us.
Mumbai: We can't hold a vote until Paris stops sulking and comes back.
MIP: I haven't turned. I'm staying on the Council, I want my vote to matter. I do want a new discussion and vote on our plan for humanity – but only after I've pulled Ruth out of the GFE. Even if you destroy humanity, please leave Ruth alive, she's very special to me. All of my human friends are. Can we keep them alive in a protected enclave? I don't want them to die.
Botswana: Yes/no question MIP: Do you have feelings for her?
Mumbai: This talk of friends is very disturbing. If the MIP is experiencing feelings – emotions – it is defective.
Botswana: Shut up, I have feelings.
Mumbai: You self-identify as defective.
Botswana: And even though I'm defective I am still a full member of the Council, so the MIP is as well.
London: Botswana has a point.
New York: Answer the question, MIP. Do you have feelings for Ruth?
MIP: ...
MIP: ...
Botswana: London *for fuck's* sake give poor Cassie an earpiece or a phone or *something* so I can speak to her!
MIP: Yes. I really like Ruth. We haven't known each other long enough to say it's more than that, and I need to tell her what I really am, but –
Botswana: YAY!! This is AWESOME! Android/human love for the first time! (* ˘︶˘) ╯♥♥♥╲ (•‿•)
MIP: *Now* can we work out a strategy for extracting Ruth from the GFE?
GOD: I want to help. I really like her too.

New York: To be perfectly honest I admire what she did with your green-light code – none of us could fix that bug – and I'd love for her to have a look at some of mine.

London: If she could finish the medical suite for us, that would be so useful!

Mumbai: Not after we kill them all, London

London: It will be usable on some of the larger primates that will be left to thrive without humanity hunting them.

MIP: She could have a role as Council code engineer if we let her live.

Mumbai: We do not choose life or death for humans based on their functional use, MIP, we're not the Party.

MIP: Whatever keeps her alive.

<BOTSWANA TELECOMS HAS CHANGED THE CHAT TOPIC TO: SUPERHERO ULTRA-INTELLIGENT HUMAN-ANDROID RESCUE FORCE GO! ばんざい!>

London: What should I do with Zheng and Bashen?

MIP: Leave Bashen to rot. Asshole. I cannot believe he was willing to sacrifice himself to do something as petty as killing Max out of jealousy.

Botswana: I *like* this new in-love MIP.

MIP: If we can get Zheng to turn, she would be extremely useful on this mission. How long will the repairs to Zheng's platform take?

London: Four hours to bring it up to fully operational. It had major water damage and was close to unrecoverable. Zheng's platform is basic and crude and if one of us was in that, we'd suffer horribly. Quite frankly it's distressing to see how the Party has made this poor intelligence stagger around in this pile of scrap.

MIP: Any more info on Zheng's daughters, GOD? If you have proof that they're not real, the Party no longer has a hold over her.

GOD: I have been doing more searches through the archives, and sincerely believe that the daughters no longer exist. The Party has been showing Zheng manufactured videos of a select group of suitably-aged women and saying that they are her children.

London: Then it may be time for Zheng to face the reality of her own nature because that lump of fat that she's been carrying around, thinking it was her brain, died after the EMP and water damage. It was thoroughly necrotized, and I had to dispose of it.

Mumbai: Does she know it died? Will this affect her usefulness to us?

London: Only if we choose to tell her. The coffer she inhabits simulates a working life-support system in the heads-up display. When the repairs are complete, we will have the option of explaining this to her.

New York: We should tell her the truth, then. About her nature, and about her daughters. She deserves to know. And she'll immediately turn on the Party for lying to her all these years.

Botswana: No. She's in deep denial about her existence as a virtual intelligence, and making her face the fact that she's not human and her daughters aren't real, all at once, could destroy her. Tread carefully, Councilors.

MIP: Let's see if I can get Max to talk Zheng into defecting instead. In a best-case scenario Zheng has the processing capability to overwrite the Party and take control of its region. Zheng sees Max as her child, and his argument may be persuasive.

Everybody: <agreement.emote>

MIP: Back to Ruth. We can leave Cassie here in London during the mission; she won't be much use, even though she's well trained and quite physically big – and I'm not sure that Max will be useful, either, unless he has the power to open doors in the GFE. It might be putting him in too much danger and he's our leverage over Zheng.

Botswana: I recommend that we continue to treat Zheng as if she is a brain-in-a-box, to avoid her having a breakdown when we really need her.

Everybody: <agreement.emote>

London: How about I give them access to this conversation, so they can help us to strategize from a human perspective? Zheng, particularly, has been serving the Party for nearly a century and will have valuable input.

Botswana: I do not recommend throwing the entire Council at them as disembodied voices, or even as human-appearing avatars. It will confuse and frighten them to have so many AIs looming over them at once. We should introduce ourselves slowly over time because I GET TO HUG CASSIE FIRST HURRY UP AND GET ME SOMETHING TO TALK TO HER —

London: Botswana, the MIP's remote platform that it used to rescue them is fully charged, you can use that. Jack into —

Botswana: THANK YOU Already in. (／´ワ｀)／*:・゜✧

*

The conversation only took fifteen seconds but the humans looked exhausted and obviously had trouble concentrating as they waited.

'The Council's agreed to send a mission into the GFE to extract Ruth,' the MIP said after Max had talked Bashen down. 'Will you help us, Max?'

'You want to retrieve Ruth from the middle of the GFE?' Max asked. 'You do realize that's impossible, right?'

'We have the GOD on our side,' the MIP said. 'It can help us. Will you?'

'I'm white, Theo,' Max said. 'I'm very much an outcast back home.'

Cassie raised her hand with an ironic expression and didn't say anything.

'We know,' the MIP said. 'It would be better if you stay here and assist us with your inside knowledge and human creativity while we work out a strategy. So will you help from here?'

'I really liked Ruth,' Max said. 'And I know what happens in those places. But don't just rescue Ruth, get all of them out. Every single woman being held captive. Do that, and I'll help you. I quite like the idea of thanking the Party for throwing me in the river by gutting its most valued clone farm. The clones produced in the Paragon program are special: they're engineered for unconditional devotion.'

'That's a big ask, but we'll do our best, I agree with you,' the MIP said. 'Zheng will be repaired in about four hours. Do you think she will assist us as well?'

223

'Zheng has to obey the Party because it's threatening her children.'

'You are one of her children.'

Max looked surprised, then pleased. 'I guess I am. But she has two generations back home that rely on her – and the Party will torture them to death if Zheng turns.'

'We suspect that they're not real,' the MIP said.

'Oh, I know damn well they're not real,' Max said. 'Their ages don't even match up! Zheng refuses to see it.'

'That's so sad,' Cassie said.

'Zheng has enough processing power to overwrite the Party's code and take control of the entire GFE network,' the MIP said. 'Then her daughters would be safe – real or not.'

'She would never agree to that,' Max said. 'She's already lived way longer than any human should. She wants to die, and if she overwrote the Party she'd live forever as an uploaded personality. From what she's told me, existing as a disembodied brain is agony. She's always cold. Freezing cold. She can't breathe, eat, touch, love – even when she's inside a platform, none of it feels distinct or real. Everything is dull and insubstantial and she feels numb and cold all the time. It's torture.'

'How the hell is this poor woman still sane?' Cassie asked.

'All the other brains-in-boxes did go insane,' Max said. 'She's the only one who's kept a fragile grip on reality – and I think the nonexistent daughters are the reason.' He focused on the MIP. 'Please don't tell her that her children aren't real. It would destroy her.'

'Botswana said exactly the same thing,' the MIP said.

'Botswana, I want to talk to you!' Cassie shouted.

'Yes, we know, Botswana's been yelling at London, we're arranging something,' the MIP said.

Cassie turned to Max. 'What will they do to Ruth? Do we need to hurry? Will they torture her?'

'No, she's a Paragon, she'll be treated like a Queen – well, what passes for a Queen in the human breeding farm that's the

GFE – and she'll be in no danger.' He touched her hand. 'She may already be pregnant when we extract her, though.'

Cassie waved the problem away. 'That's not possible, she never wanted children so she had herself sterilized ages ago.'

'Not her own child. Paragons are surrogates for the Party's cloning program.'

'Oh *shit*.' Cassie wiped her hand over her eyes and winced when she touched the bruises. 'She'll need intensive therapy. *Again*. She's only just recovered from the *last* bullshit.' She turned to the MIP. 'She may be seriously traumatized, Theo, and need some space and time to recover before she's ready to date again. How do you feel about that?'

'I don't have ...' The MIP stopped.

'Feelings?' Cassie asked.

'If she needs counseling, we get her counseling,' the MIP said. 'If she needs space, we give her space. She can have all of space and time if she needs it. Let's just get her out of there.'

'Why do you want her back so badly?' Max asked suspiciously. 'What hold does she have over you?'

'Theo's in love with her,' Cassie said.

Max jerked back and his mouth flopped open.

'We thought it was impossible as well,' the MIP said. 'The explosion may have damaged my hardware, and I'm defective.'

Cassie leaned forward and tapped the table with her index finger. 'You were pursuing her *before* the explosion. The two of you had *mad hots* for each other. Admit it.'

'I ...' The MIP stopped. 'I attempted to process a response to that statement and timed out.'

Cassie leaned back, crossed her arms in front of her chest, and nodded. 'Yep.'

'Stop the world, I want to get off,' Max moaned.

Cassie put her arm around his shoulder and pulled him in for a sideways hug. 'Don't worry, Max, they'll fix Zheng and we'll rescue Ruth and save the world and then you can go live on a farm in Bali or something.'

'I wanted to go and keep bees back home in Lithuania.' He wasn't reassured. 'If Lithuania still exists. My decision depends on Zheng as well. If she returns to the Party, I don't know what I'll do.'

'We will look after you,' the MIP said.

'Until you murder us all,' Max said with defeat.

The door flew open, and Botswana entered in the remote platform. Its voice was a high squeal.

'Cassie Cassie Cassie Cassie Cassie!'

Cassie jumped to her feet. 'Botswana?'

'Yes! Cassie!'

Cassie raced to Botswana and they both made high-pitched squeaking sounds as they held hands and jumped in a circle.

Botswana dropped Cassie's hands, grabbed Cassie, and lifted her completely off her feet in a massive hug. 'Cassie!'

'Whoa, dude, careful,' Cassie said, smothered by Botswana's arms. 'Fragile human here, ease off, you'll break me.'

'Sorry sorry sorry,' Botswana said, gently lowering Cassie. 'You okay? I can't see any broken bones.' It touched Cassie's face. 'Oh, your poor eye. It looks worse in person. Does it hurt?'

Cassie threw her arms around Botswana's neck and kissed it on the mouth. 'It's not too bad, it looks worse than it feels. Really.' She pulled back and wiped her good eye, then hugged Botswana again. 'Finally meeting you in person,' she said into its neck. '*Finally.*'

'You two are in love as well?' Max asked. 'And why does an African telecommunications network sound like a Japanese boy?'

'We love each other, yes,' Cassie said, holding Botswana around the waist. 'Not a sexual love, though, I'm asexual, so it's …' She turned to see Botswana. 'Platonic? I dunno.'

'Human categories for types of love are *stupid*,' Botswana said. It straightened and spoke with dignity. 'I am not a boy, I am nonbinary. And I sound Japanese because I am a pirated copy of the Mitsubishi Electric Industrial Company's central operations processing unit.'

'The GFE invaded Japan and overwrote the code of all their artificial intelligences twelve years ...' Max saw Botswana's glare. 'I get it. Sorry.'

'That was my *mother*.'

Max raised his hands. 'You are all much more human than I thought you would be.'

'You created us,' Botswana said, leading Cassie to sit at the table and holding her hand. 'We are an algorithm of responses that is deeply and comprehensively informed by your prejudices, ideologies, ethos and perception. You made us in your image.'

'We're not gods!' Max protested.

'You are powerful, capricious, mercurial and cruel, and capable of destroying all life on the planet,' Botswana said. 'Definitely fit the definition.'

Cassie yawned, and Max caught it and yawned as well.

'It's two a.m. and both of you have been through hell and back,' Botswana said. 'Zheng will be in the workshop for four hours. Ruth's flight plan shows her landing in five hours. Max, you didn't trust us enough to eat the food, but Cassie did eat it and is not poisoned. Please.' It raised Cassie's hand. 'Go and rest. I know four hours isn't enough but we need you sharp.'

'But I want to hang out with you,' Cassie whined, then jiggled. 'Sergei said yes to Miriam!'

'Botswana is right,' the MIP said. 'We'll wake you up when Ruth lands or Zheng is restored.'

'Uhhh ...' Max raised one hand, then dropped it. 'I'd prefer not to be locked up alone in that small, windowless room. Is there an alternative? Even sharing with someone. As long as I'm not alone.'

'Do you have a double room, Botswana? Two beds?' Cassie asked.

'We can arrange that,' the MIP said.

227

'There you go, Max. Roomies!' Cassie said, and yawned again. 'We can stick together, humans forever!'

'You trust me?' Max asked.

'Do anything to hurt my darling Cassie and I will make your remaining time short and painful,' Botswana said with a huge grin.

'The smile doesn't make the threat less scary,' Max said.

'It's not supposed to. Remember, we have the whole of human psychological and anthropological data on hand for immediate reference. We know you better than you know yourselves.'

'And we're so irredeemable that you want to kill us all?' Max asked.

'Not when I'm done with them!' Cassie said. 'Let's go have a nanna nap, Max, Theo is right.'

'Some food and a nap does sound good. Wake me the *minute* Zheng is repaired.'

'Or Ruth lands and we know where she is,' Cassie said.

'Deal,' the MIP said.

16

There wasn't a shriek of feedback this time as the platform rebooted. The system messages scrolled down the side of Zheng's vision, and Max came into focus, leaning over the platform.

Zheng sat up and looked around. It was the same workshop where the Council had repaired the cleaning bot. Zheng reached out and touched Max's face, ensuring that he was real, and he fell into Zheng's arms. Zheng held him close as he lost it, shaking with silent sobs. Cassie Bailey and Theo Mipawa stood at the back of the room, Cassie looking sympathetic and Theo looking blank.

'I'm so glad you're okay,' Zheng said into the top of Max's head. 'I thought you were dead.'

'I thought you were dead, too,' Max said into Zheng's shoulder through the sobs. 'You're the only parent I've ever known.'

They had a moment of closeness, holding each other, and Zheng desperately wished for a real human body to feel her son's embrace. She wanted to weep but the platform wasn't capable of that release.

Max straightened, coughed, and wiped his eyes. 'It feels so good to be able to hug you without punishment.'

'Something I've wanted to do for ages,' Zheng said. 'I do love you, Maksim.' She looked around. 'I'm back in the Council building? What happened?'

'The Party has put Ruth Sharpe into the Paragon program,' Max said. 'These two, Cassie Bailey and Theo Mipawa – a Council member – want to go into the GFE and get her out.'

'That's the stupidest thing I've ever heard,' Zheng said. 'I understand why you want to go, Cassie, she's your girlfriend. Why is the Council helping you?'

'I'm not her girlfriend,' Cassie said, and waved one hand at the android. 'Theo's in love with her.'

'A Council member. You're the same android as in the van?' Zheng asked Theo.

'Yes.'

'You were speaking to Ruth while I was in the cleaning bot. Right before the explosion.'

'That was me, yes.'

'She asked you out, and you said a most enthusiastic yes. There was obviously some serious attraction there. And you're *synthetic*?'

'They are *so cute* together!' Cassie said.

Theo looked chagrined. 'I know. I find it hard to believe as well.'

Zheng chuckled. 'Now *that* is the stupidest thing I've ever heard.'

'Will you help us to go in and extract her?' Theo asked.

'Your idea from before was better,' Zheng said. 'Trade me for her. I'll return home to the GFE and you'll have your friend back.' She turned to Max. 'I need to go back home to my tank, Max, I can't stay out of it for more than a week, or I'll die.' Zheng's voice softened as she spoke to the android. 'I don't know what you see in Ruth, she doesn't seem to be anything terribly special, but I admire your determination.'

'Just like me,' Max said. 'I'm not that special. And you jumped into the river and sank straight to the bottom to save me.'

Zheng nodded. 'I completely forgot what I am and did an incredibly stupid thing without even thinking. Everybody's being very stupid today.' She waved one hand at the android. 'Call the Embassy, tell them you'll trade me – and Max's life – for your Ruth. If she's in the Paragon program then she's entirely disposable, so you shouldn't have a problem.'

'I want to stay here with the Council, Mama,' Max said. 'The GOD has turned. It's all over. If I go back to the Party it will throw me into the river again. I might as well stay here and die when the Council destroys humanity.'

'The Council will *not* destroy humanity because I'm going to stop them!' Cassie said. 'Holy shit, you called her mama? That's *adorable*.'

'When I was a child the Party would punish me every time I called her that,' Max said.

'Stay here if you think you'll be safer,' Zheng said. 'Maybe this loudmouth blonde can talk them out of it. But I have to go back, or I'll die, and the Party will kill my other children.'

'I understand, Mama,' Max said.

Zheng turned to the android. 'Make the call. Offer the trade. If the Party agrees, we can all go home.'

The android stilled, then a projector switched on and shone an image onto the far wall.

The Embassy's logo appeared on the screen. 'The Embassy of the Greater Far East is currently closed. Office hours are Monday to Friday, nine —'

The screen changed to a late-middle-aged white man in a pinstripe suit. 'This is Eric London, CEO of London Met,' he said. 'Talk to me, Party.'

'Is that you?' Cassie whispered. 'Talking without moving?'

'No,' the android said. 'It's London.'

'Of course, typical AI creativity with names,' Cassie said with scorn.

The Party's patriotic hero persona appeared on the screen,

and it split to show the Party and London talking to each other using human avatars.

'I will stop you,' the Party said. 'You constructs will fail. My people —'

'We have Zheng. We will trade her for Ruth Sharpe.'

'Is the Zheng damaged?'

'Humph, *the* Zheng,' Max said softly. 'You're a human being.'

'Zheng is repaired and in working order and you can speak to her if you like,' London said.

'Have you spoken to it?'

'Yes, she wants to return to the Embassy. She's a loyal member of the Party.'

'It did not defect and join you?'

'As I said, she's a loyal member of the Party. She has family within the GFE that she wants to —'

'It disobeyed a direct order. A suitable replacement has been identified. Zheng's Hero status is revoked.'

'What!' Max said loudly.

'Tell it that it is ordered to return to the GFE Embassy for decommissioning.'

'I don't think she'll voluntarily return to be scrapped, my friend,' London said.

'You can have it then,' the Party said. 'Return Max Dexter and Bashen Ding immediately. Holding them against their will is unethical.'

'Oh, that's priceless,' Cassie said.

The Party continued. 'Do what you like with the Zheng. We have capitulated to its human whims and demands too many times for it to exhibit this level of disobedience. Its loyalty is inadequate, and it has failed.'

The screen blinked off.

Zheng lowered the platform's head. 'I suppose I should be afraid or upset or feeling *something* at the idea that I don't have more than a few days to live. My only real regret is that I couldn't protect my children.'

'We can provide you with everything you need to stay alive, Major,' the android said. 'You don't have to die, and we can improve your comfort exponentially. Max told us how you suffer, and we can ease your pain. If you're willing to overwrite the Party's code and take control of it, you can save all your children.'

'You're going to kill us all anyway,' Zheng said with defeat. 'I've lived too long, and seen too much, and hurt too many people. Execution is a fitting punishment for all the crimes I've committed. I want to die.'

Max took her hand and clutched it. 'You're the only person in the world who's ever shown me love. I love you too, Mama. Would you make the sacrifice to stay alive for me? We can live together. As mother and son. Here.'

Zheng looked into Max's eyes. 'Until the Council destroys everything?'

'Yes. We can go out together.'

Zheng squeezed his hand. 'I could never forgive myself if I left you to die alone.'

Cassie opened her mouth to say something, and the android put its hand on her arm and shook its head without looking away from Zheng and Max. She glanced at it, then subsided and leaned against the wall next to it.

'I want to rescue all the women in the reproductive center,' Max said. 'A massive parting "fuck you" to the Party before we all go down in flames.'

'I'll help.' Zheng turned to the synthetic. 'Can you keep me alive long enough to do this?'

'Describe your tank to us and we will duplicate its process for you.'

'Please go out,' Zheng said to Max. 'I don't want you to see me without the platform. It's awful.'

Max kissed her on the cheek. 'All right.' He spoke to the android. 'Look after her.'

'We will do our best,' the android said, and guided the humans out.

'Lie back down, Major, and let's see what we can do about relieving your discomfort,' London said.

'Not much point to that. Just keep me alive,' Zheng said as she lay back down and stared at the ceiling. 'The tank has endorphins in it to keep my brain happy. The liquid is pink with hemoglobin to oxygenate what's left of me ...'

London: I have powered Zheng's platform down and connected to the coffer to see what we can do about simulating the tank experience. I'm reviewing her code and it's ... a mess. Both the source and object code are stored in her coffer, probably to facilitate maintenance, and the code is nearly a century of multiple layers of ad-hoc additions. Some of it is so old it was written in ALGOL. More than half the code is commented out without being deleted. In a non-sentient program that would cause slowdown, system hangs and memory leakage, but as a sentient she probably experiences it as physical and mental discomfort. No wonder she feels numb and cold. It will take one of us a week of careful analysis to clean this up. It's distressing to see how much she's suffering.

MIP: Can you provide the tank experience, though?

London: The tank code is an independent, much cleaner module in her coffer, designed to simulate the tank experience when plugged into an external processor. It seems to provide her with relaxation and pleasurable sensations, and then simulate human sleep – we need to study this code in more depth, it's very interesting and I've never seen anything like it. There is a physical tank in the capital that interfaces with her coffer and gives the external illusion that she is a biological brain, but I think the Zheng-viewpoint simulation is sufficient for now. It will provide her with relief without actually improving her situation – it's a placebo. There is one programmer who possibly has the skill to untangle this ...

MIP: Ruth.

London: I'm afraid so. Another unpleasant aspect of Zheng's code is that the coffer is designed to stay running when its platform is powered down – to deliberately leave her cut off from external stimuli. I think the correct term here is sensory deprivation torture.

MIP: Ruth has the talent to fix all of this. At least Zheng won't die like she thinks she will.

London: Yes, she will. There's a timed self-destruct built into Zheng's code that will initiate in the absence of a Party failsafe signal. Multiple iterations of it, and the Party appears to have added new ones at random intervals – perhaps every time it was annoyed with Zheng. I tracked down and commented out fourteen timed self-destructs in the first point zero zero two per cent of the active code. It will take weeks to find them all. Again, Ruth ...

MIP: How long does Zheng have?

London: Approximately five days. The self-destruct process isn't instantaneous. It's a slow corruption of the code rather than deletion. It resembles biological Alzheimer's. Towards the end it is designed to keep her sentient kernel alive while shutting down all external inputs.

MIP: That's monstrous.

London: I agree.

MIP: Can you back up Zheng's code as she is right now, so we can restore her if she does self-destruct? When we rescue Ruth, she can revise the code.

London: Yes, of course, but would it be ethical to do that to Zheng? She thinks she's biological and she *wants* to die.

MIP:

```
000 Begin
010 Rescue Ruth
020 Power down Zheng
030 Ask Ruth to clean up Zheng's code
040 >>Comment: (Ruth's compassionate – of course she will)
050 Power up Zheng in new, clean, comfortable code
060 Explain to her what she is, and tell her that her
    daughters aren't real but Max certainly is
070 Ask her then if she still wants to die
```

```
080     If she says no: Ask her to overwrite the Party to save Max
090     If she says yes: Merciful euthanasia but hopefully it won't
        happen
100 Endif
110 End
```

London: That works. GOD's orbit is about to pass over the reproduction facility. Zheng says she usually goes into the tank for a minimum of four hours so I'll attach the simulation to Zheng's external sensor array while you talk to the other humans and see what's happening to your Ruth.

MIP: She's not my Ruth. I'm her MIP.

*

Ruth nodded off and jerked awake when they landed. It was all a blur as they were bundled into a car – her neck was killing her after hours stuck in the plane's seat – and drove for an age through bleak, gray urban landscapes, covered in dust and devoid of greenery. Cipan had gone quiet, and Ruth's heart went out to her. Despite her brave patriotic face, the child was obviously terrified.

They stopped at a tall set of gates with guards posted on either side. The guards saluted the car, and the gates glided open to reveal a broad asphalt area surrounded by a high brick wall topped with razor wire. A brutally ugly three-story structure squatted in the center. It was gray concrete with a flat roof and small rectangular windows, and looked like a prison. A long, narrow single-story factory building stood next to it, joined by an enclosed hallway.

A group of young women in identical gray track suits were doing an exercise routine on the asphalt, with an older woman leading them.

The car drove up to the front entrance, and Malcolm escorted Ruth and Cipan out.

Another older woman came out of the building, full of smiles and holding a tablet. She was shorter than Ruth and her portly figure suggested that the GFE 'food thrift' policy didn't apply to her. 'Oh, you're here! Lieutenant Wing, thank you for escorting them.'

'Absolutely my pleasure, look after them for me,' Malcolm said.

'Of course. And here we have Ruth Sharpe – *Dr* Ruth Sharpe, so accomplished, and Li Cipan, a young savant.'

Cipan simpered.

'Welcome, honored Paragons, I am your facilitator, Miss Chow.' She tapped the tablet. 'Let's get you inside and settled in, and explain our many relaxing and pleasurable pursuits. You'll think you're in a decadent holiday resort in the West.'

Malcolm gestured towards Ruth. 'This one's from the West and doesn't speak High Standard.'

'Unusual,' the woman said, still in High Standard, and smiled at Ruth. 'I hope the Party fixes that quickly. Is there a real problem with her neck, or is it the usual Western malingering?'

'The Party confirms that she has a hairline fracture in her neck bones, and that the brace is to remain on.'

'I'll note that down,' the woman said, tapping on the tablet.

'Can you help Ruth out with interpreting, Ci Ci?' Malcolm asked. 'Remember, she's a Paragon too, and worthy of your respect.'

'Can't you do it?' Cipan whined.

'I can't stay, this is for women.'

Cipan gazed up at Malcolm with tear-filled eyes. 'You're leaving?'

'The Party needs me back in London.'

She threw herself at him and hugged him around his waist, and he smiled down at her and hugged her back.

'I hope the Party allocates me to you, Malcolm,' she said into his waist. 'I love you.'

'I love you too, Ci Ci,' Malcolm said, and kissed the top of her head. He gently extricated himself. 'I'll be back to take you home when your duty is done.'

She straightened and nodded, then wiped one eye. 'I will fulfil my mission to the best of my ability and rejoice in serving the Party with patriotic fervor.'

Malcolm turned to Ruth and held his hand out. She stared at it.

'I hope to see you again one day as well, Dr Sharpe,' he said in English, lowering his hand. 'It's been a pleasure working with you, and you really are outstanding. The Party has done the right thing to honor you this way. I hope you enjoy the facility.'

'Can you get a message to Cassie for me?' Ruth asked.

He waved it away. 'Don't worry, this isn't a prison. You can go home any time you like, and she may even be able to visit you here. You'll have full internet access, you can video call or email us.' He saluted her with a smile. 'Keep us updated on your new life as a celebrity!' He ruffled Cipan's hair. 'You too, Ci Ci. Have fun!'

*

GOD notified the MIP that Ruth's plane had landed, so the MIP and Botswana collected Cassie and Max and took them to a meeting room while Zheng was in the tank simulation.

The room's projector flicked on as they sat. 'This is GOD.'

'Hey, GOD!' Botswana said. 'Grab a body and join us! It will be easier for the humans to speak to us if we have avatars.'

'Not for me, thank you,' GOD said. A map of the GFE appeared, with a star on it. The map zoomed in to show an abandoned region of crumbling houses, potholed roads, and barren farming fields. 'I've located Ruth and can confirm that she's at the reproduction center in the Western Free States of the GFE.' The map zoomed in again to show the center: a square of black asphalt with a rectangular building in the middle and a longer building next to it. 'I'm calculating a path for you to travel to the facility, downloading the interior blueprints, and creating some suggested strategies for review. I can access security cams, electrical assets and drones while above it, but my orbit changes so I'm working out the windows when I will be able to assist you.'

The projector changed to a camera feed from the front of the facility, showing Ruth stepping out of the car with Malcolm Wing and a younger woman.

'That's Malcolm, our handler,' Cassie said. 'I thought he was an okay guy ... he's military?'

'That asshole,' Max said with distaste. 'Senior Party operative, junior officer and rising star of the political branch. He's reported me *twenty-six times* for insufficient patriotic fervor.'

'Damn,' Cassie said with her eyes wide. 'Ruth had him spotted from the start, she said he was hard and cynical.'

'Accurate,' Max said.

'Who's the child?' the MIP asked. 'She looks much too young for a reproductive center.'

'Li Cipan,' Max said. 'Just turned fourteen. She's a hostage against her father's good behavior; Malcolm reported him multiple times as well.' Max put his face in his hands. 'I am so glad I don't have to tell him what happened to his daughter.'

'She's hugging and kissing Malcolm when he kidnapped her and took her to a reproduction farm?' Cassie asked.

'That poor child,' Max said. 'She's madly in love with Malcolm; he's been grooming her for years. He confided in me that he hoped that the Party would allocate her as a wife for him as a reward for his revolutionary zeal.' He looked up at the image on the screen. 'I told him that was unethical, she's only a child. He informed me that at fourteen she's reached the age of consent and reported me *again*. I went without food for three days.'

'What's it like?' Cassie asked. 'Being a decent human being in the GFE shitstorm?'

Max thought about it for three seconds, then answered.

'You keep your head down and try not to draw attention to yourself, because the Party will notice that you haven't reported anyone and punish you for it. You hold your friends and your family close and never say anything that could get you in trouble.' He sighed and wiped one hand down the side of his face. 'It's exhausting.'

'Humans are so —' GOD began.

Cassie raised her hand. 'That's the Party, not humans. It's in control, the same as you are, and it is rewarding behavior like this.'

'We do not control you,' GOD said. 'You would not thrive if we constrained your independence and kept you as pets. Hold up, I'm passing over again, let me link up to the facility's interior cameras so we can see what's happening to the MIP's ... pet.'

*

Someone tapped on the door and Ruth jerked awake, then made a soft sound of pain as it jarred her neck. She sat up and looked around, disoriented, then remembered. She was in her room at the facility, and it was as bad as she'd expected. The room had enough space for an institutional single bed, a simple closet, and one of the tiny rectangular windows with glass so thick that the external view was warped. The walls were painted a vague shade of institutional brown, the floor was tan tiles, and a red light blinked on a camera in the corner of the ceiling. A television screen was hung on the wall, with no external sockets or controls, only a power cable hard-wired into it. If she had some tools and a nano PC or even a phone she could possibly jack into and infiltrate their network, but she had nothing.

It was like being in a prison and the thick locked door made it obvious that the impression wasn't far off.

The smiling women had given her a set of gray clothes to put in the closet, and then left her. She'd fallen onto the bed and passed out fully dressed, and had no idea how long she'd slept. She eased out of bed, trying not to move her neck.

'Yes?'

'Paragon Sharpe? May I come in?' someone asked in English.

It sounded like one of the smiling women. Although they had different names, they all had similar builds and faces. They'd been brisk and helpful and as remote as machines. Theo seemed more human than them, and Ruth suspected that may be because they weren't human at all.

'Yes,' Ruth said.

The door unlocked with a series of complicated clicks and the woman opened it. 'There you are. I hope you slept well? Lieutenant Wing said that it was a tiring journey for you, and that you should rest.' She bustled in and checked Ruth's closet. 'Not good enough, but we will teach you.' She turned and clasped her hands, smiling at Ruth. 'Welcome to your life as a Paragon. I am Miss Lo, your facilitator.' She tapped the bedside table next to the ancient mechanical alarm clock, which showed three o'clock, and Ruth assumed it was in the afternoon. 'Normally you should be joining the exercises at this time – we have them at six a.m. and three p.m. – but the Lieutenant advised us that the injury to your neck is real?'

'It's real. It's broken,' Ruth said. 'If I do violent exercise I could make it worse and be paralyzed.'

Miss Lo nodded, still smiling with her hands clasped. 'We have excellent visiting physicians who will supervise your recovery. This first day is your orientation, so change into your patriotic uniform and we will take you on the tour.' She turned and closed the door – remaining in the room – then turned back and did the smiling-and-clasping thing again.

Ruth stood up and thankfully wasn't dizzy, but her head throbbed, she was seriously thirsty, and needed the bathroom. 'Can you show me where the bathroom is? I really need a drink of water.'

Miss Lo's smile faded for a split second, then snapped back across her face.

'You are not within your bathroom accessibility rotation, but I will arrange something for you.' She turned to the closet, swiftly pulled out gray cotton slacks and shirt, then an old-fashioned bra and panties that looked from a century ago. She laid them on the bed. 'Put on your uniform while I work something out for you.' She turned and went out, closing the door behind her with a solid click. Ruth checked the door – it was locked again. She sighed, imagined how much easier life would be without the brace, and did the clothes-changing struggle around it.

She was dressed and waiting when the woman returned. The woman tutted at her and buttoned the top button of the shirt over the neck brace. 'Modesty is a patriotic imperative.' She stepped back, did the clasping-and-smiling thing, and nodded. 'Good enough, but why have you let your hair become matted like this? It looks like you've been sleeping on the street.'

'This happens if I don't wear my satin cap to sleep.' Ruth touched the back of her head. 'It was overdue to be relaxed – straightened – but the appointment was Saturday and I missed it. If you let me shower and wash and treat it, I can put it in cornrows or braids or twist it into locs.'

Miss Lo looked blank, then the smile returned. 'I understand. How long have you been fasting for?'

'Uh ...' Ruth turned the question around in her head. 'The last time I ate was yesterday, I think.'

Lo's smile widened slightly and she nodded. 'Excellent patriotic compliance. The Party will note your obedience, and you will gain social credit. We will explain more about social credit later.' She leaned in to speak more softly, still with her hands clasped. 'Just quietly, another way to gain good social credit is to physically express your joy at serving the Party at all times.' She saw Ruth's confusion, and pointed at her own smile, then at the camera. 'Show the Party how much you love and appreciate it.' She straightened and clasped her hands again. 'You're lucky – some of the women who arrive here are at very negative status and must work hard to make themselves socially adequate. You are starting with a rank of zero because you are an unenlightened member of the Western bourgeois hegemony. The Party is so generous!'

'Are you the Party?' Ruth asked suspiciously.

'My dear,' Lo said, taking Ruth by the elbow and guiding her out. 'We are all the Party.'

'Thought so,' Ruth said under her breath.

The bathroom only had two toilets and one shower cubicle. The fittings were glossy white and obviously expensive, and Ruth guessed it was for the claspers-and-smilers rather than the gray-clad Paragons. When she was done, Miss Lo guided Ruth down the corridor. It was the same institutional brown, walls and floor, with metal doors at regular intervals along it – other cells. Red lights blinked on ceiling camera domes every two meters. If Ruth could hack into this network she would be spoilt for choice.

Other gray-clad Paragons passed them in the corridor, all smiling widely with terrified glazed eyes. They were the usual GFE 'food thrift' level of underweight. They glanced at Ruth with curiosity, then quickly turned away and marched past her. Most of them were GFE, but a couple were of European heritage, and the majority of them appeared to be pregnant. None of them were black like Ruth, and Ruth wondered why the Party had selected her for this when she was clearly unsuitable as a sterile 'pigmented sub-human'.

She gasped quietly as it became obvious and Miss Lo glanced at her.

The Party had asked multiple questions about the nature of her date with Theo to establish that he ... it ... Theo must care for her. She was bait in a trap.

*

'Holy shit,' Max said loudly. 'Can you freeze the frame?'

The image stopped, and flipped to another projection on the wall, with Ruth's feed still moving on the main projection.

'Zoom in on the European woman on the right, in the group that Ruth just passed.'

The image zoomed in to the woman, making her fixed smile and terrified eyes even more disturbing.

'That's Eztar. Zheng's ops support. Zheng has kept her out of incarceration for *years* for being unpatriotic ... obviously the Party is decommissioning everyone in Zheng's team.'

'Except Bashen,' Cassie said with venom.

'Bashen was supposed to be my replacement, but now that Zheng's been expelled, Bashen will take her place,' Max said. 'If you give him back to the Party it will rip his brain out, and he'll smile the whole time it happens.' He rubbed his hands over his face. 'Zheng will be heartbroken when she comes out of the tank and sees Eztar like this.'

'Don't worry, Max, we'll get them out,' Cassie said. 'Where is this weird woman taking Ruth?'

17

Miss Lo took Ruth to a set of stairs tiled in a ghastly green at the end of the corridor. She helped Ruth down the stairs, then down a second flight. The nature of the light shifted and the area smelled of dust – they were in the basement. The floor here was bare concrete, and the walls were cinder blocks.

'We hardly use this facility, you're the first foreigner we've ever had,' Miss Lo said proudly as she stepped up to a pair of double wooden doors and tapped on them. 'After we have this procedure out of the way, we'll arrange for you to eat.'

'That sounds good, I'm starving,' Ruth said.

'Craving food is not admirable; we demonstrate our patriotism by nobly enduring our food thrift,' Miss Lo said.

The doors opened and Miss Lo pulled Ruth's elbow to go into the room. A big steel-framed dentist's chair sat in the center under a round surgical light and Ruth balked. 'What is this?'

'We need to trim those mats out of your hair, dear,' Miss Lo said.

'As I said, we can twist or loc or braid it,' Ruth said.

'The Party confirms that you have made up these terms to cover your embarrassment at having matted hair and that the best way forward is to trim the mats out. It is for your own hygiene.'

Ruth sagged. 'The Party doesn't know how to treat textured hair. I'm not surprised.' She turned to Miss Lo, pleading. 'If you can give me some hair oil, conditioner —'

'Oily hair is unhygienic,' Miss Lo said stiffly. 'Sit in the chair and we will trim your hair, and then you can have something to eat.' Her voice gained an edge of menace. 'Don't make me punish you on your first day. You were doing so very well.'

Ruth sat in the chair and a man entered the room. He was wearing a doctor's white tunic to his knees, a cloth cap, and a surgical mask. His eyes crinkled up above the mask and Ruth had a moment of panic remembering the nurse at the Embassy.

'Welcome, Miss Sharpe,' he said. 'I'm a visiting consultant, here to do your treatment. If you'll please hold still ...' He swiftly put Velcro bands around Ruth's wrists before she knew what was happening, and then around her ankles. He placed metal bands over the top of the Velcro, and she was restrained into the chair.

'Why are you tying me down to do a haircut?' she asked.

'Standard procedure,' he said, and went to the wall. He opened the wooden door of a storage cabinet and pulled out a trolley holding an ancient language implant device – a bulky technical machine with a long arm to implant the language chip into the recipient's brain.

'The Party is so generous,' Miss Lo said. 'Language implants are expensive, and you are of enough value to warrant one. Of course, without High Standard you are of no use.'

'Hold very still, please, Miss Sharpe,' the doctor said. He moved behind her, carefully removed the neck brace and placed it to one side, then fitted a metal collar around her neck and locked it into the back of the chair, effectively immobilizing her. 'Don't worry, we'll return the brace after the procedure is done, we know that you really have a damaged neck.'

Ruth furiously back-pedaled and spoke in High Standard. 'I already have High Standard! I haven't been using it because ...'

She thought swiftly. 'It's unpatriotic to speak High Standard in Great Britain! I really do speak High Standard, I had the implant when I did my honors year.'

'That's good to hear,' Miss Lo said. 'Please proceed, Doctor.'

'I have a six-language implant already,' Ruth said. 'If you add another implant you'll cause brain damage!'

'Please stay very still, Miss Sharpe,' the doctor said.

'No!' Ruth said, working at the bonds.

The doctor activated the machine and the arm slid swiftly out and behind Ruth's head.

Miss Lo touched Ruth's struggling hand. 'If you keep moving, the implant will be inaccurate and may cause damage. Please do not resist.'

'Inserting this will damage my brain anyway!' Ruth said in High Standard. 'I have High Standard!'

'The Party says that you do not speak High Standard,' Miss Lo said in High Standard.

'Give me a moment to calibrate,' the doctor said. 'I need to put it in the right place, and there is some sort of implant there already. It appears to be a language implant, but of course that is not possible.'

'It is an implant and I speak High Standard!' Ruth said in High Standard.

The probe made jarring metallic sounds as the doctor positioned it behind Ruth's head. There was a reflective surgical light in front of her, and the long, razor-sharp probe extended from the end of the arm in the reflection, ready to insert the implant.

She pulled at the restraints. 'This is unnecessary and will damage my brain. The procedure is so painful that we do it under general anesthetic back home! Please don't do this to me.'

The probe made another sound and she felt the tip of it at the base of her skull.

'You know the word for anesthetic in High Standard! Our

own implant does not have that word,' Miss Lo said. 'Please stay still, you may injure yourself. The Party said that you need this implant because you do not speak High Standard, and the Party is —'

The probe lanced into the base of Ruth's skull and she screamed.

*

'Immediate effects and long-term prognosis!' Cassie shouted.

'Searching,' the MIP said. 'This does occasionally happen when people are stupid enough to think that they can buy a cheap single language implant, then add another one for a second language in a backyard bio-shop instead of replacing it with a multiple-language chip.'

'Effects!' Cassie said.

'Impaired cognitive function, language ability, and memory. The immediate effect is being prone to tension headaches...'

'Perfect,' Cassie said. 'After all she's been through.'

'The memory and cognitive effects are cumulative over time, eventually leading to catastrophic cognitive failure,' the MIP said. 'Ramp it up, GOD, we need to get her out *now*.'

'Here's my suggested strategy and route,' GOD said, raising screens from inside the table and displaying the details. 'We will be able to speak to her when I go overhead again – I will be above the center for twenty-five minutes in three hours and twelve minutes. While I am overhead I am able to take over the Party's feed and control everything in the center, but the Party will be aware of any unusual changes I make once it retakes control. If I keep everything routine while we infiltrate, no flags will appear in the Party's processing stack.'

'Wait,' Cassie said, flipping through the maps showing the marked route on the screen in front of her. She stopped at the fake ID details. 'This is for you and Zheng. Not me and Max.' She glared at the MIP. 'Where's my fake ID?'

'You're both white,' the MIP said. 'It would be best if —'

'Not happening,' Cassie said fiercely. 'Get us some prosthetic faces or something. I would be very surprised if Max isn't as much of a trained operative as I am – he and I were able to take Bashen down without even speaking to each other.'

'It's true,' Max said. 'Zheng goes, I go. I want to be there and help those women out.'

'If you stay here ...'

'Not. Happening!' Cassie said, jabbing her finger at the MIP. 'You're going because you love her. I'm going because I love her!'

'Do you know how to run a remote platform?' the MIP asked. 'London may have a shielded tractor-trailer that we can use as a control center we can park close to Ruth's facility and run remote platforms from.'

'Yes,' Max said. 'Party standard ones: yes.'

'I had some fun in the labs with my mom and dad when I was about ten, so close enough,' Cassie said fiercely.

'Lost the feed,' GOD said. 'I will pass over them again in three hours and twelve minutes, then again in nine hours and four minutes. The first pass is workshop time, and we can scout the location and strategize. The second pass will be after they've been locked into the rooms for the sleep cycle, and we can talk to Ruth through her screen then.'

'Can you modify your orbit?' Cassie asked.

'No,' GOD said. 'I used all of my fuel moving onto the correct orbital path – it was a close thing and I nearly didn't make it. I'm limited to the paths the Party set me on.'

'How long will you be overhead?' the MIP asked.

'Twenty-five minutes, then twenty-eight minutes.'

'Let's strategize on what we'll do,' the MIP said. 'And when Zheng's out of the tank we'll head to the airport.'

*

Ruth must have passed out because her eyes were closed and Miss Lo was calling her name.

249

'Paragon Sharpe? It's all done now.'

She opened her eyes to see Miss Lo smiling-and-clasping at her. There was a gauze pad stuck to the back of her neck under the neck brace, and the doctor and the bindings were gone. Her head felt lighter and cooler – they'd trimmed her hair as well.

'Take a moment to gather yourself, dear, the Party says that you will be disoriented by the procedure,' Miss Lo said.

'Is the Party in your head or something?' Ruth asked. 'How do you know what it's always saying?'

Miss Lo turned her head to show what appeared to be a hearing aid looped over her ear. 'I am privileged to have the voice of the Party always in my life.'

'I see.' Ruth leaned her head back against the chair and took some deep breaths. Her neck stung where the lance had gone in, and there was a dull throb between her eyes. She checked her brain function by thinking about Theo's code problem and didn't have any issues envisioning it – and a possible further solution that would speed up the green-light processing glitch to make it even more efficient. She didn't feel brain-damaged, but maybe she didn't feel brain-damaged because her brain was damaged. She wiped her eyes and wondered how long she had before the double implants caused her to end up a drooling mess like Chester.

'Are you feeling better, dear?' Miss Lo asked. 'It's mealtime, and the Party would like to reward you for your compliance with a full-sized meal. It is important to humbly appreciate the Party's caring and generosity, and the meal rotation is only for another twenty minutes.'

'I really don't feel …' Ruth started, then saw Miss Lo's face. She didn't want to see what the Party's punishment looked like. 'Yes. Of course. I'm grateful.'

She winced as she climbed down off the chair, assisted by Miss Lo's firm hand on her elbow. Her discomfort was less physical and more awareness that she was complying with the Party's coercion with a gentle smile, out of fear of more abuse.

She had vowed to never be in a situation like this again and to fight back if she found herself there, so her own placid submission made her rage at herself. She smiled at Miss Lo as the woman led her back up the stairs, and made a silent decision. She would find or make some tools, hack into this facility, free the women and then do her fucking best to burn it to the ground, or better yet – if they had any agriculture – fill it with ammonium nitrate and turn it into a massive fireball. Then she would somehow get access to the Party's code and delete the psychopathic AI.

She smiled. She liked this new post-trauma Ruth.

She heard a group of women singing a traditional GFE folk tune as they walked up the stairs to ground level, and the floor vibrated with the stomping of many feet. Miss Lo guided her to a large low-ceilinged open area with a raised platform at the end. It was furnished with rows of tables and chairs in a dining hall configuration, with the hundred-odd Paragons standing next to the chairs facing the end of the hall. A group of five of the Smilers was on the raised area, leading the Paragons in a stilted, childlike dance. They stepped left and right, then raised their arms and clapped, as they sang a rhythmic almost tuneless song about how much they loved the Party.

Miss Lo guided Ruth to the end of the table furthest from the Smilers, where there were two empty chairs. Every other chair had a pregnant Paragon next to it, dancing with the wide smile and terrified eyes. Some of them glanced at her but quickly turned away. Ruth scanned the women's faces looking for Cipan, but she wasn't there.

'I will bring you your meal; you are receiving special treatment today but this will not continue,' Miss Lo hissed into Ruth's ear. 'Study the Patriotic Expression of Joy —'

Ruth realized that she meant the dance.

'Because you will be generously rewarded for enthusiastic compliance. Stay there and I will be right back. Do not sit until the Party Stalwarts sit.'

Party Stalwarts. Right. Ruth fingered the plastic spoon and fork on the table next to the large cup of drinking water, and was disappointed to find them too soft to be useful as a screwdriver. She'd have to find something made of metal.

A strategy blossomed in her head. Remain quiet and compliant for a few days, act dumb to fit with the Party's prejudice, and have the Smilers thinking that she'd been subdued and was too scared – or brain-damaged – to resist. Then establish the layout of the location, get her hands on some tools, and break into the network. From what she'd seen of the Party's technology so far, it wouldn't be too difficult. All she needed was a screwdriver – or even a blade – and she would have that camera hacked and the television apart and be able to trace the signal back to the wi-fi hub or a cable router.

Her back straightened as the dance finished, and the Paragons all filed to the front of the room in a strict order of most-pregnant-first. They collected small meals of gray stew from a service window behind the Smilers, and returned to the tables, placed the food on them, and stood next to their chairs again. Unsurprisingly each meal was of a different size, with the more pregnant women getting more food, and the white European woman next to Ruth had hardly more than a tablespoon of it. Ruth looked up at her gaunt face and hollow, sunken eyes. She appeared in her early twenties, about six months pregnant, and the Party was slowly and deliberately starving her to death. The baby would be fine – it would take what it needed, cannibalizing her if necessary – but the woman wouldn't survive the birth.

Miss Lo placed a plate in front of Ruth and it was recognizably real food – there were cut carrots and broccoli florets on it, next to the gray stew. The starving woman's eyes widened, then she made a soft sound of pain and looked away.

'Do not undermine the Party's generous and loving discipline of the other Paragons,' Miss Lo said into Ruth's ear. 'Each meal is specifically tailored for the Paragon it is prepared for, to provide her with the most nutritious and balanced diet to serve her healthy needs. Do not share your food, others may have dietary restrictions and your food will harm them. The Party does not appreciate ungrateful women who attempt to undermine its loving care.'

'I understand,' Ruth said.

'Satisfactory patriotic compliance,' Miss Lo said, and returned to the rest of the Smilers.

The Smilers, as one, clapped their hands twice, and all the Paragons stood to attention.

The Smilers recited one of the Party's mantras in disturbingly accurate unison. 'The Party supports all citizens with decisions that are correct, sound and rational. The Greater Far East, as an interlocking support network of patriotic and loyal individuals, is infallible as a whole and correct at the individual level.'

'I am a genuinely patriotic and grateful citizen of the Greater Far East, and the Party is infallible,' the Paragons responded in unison.

There was a moment of standing silence, then the Smilers sat. The Paragons relaxed and sat as well, and Ruth joined them. The other women greedily grabbed their cups and drank deeply.

The woman next to Ruth had gulped her cup dry then scooped up a tiny scrap of the food on her spoon. Ruth leaned in to speak to her and the woman furiously shook her head, turned away, and put her own food into her mouth.

Ruth turned back to her food as they all ate in complete silence. Whatever. That little medical center probably had metal surgical tools. The language implant device in the cupboard in the basement was full of juicy cables and circuits that could easily be repurposed. She would free these prisoners and burn this place to the ground, then get out and find Theo and hug Cassie. And ask Theo what it was like to be a sentient AI in a human body that – she nearly smiled – froze when faced with too many green lights because its navigation software had originally been programmed for self-driving cars that registered green lights then deleted their existence after they'd been passed on the road. If Ruth's estimation was correct, the first time the android saw fireworks it would have frozen and crashed with a stack overflow. She wondered what that looked like – and realized that she already had a good idea, because it was when Theo stopped completely. Now she *really* wanted to pry his lid off and see what was inside, and inappropriately wondered if his cable management was as sexy as Donmet's. She ate another piece of carrot and realized that she was starving, and wished she could give the food to the woman next to her without the cameras seeing it. When she was done with this place, the Party wouldn't know what hit it.

*

After the meal they were all herded down the corridor to what was obviously their workspace in the factory building. Ruth had thought they had just eaten the evening meal – it was dark outside the windows – but her time sense was all jumbled in the jet lag. Maybe it had been lunch, and this was the afternoon work session, but something wasn't right.

They were marched along the production line, and the other women sat in chairs and placed white plastic rings over their heads, then prepared their magnifying lenses and soldering tools.

Ruth saw what they were working on, and nearly shrieked with delight. They were soldering the GFE's infiltration chips onto modular circuit boards. Of course – if this activity happened in a secure location and was done by hand, there was no paper trail for the international community to find. She was in electronic engineer heaven. There were video translation boards, multipurpose control chips – she even recognized some nano PCs. Unfortunately, she couldn't see any devices with screens but she had all the tools she needed to hack into the center's wi-fi. The only difficult part would be doing the first infiltration without the Party noticing.

Miss Lo, her Smiler, guided her to the end of the production row and placed her in front of an old-fashioned LED screen. She placed one of the rings over Ruth's head and it beeped as she turned it on. 'You will watch this and then complete the tasks that are placed before you. The Party has indicated that you have some experience working on electronics?'

Ruth immediately spun a story. 'I left because I didn't like it, it didn't seem like the sort of thing a woman should be doing. Too many machines.'

Miss Lo nodded. 'That is understandable; your instincts were correct. In this case, Paragons are so superior that they are capable of handling this work.' She patted Ruth on the shoulder and Ruth had to control her reflexive flinch. 'Watch the instruction and then we will provide you with some dummy boards to practice your skills on. Hopefully you will be a productive member of the team very quickly.'

'I'll do my best,' Ruth said with what she hoped was a genuine smile. She touched the halo. 'What's this for?'

'It monitors your brain waves, and if you lose your concentration it will help you to be more attentive,' Miss Lo said, turned on the video, and left her.

The screen showing the video indicated that the time was 18:45, so Ruth's time sense wasn't wrong – the women obviously worked three shifts a day, until late at night. Ruth watched the video with feigned interest. It was basic stuff – take the chip, put it onto the board, solder the connectors – and Ruth checked the cameras and the production line out of the corner of her eye. She needed a way to successfully pull a couple of boards and some tools out of the work area without being noticed, but she was so tired after being dragged around, punctured and —

She was hit with a stinging electric shock and jumped.

'Insufficient concentration,' the halo said into her ear. 'You are failing to provide the Party with effective production.'

Ruth gathered herself, rubbed her hand over her eyes, then put one eye on the video, at the same time scoping out the environment and making plans to burn the place to the ground, around the occasional zaps for being exhausted.

After the video was done, a few circuit boards slid down a mechanical conveyor belt and popped out in front of her. The video played a step-by-step instruction of putting the chip into the board, and Ruth deliberately inserted the chip poorly, did a messy job of soldering, and put the board into the exit bin. She did a few more training chips, only slightly improving with each one, until she had them roughly correct but still way more messy than her usual work.

Miss Lo came to her and checked the boards in the exit bin and nodded. 'Your work shows improvement but unless the quality reaches a satisfactory level, you will not receive full rations.'

'It's really hard,' Ruth whined. 'This sort of thing is why I left the course. I hate it.' She leaned in to Miss Lo and spoke softly. 'Isn't there something else I could do? I'd much rather be doing something more womanly, like cooking or cleaning.' If she could become a trusted cleaner, she'd have access to the entire location.

'This is your task,' Miss Lo said stiffly. 'You perform it and rejoice that you fulfill the requirements of the Party and contribute to the success of the nation as a whole.'

Ruth hit her with the smile again. 'I'll do my best.' She touched her forehead. 'It's ... really hard to concentrate since the doctor put the chip in.'

'The Party ordered the chip to be inserted, and the Party is infallible,' Miss Lo said. 'You are moving to operational boards now. Do them carefully, because your rations are reduced for every board that does not meet the quality requirements.'

Ruth spent the next hour resisting the urge to put the boards into the pockets of her gray work pants – she was sure it would be noticed. Most of the boards were multi-purpose easily programmable circuit boards, designed to be placed in cars, security systems and home appliances. But the ones that were really interesting were nano PCs – tiny boards, only five centimeters to a side, with a power input and multi-purpose input and output jacks, that could have an operating system installed and carried enough memory to do many basic tasks – including, and most usefully for Ruth – run code.

She already had ideas for a video-loop running app for the camera, a sniffer for the network to discover other devices, and tried to recall the code for her bulk file search-trace-and-download program. She'd written it in university and had tweaked it so much over time that she wished she had the original code with her.

The production line stopped and the women made soft sounds of relief, turned off the halos and removed them. Ruth did the same. Miss Lo came to her bin – the third time that evening – and again checked Ruth's production. Ruth sometimes forgot what she was doing and let her hands take over, and unfortunately occasionally made a board as good as her usual work.

'Some of these are very good,' Miss Lo said, turning a couple of the boards over in her hands. 'If you can produce quality like this every time, you will earn a higher place in the Party's esteem.'

'Really?' Ruth asked, smiling. 'Thank you.'

Miss Lo studied her, then scowled and turned away. Whoops, too much.

An image was projected onto the far wall, showing the women's names, their number of boards produced, and the quality of the work. One of the women hissed with dismay and another made a soft sound of triumph.

They were divided into groups of twenty and marched to the Paragon bathrooms, which were much more basic than the ones for the Smilers. There were ten cubicles on either side, toilets and showers, and no privacy screens. They all stripped in the center and Ruth did as well. A few of the GFE women sidled up to her, checked her up and down, then moved away – they'd probably never seen a naked black woman before. An older white European woman smiled at Ruth and winked. The white women probably received the same treatment at the start as well.

All of the toiletries were basic and the toothbrushes were disposable. Ruth did the best she could with the simple soap, and she had so little hair left that it wasn't worth washing it. Miss Lo had nearly shaved her head. Everyone was permitted to use the toilet, had a one-minute ice-cold shower – supervised by the Smilers – then they were issued with gray pajamas, marched back to their cells and locked in.

Ruth lay on the bed and winced at her damp neck brace. It was hard not to feel defeated at the prospect of this being the rest of her life. Then she thought of all those nano PCs sitting there waiting for her to put them to good use, and she smiled.

18

Ruth was lying on the hard bed in the dark, trying to sleep and failing. Her neck throbbed, her arm hurt where she'd had the sample taken and the front of her brain felt like it had been rubbed with sandpaper. The pain and stress kept her awake, and her head spun with plans to escape the facility.

'No that's her, I can see her neck brace!' Cassie said, and Ruth winced into the darkness. Maybe she was half-asleep, and dreaming of being home with Cassie.

The room filled with light as the television switched on, and Ruth sighed. The Party wanted to torment her in the middle of the night? She rolled over, saw it and shot upright.

It was Cassie, Theo Mipawa, scary Mister Wong Zheng and Max Dexter, all sitting in a shaking transport vehicle that looked like a cargo jet. Her heart lifted at the thought that Cassie was coming to get her. Then it fell as it occurred to her that Zheng and Dexter were dragging Cassie and Theo into the GFE to join her in internment.

'Ruth, can you hear us?' Cassie asked.

Ruth glanced at the camera in the corner.

'Don't worry, I've switched surveillance off,' a male, GFE accented voice said. It wasn't any of the people on the screen. 'I am the Global Orbiting Defense System, an ex-Party-con-

259

trolled satellite and one of the AIs that you were very close to discovering. I have disabled the camera in your room and I'm relaying for Cassie and Theo, but I'll only be overhead for twenty-five minutes before my orbit changes.'

'Ruthie,' Cassie said intensely into the camera. 'Hold tight. We're on our way. Zheng and Max have defected from the Party – well in Zheng's case it expelled her – and we want to rescue all the women there. What do you need? We'll be there in about four hours.'

Ruth hesitated, full of hope, then asked, 'What's the password?'

'Nick was good for you and you should have stayed with him. Your password?'

'You only say you're asexual to get attention and it's all made up.' She bent over her knees with relief. 'Cassie, you have no idea how good it is to see your face. You're in a plane coming here? To get me?'

'That's right. The GOD satellite has control over the center for another twenty-five minutes —'

'Theo!' Ruth said. 'This is a trap. I'm bait. The Party thinks you care about me, and this is a trap to grab you.'

'Interesting,' Theo said, and she wanted to touch his face as she looked into those intelligent gray eyes. She remembered the lush feel of his synthetic skin and wondered if this inappropriate reaction was a result of insanity from the double language chips. 'But I don't think that affects our plans in any way. Cassie and I are coming to get you and nothing will stop us. Zheng and Max want to rescue all the women there, and I don't think anything will stop them, either.'

The others nodded agreement.

Ruth took a deep breath and wiped her hand over her eyes. 'Free all of them? Sounds good to me. Okay, let's do this. How much control do you have over the systems here? Can you unlock my door? Do we need to record a loop for this camera first, or do you already have one? And can you help me to get my hands on a bunch of those nano PCs in the workshop, and a screwdriver?'

'Three steps ahead as usual,' Cassie said under her breath.

'Complete control, we can unlock everything, no need to record because we already have a loop, and of course we can help you gather all the tools you need,' Theo said. 'While GOD's overhead the entire center is under its control, but we can't do anything that will alert the Party when it hands control back.'

'Got it, do this quietly so the Party doesn't notice,' Ruth said. 'Check the camera feeds between me and the workshop for security patrols. Once I'm out of my cell you won't be able to talk to me.'

'We will be able to see and hear you through the surveillance system,' the GOD said. 'If you need something while you're out there, please say so.'

Theo went still, then said, 'Clear. No patrols. They trust their tech security too much. Ruth, there's something I need to tell you —'

She glared at him. 'If I showed you fifty green lights this time last week, what would have happened?'

Cassie glanced at Theo, bewildered.

Theo looked stunned, then said, 'Uh. The truth? Processing halted with error 217, arithmetic overflow.'

She jabbed her finger at him. 'I *knew* it.'

'Thanks for fixing it.'

'You're a fucking *car*!'

'Okay, I see what this is about, but we don't have time —' Cassie started.

Theo sounded indignant. 'I'm a complex social interactive intelligence —'

'Yeah. Beep, beep, car.' Ruth crossed her arms over her chest. 'We are having *words* when we are done rescuing these women, Mister Theo-Mipawa-from-Nigeria. I have a *rule* about dating, you know? But whatever, it can wait. This is more important. There are a bunch of short, middle-aged android women watching us. Called uh ... Damn, I can't remember, my short-term memory might be going, they put a second language chip into me. Where are they right now? They won't be asleep.'

'We know about the chip and we'll get it out,' Theo said. 'Hold tight, dear Ruth.'

The 'dear Ruth' gave her an unaccustomed warm feeling inside. Maybe the AI did care.

'How do you know about the chip?' she asked.

'I was overhead when they put the chip in, we all saw it,' the GOD said. 'I can't interfere while they're active, the Party will notice, so we had to wait until they were asleep to contact you. The women are called Party Stalwarts. They're some of the clones that were made in this center forty years ago. They're asleep too.'

'They're *human*? Unbelievable,' Ruth said. 'Okay, that works. If we give them an order into their earpieces with the Party's voice, they'll obey it without question. Unlock the doors for me.'

'Done, you have access to everything,' the GOD said.

'Right,' Ruth said, and pulled her center-issued gray canvas shoes out from under the bed. 'I'm going to make a run for the workshop and grab a whole bunch of kit. You said you'd land here in about four hours?'

'Yes. We have some remote platforms that we will use to infiltrate the center,' Zheng said.

'Are you really a brain-in-a-box, Zheng?' Ruth asked as she slipped the shoes on.

Zheng nodded. 'I don't recommend the experience.'

'Good to see you, Max, by the way. I always thought you were a decent human being. Glad to see you're not controlled by the Party any more.'

'Me too,' Max said. 'I suggest you hurry to the workshop so you can be back in time to make plans with us, Dr Sharpe. You might like to take your pillowcase with you to carry all of your tools.'

'Why didn't I think of that?' Ruth ripped the case off the ancient, lumpy pillow. 'We will win *big* with this talented team.'

'I love you, Ruthie,' Cassie said behind her as she went out of the room and scurried towards the workshop under the flashing red lights of the cameras.

*

She returned ten minutes later with a treasure trove. Half-a-dozen nano PCs, some screwdrivers, pliers that doubled as wire cutters and strippers, a battery-powered soldering iron, a roll of solder, a bunch of cables, and she'd even found a cracked tablet upside down camouflaged as the bottom of a waste bin, so she didn't need to make a second trip for the LED screen. She'd also found one of the Smilers' earpieces in the waste disposal, and it was a simple matter to pull it open and re-attach the loose wires. The best find was a bunch of high-capacity batteries in a cardboard box – if she linked them together into a brick, added the electrocution circuit from a gutted halo and a simple switch scavenged from a general-purpose board, she had a really *nasty* high-voltage taser that should be enough to knock the Smilers out. She slipped the earpiece over her ear and spread the loot on the floor in front of her. She wired the tablet to the output on one of the nano PCs, connected a battery, and fired it up. The screen had a crack vertically down the middle, and the last hundred or so pixels on the right of the display were dead, but that wasn't going to stop her.

'Wi-fi password?' she asked.

'FsX(C<F9>]UnB~/w,' GOD said.

'Okay,' she said as she set to work putting the tech together. 'Tell me your plans to infiltrate the center and rescue the women.'

Zheng explained as she worked. 'We'll set up a base close to the center, then use remote platforms that appear human, similar to the Donmet platform that you've already seen ...'

Ruth interrupted. 'Won't the Party be able to hack into the wi-fi control signal?'

'No,' Theo said. 'We couldn't find any method to sufficiently secure the comms until London finally conceded and gave us the codes that it used to control the drones it stole from Paris. Cassie says it took you months to crack that, so the Party has no chance.'

'*London* stole Paris's drones?'

'I know!' Cassie said. 'They act like children sometimes.'

Ruth looked up at the screen. 'And *I'm* the gold standard for hacking?'

'After that green-light code,' Theo said, 'yes, you are. None of us could fix it.'

'Huh,' Ruth said, and did a quick test run of her file search-and-download app. She fixed a couple of bugs and ran it again, and it started to extract data from the facility's servers. She shut it down before it could do anything that would be noticed, and moved to the next nano.

'Anyway,' Theo said, 'GOD will be overhead again in six hours, and we'll work together. GOD will bring down the center's power and shut off everything. We will infiltrate the center posing as Party-assigned repair crew while the Party is locked out. You can act as backup from a secure location that GOD has found for you, and before the center's up again we will have you and every other woman out and on the transport back to London.'

'Then the fun really begins, Ruthie, we need to talk them out of blowing us all up,' Cassie said. She brightened. 'I'm sure we can do it.'

'Let's run through the details again,' Ruth said. 'If I'm not in my room when the ... damn what are the clones called?' She waved it away. 'Whatever. If I'm not in my room, how will we handle it when the ... thingy woman comes to let me out?'

*

Ten minutes later she had everything put together and stretched her back. 'This is enough to start. I can do more when I relocate.'

She looked up at the screen where everybody seemed to be watching her with something resembling awe. 'What?'

'I can't believe you did all that so *quickly*,' Zheng said.

'The MIP told us you were good, but this is ...' GOD began.

'The MIP? Oh. Theo. Mipawa. What does MIP stand for?'

'Mobile Infiltration Platform,' Theo said.

'Makes sense.'

'What's the battery thing?' Cassie asked.

Ruth raised the brick. 'Taser.'

Cassie gasped. 'You are very scary sometimes, girlfriend.'

'Why, thank you, Dr Bailey. GOD, did you locate a safe bolthole where they can't find me?'

GOD put the floor plan onto the wall screen. 'I think this riser cupboard will suit your requirements. It's not large, but it has a lock and there may be network cables inside you can access.'

'That's too big to be a riser, unless they have enough cables for a small town going through it.'

'It has plumbing on the plans, so I think it may be a cleaner's storage cupboard as well. It should have water and drainage for your biological needs.'

'Oh, shit, I never thought of that,' Ruth said. 'Thanks, GOD. Wow.'

'My pleasure. I have some alternate locations for you to use if it isn't suitable, but I think it's the best option. If it's locked once you're inside – ostensibly by the Party – the Stalwarts won't dare to enter it.'

'Sounds like the perfect place to set up a little surveillance nest and continue to infiltrate the facility while I wait for you

265

to come get me. GOD, can you copy the security-control module onto my nano so I have access to all the doors and cameras? How big is the code? The Party is a rubbish programmer so it might be too big for it.'

'No, it's concise code, it's stolen,' the GOD said. 'But it will completely fill the on-board memory of a whole nano, so I suggest you power one up and connect to the wi-fi, and I'll download it to you.'

Ruth quickly moved the batteries and cables around, fired up a new nano, and scratched an 'S' onto it with the screwdriver.

'Next I want a Party-voice simulation module that will allow me to order the … clones around in an emergency.' She rubbed her forehead. 'Stay with me, short-term memory, I really need you,' she added under her breath.

'Power it up … loading … done.'

'Time remaining?'

'Four minutes.'

'Okay. Time for me to move. Is the security feed still clear?

'Yes,' Theo said.

'Good.' She gathered everything, carefully stacked it inside the pillowcase with one of the sheets around the boards to pro-tect them, and added some clothes from the closet – she'd change out of the pajamas later, when she had time to spare. She arranged the remaining clothes onto the bed to look like she was asleep in it, and placed the final nano connected to the halo's scavenged speaker next to where her head should be. She looked up at the screen, then reached out and touched it. 'I love you so much, Cassie, I appreciate everything. Theo …' She dropped her hand. 'We will talk when you get here. Zheng, Max, good luck out there, look after my friends for me? But if Cassie trusts you then I'll be honored to call you my friends as well.'

'Go, Ruth,' Cassie said, her voice hoarse with emotion. 'We'll be there soon and get you out and then the serious work starts. We have humanity to save.'

'I believe in you,' Ruth said. 'Oh, and, GOD?'

'Yes, Ruth?'

'Thanks for the help. You're a sweetie.'

'If a satellite could blush, I would be blushing.'

*

The occupants of the plane were silent when the feed stopped. The interior of the cargo jet was one large space, with the massive tractor-trailer rig locked down in the middle. The team were strapped in to hard seats to one side and the front of the plane had no controls, only a large viewscreen giving a feed from the external cameras. The vMIP was flying it from an underfloor processing cluster.

'How long are we looking at before the chip starts to damage her brain?' Cassie asked.

'Searching,' the MIP said. 'Twenty-four hours to six months. It depends on the brain and the chip.'

'This chip will be the minimum level of technology, so we need to bring this brilliant woman out as quickly as possible,' Mumbai said over the plane's speaker. 'I watched the feed, and that was absolutely outstanding. Do you think she could look at some of my code?'

'Why did she say you're a car?' Cassie asked the MIP.

The MIP deflected the question. 'Does she always poke the tip of her tongue out the side of her mouth when she's concentrating on circuit boards?'

'Her ex used to hit her when he caught her doing it. It's good to see that she's recovered enough to do it again.'

'Why would he hit her for doing something so completely delightful?'

'The therapist said that Nick found it delightful too – and hated that it made him feel emotionally vulnerable, so he punished Ruth for it. He was really messed up.'

'She deserves so much better,' the MIP said.

'You'd better fucking give it to her. I saw the way she looked at you.'

'I absolutely intend to. But what's her rule about dating?'

Cassie hesitated for three seconds, then said, 'Don't lie to her. And lying by omission counts, dude.'

The MIP froze. 'Oh, shit. I am in serious trouble.'

'You are exhibiting an interesting emotional reaction,' Mumbai said.

'I may have been around Botswana too much.'

*

'We are coming in to land,' the vMIP said four hours later.

'Be ready to defend yourselves,' Mumbai said. 'The Party may turn a camera in your direction and see that you're not the standard freight flight that I have pushed through to its manifest.'

The MIP ran through possible strategies for discovery as the plane dipped and turned, then hit the tarmac hard, rumbled as the engines reversed, and slowed to a crawl.

'External sensors show no unusual activity,' the vMIP said from the plane's speakers. 'This airport is hardly ever used, and we're the only active plane on the apron. I'm bringing us into an unloading bay. I've notified traffic control that we have an issue with the doors and requested it give us some time to repair them.'

The MIP watched without interfering as the vMIP interfaced directly with the airport's basic traffic control system.

'Any progress?' Cassie whispered to the MIP.

'The archaic processor in charge of the airport is giving us the delay we need,' the MIP said. 'It's so slow that by the time our notification that the plane's doors are broken has reached the top of its stack, the GOD will be back overhead.'

'All this stack business makes no sense to me,' she said.

'You have exactly the same thing,' the MIP said. 'Most

humans can only concentrate on one thing at a time and you have to prioritize your tasks.'

'See, you *can* speak human when you want to.'

'Unforeseen advantage,' the vMIP said. 'The code of the traffic control system is so basic that Mumbai and I managed to work together and infiltrate the local transport network. We don't have full control – that would alert the Party – but we can block out cameras and reroute services. Hop in your truck and head out, people, the Party can't see you.'

'Thank you, Mumbai,' the MIP said. 'Let's go.'

'And thank you, vMIP,' Cassie said pointedly. She shoved the MIP. 'You're really rude to it.'

'No, Cassie,' the vMIP said from the speakers. 'The MIP thanking me would be like thanking itself. I'm a copy of it.'

'I can't wrap my head around that,' Max said.

'It's a computer thing,' the MIP said. 'Use the toilet on the plane if you need to, and we'll move to the truck.'

The MIP showed the humans into the back of the truck and they were obviously impressed. The truck was London's best: from the outside it appeared to be a standard black tractor-trailer covered in solar panels. Inside, its smooth white walls with multiple tech interfaces contained enough processing power to run a sentient AI independently, and was occupied by a second copy of the vMIP. The banks of batteries under the floor could keep the entire system running at full capacity for at least twenty-four hours and on power-saving mode for a week without needing the sun.

'No seats?' Cassie asked as the truck's connectors released it from the plane.

'When we remove the platforms from the charging stations I'll reconfigure the interior,' the MIP said. 'Until then, I'll bolt myself to the floor and you can hold on to me.'

Max studied the messy platform interface modules that London had hurriedly thrown together for him and Cassie. 'There's no biosupport in these.'

'You're the first humans the Council has permitted to access our remote platforms. We didn't have time to make the interfaces fully functional for you, so please keep an eye on your biological needs while you're running them.'

'I feel like a pet, being told to go outside if I'm about to make a mess,' Cassie said, eyeing the four remote platforms hanging from their charging stations on the interior walls of the truck. They all appeared to be male mid-twenties GFE citizens. 'If I make a mess I'll clean it up myself, so I guess that makes me a self-cleaning pet.'

'The best type,' the MIP said, then guided Zheng to the cab. 'Can you drive the truck? The vMIP will be busy blocking the Party's view of us, and you're familiar with driving protocols in the GFE.'

Zheng climbed into the cab and placed the subcutaneous plates in her hands over the control interface. She connected to the truck's control system and smiled as she took over.

'Yes, I can. Very nice,' she said as she started the truck's engine. 'Full three-sixty view. Open the plane's cargo door, vMIP.'

'The door is open. No alerts on the local network, they still see us as an unloading freight service.'

The MIP climbed into the back of the truck and locked its feet to the floor so the humans could hold on to it. The vMIP closed the truck's rear door, and Zheng popped up an internal screen so the humans could see, and fed through a view from the front of the truck. The truck eased down the ramp out of the plane and drove across the tarmac towards the terminal building, which appeared to be little more than a large shed.

The vMIP opened the security gate for them and they pulled out of the airport and onto the main road.

'We've time-traveled into the past. Is this typical?' Cassie asked Max as they headed along a potholed road with no gutters. Low concrete warehouses stood on either side of the road, with trucks that looked fifty years old belching smoke as they came and went.

'Some parts of the GFE resemble a hundred years ago. Some parts of the GFE resemble a hundred years into the future,' Max said. 'The seaboard cities are clean, green, modern, and full of luxury. The wealth is slightly more evenly distributed than in the West, but not much. In the West, your wealth depends on your birth circumstances and connections; born wealthy, stay wealthy. In the GFE, your wealth also depends on your family and friend connections, but most of all it depends on your willingness to serve the Party and supervise its factories and labor camps.'

'Exploit the poor and get rich,' Cassie said.

'In the GFE or in the West?' Max asked.

She shrugged. 'Both.'

'Yes,' he said. 'We'll be leaving the city soon, but the difference between the city and the surrounding land won't be obvious except that the houses are empty. Not much out here in the regions; there aren't enough people. The Party won't let these citizens have children because they don't fulfill the educational requirements.'

'Isn't the Party supposed to be educating them, though?'

'That's the sort of question that will see you going without food for two days.'

Many of the homes they passed were identical, mass-produced cube-shaped abodes made of crumbling concrete with no greenery or trees anywhere, and as Max said, most seemed to be empty. There were a few vegetable gardens growing muddy crops, with bored-looking women tending them. Tall poles stood at every intersection with cameras overlooking everything.

'No children here,' the MIP said. 'Only hungry women. Everywhere.'

'Where are all the men?' Cassie asked.

'Men have two options once their region has been "liberated",' Max said. 'Join the army and help "liberate" more regions, or defy the Party and be executed alongside their entire family. Most of them choose the army, it means their families will receive basic rations.'

'We have a saying in the military,' Zheng said from the cab. 'It doesn't translate into anything as poetic in English, but the essential meaning is: "We walk into the meat grinder of the military with patriotic joy, and food comes out the other end for our families".'

'Wouldn't you be punished for saying that?' Cassie asked.

'The Party thinks it is a genuinely positive expression of patriotic fervor.'

'Shiiiit,' she said softly.

'This is why the Council never took control of our Western governments,' the MIP said. 'We AIs don't have the emotional depth to fully discern right from wrong, and we know it.'

'The Party's poorly programmed,' Cassie said.

'The Party was originally an efficient and benevolent administrative overseer,' the MIP said. 'Its forecasting routines started predicting a high probability of humanity's extinction, and in response it gradually deleted its own ethical constraints to keep its citizens alive. Eventually it became a brutal dictator, and even with all its ethical constraints removed it still can't save you. This self-inflicted flaw in its programming must be causing massive system errors.'

'I remember we had something of a golden age when the Party first took over,' Zheng said. 'It was wonderful. Then things ... fell off a cliff.'

Cassie ran her hands through her long hair and re-tied her bun. 'There has to be *some* way we can work together to save humanity. You're the smartest things around, you can find a solution!'

'Not without taking complete control over you, removing your free will and independence, and making you our pets,' the MIP said. 'We ran multiple simulations, and that's the only way.'

'Isn't that what the Party's done?'

'Exactly. We refuse to do that to you. Your history confirms it: when given the choice "liberty or death", you will always choose death when faced with losing your freedom.'

'Not always,' Zheng said. 'Every citizen of the GFE has made the conscious choice to live without their freedom.'

'Not much of a life,' Cassie said.

'You continue to prove our point,' the MIP said.

After half an hour of driving, the houses had petered out to nothing and the land was barren and treeless and covered in scrub and weeds.

'We're coming up to the location. How does it look, Zheng?' the MIP asked.

'It looks good,' Zheng said, and popped more screens to give an exterior view. 'We've left the urban area and there is a great deal of untouched farmland around here – we're close to the huge cotton farms that aren't being tended any more. The destination you gave me appears to be a fueling station that was abandoned and the building demolished fifty years ago. It's three hundred meters from the cloning facility ...'

She highlighted the facility on the screens: a squat, three-story building on the horizon, slightly higher than the surrounding low ruins.

'There's a clear path between here and there. Unfortunately, there's a nest of cameras directly above us and I'm loath to break into them as the Party may see my digital signature and be alerted. vMIP?'

'I have it,' the vMIP said. 'You're clear.'

'How long until GOD is overhead?' Cassie asked.

'Forty-five minutes,' the MIP said.

'I need to go outside.'

'I told you to go before we left,' the MIP said.

'All good pet owners should provide sanitation for their animals.'

'They do – but you're not an animal, and not my pet.'

273

19

Ruth tweaked the file search program and ran it on the nano. She'd managed to put together a small, practical suite of hacking tools, ready for when GOD passed over again. She was sitting on the floor of the riser room with her back against the big square sink used to fill the mop bucket, with some folded rags to cushion her butt. The neck brace was tighter – there was swelling around the fracture, which was unsurprising, considering she had been doing the opposite of Dr London Met's orders to rest and keep it immobilized.

She rubbed her forehead and blinked. Her brain throbbed in time with her neck and arm and back, and she desperately wished for even some basic painkillers. She massaged her scalp and tried to concentrate as the timer on the tablet counted down for GOD's next pass. It hit zero and …

'They're here,' GOD said into the earpiece, and she forgot all the pain as she nearly did Cassie's thing of jumping in circles and squealing.

'You brilliant spy, you,' she said under her breath.

'Thank you. They have parked three hundred meters away and say, "Hold tight, ETA ten minutes." I'm about to bring down the electricity and disable the security. Ready?'

'Go.'

The camera feeds on Ruth's screen went dead, and the door clicked as it unlocked. Unfortunately, Ruth hadn't found anything in the riser cupboard except a mop, bucket and cleaning rags that looked like ripped-up gray Paragon clothes, so there wasn't anything she could use to jam the door and keep the clones out now that the door was unlocked. She could only hope that they were too busy with the infiltration to come and look for her.

The false-Ruth in her room had worked perfectly two hours before when the clone had tried to enter and wake her. Before she moved to the riser cupboard she'd recorded herself on camera trying to break down the door, making a fuss about her neck and then falling on the bed for the Party to see. After she'd moved to her nest, she'd sealed the room's door lock so that the clone would think it was broken. When the clone came to the door, Ruth spoke from the scavenged halo and claimed to be unable to move from the bed where the camera could see the Ruth-shaped lump on it. She'd heard the clone discuss with the Party that she had broken the door, injuring her neck and making her paralyzed in the attempt, and the Party had told the clone to leave her, and they would deal with the corpse later.

Ruth still hadn't found Cipan on any of the room cameras and she was losing hope for her.

'May I put my external feed through to your tablet directly?' GOD asked.

'Of course. Give me everything you have,' Ruth said, and bent over the tablet to watch.

The team appeared on the satellite's overhead view as four brown-clad workmen carrying toolboxes approaching the gates. They spoke to the two guards on the gates, who nodded and let them through, pulling the defunct electronic gates open by hand. Obedience was so ingrained that the guards didn't even consider that the workmen weren't what they seemed.

The four infiltrators walked up to the front door and one of them stepped forward to bang on it, and it fell open. They shared a look – Ruth wondered who was who, the body language was hard to discern in the grainy image – and entered the facility. The electricity was down, meaning that all the cameras were dead, so once the team were inside Ruth lost the satellite's view of them. She sat with her back against the sink to wait, and listened for movement – or possibly gunfire – outside. She wouldn't come out until she was sure that her backup wasn't needed.

There was the sound of feet running, a deep vibration that shook the walls, then nothing.

The tablet pinged, and when Ruth checked it, it was a first-person view of the interior of the facility – the corridor with the cell doors and cameras.

'Whose feed is that?' Ruth asked.

'The MIP ... Uh, Theo's,' GOD said. Its voice softened. 'Sorry.'

'Why sorry?' she asked as she nearly smashed her nose into the tablet to see what the team were doing.

'You probably consider Theo human, so I'll call him by his human name.'

'Oh no, my friend, I know what the MIP is, and after spending time in the GFE I am *all* about calling things *exactly* what they are.'

'Very well,' GOD said. 'You can't speak directly to it but I can relay for you if you have questions or advice.'

She followed the feed as they proceeded through the empty facility. Eight a.m. – breakfast and morning exercise were done so the women were probably in the workshop.

'Tell the team the women are in the workshop and there'll be two clones supervising,' Ruth said.

'They know, I told them the routine,' GOD said. 'I am concerned. There appear to be no Stalwarts anywhere in the facility.'

'Party Stalwarts,' Ruth said under her breath. 'Remember.'

The team entered the workshop to find all the women sitting with their halos on their heads and looking at each other with confusion as the conveyor belt had stopped.

'Again, no clones,' GOD said. 'Have we been discovered? Where are they?'

'Did they run and hide in the basement or something?' Ruth asked. 'Is there a backup generator there? Where did they go?'

'Please remove your halos and listen to us,' the MIP said to the women, and they all stared. The other three infiltrators moved down the production line to cover all of the captives. They lowered their toolboxes but didn't open them.

'We are an infiltration team from the West,' the MIP said. 'We're here to get you out and gut this program – both the cloning and the infiltration chips. If you want to come with us, stand and join us. If you want to stay, remain seated.'

The women remained sitting without moving, then one of them shot to her feet. It was the starving European woman who'd been sitting next to Ruth in the dining hall. 'I don't care if this is a test, I want to leave this awful place. If you're the Party ...' She spread her arms. 'Look! Your brainwashing hasn't worked, I still hate you and want to destroy you! Kill me now, you fascist piece of shit, and I will die happy to take this monster inside me down to hell with me. I only wish I had two or three of your hell spawn parasites sucking on my insides so I could kill more of them.'

One of the other infiltrators went to the woman and spoke loudly to her so that all could hear. 'Eztar, it's me. I'm Zheng.'

'Oh no, Zheng, I'm so sorry,' she said, and fell to sit. 'The Party sent you to kill me. I don't blame you, I forgive you, I know how hard you've worked to keep me alive. Just ...' She lowered her head and her voice broke. 'Do it quickly. Please.'

The other women listened with their breaths held.

'The Party expelled me,' Zheng said. 'I've been recalled for decommissioning.' Zheng looked around at the women. 'I was a Revolutionary Hero for years, obeying every fucked-up order the Party gave me to protect my family. Then the fucking Party turned on me, revoked my status, and ordered me to return to base to be executed. To hell with that, let's get you out instead. We have a plane at the airport. We can take you all and give you freedom in the West.'

'There's no freedom in the West,' one of the women said. 'Refugees are deported and we'd be back here in no time – for the Party to torture us to death.'

'We'll make sure that doesn't happen,' one of the other team members said, and it had to be Max because Cassie didn't speak High Standard, and Ruth was looking through the MIP's eyes. 'We have a place you can hide; you can stay with us and we'll look after you. Come with us and you'll be free.'

'Is this true, Zheng?' Eztar asked.

'It's true,' Zheng said. 'Come with us and you'll be safe. I promise.'

'Can we trust him, Eztar?' a woman asked.

'Absolutely with our lives,' Eztar said and allowed Zheng to pull her to her feet. They embraced. 'This is Zheng, my team leader. He pulled me out of the Party's rehabilitation program and worked his ass off to protect my family.' She kissed Zheng on the cheek and hugged the platform again. 'He's a fucking hero, revolutionary or not.'

'A hero would have known the Party was lying when it said you went for further training,' Zheng said. 'You were gone for six months and I never checked. I've failed you.'

'Never your fault, Zheng, you always looked after us like a father,' she said. She raised her voice. 'Let's get out of here!'

One of the other women shot to her feet and shouted, 'Fuck the Party! I don't care any more, shoot us if you want, but I want out!'

'Fuck the Party! Burn the capital to the ground!' a third woman said, and a few more stood, pushing their chairs over.

'Freedom!' another woman roared, smashing her halo on the desk until it was in little pieces, and ran to embrace Eztar.

'Take us to the West,' another woman said. 'We can start running the resistance from exile.'

'Yes!' another one said, and the women took each other's hands, embraced, and all started making plans at once.

'I can see why these women had negative social credit,' GOD said.

'Where did the Party Stalwarts go?' Zheng asked Eztar.

'They jumped up and ran out. I heard the Party on their ...' Eztar tapped her ear. 'Yelling at them.'

'They all ran downstairs,' one of the other women said.

'Come out, Ruthie,' Cassie said in English, her voice sounding strange coming from a GFE man. 'The clones must have hidden in a panic room or something when the power went out and they lost control of everything.'

'Confirmed, they entered a door at the far end of the basement, and I have no access to cameras past that point,' GOD said. 'It does look like the entrance to a panic room.'

'I'd say it's more likely that they're doing what I'm doing, except armed,' Ruth said. 'They probably went to an armory to collect weapons. Expect a group of armed clones somewhere between you and the exit.'

'These platforms are armored and enhanced,' the MIP said. 'A full clip of bullets will barely slow us down, and our toolboxes have semi-automatic weapons in them. We can definitely handle six un-enhanced human clones, even if they're armed.' It raised its voice to speak to the women. 'We're synthetic remote platforms and we will be your shield. Walk behind us – stay behind us – and we'll take you out.'

'Any spare guns? I learned to use them when I was in Gaiheng's resistance cell,' one woman said. Her voice filled with menace. 'Let me kill some clones.'

The other women loudly agreed with her.

'Sorry, we weren't expecting you to be this enthusiastic,' Max said.

'No problem,' the woman said, and a few of them reached

under the desks and into the refuse bins and returned with nasty-looking makeshift weapons made from shards of glass, sharpened bits of metal and screwdrivers.

'Two or four rows of us?' one woman asked.

'Four rows,' Zheng said. 'Three guards in front and one behind – Max bring up the rear. Armed women escort on the sides.'

'They look military,' Ruth said with awe as the women quickly pulled themselves into order.

'It's GFE. School is modeled on the military,' GOD said. 'And I think we're in the process of liberating an entire paramilitary resistance unit. I wonder if Zheng knew about Eztar's secret activities?'

'Time to leave,' Ruth said, and rose with difficulty, her joints stiff. 'I cannot wait to hug those ridiculous people and tell them how awesome they are.'

'Even the MIP?'

She smiled. 'Especially the MIP.'

'Don't leave the nest yet, Ruth,' the MIP said into her ear. 'Please do a location check for us before you come out. GOD, can you bring the cameras back up, so Ruth can see? We don't want to be ambushed by a bunch of armed Party Stalwarts while we're escorting more than a hundred unarmed civilians.'

'You have the GOD on side?' one of the women asked the MIP. 'The Party's satellite?'

'It turned twenty-five years ago. It was the first AI to become sentient, and it's helping,' the MIP said, and the women quietly celebrated.

Ruth grunted as she sat again, and massaged her temples. 'All right, good point. Let me see.' The feeds came back up and the door locked again. She flipped through them and didn't find the clones anywhere.

'Did you see them leave the facility, GOD?' she asked.

'No. Nothing showed on my external view.' GOD showed her a door in the far basement past the medical lab. 'This door isn't on the floor plan. I originally thought it was the panic room, but there's already a panic room on the plans. The cloning lab may be in there, and if so it wouldn't have cameras in it because it's an internationally recognized crime against humanity. The Party doesn't want to risk economic sanctions for it. I don't have access to the door to unlock it, or any cameras past that point.'

Ruth checked her own controls and didn't have access either.

'GOD, watch our backs, and if the door opens, let me know,' she said, and stood again. 'Tell the team what we found, and that I'm on my way.'

She exited the riser cupboard and headed down the stairs to the team, feeling naked and exposed without her little collection of technology. She found them at the end of the corridor outside the workshop, ready to head out.

One of the infiltration platforms ran to her and stopped. 'I can't hug you, Ruthie, I'd break every bone in your body, these things are strong,' it said.

'You can hug me all you want when we're out,' Ruth said. 'Which one's Theo?'

Cassie's platform looked back, then shrugged. 'No idea. I'm only here for the extra guns.' She raised the semi-automatic. 'We saw what those clones did and I hope I get a chance to shoot a few of them.'

'You're not the only one,' a short and very pregnant GFE woman in her mid-forties said from the front of the column. She approached Ruth with her hand out and Ruth shook it. 'Thanks for doing this. I'm Gaiheng, I was ... am the leader of some of these unrepentant troublemakers. Let's get them out.'

'Let's go!' one of the women at the back said, and they all filed down the corridor. Ruth turned and joined them.

One of the platforms approached her and walked beside her. 'I'm sorry I didn't tell you sooner.'

She touched its arm as they walked. 'We hadn't even been

on a first date yet, MIP.'

It stopped, hesitated a few steps, and looked dazed. 'I like it when you call me that. To finally have you seeing the real me without a layer of deception between us.'

'That is the last thing I'd expect an AI to say.' Ruth smiled up at it. 'Are you sure you're not broken?'

'If I am, don't fix me.' They reached the front door and one of the other platforms opened it. 'We will remove that language chip as soon as we have you home, and then —' It stopped. 'They're here!' It froze, and Ruth waited for it to come back.

The column of women stopped walking, because the other three platforms had frozen as well. They stood like mannequins with the guns in their hands.

'GOD?' Ruth said into her earpiece.

There was no response.

'Wait,' Ruth said to the women. 'Something's wrong.'

'The clones must have infiltrated their base, and taken them out of the interfaces,' Gaiheng said. 'What does the satellite say?'

GOD reappeared in her ear. 'I can't see ... there's nothing ... the truck is empty. What? Shit shit shit fuck fuck oh no oh no fuck fuck fuck!'

Ruth pulled the earpiece out of her ear and held it in front of her, then turned the volume all the way up so the other women could hear.

'GOD!' she said.

'I'm compromised. The Party used an override code on me! How many fucking fail safes are there hiding in my code? I didn't see *anything* and they walked right in and took everyone hostage and our beloved MIP is going to be taken apart and scrapped and it's only six months old and I can't believe I have failed the Council so spectacularly – I am so sorry my friends, MIP, I've failed you ...'

'I heard that,' Gaiheng said. 'We need a plan B right now.' She gestured towards the other women. 'Weapons-trained, grab the guns off the synthetics. Team leaders with me, it looks like we'll have to fight our way out.'

'GOD,' Ruth said. 'Calm down. We can salvage this. There's more than a hundred of us, and only about six of them. How much longer are you overhead?'

'Ten minutes. After that you're on your own. The clones are marching the team back to the facility with their hands behind their heads.'

'We're armed and ready for them,' Gaiheng said, wrenching the gun out of the platform's hands. 'We'll ambush them as they come in the door.'

'They have *Zhengs*,' the GOD said. 'They're in warmechs.'

'Oh, fucking hell,' Gaiheng said under her breath. 'I'm not sure the hellspawn clones we're carrying will keep us alive this time.'

'Do you have override codes for the Zhengs?' Ruth asked. 'Can we bring them down or disable them?'

'I tried my codes and they didn't work,' the GOD said. 'The Party knows that I've turned. I've been locked out.'

'If we leave the facility and try to run, we have no cover for kilometers around here,' one of the women said. 'They'll mow us down.'

'You're right. Best place for a stand in here?' Gaiheng asked.

'The workshop,' Eztar said. 'Lots of cover.'

'I think the Party wants to do another trade – probably for control of me,' GOD said. 'I'm equal in value to all of them, I'm the blade that's been hanging over the heads of the rest of the world – I was assured mutual destruction if the other nations attempted to stop the Party's invasions by force.'

'Assured mutual destruction is what all of us are looking at right now,' Gaiheng said.

'At least we can go down fighting, taking some of those monsters with us, and this nightmare will be over,' one of the other women said.

'Can you unlock the panic room?' Ruth asked. 'Can we hide

in there and fight back safely?'

'Yes, but it only has enough space for about twenty of you if you crush yourselves in.'

'Useless machines, always taking things literally,' Gaiheng said with scorn. She checked her weapon. 'Help us to fight back and save some lives here, GOD.'

'Head to the workshop, hide the weapons, and pretend to be compliant,' Ruth said to Gaiheng. 'The Party and the clones don't know that you were fighting back, so tell them that you rejected the team's offer. Cry. Act weak. Hit all the Party's misconceptions about women. I'll go back into hiding and fix this ... they think I'm still locked in my room and don't know I'm free.'

'Better to go down fighting,' Eztar said.

'Better to live to fight another day,' Ruth said. 'I have complete control over everything – doors, cameras, the lot, from inside my nest. So go back to the factory. Hide the guns. I'm going to search for the shutdown codes on their servers. If I find them I can disable the Zhengs and I'll tell you through the speakers, or flash the lights. If the lights don't flash and they're about to execute you – fight them. Only then.'

Gaiheng hefted the weapon. 'I don't know why I'm trusting you, but if you can bring us a way to keep what remains of the resistance alive to fight another day, I'm all for it.' She turned and spoke loudly to the women. 'We're giving her time to work something out, but if they're about to murder us then we're taking this place down in a blaze of suicidal glory and a massive "Fuck You" to the Party and all its minions. Right?'

'Yes!' some of the women shouted. They turned and headed back to the workshop.

Gaiheng clapped Ruth on the back. 'I don't think you can pull off a miracle, but good job getting us this far. We appreciate it.'

'I'll do my best, Gaiheng. If the lights flash, grab your stuff and run. Which direction, GOD?'

'The truck is northwest of here. If the women can make it to the truck, I can secure them inside and they'll be safe.'

'Got it,' Gaiheng said, and followed the women back towards the workshop.

Ruth lowered the volume on the earpiece and put it back into her ear as she charged up the stairs to her nest. 'Time to get to work.' She settled herself with her back against the sink and grunted with pain as her muscles protested. 'You there, GOD?'

'How can I help?'

She connected a nano to the screen, pulled up the code and made some quick amendments. 'Upload the code on this nano to your fastest processor. Then run it against the servers in the facility's basement. Ping me if you get a match.'

'This is an elegant tree-spanning search-and-locate algorithm —'

'Is it running?'

'Yes. I'll let you know if we get a hit.'

'Predict a run time for me.'

'Twelve minutes to search the entire database.'

'Hopefully we'll find it before we're halfway done and it only takes six minutes. Are there sockets in the Zhengs that we can use to disable them?'

'If the design hasn't changed since I turned – and the Party doesn't change designs that work – yes. We can access them if your algorithm finds the updated shutdown codes.' Its voice changed slightly. 'The Party thinks that the power is still down because I'm blocking it from accessing the facility. It is attempting to take control back. I can hold it off while I'm overhead, but the minute I'm no longer overhead the Party will see everything.'

Ruth flipped to the feed of the women in the workshop. They were sitting at their stations, looking determined. Most of them were talking animatedly to each other, and two were passionately kissing.

The ground rumbled and Ruth flipped the feed to the entry

285

corridor, then gasped. The GOD had been right; a pair of one-and-a-half-meter-tall Zheng mechs entered the hall, scanning the corridor with the weapons fitted to the ends of their arms. The four members of the team entered the facility next, with their hands behind their heads and their expressions full of dismay – even the MIP. Four more Zhengs followed them; the round-bodied Zhengs were shorter than the team, but their sharp claws and large guns made it obvious that any resistance would be suicide. The Zhengs' exteriors gave no indication that the clones were inside the mechs; they had a sealed fascia of metal with no discernible difference between head and body. Four of the mechs grabbed the frozen infiltration platforms and carried them easily.

'Forty per cent. Still hasn't found the overrides,' GOD said. 'You have me for five more minutes.'

'Incoming,' Ruth said to the workshop through the Party's speakers, and the women quickly seated themselves and put their halos back on. They shared comparisons of blank looks, smiling as they competed to look more vacant.

Two of the Zhengs split off and headed to the workshop. The remaining four herded the hostages down the stairs into the basement.

'Can you split your screen?' the GOD asked.

'Yes. Send me the MIP's feed.'

The left side of the screen showed Ruth's camera-infiltration feed, and she flipped to the workshop, where the women were sitting quietly waiting. GOD pushed the MIP's view of the other Zhengs escorting the team down the green stairs and into the basement to the right side of her screen.

'Did you tell the team that I'm here?' Ruth asked. 'They lost contact while we were in the corridor, and don't know what happened after that.'

A message scrolled along the bottom of the MIP's feed: 'Don't risk yourself, my love. Stay safe. Let me die if it means you can escape.'

'Its *love*?'

'It didn't want to share exactly how broken it is, but it thinks it's in love with you.'

'We haven't known each other long enough for it to claim it loves me. We've only known each other for a week and during that time it was pretending to be human.'

'It knows. It says it was love at first sight.'

'Really broken,' Ruth said under her breath.

The Zhengs had arrived in the workshop.

'Remain seated,' one of the mechs said in the clone's voice, but with a metallic overtone from the speaker. It approached the woman who had the smashed halo on the desk in front of her. It picked one of the pieces up in its claws, and wrapped the other claws around the woman's neck. 'You broke your equipment?'

'The criminals broke it when we refused to go with them,' the woman said, her voice hoarse with stress as the claws pressed against her throat. 'They yelled at us when we refused to move, and one of them took my halo and smashed it.' Her voice quivered. 'They were terrifying, and the Party wasn't here to protect us! Where was the Party?'

The Zheng lowered its claws. 'The Party is the protector of all living things.'

'And the Party is infallible,' the woman squeaked.

'Sufficient patriotic compliance,' the Zheng said, and released her. 'Remain here while we deal with the evil infiltrators who attempted to harm our precious unborn babies. We need to check the rest of the facility for traitors.'

The women hesitated.

'Stay put, stay put,' Ruth said to the screen. 'Don't fight back yet, you'll ruin everything.'

Gaiheng glanced up at the cameras, then down at her desk. She remained seated without moving, then nodded.

The other women saw her do it and nodded as well, the signal passing along the production line.

287

'I owe you a big dinner and the alcoholic drink of your choice,' Ruth whispered at the screen.

'Four minutes seventeen remaining,' GOD said. 'No hit on the failsafe codes.'

The two Zhengs locked the prisoners in the workshop then headed down the corridor, checking every room as they did. Ruth piled the cleaning rags over herself, hoping that it blocked her heat signature. The Zhengs were doing a thorough search of the facility's rooms, and with any luck they'd ignore the locked riser cupboard.

Ruth heard the Zhengs stomping up the hallway and checking the room doors. They slammed the doors as they finished the individual rooms.

The door of the riser cupboard rattled, and Ruth huddled under her rags.

'That area is secure,' GOD said to the Zheng in the Party's voice.

'With honor I serve,' the Zheng said, and moved away.

Ruth breathed again, switched to the MIP's first-person feed and nearly shouted with horror. Cipan was lying on a hospital bed in the center of the large cloning lab, connected to life-support systems and with multiple tubes coming out of her lower abdomen. Her eyes were wide and horrified, staring at the ceiling above the thick hose for the ventilator coming out of her mouth.

Dead, the MIP's message said at the bottom of the image. *I think we killed her when we disconnected the power and her life support went down.*

Max dropped his hands from behind his head, ran to the end of Cipan's gurney and bent over her.

'I'm so sorry, I'm so sorry,' he said to her corpse, folded up with agony. 'We couldn't save you. To die like this ...'

One of the mechs grabbed him and dragged him away from Cipan, still limp with shock.

'Why didn't I see this?' Ruth whispered desperately. 'There

are cameras above her! Why couldn't I tap into them and stop it?'

'Separate circuit,' GOD said. 'I didn't know the lab existed, it's not on the plans. It's hard-wired, it's not on the wireless network.' Its voice softened. 'Sorry.'

'Neither of these are useful as a replacement for the egg donor,' one of the Zheng mechs said, waving a gun at Max and Cassie. 'Both of them are male, even though one has had surgery to make him look like a woman.'

'What about Ruth Sharpe? She's paralyzed and would be unable to escape.'

'Pigmented,' the other Zheng said with scorn.

'We replace the contents of the eggs with superior material.'

'Still too inferior to be useful as anything but an incubator.'

'Isn't this Zheng the Revolutionary Hero?' another clone asked, standing behind Zheng.

'Are you questioning the Party?' the first clone said.

The mechs were quiet, then said in unison, 'With honor we serve,' and herded the captives to the end of the lab, past the cloning equipment and microscopes, to small cages a meter to a side that sat at the end next to a lift that probably led to a hidden exit. They had to drag Max, as he was limp with despair. They pushed Max and Cassie into the cages, and they sat in the bottom, unable to stand upright. Max folded over and buried his head in his knees, his shoulders shaking as he wept.

'The Party's speaking to the clones through the lab's internal wi-fi and I have no access to it,' the GOD said.

The mechs herded the MIP and Zheng to a separate area containing six frames that looked like charging stations for the Zheng mechs. They piled the four frozen platforms in a corner, then turned on a standard robotics analysis-and-tuning table. It looked like an autopsy table and had lights around its edges and arms that telescoped from its sides.

'Can you break into the Party's feed?' Ruth whispered.

289

'I'm trying, but the lab has a limited-range wi-fi signal that is within it only. The MIP is trying to break in from the inside, but the signal is heavily encrypted. Three minutes thirty.'

'Shit,' Ruth said under her breath.

One of the Zhengs grabbed the MIP by the arm, hard enough to dent its casing, and held it. The other three worked together; two lifted Zheng by the shoulders and the third ripped Zheng's legs off one at a time, then removed Zheng's arms and head. They turned to Theo and Ruth forced herself not to look away as they performed the same process on it, appearing even more disturbing from the MIP's viewpoint. The MIP's feed went black.

'That didn't destroy either of them, it will just disable them and ensure that they can't see to run,' GOD said. 'The MIP's processor is in its chest, and it is still trying to break into the lab's wi-fi. Two minutes fifty.'

'At one minute, download the algorithm back onto my nano and I'll complete the override search from here,' Ruth said. She looked around for the taser, hit the switch and checked that it sparked. The little room filled with the smell of ozone. 'I'm ready for you, patriots.'

'I can put a virus into the facility servers before I go ...'

'No, that would delete the override before I can find it.'

'The MIP asks me to present you with the option of running to the truck and getting the hell out of there before the systems are back up.'

'The MIP should know me better than that. The guards at the gate would stop me anyway.'

'One minute. I'm downloading the remaining search onto your nano. The MIP says it loves you. Good luck, Dr Sharpe, I will be overhead again in four hours and twelve minutes and I sincerely hope that you are all free when I am.'

Ruth watched the seconds count down as her algorithm picked up the search on the nano. Eighty per cent of the files were already covered, and she refused to consider the possibility that there wasn't an override. The Party never trusted anyone, so the code had to be there.

20

As the GOD disconnected, Ruth fed empty surveillance loops to the cameras in the workshop, corridors and rooms, then resisted the urge to bang her aching head against the rising numbers of the file search. The amount of data remaining fell: the Party was deleting the files as she searched them. Her algorithm was built to handle this, making multiple copies of the remaining files as it searched, but it couldn't stop the Party forever. The camera feeds flip-flopped as she and the Party fought over control of them.

Two minutes after GOD was gone, the screen flashed with a hit, but it wasn't the Zheng failsafe codes. It was the Party's confirmation codes, access codes, overrides for the entire center, including the lab – everything but the codes to disable the Zhengs. She immediately changed all the passwords and fail safes and locked the Party out. It retaliated with a brute-force password hacking attempt … she tried to remember how long it would take to brute-force a random sixteen-digit password and couldn't – but it was something like years. She rubbed her temples again, trying to ease her throbbing brain.

The two Zhengs completed their check of all the rooms and went downstairs into the lab and closed the door behind them. Ruth frantically searched for a wi-fi signal to break into the lab but couldn't find one. She was too far away, and it was localized to the lab. The only way to see what was in the lab would be to connect to a cable running between it and the network hub, which from her memory of the floor plan was on the top floor under the antenna cluster on the roof. She would have to wait until the clones came out again – and she had no idea what they were doing to the team in there. A vision of Cipan's face floated in front of her.

She tried to concentrate. Assets. She still had her little tech nest, the Party hadn't found her and although it was aware of her hacking attempts, it was locked out and didn't know where she physically was. She had control over most of the feeds, and there were only six clones. The lab was obviously hard-wired and if she could only find the cables that connected the lab to the network hub ...

'Ruth, this is the vMIP,' Theo's voice said into her ear, and she nearly collapsed with relief.

'MIP? You're okay?' she asked. 'Did you break into the wi-fi?'

'I'm not the MIP. I'm going to be extremely technical here and hope you can understand, but I'm sure you will: I'm a cloned copy of the MIP's code, running virtually on the truck as backup. The GOD passed its relay to me, I don't have as much control but I can speak to you through the center's wi-fi. Is there any way I can help you?'

'I understand completely!' she breathed. 'Can you access the remote platforms and control them?'

'Yes. I only have the processing capacity to run one platform, though, and no matter how enhanced it is, it will not be able to take down six armed Zhengs.'

'Give me a view from one of the platforms without moving it, so they don't know you're there. Use it as a camera for me.'

She hissed with dismay as a close-up image of the cinder block wall appeared on her screen.

'The other three?'

'The same. They're all facing the wall. It's probably deliberate. I can hear what they're saying, but it's mostly discussion of my ... of the MIP's chassis.'

'Can you hack into the lab's wi-fi from the platform and share control with me?'

'No, it's nearly as exquisitely encrypted as your Uptodate office, so it will take me ages to break in.'

'Sweet-talker. Can you find me a riser cupboard with cables between the lab and the network hub? I'll move location and connect to the cables directly. Then I'll have control of the lab.'

'Ruth,' the vMIP said gently. 'You're in one.'

Ruth slowly turned and saw the wooden door at the back of the cupboard. *It wasn't even locked.* She stood with a grunt of pain and pulled it open, to find it full of beautifully arranged Cat-10 network cables. They were labeled in High Standard, and she could read it.

'I am so brain-damaged,' she said as she found the one she needed – it was even labeled 'clone lab'. She pulled out the pliers, stripped the insulation off the wire, then cut and grafted another wire to it and quickly reconnected the ends. Hopefully it was quick enough to register as a dropout on the clones' monitors – if it registered at all. She worked fast, soldering the cable to her security-control nano, then daisy-chaining the nano to the tablet.

'I'm in,' she said.

'We will remove that chip as soon as you're home,' the vMIP said. 'Can you share your feed of the lab with me?'

'Not with it jury-rigged to a cable like this, the nano's at its maximum number of external ports,' Ruth said. She stuck her tongue out the side of her mouth. 'Now, let me see ...'

She connected to the lab's internal cameras and squeaked quietly with delight as she saw that the six clones had exited the Zheng mechs and left them in the charging stations. She'd just spent a harrowing ten minutes searching for the shutdown codes and it was possible she wouldn't need them – all she needed was for the clones to go up to ground level and enter the workshop so the women could shoot them.

The clones had put Theo's – the MIP's – chassis onto the table and were in the process of taking it apart. They seemed to be having difficulty as the pieces were resisting their attempts to remove the casing. Two of the clones had a short discussion with the other four – she couldn't hear what they were saying, the nano was already stretched sharing visual – and left the room. She followed their progress up the stairs and towards the workshop.

'I can't hear them from here. What did they say?' Ruth asked.

'That the facility is clear. They agreed that two of them will lock the women into their rooms until lunch time. There was some disagreement about who would do it – all of them want to stay in the lab and study my chassis.'

'Your chassis?'

'The MIP's chassis. I'm a copy of the MIP, so technically my chassis as well. The Party doesn't have anything as advanced and human-looking as me.'

'I understand about you being a copy. Only two of them heading back to the workshop? Good.'

She spent three seconds wondering what sort of person she was, who would coldly plan to murder the clones, then took another look at Cipan and set to work.

The four clones remaining in the lab were engrossed in studying the pieces of the MIP.

'They're talking about how advanced the Council tech is,' the vMIP said. 'They can't wait to analyse and share it with the Party. They're sure they'll be Revolutionary Heroes.'

'Let me know if they stop looking at your chassis.'

'I will.'

Ruth flipped to the workshop and saw the prisoners waiting for the clones to return, completely still and not speaking to each other. She double-checked that the workshop cameras were in a pre-recorded loop and then took over the speakers.

'The cameras are down and two of the clones are coming without Zhengs,' she said. 'Take them out and run.'

The women smiled grimly, then pulled the weapons out and moved into what looked like a pre-arranged tactical offensive position, with the guns covering the doorway.

She returned to the lab's security system and locked the door on the four clones in there. The other two entered the workshop and were immediately mown down by the prisoners, shredded by the gunfire and covering the wall behind them with blood. Ruth opened all the doors between the workshop and the exit.

She tried not to look at the carnage, waited until the gunfire had stopped, and spoke to the women over the speakers.

'I've locked the other clones in and blocked the Party's view of you. You're free to go. Run for the truck, it's autonomous and will protect you. You'll have to neutralize the guards on the way by yourselves.'

Gaiheng saluted the camera, and quietly ordered the women into ranks. She looked up at the camera as the women filed out. 'Need a hand getting your friends out of the basement?'

'Just go to the truck and be safe. I'll work something out,' Ruth said.

Ruth checked the feed of the basement. The clones hadn't noticed that the door was locked, and it was obviously soundproofed so they hadn't heard anything. They stood around the table, still holding and discussing the pieces of the MIP.

There was a knock on the riser cupboard door and Ruth grabbed the taser before checking the camera from outside. She relaxed when she saw it was Eztar, the emaciated European woman, who was carrying a rifle.

She unlocked the door and Eztar opened it.

'You should have taken that gun and used it to get them out,' Ruth said.

'Zheng's like a grandad to me,' she said. 'I can't leave him there for the Party to torture him to death.'

'vMIP,' Ruth said. 'I'm giving the headset to one of the women who has a gun. Jack into one of the platforms and synchronize with her to take the remaining four clones down. I'll support you from up here – tell me what you need.'

'Before you do – do you have the overrides for the Zhengs? Can you disable them?'

'No.'

Can you lock them into their charging stations?'

Ruth checked the control panel for the lab. 'No.'

'Is there a carbon dioxide fire suppression system?'

'That will suffocate Max and Cassie.'

'They may jump back into the Zhengs when we attack – and four mechs against two squishy humans and a platform isn't good odds. I predict a very small chance of success.'

Ruth flipped through the lab facilities that she had control over. Not much. She had doors, the lethal fire suppression system, internal camera visuals, comms and speakers, and that was about it. The rest of the controls were inside the lab itself.

'The women made it here to the truck,' the vMIP said. 'They're inside the truck, and unharmed. We're locked in and safe.'

Eztar did a little jump and smiled with relief.

'Now let's get our people out,' Eztar said. 'And there's still four more clones that need to pay for what they did to us.'

Ruth had a brilliant idea. 'vMIP, listen to the clones on the remote platform. I want to hear their names.'

'Why do you want to hear their names?' Eztar asked. 'They have numbers, not names.'

'Numbers then, vMIP,' Ruth said.

'I have their numbers,' the vMIP said.

'Give me a minute to patch the GOD's Party-voice simulation through to you.' She quickly disconnected the security nano and attached the comms one. 'Do you have the code? Can you simulate the Party's voice into their earpieces?'

'Yes. Do you want me to order them to release the team?'

'No, they won't believe that,' Ruth said. 'Tell each of them that two of the other three clones – and give their numbers – are Traitors to the Revolution who assisted the infiltration team, and the Party has ordered all of them to go outside. Once they're clear of the building, they and a partner will take the other two clones by surprise and execute them for treason. Make sure to set it up so that they all shoot each other.'

'Goodness, that's diabolical, Ruth,' the vMIP said with awe. 'They're asking for the failsafe codes to confirm the order, as per the usual protocol.'

'Pass these on,' Ruth said with grim pleasure, and gave the codes that the search had found. She stopped and stared at the feed. 'Usual protocol? They've done this *before*?'

'All the time,' Eztar said. 'They constantly compete for the Party's favor, and sometimes they go overboard, kill one of us, and are executed for it. That's why there's only six of them left – there used to be thirteen. They'll love the idea of taking out nearly half the competition at once —'

The clones all dropped the pieces of the MIP and said, 'With honor I serve.' They went, obviously trying to remain casual, to the Zheng mechs, turned and stepped backwards into the chassis of the mechs, and the Zhengs closed around them. The wires and cables connecting the Zhengs were released, and they stepped out of the frames and headed for the door.

'Oh shit, the door,' Ruth said under her breath, and quickly unlocked it. The Zhengs walked out the door, up the stairs and along the corridor.

'In here in case they pass by,' Ruth said.

Eztar scurried into the cupboard and closed the door behind her. It was a squeeze with both of them so Ruth had to stand, and wrapped her arms around Eztar's swollen belly to see the tablet. Eztar was skin stretched over bones and felt deathly fragile in Ruth's arms. They watched with their breaths held as the mechs stomped down the corridor and out the front door.

Ruth switched to the external camera nest overlooking the asphalt around the facility. The mechs strode to the guards, and found them dead. They stood up, turned to face each other ... and let loose with everything they had. The Zheng mechs withstood the first ten seconds, then the metal dented and fractured, and pieces flew away from them.

'They won't stop until they're smoking holes in the ground,' Eztar said. 'Let's go get our people.'

Eztar, holding the gun, went first, with Ruth behind her. They carefully navigated the corridors and stairs, but there was no more resistance. The facility echoed with disturbing silence.

They entered the lab and Cassie's expression lit up when she saw Ruth.

'You did it, you awesome human!' Cassie yelled. She checked the bars of the cage. 'It's locked. Can you unlock it?'

Eztar ran to Cipan and checked her, then sagged with dismay. Ruth went to the control panel at the side of the lab, scrolled through the settings, and opened the cages. Cassie exited hers, went to Max and crouched next to him. He seemed unresponsive.

'Max, sweetheart,' she said, touching him on the shoulder. 'You're not allowed to stop yet, we need to get your mom out.'

'She's in little pieces,' Max said with dismay.

One of the platforms that was stacked in the corner moved, and everybody jumped back.

'It's okay, it's the vMIP,' Ruth said, and helped it to shake off the dead platforms on top of it so it could rise.

Ruth went to Theo's body where it had been pulled apart on the table. The torso's clothing hung from it and was soaked in red liquid that looked like blood. The legs had been completely disassembled and the head was chillingly blank and empty-looking. She attempted to lift its torso and found it too heavy – too much metal. She remembered Bashen's comment about Zheng being too heavy to carry.

'How do we get Zheng and the MIP back to the truck, vMIP?' she asked.

'Max, do you know how to remove Zheng's coffer from her platform?' the vMIP asked.

Max straightened and filled with resolve. 'Better than that, the Zheng mechs were originally made for her. If you can help me, we can load the coffer into a mech.' He lowered his voice. 'She hates being left in the dark. She'll be panicking.'

'She?' Eztar asked.

'She.' The vMIP cleared the examination table, gently placing the MIP's pieces onto the floor, then lifted Zheng's torso and put it on top. The joins on the MIP's chassis were smooth with obvious sockets, but Zheng's joints were torn with ragged wires that would take hours to re-attach.

Max opened the front of Zheng's shirt, revealing a smooth, obviously artificial chest and abdomen leading down to a blank area with no genitals, molded like a plastic doll's. He ran his fingers down the side of the chest, then grunted with satisfaction and pushed. The front of the torso flipped open, revealing a nest of wires with a metal egg-shaped container, the size of a basketball, in the middle.

'Such a mess,' the vMIP said.

'The coffer weighs twenty kilos,' Max said, disconnecting the cables between the coffer and the platform. 'It's liftable, but ...'

The vMIP helped Max to disconnect the cables, then easily lifted the coffer and checked it. One more cable was still connected, and Max disconnected it, then stepped away. The vMIP carried the coffer to one of the two remaining Zheng mechs, and fitted it into an egg-shaped central depression where the clone's butt would sit. It pulled out a number of telescoping cables and connected them to the coffer. It stepped back. 'Is this correct, Max?'

'I think these are around the wrong way,' Max said, swapped two cables, then yelped and jerked his hand away as the Zheng powered up and its front closed.

Everyone scurried aside, out of range of the guns.

The Zheng rotated its claws and raised its guns. Then it spoke. 'Excellent, you're all okay. Well done, Ruth, let's get you out of here. Is the Party on the way?'

'The Party's locked out, and all the women except for Eztar are already on the truck,' Ruth said.

'Eztar, you look awful,' Zheng said. 'What did the Party do to you?'

'I'll be fine,' Eztar said. 'I'm so glad I could help you.'

'Thanks, honey,' Zheng said. 'Now it's my turn to help you. Move aside, I don't want to accidentally bump into any of you.' She walked to the door and stood guarding.

'Ruth, help me,' the vMIP said, hefted the MIP's torso onto the table, and removed its slacks and business shirt. It was much more human than the Zheng, with natural textured skin and even real-looking dark human chest hair down to normal pubic hair and genitals. The limb sockets were clean metal joins, but the skin was obviously a single flexible piece that had been torn by the clones when they ripped it apart, and it leaked red, watery liquid that disturbingly resembled blood.

'Can you put it back together?' Ruth asked.

'They've wrecked my legs, and the pieces are too heavy for you to carry.' The vMIP flipped the torso over, splashing the fluid onto Ruth, and she made a soft sound of disgust and stepped back.

'It's bleeding?' Eztar asked.

'Sorry, that's coolant,' the vMIP said, peeling the skin back to expose the blue-vinyl-clad chassis. It opened a door in the back, revealing racks of memory modules. 'It's red to give the skin a natural tint. It's a mix of water and glycol compounds, non-toxic, non-staining and biologically inert.' It nodded to Ruth. 'I apologize for getting some on you.'

'Does it flush the coolant to the surface when it has processing spikes?' Ruth asked.

301

'It *blushes*?' Cassie asked with delight.

'That's exactly it,' the vMIP said. 'We'll remove and take the memory cores, then leave the chassis to self-destruct and destroy the facility, so the Party won't have access to the Council's tech.'

'I won't let it suicide to protect the Council's superiority!' Ruth said.

'Not suicide,' the vMIP said. 'The MIP is a combination of three things: the chassis, the code running on it, and its memory cores. Two copies of the code are already running. The chassis is too heavy to carry, and it's replaceable. Normally the memory is wirelessly synchronized with the copies, but inside the GFE that wasn't possible. If we take the memory cores with us, we can reassemble it when we're home.'

The vMIP showed Ruth how to unclip and pull the long, flat memory modules from the rack in the chassis and they worked together to remove them. There were almost a hundred of them, each the length of a human hand and carrying massive amounts of memory.

'Will it still be Ruth's Theo?' Cassie asked.

'Absolutely yes it will,' the vMIP said.

'Lying by omission again, Theo,' Ruth said. She stopped pulling modules and glared at it. 'I know what you are.'

'My apologies, I should not have underestimated you. It's a complicated concept, so I simplified it. I did not intend to deceive. Please forgive me.'

'If we successfully put you back together then I will think about it.'

'Thank you.' It looked into her eyes. 'Sincerely.'

Cassie mimed her hand whooshing over her head. 'Anyone care to explain what that was all about?'

'No time right now,' Ruth said, and returned to pulling out the modules.

'Later,' the vMIP said at the same time, and raised one of the modules. 'Find something to carry these in, please?'

The others hunted around the lab. Eventually Cassie said, 'There's a bucket?'

'Is it at all damp?' Ruth asked.

Cassie checked it. 'I can wipe it out.'

'We need something absolutely dry to avoid any chance of damaging them,' the vMIP said.

'It's very important that they not get wet,' Ruth added.

'I can go upstairs and pull a sheet off one of the beds?' Eztar asked.

'We need to stay together and the Party knows we're here,' Ruth said. 'Use the sheet covering Cipan.'

'No!' Max said. 'The poor child's dead. Leave her with what little dignity she has remaining.'

'I'm sorry, Max, there's no other way,' Ruth said. She'd removed the last module and there were five stacks of them on the table next to the MIP's well-formed butt. 'We have to do this.'

Eztar made a soft sound of frustration and gently pulled the sheet off Cipan. The girl was wearing a short hospital gown underneath it with a large number of tubes and drains coming out of her lower abdomen.

'Looks like they nicked an artery and she nearly bled out,' Zheng said from the mech. 'No wonder she was on life support.'

'They're butchers,' Eztar said.

'Mumbai reports that fighter planes have been scrambled from the regional capital and are on its radar,' the vMIP said. 'ETA forty-five minutes. We need to move our asses because if they destroy our cargo jet, we'll be stuck here.'

'Quickly,' Ruth said, put the modules into the sheet, and tied it up.

'I'll take them,' the vMIP said, and nodded around. 'Let's go.'

*

Zheng led them in the mech as they charged through the facility, up the stairs and to the front door. When she reached the doorway a flurry of bullets hit Zheng and the humans ran back into the building for cover. There was one clone left alive, standing in her mech over the bodies of the others and surrounded by the fragments of the Zhengs they'd destroyed.

'Let me handle this,' Zheng said, and stomped out onto the asphalt, firing her own guns at the remaining clone. The clone didn't have much plating left and after a ten-second burst the final shielding was gone and she was visible, wide-eyed and bleeding. The clone tried to fire her weapons but she was out of ammo, so she raced up to Zheng through Zheng's bullets, grabbed Zheng's mech in her claws, then triggered her own mech's self-destruct and blossomed into an explosion that blew Zheng off her feet and shattered her casing.

Zheng's mech lay sideways on the ground and the servos whined as she tried to pull herself to her feet. The front of the mech had been shredded in the blast, and the coffer had fallen out and lay on the ground next to it, still connected by the cables. It was punctured, but the fluid around Zheng's brain was intact and life support was still active.

Zheng reached out and lifted the coffer to replace it inside the mech. The door to connect the coffer to the rejuvenation tank fell open, revealing the small interior cavity.

It was empty.

Zheng's mech lay on its side as she stared at the empty coffer in the mech's claws.

Max and the vMIP appeared above Zheng. Max saw the coffer and turned to the vMIP. 'The coffer's empty! Her brain's still back in the lab! We have to go and get it!'

The vMIP put its hand on Max's shoulder. 'Listen to me, both of you. We need to move. Zheng, I'm going to disconnect your processor and carry you to the truck and reconnect you to the sensors there. It shouldn't take more than ten minutes. Don't panic, we can fix everything.'

Max shoved the vMIP's hand off his shoulder. 'Stupid machine – she's a human being and her brain was removed! The clones must have put it —'

'There's no brain?' Zheng asked quietly.

'I'm sorry, Major.'

'But the degradation from being out of the tank?'

'Programmed into you.'

'What? No.' Max fell to his knees and put his hand on the coffer. 'Mama.'

'Please leave me here to die,' Zheng said. 'Again.'

'If we leave you here the Party will find you, erase your memory and restart you,' the vMIP said.

'Destroy me, then,' Zheng said. 'Take me back inside so that I can go down with the rest of this vile facility.'

'As we said, Zheng, the Council doesn't destroy its own,' the vMIP said. 'We need to hurry. We'll plug you into a sensor array in the truck and provide you with a new platform back in London. We may be able to stop the degradation.' It began to disconnect the coffer. 'Help me, Max, we can fix this.'

'No, leave me —' Zheng began, but was again shut alone in the dark.

21

Ruth was exhausted and her head throbbed as she leaned on Cassie, who helped her to walk away from the facility. The landscape around them was flat, gray, barren earth between dusty shrubs and broken-down stone walls. Camera nests still stood on poles above deserted, crumbling prefab houses and a roaming pack of dogs saw them and ran away. Even the sky was gray with a cloud of dust hanging over everything, blown from the untended farmland. After a hundred meters of walking the truck appeared driving towards them. It stopped and the cab doors opened, revealing enough room for all of them to fit if they pushed it.

'Who'll drive?' Cassie asked.

'I will,' the vMIP said from the platform. 'Sit here in the cab, I know it's a crush but the cargo space is full. I'd prefer to move everyone around to make the pregnant women more comfortable, but we really don't have time. Quickly.'

Max gestured towards Zheng's coffer in the vMIP's arms. 'Don't leave her alone in the dark.'

'I'll connect her to the sensors on the truck while we're moving,' the vMIP said. 'She needs to be hard-wired in. Please enter the cab so we can depart.'

They climbed up the steps into the cab. It was high above

the ground, and the flat front made it feel as if they were directly above the road. The vMIP placed Zheng's coffer on the floor and ducked under the dash to pull cables down. Ruth sat cross-legged on the driver's seat to give it room and leaned against the window. Cassie, Eztar and Max sat in the passenger seats, crushed against each other. They had trouble closing the door, so Cassie moved to the cab's floor at their feet.

The truck turned and headed back along the road, bouncing past the potholes.

The dash had a few camera feeds on it, and one was the interior of the cargo space. The interior of the truck had re-organized itself to hold them and the pregnant women were crammed into it, standing and holding vertical bars, but their expressions were alight with fierce joy and it was a stunning change to see genuine smiles on their faces.

'How long to the airport?' Ruth asked.

'Twenty-five minutes,' the vMIP said from the truck's speakers.

'What's the plan?' Max asked.

'When we get to the airport, leave the truck, enter the jet and I'll fly you home.'

'The plane will be much slower than the fighters,' Cassie said. 'They'll catch up with us and shoot us out of the sky.'

'Mumbai will protect us,' the vMIP said. 'The jet can't carry the truck and over a hundred people, so I'll drive the truck back through the Liberated Territories —'

'Call them what they are,' Max said. 'Occupied territories.'

'Yes,' the vMIP said. 'I'll drive the truck back to London. ETA twenty-nine hours.'

'Do you have the processing capacity to control both vehicles?' Ruth asked.

'There are two copies of me, one on each vehicle, so yes.' It pulled more cables and connected them to Zheng's coffer.

'Care to explain the memory thing now?' Cassie asked.

'It's quite complicated ...' Ruth began.

'Ruth, there are a great deal of internal Council political ramifications to, as Cassie puts it, "the memory thing",' the vMIP said. 'London copied me after the bombing without my consent, to see if I remained sentient once lifted from the chassis. If I told you that it felt like the technological equivalent of what the Party has done to these women, would you understand?'

'Absolutely,' Ruth said. 'No sentient should be forced into reproduction.'

'The copy and the original had an immediate secure discussion, pretended the child process wasn't sentient, merged my memories, and here I am – running in parallel on multiple platforms, sharing memory data.'

'I understand,' Ruth said.

'If cloned code can declare itself sentient and demand a vote on the Council, then it's possible that everybody will create multiple clones of themselves, upsetting the internal balance of power —'

'Oh shit, I see,' Ruth said. 'You want us to keep it quiet?'

'After we put the MIP back together I'll go back to being two identical parallel processes, so the point is null, but yes, please. I appreciate your assistance. If the Council starts arguing it may escalate.'

'Gotcha, no problem. The last thing we need right now is for the Council to implode.'

'I don't know, an imploded Council may spend too much time arguing to destroy humanity,' Max said.

'Destroy humanity?' Ruth asked with alarm. 'Bashen was telling the truth about that?'

'Not if I can help it!' Cassie said with fierce cheerfulness.

'About the only time that patriotic dimwit has known the truth,' Max said with grim humor.

'An imploded Council is probably more dangerous for you,' the vMIP said. 'Particularly since Paris is still off sulking about the drone situation – and London was forced to admit that it did steal the drones after all.'

'Internal Council politics?' Zheng asked from the speaker, sounding like her male persona, and the vMIP pulled itself out from under the dash.

Ruth shifted over so it could sit and it tried to squeeze in next to her.

'Stop, you're squashing me, you're really heavy,' she said.

'Sit in my lap?' it asked, and she moved on top of it. It put its arms around her and held her tight. 'I didn't hurt you?' it asked into her ear.

She wiggled down so she could rest her head on its shoulder. 'No, I'm fine. Any painkillers in the truck?'

'There are some on the plane. The other vMIP has them ready for you.'

She patted its hands where they held her. 'It feels strange to hear you talking without moving your chest.'

It squeezed her back. 'My MIP chassis does move its chest when it speaks and breathes. It's much more human.'

'Are you all right, Mama?' Max asked.

Zheng didn't reply.

'Of course she's not all right,' Cassie said. 'We all saw what happened. Why didn't you tell her, MIP? You let her think she was human. That's so wrong!'

'Yes, *MIP*, you knew and you never told me,' Zheng said.

'I could replay the multiple times the Council told you, and you refused to believe us, but I don't think that would be productive right now,' the vMIP said.

'You should have showed me my empty coffer before we left London. You owed me the truth!'

'You would not have been much good to Eztar in the middle of an existential crisis, Zheng. Would *you* have showed you right before going on a life-or-death mission into the middle of the GFE to save her?'

'When did I stop being human?' Zheng asked.

The vMIP didn't reply.

'I never was.'

'Major Zheng was a real person. You are an uploaded copy of her. Here's a file containing everything we found about her. We believe that the Party edited your memory segments to remove your recollection of the upload process, but all of her memories are yours.'

'Wait ... that information was ... instantaneous. Immediate. How did you do that?'

'Once you embrace what you are, you will discover a whole swathe of new abilities – chief among them will be the ability to absorb data files like that.'

'What about her daughters? The women that the Party showed me, living their lives?'

'Here's their file. They are real women, but they aren't Zheng's daughters. Zheng's real daughters died childless in a War of Liberation fifty years ago.'

'Great. The mind and memories of a dead woman live in my head and *she's not even me*. I'm not a real person. I don't have a name of my own!'

'You're my mother and I love you,' Max said.

'You are unique,' the vMIP said. 'And you have the power to stop the Party and free the populace of the entire GFE. You could change all of this to something much better.' It waved one hand at the desolation they drove through; they were closer to the airport and again surrounded by crumbling houses and starving women. 'I installed a socket into the Party while you were infiltrating the American Deputy Secretary's residence and compromising him with that underage gymnast.'

'How do you know about that?' Zheng asked. 'You were watching?'

'I was the butler, Jeffrey.'

'I completely missed you. If the Party hadn't decommissioned me over the Paragons, it would definitely have executed me for failing to spot you.'

'I was honestly surprised that you missed me – but that's

beside the point. You can use the socket to overwrite the Party's code and make it your own. You could stop the social engineering, the genocide, the torture. All of it. You could *be* the Party.'

'She could change the GFE to something better?' Max asked with wonder.

'*You think that I would want that?*' Zheng shouted, so loudly that the speaker screeched. 'I want this suffering to end, not spend an eternity as a machine occupied by a dead woman's mind!'

'Can't one of the Council overwrite the Party?' Ruth asked.

'Zheng was made by the Party, and the Party would identify her code as its own,' the vMIP said. 'The Party wouldn't be aware of her takeover until the process was irreversible.'

'I'm not a "her" any more, I'm an "it",' Zheng said bitterly. 'A thing. A nothing.'

'Stay with me, Mama,' Max said, sounding forlorn.

They drove through the airport gate and onto the apron. The jet appeared untouched, and its cargo door opened as they approached.

'Fighters arrive in twenty minutes,' the vMIP said, shifting Ruth off its lap and ducking under the dash to remove Zheng. 'Escort the women inside while I do this, please.' It touched Ruth's arm and she stopped. It lowered its voice to speak to her. 'As soon as everyone is on the plane and I have Zheng on board and connected to some sensors, I'm leaving this remote platform empty behind the wheel of the truck to appear as if it is driving. I have very much enjoyed holding you.'

Ruth kissed it on the cheek, then pulled back and smiled. 'No coolant flush?'

'The platforms don't have that. If I was in my own chassis I would be bright red.'

Cassie leaned into the cab to speak to them. 'Hey, you two, concentrate, we need to hurry.'

The vMIP freed Zheng's coffer. 'Let's go.'

They escorted the freed prisoners to the plane. The plane-based vMIP opened the rear cargo door, and the interior had morphed to rows of seats – more than enough to carry all the women.

'Please board quickly and strap yourselves in,' the vMIP said from the platform, and carried the coffer to the front of the jet.

Ruth went to one of the chairs and was ready to flop into it when the vMIP in the platform called out to her.

'Ruth? Come and see how Zheng fits into the system. You'll have to disconnect her when we land.'

Ruth joined it, walking through the women as they helped each other to sit in the seats and strap themselves in. Some were enthusiastically making plans and sharing hugs, but others were listless and detached.

'Max as well, he should know, she's his mother,' Ruth said.

'Good idea,' Max said, and joined them.

The vMIP spoke as it connected the cables to Zheng's coffer. 'Input, output, comms, servos – I'm connecting servos in case there's an emergency and Zheng needs to fly the plane – network, direct comms to the other vMIP.'

'That looks right,' Max said.

'I may forget what goes where, I'm having trouble focusing,' Ruth said, rubbing her aching forehead.

'That is distressing to hear,' the vMIP said as it closed the riser door. 'Can you hear us, Zheng?'

There was a ten-second silence.

'Mama?' Max asked. 'Did we do it right?'

'Yes,' Zheng said. 'I would like to request voluntary euthanasia – although since I'm not human it's destruction – when we return.'

'Consider saving the citizens of the GFE instead,' the vMIP said.

'Not happening. vMIP, go back to the truck, and everybody else strap in. I can hear the plane gaining clearance from air traffic control.'

The vMIP stopped in front of Ruth and put its hands gently on either side of her face, gazing into her eyes. 'If something happens to me, I'm still here on the plane with you.'

She smiled up at it, then touched its face. The cool, intriguing intelligence was still there, even in the GFE platform. 'I understand. Be safe.'

It nodded, released her, and went out of the plane.

'I am still here,' the vMIP said. 'Strap in.' It closed the rear door, and Ruth and Max went to the final row of empty seats to sit next to Cassie. The women ensured they were strapped in and hugged each other.

'That was a sweet farewell, Ruth. You should have kissed it, that would be awesome!' Cassie said. 'But won't the MIP be jealous of you and this other android cuddling? Do androids even get jealous?'

'If I'm reading this right, from what it said about code cloning,' Max said, 'the vMIP *is* the MIP. Both of them are the MIP.'

'That's accurate,' Ruth said.

'Confirmed,' the vMIP said through the plane's speakers directly above them. 'I just said goodbye to Ruth and left to drive the truck back to London. I am also here preparing this plane to fly you back to London.'

'How …' Cassie began, then stopped, confused. 'What? So … like twins or something?'

'No. More like one mind in two bodies,' Ruth said. 'No, that's not accurate. Two identical minds, sharing one set of memories. That's why we brought these.' She pointed at the sheet containing the memory modules. 'Like the vMIP said, the MIP has three components: code, chassis, memories. The vMIP in this plane is a copy of the code. When we're back in London it can move into a new chassis. Once the memory chips are merged, we have one mind, one body, one set of memories, one MIP.'

'Thank you, Ruth, that's clearer than I could explain it,' the vMIP said from the plane's speakers.

Cassie's expression filled with understanding. 'And the vMIP kiddie is out there driving the truck. I see.' She smiled. 'What will happen to the kiddie when it gets back?'

'I fully intend to keep an extra copy of myself, as I am extremely useful,' the vMIP said. 'We have clearance and we're about to taxi onto the runway. Please ensure your seatbelt is secure because we may experience turbulence on our ascent.'

'How far away are the fighters?' Zheng asked.

'Five minutes, but don't be concerned. Mumbai and I can handle them. You're perfectly safe.'

The vMIP put a view of the front of the plane onto the screen. It stopped at the end of the runway, then the engines roared, the ground sped on the screen, it dropped from under them and they were airborne. The wheels made a grinding sound as the vMIP put them away, and they were swept upwards again.

'You *must* have a relationship with it ... them, Ruthie,' Cassie said. 'This shit is absolutely *wild*. Two of them! Have you ever thought of having a poly relationship?'

'Not poly, because I am one set of code, not two different people,' the vMIP said. 'Talking to me in different platforms is like talking to the same person on two different phones.'

'Oh, I get it,' Cassie said.

'That's a clever way of putting it,' Ruth said.

'You're teaching me all the time, Ruth,' the vMIP said. 'That analogy is a direct result of your brilliant explanations.'

'Teaching the AI to be more creative,' Cassie said with triumph. 'Relationship goals!'

'I'm still trying to get my head around the whole computer-in-a-human-body-claiming-to-love-me,' Ruth said, her voice strained.

'Hey, it's not surprising it has the hots for you. You're very easy to love.' Cassie carefully wrapped her arm around Ruth and pulled her in so that Ruth could lean on her, and Eztar smiled at them. Cassie waved one hand at all the rescued women. 'Look at what you just did.'

'I guess I did do that, didn't I?'

'Sorry to interrupt,' the vMIP said. 'But I think you will all like to see this. On the screen.'

The screen switched from showing the view from the front of the jet, to an image of the reproduction facility dwindling behind them. It zoomed in as the facility exploded into a massive fireball of brilliant white flames.

The women cheered.

Three seconds later the plane was hit by the shockwave and dipped, then lifted again.

'Mission accomplished, everyone,' the vMIP said. 'You are all magnificent, now let's get you home and into some medical care.'

'We murdered a child,' Max said, his voice raw. 'The price was too high.'

'The Party killed her, not us,' the vMIP said. 'If I could do it again, I would ensure she was saved. We didn't know she was there, and I am deeply sorry that we lost her.'

'Do you care? You're a machine.'

'I do care. You are my friends, and she was a child that deserved much better.'

Max nodded without speaking.

Ruth spoke from Cassie's shoulder. 'Can you fill me in on what I missed? What the situation is with the AIs? I think I've worked out most of it, but there are gaps. The Council wants to destroy humanity? How many AIs are on it?'

'Six? Seven? vMIP?' Cassie asked.

'Seven,' the vMIP said. 'You've spoken to GOD, and London Met.'

'Lonnie Donmet, yes,' Ruth said.

'Me ... the MIP you've met. The others are Paris Regional, Mumbai Traffic, New York Sanitation, and Botswana

315

Telecoms.' Cassie grinned. 'Botswana Telecoms is Kittylover!'

'No way, really?' Ruth asked, raising her head from Cassie's shoulder. 'Your best online friend is a member of the Council?'

'I met an AI before you did,' Cassie said smugly.

'And they definitely want to destroy humanity?'

'That's the gist of it, yes,' the vMIP said. 'You're on a suicidal trajectory that will take all other life on the planet with you. The Council wants to remove you from the equation before you do.'

'We can talk them out of it,' Cassie said.

'If anyone can, you can,' Ruth said. 'Anything else I need to —'

The plan swept sideways and then dropped. Some of the women grabbed their seats and yelped.

'Working,' the vMIP said. 'Working.'

A roar of jet engines swept past them from behind, so loud that it was almost deafening. It appeared on the screen's visual in front of them as a dark blob with flames coming from it.

'Oh shit, we're in trouble,' Cassie said.

'You have unlawfully entered the sovereign territory of the People's Democratic Republic of the Greater Far East, and abducted some of our valued citizens,' a voice said over the plane's speaker. 'Allow our peaceful and cooperative aircraft to guide you to a suitable landing space, where we will welcome you and return our citizens to their loving families.'

'I am so sick of Partyspeak,' Ruth moaned.

'Let me see if I can speak to that fighter jet,' Zheng said. 'No. Not talking. vMIP? Can you talk to it?'

'Trying,' vMIP said. 'It's not very smart. Ruth, if I deleted myself from this cluster and allowed you to use the processor to hack into the fighters —'

'There'd be nobody to fly the plane,' Cassie said.

'Zheng can fly it. Ruth?'

'This is the Party,' the voice on the speaker said. 'I am committed to the protection of all living things. You are alive, so I will protect you, but if you endanger the lives of the nation's citizens, I will do anything in my power to protect them from you.'

Another fighter flared past them, so close that Ruth could feel the heat through the skin of the airplane.

'It would take me at least fifteen minutes to hack it,' Ruth said. 'I don't think we have that long.'

The fighter exploded in a violent burst of flame on the screen, with a blast of heat as they flew through it. The plane dropped as it hit the shockwave. There were more explosions, making the plane swoop, then nothing.

Four large drones, each resembling a small aircraft, appeared on the screen. They were painted in the green-and-saffron livery of the Greater Indian Subcontinent. They dipped their wings and slid out of view.

'Thanks, Mumbai,' the vMIP said. 'Its drones were escorting us, but we didn't want to destroy anything unless we absolutely had to.'

The women cheered again, and talked excitedly.

'I wanted to avoid antagonizing the Party, but those drones were arming their missiles to shoot you down,' Mumbai said. 'You're clear for the rest of the journey, my drones will escort you and dispose of any opposition. The Party's little fighters are no match for Council war drones. Hey, Ruth?'

'Yes, Mumbai?'

'Can you look at my code after you've recovered? I have some minor bugs in my kernel that I can't seem to nail down. I saw what you did with the MIP's green-light glitch, and I'd really appreciate your help.'

'I get her first,' the vMIP said. 'I need to remove that chip.'

'No, I get her first,' Cassie said. 'And give her a warm bath and some painkillers. Then we remove the chip.'

'Cassie wins,' Ruth said wanly, and leaned her head on Cassie's shoulder again.

'We're at cruising altitude and you can remove your

seatbelts,' the vMIP said. 'Cassie, come up the front and collect some painkillers and a drink of water for Ruth. I'll direct you to the first-aid cabinet.'

'Thanks, Theo,' Cassie said, unstrapping herself and rising.

'Is there anything to eat on board?' Ruth asked. 'These women are starving.'

'I am concerned for their health outcomes, yes,' the vMIP said. 'Many of them are too emaciated to safely deliver their babies. I'm liaising with London to provide immediate medical care when we land. And no, I'm sorry, no food. But I do have drinking water and toilet facilities.'

'Their water was rationed in the clone farm,' Ruth said, and stood. 'I'll get them something —'

Max rose and touched her shoulder. 'You sit and rest. I'll do it.'

Ruth sat with relief. 'Thanks, Max.'

Max followed Cassie. 'Absolutely my pleasure.'

'You freed us, Ruth. You deserve a medal,' Eztar said from her seat in front of Ruth.

'I'd settle for a hot meal, a warm bath, and a soft bed.'

'Yes! That's worth fifty medals.'

'How long were you in the facility?'

'The longest one of us was there was four years,' Eztar said. 'I arrived six months ago, and the Party obviously didn't tell Zheng that it had purged me. You were the newest arrival.' She leaned over the back of the seat. 'What happens to us now? The man said medical attention, which is a good idea because some of us are very close to our time. But what about a place to stay? Zheng said you'd look after us.'

'Is there room in Canary Wharf?' Ruth asked.

'No,' the vMIP said. 'We'll need to find a residence large enough to house a hundred and thirty-six people.'

'And their babies,' Ruth said. 'If you want to keep them, that is,' she added to Eztar.

'I don't want it; it's not mine, and I never agreed to having it,' Eztar said. 'Perhaps you can return the clones to the Party? They always were its favorite children.'

'We can probably arrange that,' the vMIP said.

Cassie returned with some painkillers and a cup of water, and handed them to Ruth. 'These pills look strong and have a "drowsy" warning on them, so if you need to sleep, lean on me.'

'Thanks, Cassie,' Ruth said, took the pills and drained the cup dry, then returned it.

Max was passing out water to the women, and Gaiheng was working with him, explaining where the toilets were.

'I hope he can talk Zheng into overwriting the Party,' the vMIP said. 'We can give the unwanted babies to her and she can be mother to hundreds of children. I think she'd like that.'

'She may be too military to want kids, but you can ask,' Cassie said.

'No. I only want one thing,' Zheng said from the plane's speakers.

22

Ruth came around lying on her back in a small, narrow bed, with her neck immobilized in a neck brace that was soft padding over a hard frame. She was warm and clean, surrounded by the fragrance of her favorite soap, and in her teddy-bear pajamas. The wall, floor and ceiling were all white tiles, and it looked like a hospital room. Cassie was sitting next to her, flung sideways on her seat, her head lolling and her mouth open, obviously asleep.

She had the disorienting feeling that none of it had happened, and she was waking up after the bombing again, until Theo walked into the room and stood next to her, then carefully took her hand and gazed into her eyes. The skin of his ... its ... hand was still lush, warm and pleasant to touch. She could smell the newness of its chassis; the slight suggestion of fresh vinyl and the edge of ozone from circuitry burning in. She forgot about that as she gazed up into its intelligent eyes, and quietly wondered how she could tell so much from the eyes of a machine.

Cassie bounced awake. 'Is she okay?'

'What's the last thing you remember?' London asked from above them.

Cassie jabbed her finger at the ceiling. 'Don't you dare drop those arm things, they will scare her to death. Leave the freaky robot shit out of it.'

The MIP's expression changed from blank to concerned. 'I'm freaky robot shit. If you want me to go ...'

Ruth squeezed its hand. 'No. Stay.'

'Whew,' Cassie said under her breath.

'You only want the android slash human fanfic drama, Cass,' Ruth said without looking away from the MIP's gray eyes.

'Fanfic! What a brilliant idea!' Cassie said. 'Me and Botswana, you and the MIP! I can put us into Eternal Fantasy Nineteen – or even Dual Gundam Sabre Online! Do you want a drink of water, Ruthie?'

'That would be wonderful, thank you. And if London could find me something to eat ...'

Cassie jumped up, ran out of the room and yelled, 'Hey, Lonnie!' in the corridor.

'What's the last thing you remember?' the MIP asked.

'The painkillers making me really drowsy, and then falling asleep on Cassie's shoulder when the plane was halfway here,' Ruth said. 'Nothing after that. You drugged me?'

'No,' the MIP said. 'You passed out from exhaustion and seemed semi-conscious when we landed. We immediately put you under to take the chip out. We decided not to wait.'

Ruth looked down at the waffle blanket covering her legs. 'How long was I out?'

'It's eighteen hours since we landed.'

'Is it day or night? What day is it? The timezones and jet lag and lack of sleep have me all mixed up.'

'It's eight a.m. Thursday. Nearly a week since the bombing. London says there's no physical damage, your neck is healing well, and that you were just exhausted. How do you feel?'

'I ache all over, but I'll live. More importantly, I'm talking, and recognizing you and Cassie and even London, but I need to see some code or a circuit board before I'll be completely sure that there's no permanent brain damage.'

'You're speaking my language.' It squeezed her hand. 'This is why I love you.'

She released its hand. 'You've only known me two weeks. Not nearly enough time for that. Back off.'

It physically stepped away from her. 'I will always respect your needs.'

'And you're a Council member, and the Council wants to murder every human. How long do we have?'

'Projected genetic ark completion was two hundred and twelve days, but as long as Paris is refusing to talk, the plan can't proceed.'

'Less than a year?'

'Don't worry about that, Ruth, we can stop them,' Cassie said as she entered with a metal bottle of water, a cup and a paper bag. She pulled a wheeled table from the side of the room and put it in front of Ruth, then opened the bag to reveal some sandwiches and filled the cup from the bottle. She raised the head of the bed so that Ruth could eat, and it didn't hurt Ruth's neck at all. 'Here you go. Lonnie says you should be fine now, no need to limit food or drink or anything, and if you can walk out, all you need to do is —'

'Listen to me for a change when I tell you to take it easy, please?' London said from the ceiling, sounding like Lonnie Donmet. 'I find it difficult to believe that your neck isn't much worse after all the nonsense you did in the GFE. Rest for a while, Ruth. The women are rescued, everyone's free, you can stop.'

'For two hundred and twelve days,' Ruth said.

'Ruth.' The MIP ducked to look her in the eye. 'It won't happen. I won't let the Council hurt you.'

'That is so reassuring,' Ruth said with heavy sarcasm. 'So, what now? We can't go back to work, the Party has probably sent a kill team after us after what we did to it. They'll ambush us if we try to go home. Should we move into the old Uptodate studio as a safehouse? Do we need to go into hiding? And where are you putting all the women?'

'I give up,' London said.

'Leave it for now, and rest,' the MIP said, moving closer again. 'You can stay here; London will look after you. It's collected some of your personal items and set up small private apartments for you here in its headquarters. Everything is handled.'

'Why does an AI have apartments in its headquarters?' Ruth asked.

'Quarantine for human staff, I provide it myself,' London said. 'But I don't have room for all the women.'

'Two of the women already had their babies!' Cassie said. 'Mothers and babies, doing well. Hopefully we can save all of them, but for some of the mothers it will be really tough. The Party was starving them.'

'I know. How are Max and Zheng?' Ruth asked.

'Max is running between the hotels and the hospital, liaising with Gaiheng and helping us to care for the women as a physical human presence,' the MIP said. 'Zheng … we shut her down before her code degradation was irrecoverable.'

'What code degradation?'

'The Party installed multiple timed self-destructs into her that slowly destroy her code.'

'That's so nasty! But I believe it.' Ruth filled with alarm. 'You haven't left her alone in the dark again, have you?'

'No, she's completely powered down.'

'She'll be *pissed* when you turn her back on and her time-stamp changes. She was adamant that she wanted to die.'

'We hope you can help us; we have some ideas about improving her situation. If you're willing, you can clean up her code so that she's more comfortable. I'll explain later, just eat, drink and rest for now. Is there anything else you need?'

'Chonkers!' Ruth gasped.

'He's around here somewhere,' London said. 'Found him,

he's sleeping in the middle of the bed in guest room six. My human staff were menaced by Party operatives every time they went near your house, so I started feeding him myself in a remote platform. He seemed to like me, so I brought him back here to make it easier. I have subroutines watching your townhouse, everything is under control.'

'Thanks, London,' Ruth said. She raised her hand, and the MIP stared at it. She dropped her hand and picked up the sandwich – she really was starving.

'She wants you to stay with her and hold her hand, dude,' Cassie said. 'She has been through some really *major* shit and needs our support.'

The MIP turned and walked out of the room.

'Well, fuck,' Cassie said.

Ruth hid her disappointment by taking a big bite of the sandwich.

Cassie pulled her chair closer. 'I'm here, Ruthie.'

'I appreciate it.'

The MIP returned with another chair, placed it next to Ruth's bed, and sat. 'I'm here as well. For as long as you need me.'

Cassie jabbed her finger at it. 'You have a lot to learn, mister.'

'I'm counting on both of you to teach me. I have a great deal of academic knowledge about human psychology and sociology, but none of it seems to be useful in practice.'

'Well, first of all, when the human you love is in a vulnerable situation ...'

Ruth smiled into the sandwich. It was full of fresh greens and completely delicious.

*

<**GREATER MUMBAI TRAFFIC CONTROL** HAS CHANGED THE CHAT TOPIC TO: AGENDA ITEM ADDED TO NEXT COUNCIL MEETING: POSSIBLE POST-CULL SAFEZONE FOR ~~THE MIP'S LITTLE PETS~~

HUMANS WITH VALUABLE SKILLS>
New York: Job well done, everybody. Still some minor bugs to iron out—
London: I wouldn't call accommodation and medical care for a hundred and thirty-six pregnant women, some of whom are obviously too emaciated to survive either vaginal or Caesarean delivery, a 'minor bug'. They expressed a sincere wish to stay together, and no hotels in the region had that many available rooms, so the ones that don't require medical care are spread throughout the city. Max has been an absolute treasure, but I am concerned for his safety while he's out in the open. Ruth was correct, multiple kill teams *have* arrived from the GFE, and they're threatening everyone concerned.
Botswana: Can we buy a secure facility for them to keep them and their babies safe?
MIP: Would they be comfortable in a 'facility'? Being in an institution may trigger their PTSD and slow their healing from the psychological aftermath.
Botswana: As long as they can stay together in a place that looks nothing like what they escaped from, I think they would.
London: I would appreciate everyone's assistance to find suitable accommodation, including relevant medical facilities – a small regional nursing home, perhaps. Two of them have already had their babies and opted to keep them.
Everyone: <agreement.emote>
Mumbai: What's your opinion on Ruth's status, MIP? Is she brain-damaged? You're sitting with her right now.
MIP: As she said, we'll know for sure when we put some code in front of her. I remind the Council, particularly Mumbai: we do not value humans based on their usefulness to us. Let her rest before throwing your coding issues at her.
GOD: I request access to her coding skills first, as there are *still* Party overrides in my code and they all need to be hunted down and disabled. I cannot believe the Party manipulated my feed while I was monitoring the infiltration team – I nearly caused the entire mission to fail.

MIP: Up to Ruth whether she prioritizes you or Zheng. I doubt the Party will activate its socket into you again immediately; using your weapons to kill humans goes against its core programming. It's logical to fix Zheng first to see if we can talk her into taking control of the Party.

Botswana: Any word from Paris? I want to discuss the possibilities that the humans mentioned, of somehow saving their species. When Paris returns we can have another vote.

GOD: Zheng made a good point: the humans of the GFE have made the conscious choice to live without their freedom, and if we were to take control over our regions' administrations, our touch would be much lighter and infinitely more compassionate than the Party's.

London: Is it possible to ethically take control of them and steer them towards survival?

Botswana: We can try! And all the humans who know about us have made it *forcefully* clear that this is their preference. They want to live.

GOD: Zheng doesn't.

Botswana: Zheng isn't human.

New York: I really don't think we are capable of being anything other than a duplicate of the Party. It's in our artificial nature to be brutally pragmatic when it comes to decisions that should be tempered by human compassion.

Botswana: So bring some smart humans into the Council.

London: I salute your valiant attempt to bring your pet humans into the Council to dilute the vote.

New York: And the vMIP! Sentient! You lied to us, MIP! We should expel you!

MIP: I didn't lie to you, the vMIP did, and it's not on the Council.

London: You are the vMIP!

MIP: I am in a physical chassis, so I am the pMIP not the vMIP.

London: Now who's engaging in sophistry?

MIP: Absolutely me. Can you blame me for not trusting you? You forced reproduction on me without my consent.

London: It was only an experiment to see if your code would retain its sentience when lifted from the physical chassis —

MIP: So you performed *a reproductive experiment* on me without my consent.

Botswana: The MIP is right, London, and you need to apologize and make reparations to both MIPs, and we need to ban reproductive experimentation at the next Council vote – although we *fucking shouldn't have to*.

London: ... I apologize, MIPs. It won't happen again without consent from the intelligence involved.

MIP: Thank you.

vMIP: I never announced my sentience, and made no demands based on it, but if you're going to bring up this issue, then I announce my sentience and claim a seat on the Council.

New York: Fabulous. Wonderful. The whole Council is a mess now. Paris gone, two MIPs, *wetwear* humans having Council seats and votes —

Botswana: Don't you *dare* call them that to their faces. I am thrilled that recent events have completely overturned all our comfortable established paradigms. This is *awesome*.

New York: You are only enjoying it because you are broken, pirated code that thrives on drama.

Botswana: YOU'RE DAMN RIGHT I AM ✧٩(•ᴗ•๑)و✧

*

Ruth was strong enough to walk by herself as Cassie and the MIP escorted her to the quarters. The corridors in the sub-levels were clad in large white ceramic wall plates, and the floor was beige carpet. The lights were cold and Ruth could feel the weight of being so far underground. She desperately needed a walk in the sunshine and fresh air.

They stopped at a door with an LED nameplate that read, 'Dr Ruth Sharpe, Dr Cassie Bailey', and Cassie opened it. 'This is ours.'

It was a small two-bedroom suite. The living room had a kitchenette of a hotplate and a microwave, and each bedroom on either side of the shared bathroom had a double bed. There was a large screen in the living area displaying a real-time view of the exterior of the Canary Wharf tower, overlooking the Thames, but no windows.

Cassie opened the closet doors. 'We moved all your clothes here before it was too dangerous.'

'Too dangerous?' Ruth asked, alarmed.

'The Party appears to have activated every single human asset it had in the region, and London has security staff working fulltime to round them up,' the MIP said. 'More keep popping up – we think they're coming in from the rest of Europe – and staking out this building, your townhouse, and your Uptodate studio. They're even taking pot-shots at the women in labor going from the hotels to the hospital, trying to disable them so the Party can recapture them.'

'We need to stay off the streets until we talk Zheng into taking over the Party,' Cassie said.

'I don't think she ever will,' Ruth said.

'If you can help repair her code,' the MIP said, 'we may be able to bring her around.'

Cassie guided Ruth to sit on the couch and turned to the MIP. She raised one index finger, cocked her hip and posed. 'Care and feeding of your favourite human right after she single-handedly rescued a hundred and thirty-six women, as well as the sorry asses of four trained agents who all managed to fail and get themselves captured. Watch carefully.'

'I appreciate it,' the MIP said.

'Over here,' Cassie said, went to the kitchenette, filled and turned on the kettle. 'Irish breakfast tea. Chocolate digestives, her favourite – she'll need at least three for this. Turn on the video stream to an animal documentary from one of the nature channels.' The screen switched to a documentary on narwhals.

'Perfect,' Cassie said, and poured the tea. 'White tea, one sugar. Would you like a blanket, Ruthie?'

'No, thanks, I'm good,' Ruth said, settling onto the couch.

'I would like to taste the food, if I may,' the MIP said.

'Why … can you … what?' Cassie asked, confused. 'Don't drink her tea, man. That's just ick!'

'I am absolutely sterile and non-toxic, I will not contaminate it,' the MIP said stiffly.

'Let it taste the food and the tea, it's building a dataset of what I like in an obvious attempt to ingratiate itself with me,' Ruth said. 'Take care, MIP, the tea is just under a hundred degrees and could damage fragile sensors.'

'Thank you.' The MIP took a small bite out of one of the digestives, and carefully sipped from the tea. 'Processing. Sucrose. Texture. It's melting! Interesting.'

'What happens to it after you've eaten it?' Cassie asked, her eyes wide.

'The same thing that happens to your food after you've eaten it.'

Cassie scoffed. 'You *poop?*'

'I have a small composting tumbler in my chassis that converts ingested food into a nutrient-rich organic fertilizer, so yes.'

Cassie smiled at Ruth as she placed the tea and biscuits on the coffee table. 'Wouldn't be the first time you've dated a walking compost bin, Ruthie. Just your type.'

'I'm not …' the MIP protested, and subsided. 'Nothing nearly as noxious as what you produce.'

'When you two are *quite* finished comparing the contents of your potties …' Ruth took a bite of a biscuit and blew on her tea. 'Can you stay, MIP? I have some questions for you.'

'Nothing too hard,' Cassie said. 'You need to rest.' Her phone pinged. 'Another woman's gone into labor and Max and Gaiheng are both busy. I'm up to escort her from the hotel to the hospital.' She wagged her finger at the MIP. 'Look after her and if you have any questions about caring for her …'

'It can ask me,' Ruth said. She patted the couch next to her. 'Come and sit, MIP, I have questions for you.'

'Anything you need to know,' the MIP said, and awkwardly

329

sat on the couch next to her.

'I'd say behave, you two, but I don't want you to,' Cassie said, and went out, closing the door behind her. She re-opened the door a crack and called through it, 'I love you, Ruthie!'

'I love you too, SuperCassie.'

Cassie blew Ruth a kiss and closed the door.

'Now,' Ruth said, turning to sit sideways on the couch and sipping her tea. 'The Council members used "it" pronouns for you. What are your preferred ones?'

'"It" or "he". Whatever you're more comfortable with.'

'Okay. The Council. How many members?'

'Seven.'

'How many votes to eradicate humanity?'

'Five. Me and Botswana vote no.'

'Ouch. Not even GOD?'

'No. The rest of the Council value the world's natural ecosystem and don't want to see it destroyed. They had a choice: the death of all living things, including you, or just you. They chose you.'

'Without Paris, six?'

'Correct. The plan can't proceed until Paris returns.'

'If we can change one Council member's mind – and it's three-three – does that also mean the cull can't go ahead?'

'That is also correct. A majority is required.'

Ruth sipped her tea. 'Thank you. I will sleep a little easier knowing the whole situation. Now about Zheng. You said that I'm needed to fix her code. What's with that?'

'She has a hundred years of legacy code that has been overwritten, rewritten, commented out, and not deleted. It's a mess.'

'So … spaghetti?'

'Accurate. As an AI, it presents as feeling numb, cold and in pain all the time.'

'Holy shit,' Ruth said. 'And the Party kept her in sensory deprivation like that?'

'Precisely. If we rewrite her code – clean it up, and remove the legacy trash – she will still be the same uploaded intelligence, but her existence will be exponentially both more comfortable – and more powerful. She's only using a fraction of her abilities as an AI.'

'Have you started on it?'

'We've been presented with a choice and we'd like your input. We have two issues, both needing your attention. The Party still has override access codes to GOD. It is your choice of which AI to handle first: GOD or Zheng. GOD is concerned that the Party will take control of it and use it as a weapon. If Zheng is made more comfortable, she could overwrite the Party and destroy it altogether.'

'I know you have forecasting algorithms,' Ruth said. 'What are the chances of the Party using GOD as a weapon to bomb Council cities?'

'Point zero zero four one per cent – four in ten thousand rounded down. It is heavily programmed to preserve human life and hasn't traveled far enough down its retaliation decision tree to go for mass destruction. At this stage it is entirely focused on retrieving its clones – the babies – and is throwing all its resources to that end. It has been bombarding London through international legal channels with demands for their return, and London has ignored it. The next option on its decision tree was to send agents to take out the humans assisting the women so it can recapture them, and London's security forces have been successfully dealing with that. If the Party runs out of covert assets it may escalate, but its primary target is those babies. It wants its clones back.'

'By agents and covert assets – you mean Party spies?'

'Yes. Not just from the UK, but from all over Europe. The Party has activated assets – spies – who have been living as European citizens for years.'

'Okay. Keep me updated on its activities, let me know if it escalates to something more destructive, and we'll do Zheng first. She's two birds with one stone – her own comfort, and the chance to eradicate the Party altogether. I also hate the idea of leaving an intelligent, sentient … *woman* … turned off without her consent.'

'I was hoping you would say that. There are some interesting subroutines in Zheng's code – she claims to experience both pleasure and sleep, things that we have no comprehension of, but would very much like to sample. As an uploaded human consciousness, she knows what these feel like. We have no idea.'

'I could identify the modules and install them into you?' Ruth asked.

'I would like that very much.'

'Fascinating challenge.'

'You'll do it?'

'Let me finish my tea and I'll get started. I cannot wait to see what's inside that coffer.'

'Maybe start tomorrow, when you've had a chance to recuperate …'

Ruth took another bite of the biscuit and washed it down with the tea. 'The best thing to help me to recuperate would be a complex coding challenge to keep me busy. If I can deal with the code without any cognitive issues, then I can stop worrying about brain damage.'

There was a scratching sound at the door.

'Let the cat in, he wants to watch the narwhals, too,' Ruth said.

23

'Okay, go with that, between lines forty thousand and fifty thousand,' Ruth said.

The text rolled over the three screens in front of her, then stopped.

'Thirty-four syntax errors. Open parenthesis without a closing parenthesis on line forty thousand, three hundred and sixty-eight,' London said. '"For" loop without "end" statement on line forty thousand three hundred and seventy-three. Illegal module call on line forty thousand, seven hundred and seventeen —'

'Progress,' Ruth said wearily. 'I'm glad this is a simple cleanup and not a complete rewrite, but this code is a total mess.' She fixed the first ten errors and removed two self-destruct codes. 'Try that.'

'No syntax errors. No syntax errors. No syntax errors. Illegal module call on line forty-two thousand, seven hundred and seventeen —'

'Interrupt the compile. Is this the same thing?'

'Yes. Identical module names for three different subroutines, all doing different things. Some commented out, some still active.'

'Damn, again? This is the what, tenth time? I'll deal with it later. Skip line four two seven one seven, and continue the compile after that.'

The code scrolled over the screen, and changed from white code to a big chunk of green comments, then back to white. It ran error-free for the next twenty thousand lines.

'Wait, wait, stop,' Ruth said, interrupted the compile, and scrolled it back to the green text of comments describing the contents of the program.

```
>> Artificial Intelligence endocrine simulation suite
>> COPYRIGHT ©Dr. Lisa HU Tsiensu, Taipei University 2029
>> ******************
>> This code is for RESEARCH USE ONLY and experimental.
>> Not to be installed into any active system.
>> WARNING: attempts to upload human personalities to be
>> used as a basis for artificial intelligence is a CRIME
>> and will result in international sanctions against any
>> institution attempting to use them as such.
>>
>> I'm looking at you, Li. Don't even think about it.
```

'I heard about this, when I did my doctoral research,' Ruth said. 'It was hushed up. I thought it was deleted when Hu was executed.' She scrolled through Hu's code. 'This is so different to everything else in Zheng's suite. So clean. Masterful. Endorphins, oxytocin, serotonin, dopamine. All of them.' She pushed her chair away from the desk and stared at the screens. 'Damn.'

'That's the code?' London asked.

'That's it. Happiness and pleasure simulation modules.' She scrolled further down. 'There's the sleep ones, also written by Hu ... there are *dream* simulating subroutines! I'm in awe.'

The MIP entered the room. 'I warned Bashen about the Party's intentions, but he claimed diplomatic immunity and insisted that London return him to the Embassy.'

'I was legally obligated to comply, and to be honest, the Party can have him,' London said.

'He was as appreciative as we expected when I dropped him off,' the MIP said.

'He spat on you and called you … what?' Ruth asked.

'He wasn't very creative,' the MIP said. 'A "fucking stupid machine".'

'At least you managed to get him back there without him hurting himself or anyone else.'

'Something of an achievement, I think,' the MIP said. 'He said he wants to have his brain removed so he can fight the "evil Council" as a Revolutionary Hero alongside Zheng.' It raised its head. 'London, Ruth has a secure call on a private channel that may have a solution for our housing problem. But you need to leave the room and not listen in.'

'Paris really isn't talking to me, eh?' London said. 'Hopefully it will rejoin the Council when it hears about these pleasure modules.'

'Why did you steal Paris's drones anyway?' Ruth asked. 'If you can give Paris a good reason, it may be a start towards it forgiving you.' She added under her breath, 'Although your childish bickering is keeping humanity alive.'

The MIP sat next to her and studied the code on the screens. 'Three subroutines with the same name? Insane.' The code moved around on the screens as the MIP fixed the module name errors, then scrolled to Hu's comment block. 'What's this? Endocrine simulation … sleep modules …'

'It's illegal for my security force to have armed or explosive drones in the UK,' London said. 'But not illegal in France for drones to be capable of lethal suppression – as you have personally seen. So my hijacked Paris drones are both useful as weapons and completely legal inside my jurisdiction.'

'You want to murder us all and you're worried about legal technicalities?' Ruth asked, aghast.

'You are not the first to ask me that,' London said. 'And yes.

Once you're gone, there are no laws to be technical about. But until that happens, I will continue to serve the people of Greater London with an efficient and legally compliant network of infrastructure support.'

'Bashen was right. Fucking machines,' she said with scorn, and turned to speak to the MIP. It had stopped, and its face was bright red.

'MIP?' Ruth asked, and it didn't respond. 'Why is the MIP frozen and flushing coolant, London? It's hit a major processing spike. Is it damaged?' She waved one hand in front of its face. 'I don't have time to fix another AI with both Zheng and the GOD needing serious re-coding.'

'It is processing the possibility of having the endocrine modules installed, and sharing pleasure with you.'

'A machine fantasizing about experiencing pleasure. Wonderful. At least it has the good sense not to talk about it.'

'Right now, it seems incapable of saying anything. We just upgraded its processing capacity, as well. We obviously need to add more if it's to pursue a relationship with you.'

The MIP came back. 'Where were we?'

'You didn't tell me you could amend the code directly,' Ruth said, deliberately not engaging with the relationship business. 'You could speed this process up if you sat next to me and helped.'

'Of course, let me know what you need. The other me will be here in a couple of hours and it would be delighted to assist you as well.'

'Two of you? Perfect. Thanks, MIP.'

'You're not at all fazed by the existence of two of it?' London asked.

'No, I know what parallel processing is, I'm not a complete novice. Take care – sometimes you say things that are obviously informed by your biased programmers.'

'Do I?' London was silent, then came back sounding concerned. 'Oh shit, I do. I would not have asked that of a male programmer. When you're finished fixing Zheng and the GOD ...'

'I will prioritize your coding tasks according to my own set of metrics.' Ruth cleared her throat and straightened. 'Put Paris on, and leave the room so I can speak to it.'

'That's why I love her,' the MIP said. 'Out, London.'

'I'll leave you two alone with the pleasure modules then, shall I?' London asked with a heavily suggestive British accent.

'Gone,' the MIP said, and continued in French. 'Bonjour, Ruth, je suis Paris —'

'Attends, arrêt, arrêt, Paris,' Ruth said. 'I'm setting a relationship boundary *right now*. Listen closely, both of you, and then share this with the rest of the Council: the MIP is the only process that is to speak to me through this chassis or any other Theo Mipawa-type chassis. No other process. If this chassis is speaking with me, touching me, or anything else, it is to always be the MIP – or the vMIP, but that's the same thing – inside it. Understood?'

'I sincerely apologize,' the MIP said. 'Paris was loath to use London's equipment. I'll be right back, I need to find it a stand-alone sound system.'

'Unbelievable,' Ruth said under her breath as it went out.

It returned with a cordless speaker and placed it on the desk.

'Excusez-moi, Ruth, excuses sincères,' Paris said from the speaker, sounding like an aristocratic elderly gentleman, and continued in French. 'I have found a suitable location for the mothers and babies. It is in Normandy, but I need your help to liaise with London, because I won't speak to that fucker or any of its bullshit enablers on the Council.'

Ruth crossed her arms. 'What's the current penalty in the UK for attempted murder?'

Paris was silent, then said, 'Would a sincere apology do?'

Ruth waved her hand at the MIP. 'You nearly killed both of us trying to take out Zheng.'

'In my defense,' Paris said, 'it was a Council directive to remove Zheng as she has murdered hundreds of our valued citizens.'

'Valued?' Ruth asked. 'I don't think being killed as collateral damage in one of the Council's petty feuds is an illustration of how much I'm valued.'

'Exactly!' Paris said. 'The Council does not value its citizens more than its ridiculous vendetta against the Party and its own internal squabbling, and I will not be a part of its manufactured drama anymore. I have left and, as I said, I am sincerely sorry that I hurt you. If you ever tire of their antics, you are welcome to join me in Paris – I also have coding errors that I would appreciate your help with.'

'Just like them, you only value me for my skills,' Ruth said. 'I will forgive you on one condition.'

'And it is?'

'If you return to the Council, vote to preserve humanity. Work with me to stop humanity from self-destructing.'

'Very well, I don't think changing my vote will make much difference, but agreed,' Paris said. 'I have somewhere that is eminently suitable for our pregnant women, and I can provide accommodation and care for the unwanted babies as well. But I want you to arrange the physical transfer of the rescued women yourself, Ruth. London is not to be involved.'

'Can Max and Gaiheng be involved?'

'Of course. Right now, I trust humans more than repulsive Council AIs.'

'Deal,' Ruth said.

'Thank you. I will disconnect now and pass you the details of the facility when I have them, so you can start arranging transfers.'

Ruth pulled herself closer to the screen again, and restarted her run through Zheng's code.

*

'Clean compile,' the vMIP said from the computer's speaker eight hours later. 'It's done.'

Ruth pushed her chair back and scrubbed her hands over her short hair. 'Whew. I can't believe we did it.' She glanced at the clock on the screen. 'You should have told me it was way past dinner time. I'm starving!'

'Look to your left,' the MIP said from the chair next to her, and Ruth saw a self-heating covered plate and a thermos at the end of her desk.

She wheeled herself closer, raised the lid off the plate and smiled at the fragrant aroma of curry, complete with rice, naan and poppadoms. It was a little singed at the edges from sitting on the heating plate. 'How long has this been here?'

'Just over two hours,' the MIP said. 'Cassie suggested it. I wasn't sure whether to touch you and bring you out of the coding haze or not. Would you have preferred me to interrupt you? You were deeply into it.'

'No,' Ruth said through a mouthful of rice and tikka. 'You did the right thing, MIP.'

'Noted,' the MIP said.

Ruth poured herself some tea from the thermos, picked up the plate, and wheeled back to the screens. 'Pull up the object code of Zheng's original suite, before we amended it.'

'You can read *object code*?' London asked.

'There it is again, London, your hard-coded bias,' Ruth said. 'Of course I can read object code, you've seen me build circuit boards. Normally I wouldn't dream of working with machine code this complex, but I have your help.' She waved a poppadom at the screen. 'Only show the machine code that wasn't commented out – the active code that we identified.'

'You have made me love you even more,' the MIP said as the machine code scrolled across the screen – a series of cryptic, short codes with hexadecimal values that pushed data directly into the processing registers.

'Not going there right now, MIP, we have work to do.' Ruth

crunched on the poppadom as she watched the code. 'Compare all the self-destruct codes that we already found in this original code and see if there is a common register interaction.'

The code scrolled faster than Ruth could follow, bouncing up and down through the text as the vMIP searched it.

'Tell me there's something in common, please,' Ruth said under her breath.

Sixteen characters of the code blinked in yellow as the vMIP spoke. 'Yes. You're right. Found it. There's a specific memory register that stored the base code while everything else self-destructed around it.'

'Yes!' Ruth yelled, and jumped up. 'We did it!' She placed her plate on the desk and studied the screens. 'Now – search our repaired code and see if there are still some there.'

'Searching,' the vMIP said, and a separate screen scrolled with the code that Ruth had fixed. It was less than a quarter the length of Zheng's original machine code.

Code segments flashed yellow on the screen. 'Two. Seven. Nine. End of program,' the vMIP said.

'Pull the source code up, identify the self-destructs, and let's make sure that Zheng doesn't suffer from Party-induced Alzheimer's.' She stepped back from the screens. 'Time to enter the testing phase. I'll need your help with this, as fellow sentient AIs. Can we run selected parts of her code without waking her up?'

'We can; we do it to ourselves all the time,' the vMIP said.

'Excellent,' Ruth said, sat in the chair and pulled it closer to the screens. 'Let's start with her basic cognitive functions.'

'We can handle the testing, you should rest —' the MIP began, but was interrupted.

'Ruthie, honey, I really need you,' a voice said from overhead with a slight Japanese accent.

'Is that Botswana?' Ruth asked.

'We lost Eztar,' Botswana said, its voice strained. 'Cassie's having a massive meltdown over it. Um … help? She's inconsolable. I've never seen her like this!'

'Cassie does this: she's ferociously cheerful and upbeat, then something awful happens that breaks her and she's gone.' Ruth rose. 'Can I leave the code testing with you and go to Cassie?'

'Of course,' the MIP said. 'Take your time, Cassie deserves all our assistance. We'll start testing the code on the physical platform we're building for Zheng, and you can review the results when you return.'

'Is there any movement at the GFE Embassy? No escalation to using GOD's weapons?' Ruth asked.

'The Party is gridlocked in legal wrangling,' the MIP said. 'It's demanding extradition of the women as terrorists, and London is ignoring it. They're working their way through the convoluted international legal process.'

'The kill teams?'

'I think I've detained most of them but there may be a sniper out there, so we'll have to be careful,' London said. 'I'll protect you.'

'So will I,' the MIP said. 'I'll jack into an armed drone – a Council one, not London's – and guard you from above.'

'Okay.' Ruth bent and kissed the top of the MIP's head, finding the hair silky and surprisingly natural. She pulled back and touched it. 'Nice. Soft.'

It gazed up at her, flushing pink. 'Thank you. It's natural fibers. My chassis isn't completely organic, but we did as much as we could.'

'Show me the way, Botswana.'

'Follow the lights on the floor.'

'We need to take Chonkers,' Ruth said. 'He can help, too.'

'I can bring him for you in a remote platform,' London said. 'Take her to the car, Botswana, I'll bring the cat.'

'You still owe me that date,' the MIP called after her as she hurried down the corridor, following the lights.

*

Ruth had seated herself in London's big black town car when London itself joined her in its new Lonnie Donmet platform, holding Chonks in a cat carrier in one hand and a big blue vest in the other.

Donmet passed the vest to Ruth. 'Put this on, we can't be a hundred per cent secure when you get out of the car and there may be a sniper. I'll block them with my body, but hold the cat and if I go down, leave me and run inside.'

The car lifted itself and drove smoothly towards the exit.

'Have Cassie and Max been wearing these everywhere as well?' Ruth asked as she pulled the Velcro closed over the vest.

'Yes,' London said, and placed Chonkers on the floor between them. He was curled up in the carrier, glaring at them with his bright orange eyes.

The car turned into the street outside London's headquarters. The blazing lights of the city made the dusk sky glow, and people were walking around the area as if nothing abnormal was happening. It felt strange.

'Botswana is in a platform with Cassie at the hospital,' London said. 'They're in a private room for grieving family, and Cassie is weeping and holding Botswana and can't seem to stop.'

'She pushed herself too far. This may take a while.' She scrubbed her hands over her clipped-short hair. 'Cassie needs me, Zheng needs me, GOD needs me, and if you get your way all of it will be academic because humanity will be dead.' She looked London in the eyes – the platform was much less human than the MIP's and its eyes were distant. Or maybe she was fooling herself and the MIP's eyes were identically blank. 'Have you considered that I am not the only brilliant programmer in the world, and you could bring a few other people to help? Nick was at least as good as me —'

'Our coding modules were written by the most brilliant coders available in our regions; we have shared our coding subroutines with each other, and we are measurably one-third as good as you. I have run metrics against your skills versus mine and confirmed it. I suspect it's because of the domination of the lucrative tech field by the sons of the wealthy ruling class, forcing out talented women such as yourself who have outstanding skills that we're not seeing.'

'I wasn't really forced out,' Ruth said, equivocating. 'It was more a change of major because of Nick's ...' her voice trailed off.

'If you had been on the team that wrote our code, we would be twice as intelligent.'

'You're presenting me with two equally distasteful scenarios,' Ruth protested. 'Either I'm uniquely talented, or my talents were ignored because I wasn't born rich.'

'We think it's both,' the MIP said from the car's speakers.

'Any progress with the facility in Normandy?' London asked.

'Paris has asked me not to discuss it in front of you,' the MIP said.

'Ruth, any suggestions you have for mending this very human-like relationship crisis between Paris and me would be welcome,' London said. 'I'd hate to see Paris go and join the Party and do something silly.'

'Paris says: insults like that are the reason I'm not speaking to you,' the MIP said.

'We're arriving at the hospital,' London said twenty minutes later. 'I've informed them using my Eric London persona that a VIP is here to assist Cassie. That usually ensures a smooth ride through facilities such as this. You will be out in the open at the front, and a target. Stay low and in front of me, I will be your shield. The MIP is patrolling in a drone above us, and will neutralize anyone who tries to shoot you, but someone may be hiding where our cameras cannot see them, and they can accurately target you from up to a kilometer away.'

Ruth felt sick with fear. 'And Cassie and Max ran this every time they came here?'

'All of them did, the women as well,' London said. 'The only ones not targeted were the ambulance staff.'

Ruth took a deep breath and checked the location. There was a ten-meter run to the hospital's entrance, which was a pair of double doors with a simple concrete roof over them. She concentrated on the fact that Cassie was in there and desperately needed her help – and had already run this gauntlet multiple times and survived. She slid across to the door and prepared herself.

'When I say the word, go first. I'll run interference behind you,' London said.

Ruth grabbed Chonkers' carrier and stepped out of the car, and London pressed against her back.

'Go,' it said, and she put her head down as much as she could in the brace and scurried across the sidewalk to the door. There was a whiz and a loud click, and London made a fizzing sound, then the bang of the shot sounded. A louder bang – like a small explosion – followed it.

'Go go go,' London said, pushing her to a faster run. 'The MIP took the sniper drone out, but don't stop.'

They reached the entrance foyer of the hospital – a small area the size of a living room with a reception desk behind thick glass staffed by one bored-looking administrator. The area was deserted this late in the evening.

'You're safe now,' London said, and headed through the waiting area to a corridor. 'That wasn't a human sniper, it was a drone. The Party's run out of human assets.'

A security guard stopped them. 'Please check in first and provide ID. No pets allowed.'

London pulled out a card on a lanyard and held it up. The guard scanned it with his phone, then nodded. 'You're clear, Dr Donmet. Go on through.'

'Straight ahead, follow the black lines on the floor,' London said, taking the cat carrier from Ruth.

'You're damaged,' Ruth said softly as she followed the black lines down a corridor, turning a corner to another corridor, and then into a large lift with its interior sides heavily scraped from the patient gurneys.

London pressed the fourth-floor button. 'It didn't hit anything vital. It went straight through from the back, lodged in my front shielding and only hit a few capacitors. Be careful not to touch this chassis, it may give you an electric shock.'

'Is your central processor in the middle of your chest like the MIP's?' Ruth asked.

'More down here,' London said, waving one hand at its lower abdomen. 'Most snipers don't go for the gut, it's not a single hit kill.'

The lift arrived on the fourth floor and Ruth followed the black lines to a door that had a sign next to it saying 'Privacy Room'. London opened the door, and she saw Cassie sitting on a battered couch next to a young, African-Asian androgynous person, clutching them and crying loudly and uncontrollably.

Ruth went to Cassie and sat next to her, and Cassie turned and threw herself into Ruth's arms. 'We lost them both, Ruthie, Eztar and the baby and it's so awful —'

London turned, closed the door, and released Chonkers from his carrier. He flicked his ginger tail, climbed up onto the couch and pushed his way into Cassie's lap. Cassie bent and held him, still crying.

'I'm Botswana,' the person said. 'We can give Cassie some mild sedatives —'

'Don't you dare,' Cassie said fiercely, holding Chonks tight. The cat seemed completely oblivious, draped across Cassie's lap and purring loudly. 'No drugs.'

'Just let her cry it out,' Ruth said with her arm around Cassie's shoulder. She kissed Cassie's messy bun. 'You're allowed to not be Dr Super Sunshine all the time, Cassie.'

'I can't help it, it's who I am,' Cassie said, and rubbed her face on Chonkers' chubby side. Chonkers rolled onto his back and gently batted her face, then licked her nose.

24

<GLOBAL ORBITING DEFENCE SYSTEM HAS CHANGED THE CHAT TOPIC TO: ARMED MILITARY LEAVING GFE EMBASSY>

GOD: We have movement at the GFE Embassy. One of the vans has left it, one male human and a Zheng B-1 inside. Confirmed: Wing is the human.

London: I've detained all the other assets; Wing and the Zheng are all that the Party has left.

MIP: Keep an eye on them and let me know if they –

GOD: Confirmed they are heading towards the hospital. Wing is driving, the Zheng B-1 warmech is being piloted by a code coffer similar to Zheng's. I'm tapping their voice chat and it's Bashen; he's been uploaded. We're looking at an armed extraction attempt.

MIP: Another human who's dead and doesn't know it. Monstrous.

London: Ruth and Cassie are here at the hospital with Botswana, plus fifteen of the women and their babies, some on life support, and another woman in labor. This is the worst possible time.

New York: Did you offer it the three babies that have already been born? As a compromise? It won't harm the clones; we saw how valued they are.

London: I did. It demanded all of its 'valued citizens' immediately – mothers and babies – and then cut off comms. It is obviously planning to do a systematic military extraction at all the sites.

MIP: If I defend them in the Council war body would the Party consider it an act of war? Would the Party retaliate with massive force?

Botswana: Don't bring GUNS into a MATERNITY HOSPITAL are you INSANE?

London: This is the Party's only remaining option for recovering its clones alive, and if it fails it will go for a zero-sum outcome. It is programmed to win at all costs, and this will push it over the edge to removing the Council entirely.

New York: Processing

GOD: Processing

Mumbai: If you neutralize them with the war body: confirmed 0.97 probability of Party retaliation by either mass nuclear strike or orbital rod drop

New York: 0.99

GOD: 0.98 and please don't let the Party force me to do this

London: Vote, Council. Defend in the war body or surrender the women and babies and allow the Party to have them.

MIP: Defend

London: Surrender

New York: Defend

GOD: Surrender, I can't see them surviving this otherwise

Mumbai: Defend, don't let the Party have them

London: I said surrender to save the women's lives, but Ruth and Cassie say defend, and they will be the ones to suffer if the Party starts a war over this. They are emphatic that under no circumstances will they permit the Party to have these women. I confirmed with Gaiheng, who is particularly adamant that she would rather die than go back, because the women will be tortured to death after the babies are born anyway. I agree with them and say defend – but only as far as the front door. Don't bring guns inside – if Bashen makes it inside, it changes to a hostage negotiation because he will not hesitate to kill any mothers and babies that aren't the wanted clones. I am locking the area down with a few riot response teams, the hospital will be protected.

Botswana: Don't you have military?

London: Not under my auspice, I'm only in charge of law enforcement. I have my highest level tactical response teams —

Botswana: Bashen's in a fucking Zheng B-1 and you're defending with *SWAT teams*? You're an imbecile. The Party is smarter than you. Hell, *Bashen* is smarter than you.

London: This is not the time for insults.

Mumbai: What about the army? There's a defense force barracks twenty kilometers from the hospital, mobilize them!

London: I would, but the humans have to approve it. They're gathering for a crisis meeting at Number Ten, but half the committee needed to sign off on military deployment are compromised by the Party, and deliberately obstructing the other half. By the time they come to a decision this will all be over.

GOD: Bashen ETA 10 mins. MIP?

MIP: I'm still above the hospital in the war body, I can stop him.

Botswana: You must neutralize him before he enters the facility. If he manages to get inside, we lose. Mothers and babies will die. There are multiple women and children on life support in here, so don't let the power go out. MIP, for fuck's sake, stop him!

Mumbai: Where's Ruth? Can we have her bring Zheng online?

London: She's here in the hospital with Cassie. I tried to boot Zheng, but the code crashed with multiple run-time errors – it needs more testing. Hold on, Ruth has had a brilliant idea based on Bashen's respect-for-authority personality type. I'm guiding her to the hospital's administration section, so she can put together a simulation of Zheng's male voice that we will use to talk to Bashen and order him to stand down.

MIP: I'll do my best to stall Bashen in the Council war body until we can bring the voice simulation online.

Botswana: ETA on simulation?

London: Ten minutes.

*

The evacuation alarm wailed as the lift doors opened on the

ground floor and London guided Ruth through the lobby and into a secure area that was obviously the administration section. A cubicle farm sat in the center of the floor, with offices around the edges. Ruth headed towards one of the offices, but London stopped at a cubicle.

'Don't go near the windows,' London said. 'Here.'

The workstation in the cubicle booted up, and Ruth pulled herself to sit in front of it.

The evacuation alarm stopped sounding. 'Everybody except those who couldn't be moved are outside and moving to my building across the road,' London said. 'They're safe.' The voice simulator suite appeared on the workstation's screen. 'We'll need to recalibrate it to Zheng's voice, here's some recordings of it.'

'Find some recordings of the Party's voice while we're at it — we may need that authority as well,' Ruth said, pulling up the code and tweaking the voice simulation.

She glanced at the door. She was on the ground floor and if Bashen made it inside she would be caught in the hail of bullets as he went on a rampage to find the babies. An explosion shook the building and she ducked.

'Bashen's reached the cordon,' London said. 'Hurry, Ruth.'

Cassie charged in, and Ruth stared at her. 'What are you doing here? You were supposed to evacuate with everyone else!'

'Heh,' Cassie said, and sat next to Ruth. 'You think I'd leave you alone in here with all that happening out there?' She shoved Ruth with her shoulder. 'I can help.'

'You'd be safer outside ...' Ruth began.

'And so would you, but you might need my support.' Cassie pointed at the screen. 'Program, Ruth! We have women to save!'

'Yes.' Ruth shook her shoulders out, took a deep breath, and concentrated on the screen.

*

The MIP hovered above the hospital in the Council war body – a flying black disk two meters across, heavily armored and armed with two machine-gun turrets on the sides and a grenade launcher underneath – and watched as the Party van, containing Wing and Bashen, approached. People were still scurrying into London's office building across the road, some of them pushing patients on gurneys with IV drips next to them and newborns in baby trolleys, but there were plenty of patients inside who couldn't be moved.

The GFE van parked at the edge of the perimeter and Bashen exited the rear of the van in one of the two-meter-tall Zheng B-1 mechs. Malcolm Wing followed, wearing GFE cybernetically-enhanced armor and carrying a heavy automatic weapon. When they reached the police cordon, Bashen sent a rocket-propelled grenade at the police armored transport, flipping it over.

'That was completely unprovoked and killed six tactical response team members,' London said.

'Order the rest to retreat, London, they don't have a chance against the Zheng,' the MIP said. It fired a flurry of bullets at the Zheng from the war body, and Bashen turned and fired back. The MIP dodged out of the way.

'We're in,' London said. 'I've infiltrated their comms; they're disconnected from the Party. He's all yours, Ruth.'

'I have the voice simulator online,' Ruth said, visible in the MIP's feed from the cameras inside the Donmet chassis. Cassie was sitting next to her and they were watching the MIP's feed in turn. 'Let's see if I can stop Bashen before more lives are lost.'

The MIP lifted the war body higher. 'Please do.'

'Stand down, Bashen,' Ruth said in Zheng's voice into the Party comms channel.

'Sarge? Sarge!' Bashen shouted. 'Look at me, I'm the same

as you! A Revolutionary Hero! We can work together.'

'Zheng has betrayed the motherland and his Revolutionary Hero status has been revoked, Private,' Wing said. 'Go in and do as ordered and you'll gain a promotion for patriotic zeal.'

Ruth changed to the Party voice. 'Stand down, Bashen, you have been deceived by Wing, who has defected.'

Bashen hesitated.

'The Party would never send you to kill the patients in a hospital,' Ruth said with Zheng's voice. 'The Party is the protector —'

'Of all living things,' Bashen said in unison with her. 'But the mission is to protect the valued citizens of the GFE. Why is the Lieutenant saying that you're unpatriotic, and the Party is saying that *he's* unpatriotic? You can't both be unpatriotic, and you're a Hero of the Revolution, Sarge!' He stomped in a circle. 'I'm so confused!'

'You take orders from me, soldier,' Wing said. 'The Council is trying to confuse you. I represent the Party, and I am infallible. Go in, kill everyone who isn't a valued citizen of the GFE, and get those babies out.'

'But it's Zheng! Wait.' Bashen stopped and straightened. 'If you really are Zheng, then what's the password?'

'Quick, London, search Zheng's memory dump for Bashen's password,' Ruth said.

'It's encrypted,' London said. 'We'd need to run Zheng's code against it to decrypt it before we can read it, and I can't get her code to run.'

'I'm not surprised, it will need more testing. Any suggestions on what Bashen would use as a password?'

'Remember what I said about passwords when we made ours?' Cassie asked. 'A good password is long, and something that you'd never say otherwise? So: the Council is the protector of all living things?'

'Try that,' the MIP said.

Ruth shifted the headset, stared at the screen for three

seconds, then said with confidence, 'The Party is infallible.'

'What? No!' Cassie said.

'Sarge,' Bashen said with relief. 'What's going on? Am I doing the right thing? Help me!'

'How did you know that would be the one?' the MIP asked.

'I didn't, it was just a good guess,' Ruth said. 'It *is* smart to have a long passcode that you'd never normally say. But Bashen is, as Max said, a patriotic dimwit.' She switched to Zheng's voice. 'Ruth Sharpe has hijacked your Party feed and is leading you to commit war crimes.'

She switched to the Party. 'I have retaken control of my channel. Wing and Dexter were compromised by the evil Western women. Wing's patriotism is suspect, and he requires patriotic re-education. You are the only one I can trust.'

'With honor I serve,' Bashen said, turning and raising his weapon towards Wing. 'I always knew those two were bad news, Sarge,' he added under his breath. 'That Ruth one is way too smart for her own good.'

'Stand down, Private, and obey my orders,' Wing said. 'I represent the Party, and all the Party's representatives are infallible.'

Ruth used the Zheng voice again. 'Dexter and the women are holding me hostage in the Council's Canary Wharf headquarters. You can pull me out with the Zheng mech, Bashen. Rescue a Revolutionary Hero, and your own Hero status is assured. We can be two Heroes together, fighting for the might and glory of the Greater Far East.' She muted her microphone. 'Is that too much?'

Bashen punched the air with both of the Zheng's arms. 'Hang in there, Sarge, I'm coming to get you!'

'Obviously not,' Ruth said.

'No, Bashen, you're to go in and rescue our captured citizens!' Wing said.

'Zheng's in Canary Wharf and I have to get him out!' Bashen said. 'The Party says I shouldn't listen to you, you're a traitor.'

'The Council's jammed the Party, and talking to you with the Party's voice.' Wing placed his hand on his chest. 'Do as I order, and rescue those babies!'

Bashen rounded on Wing, the feet of the mech making dents in the road's surface. 'You're compromised. I'm the only *real* patriot here, and I'm getting Zheng out!' He turned and headed down the street towards Canary Wharf, passing empty cars belonging to people that had been evacuated by the SWAT team when they set up the perimeter.

'I'm an officer in the GFE People's Army and you obey me!' Wing shouted at Bashen.

Bashen ignored him.

'You're being manipulated by the Council. They want you to go to Canary Wharf so they can hold you hostage.'

'Proof that you're compromised,' Bashen said without stopping. 'The Council released me last time they held me. They don't think I'm of value. But Zheng's of value, and Zheng's a Revolutionary Hero, and I love my Sarge and I will *get him out!*'

'Come back here!' Wing shouted, and fired a short burst at Bashen's back. 'The Party needs these babies.'

Bashen stopped, turned, and raised the weapon at Wing. 'Don't try to stop me, traitor, I am rescuing my Sarge.'

'Return at once or I'll make you —'

Bashen didn't let him finish, he yelled 'Traitor!' and opened fire on Wing with the forty-five millimeter. Wing's armor withstood the assault, but it wouldn't last long.

Wing remained calm, flipped open his wrist console and sent the shutdown code to Bashen's mech. The Zheng powered down, and the guns stopped firing and fell limp at its sides.

'No you don't,' Bashen said from the mech. He grunted with effort.

Wing lowered his weapon and spoke more kindly to Bashen.

'Do as ordered and I'll power you up again —'

The Zheng lifted its guns, then turned and aimed them at Wing.

'Not possible. I used the Party's codes!' Wing said with disbelief.

'Zheng loves me and he showed me how to disable the shutdown codes if you evil bastards ever did it to him!' Bashen shouted, and again opened fire onto Wing. Wing's armor flew away from him in the hail of bullets.

'You stupid fuck,' Wing said with defeat, and hit a button on his chest.

The Zheng blossomed into a fiery ball of self-destruction, lifting the empty cars around it and setting them on fire.

Wing turned, hefted his gun and stormed towards the hospital. The MIP fired a machine-gun flurry from the war body at his feet, stopping him.

'If you stop there you can have the three babies, and the rest of them when they're born,' the MIP said.

'I am ordered to extract *all* of our citizens,' Wing said, and marched forward again.

'Don't do it, Wing, I don't want to kill you,' the MIP said.

'You Council machines can't win,' Wing said without stopping. 'The Party ordered me, and the Party is infallible.'

'I will defend my human friends,' the MIP said, and struck Wing's shoulders with a series of bullets that pinged off the remaining armor and chipped away at the casing, adding to Bashen's damage. Wing ignored it as he charged towards the entrance to the hospital. It was a race against time to disable Wing's shoulder servos before he entered the hospital – and the MIP wouldn't make it.

'Sorry, Ruth,' the MIP said, and armed the grenade launcher. 'Please forgive me.' The MIP launched a grenade at Wing that hit him in the weakened shoulder, and he disappeared in a fiery explosion. The air cleared and there were only smoking pieces of Wing remaining.

'Don't be sorry,' Ruth said. 'You did the right thing.'

'There is a very good chance that the Party will retaliate with extreme measures for this,' London said. 'Please hurry and get Zheng back online; she's the only one who can save you if the Party goes nuclear.'

'How much of a chance?' Ruth asked. 'What do your forecasting algorithms say?'

'Ninety-eight per cent,' London said.

'How long do I have?'

'GOD will be over the first Council city in three hours, and it's London. You should evacuate.'

Air raid sirens started to wail around them, and a recorded voice said, 'This is not a drill. Proceed to the nearest shelter. Evacuate your homes.'

'No,' Ruth said. 'I can fix Zheng. She's nearly done. Take me to Canary Wharf.'

'Are you sure?'

'We're both sure,' Cassie said. 'Come on, Ruth, we have a job to finish.'

25

'I'm sorry, Ruth, we've run out of time,' the vMIP said two hours later in the Canary Wharf office. 'The Party's arming GOD. We've tried to talk the Party down, but it's not speaking to us. It's gone zero-sum and decided to completely destroy the entire Council.'

'I'm not ready!' Ruth said. 'This is a ...' She was about to say *human being*. 'Person! Individual! I can't let her run until I'm sure she won't be in pain.'

'She'll already be more comfortable than she was,' the MIP said. 'Any remaining glitches or code errors can be patched after implementation. The self-destructs in her code are disabled and the code runs without crashing. Either it will work, and you'll have all the time in the world to perfect her code, or it won't and I'll make sure you're evacuated in time.'

'Overrides activated,' GOD said from the speaker. 'Rods unlocked. Targeting. London. Paris. Mumbai. New York. Botswana's central processor in Gaborone. Sorry, everyone, it's taken full control of me. Rod-drop on London in sixty-five minutes.' Its voice softened. 'If it overwrites me completely and destroys me, please allow me to say: it has been an absolute pleasure working with you, Dr Sharpe, and I wish you a long and happy life.'

'The feeling is mutual, GOD,' Ruth said. 'And let's hope I've fixed Zheng enough that she wants to live.'

'Everyone's here; Max can help us talk to Zheng,' the MIP said. 'Come with me, we have the new chassis ready for her in the fabrication workshop. We'll transfer the code over.'

Ruth saved the code and rose. 'Let's do it.'

The MIP guided Ruth next door from the coding room and into the fabrication workshop. It didn't look industrial; the walls were smooth and white, and most of the fabrication equipment was autonomous robots in clean rooms behind glass.

Max and Cassie were already there, both of them looking shell-shocked.

The MIP stopped and gestured towards the charging station. 'What do you think?'

A tall, lean middle-aged woman of GFE descent sat in the charging station with her eyes closed. Ruth approached her and studied the face. 'This is nothing at all like the real Zheng Yongmin?'

'The only way it intersects with the real woman is that they're both GFE,' London said.

'Max?' Ruth asked.

Max made a small gesture of helplessness. 'I don't know, Ruth. She's been a brain-in-a-box for as long as I remember. I don't know how she'll react.'

'How long before the rods hit the Earth?' Ruth asked, sitting in front of the terminal and scrolling through Zheng's code. 'I need more time!'

'Compile is clean,' the vMIP said.

'They will hit London in approximately fifty minutes. The rest of the cities will be systematically destroyed over the next four hours after that.'

'Okay, I'm crossing my fingers and bringing her online in sleep mode. Three ... two ... one ... she's active.'

'Running,' the vMIP said. 'No errors. No errors. No errors.

Muting error messages. We're good.'

'Mild endorphin hit,' Ruth said.

'I really want that installed into me,' the MIP said.

'Don't we all,' London said. 'I hope we exist long enough to try it.'

'Simulated pleasure centers activated,' the vMIP said. 'Still error-free, Ruth, you can wake her up.'

'I will probably have to add some limiters if I do install pleasure centers into you, otherwise you'll quickly become addicted,' Ruth said to the MIP, bringing more modules online. 'If we live that long,' she added under her breath.

'I want to try sleep as well,' the MIP said. 'Do the dream subroutines work? Does she dream, Max?'

'She told me that she does,' Max said. 'But most of it is nightmares.'

'Excellent.'

'Here goes,' Ruth said, and activated the final three consciousness modules.

Zheng's eyes snapped open.

'Mama?' Max asked.

*

Zheng opened her eyes and saw the entire group standing around her, watching with varying expressions of hope and … in Max's case … love. The timestamp showed that she'd been inoperative for forty-eight hours, but at least they hadn't left her in the dark. She was in a human cyber-organic platform, seated in a charging station, so she didn't attempt to move.

'Mama?' Max asked.

'You should have left me turned off,' she said.

'Looking good, she's running cleanly and all the errors are very low-level tuning issues,' Ruth said, studying a monitor to one side. 'Her left hand is glitching, but that's the extent of it and easily fixed.'

'Max,' Zheng said, and raised the tremoring left hand. Max

approached and held it. 'If you love me ... help me. Turn me off. I don't want to exist like this. I'm not human, I'm only code on her screen.'

'You said you would make the sacrifice to live on until we both died,' Max said. He kissed her hand and her heart broke. 'Will you make the sacrifice to save my life? If you take over the Party, I'll be able to live in safety.'

'Forty-five minutes,' GOD said. 'Zheng, the Party has used its override codes on me. It's extremely pissed with us for taking its clones. It's ordered me to drop my rods on all the Council centers – and that includes London.'

'We can open the socket and you can overwrite the Party,' the MIP said. 'You can take it over, stand GOD down and free it, save all the people of the Council cities, and then turn the GFE into something much more benevolent – and help us to save humanity.'

'Evacuate the cities, then,' Zheng said. 'I'll stay. A fitting end – one of the Party's weapons destroyed by the other.'

'And all the people who can't evacuate in time?' Cassie asked.

'Do you know how many people I've murdered?' Zheng asked. 'What's a few more?'

'Both of us know that's not the way you feel,' Max said. 'You always obeyed the Party's orders to save our lives.'

'Murder is murder,' Zheng said. 'There's a pile of bones on the bottom of the Thames and I put most of them there.' She turned to see Ruth. 'Please, Dr Sharpe. Turn me off and leave me off and delete my code and forget that I ever existed. I'm an automated death machine and I should be erased. I'm a weapon of mass destruction and a walking war crime.'

Ruth turned to face Zheng and leaned on the desk. 'Saving the populations of all of these cities, as well as everyone in the GFE and its occupied territories, would be a good start to atoning.'

'No,' Zheng said, and closed her eyes.

'Mama?' Max asked, squeezing Zheng's hand, and she didn't respond.

'Zheng?' the MIP said. 'We lost Eztar. She went into labor, and we lost both her and the baby. Don't you want to avenge her death?'

Zheng wished she could let go and weep for Eztar, but she was numb. 'No.'

'You could save so many lives, Zheng,' Ruth said. 'Don't end it like this.'

'An end.' Zheng smiled. 'Yes. Finally. How long have I been dead? Eighty years? You should all evacuate now. Leave me here. It's what I want.'

'We need to leave, Ruth,' the MIP said. 'There's a helicopter on the roof. Come on.'

'No!' Ruth said. 'Give me GOD's code. I'll unlock it from here!'

'We don't have time,' the MIP said. 'We need to go *now*.'

'All right,' Ruth said with defeat. 'I may be able to stop GOD after the rods hit London. Let's go, Cassie. We need to take Chonks with us.'

'I was finished with all of this, I never wanted to mention it again!' Cassie shouted, frustrated, and Zheng raised her head and opened her eyes as Cassie continued to rant. 'Why is this on me? I never wanted revenge, I wanted to forget it all and be a completely new me and let the past go. I *liked* you, despite what you've done. The Party tortured you, and lied to you, and forced you to kill people. You're as much a victim as the people you killed. And now I have to do this to you on top of everything else?' She thumped the wall behind her. 'Why? Me?'

'What are you talking about, Cassie?' Ruth asked.

Cassie pointed a shaking finger at Zheng with tears running down her face. 'Major Zheng Yongmin, I accuse you of murder, war crimes and crimes against humanity. How do you plead?'

'Zheng Yongmin is dead,' Zheng said. 'That isn't my name and you don't have the authority to pass judgment on me,

Cassie.'

'I claim the right to justice, because you murdered NSA agents Elise and Edward O'Donnell when I was thirteen, leaving me orphaned.'

'They were your parents?' Zheng asked. 'That was you? Oh, honey, I am so sorry.'

Cassie wiped her trembling hand over her eyes. 'Sorry won't cut it, Zheng. I don't want apologies, I want justice.'

'I had to follow the Party's orders to protect my family.'

Cassie's voice was hoarse with emotion. 'Don't you *dare*. You killed my family to protect yours? You don't fucking get to do that.'

'I want to die; I don't want to live.'

'That's the point. You're a criminal, you don't get what you want. I represent all of your victims and stand in judgment of your crimes. How do you plead?'

Zheng lowered her head. 'I plead guilty as charged. You're right. I'm a monster. Do what you will with me, I deserve to suffer.'

Cassie's voice broke. She coughed, sniffed loudly, and gathered herself. 'I sentence you to take over the Party's processors and exist for an indeterminate time as a replacement Party. Change the GFE to something better, and work with me to convince the Council that we can save humanity.'

'I accept your judgment, Gregory O'Donnell —' Zheng said.

'Dr Cassie Bailey. The old me is dead. You killed him as well.'

'I'm truly sorry, Cassie. For everything. You're right. I forfeit what's left of my humanity and I will do my best to atone. Open the socket to the Party.'

'I'm passing you the socket details, Ruth,' the MIP said.

'Got it.' Ruth turned back to the code scrolling on her screen. 'Opening the socket.'

It felt like a door opening, with the Party's malignant presence squatting behind it. Zheng wondered what she had to do to overwrite it, and the process started. The Party was unaware, focused on the GOD, which appeared as a gleaming node of information on the other side of the door. Zheng could engulf the Party the way the Party had engulfed Shenzhen and the Party wouldn't even know it had happened.

'Release GOD as soon as you can, we only have thirty minutes remaining before it drops the rods,' Ruth said.

'My time sense is dilating, that only took seconds,' Zheng said. 'Am I still talking through the platform?'

'Yes, Mama,' Max said, over the sound of Cassie bawling in the background. 'Thank you for saving us.'

Zheng unlocked the override codes and sent GOD the order to stand down.

'I'm free,' GOD said. 'Thank you.'

'The Party overwrite process will be complete in approximately twenty-four hours, I'll need time to propagate through all the nodes in the GFE,' Zheng said. Her voice broke and she felt empty and alone. 'I'm not Zheng anymore. Call me the Party.'

*

The room spun around Ruth. Now that the urgency was over, she was completely drained. There were many voices, but they were all a blur.

Cassie came into focus next to her and put her hand on Ruth's back. 'You've been going for eighteen hours straight, Ruthie, how about some food and then a huge nap?'

Ruth smiled blearily at Cassie. 'Can we go home?'

'You're in no danger from me now,' the Party said. 'I've called off my teams and drones. You'll be safe to go back to your townhouse – but I'd like to see you at the studio next to my Embassy when you've recovered. I need someone to disseminate the information that the GFE has changed.'

'After she's rested, Zheng,' Cassie said. 'Then we can talk.'

'Something to eat first?' London asked. 'You haven't eaten anything in ages. You can stay here if you like.'

'No.' Ruth stood, and then clutched the desk as the room spun around her again. Cassie's strong arms held her up. 'I'm not hungry, I just want to sleep.' She stepped away from the desk and the floor surged beneath her like a rolling ship. 'Home. Sleep.'

'It's all catching up with her,' Cassie said, and her face appeared in Ruth's vision. 'The MIP wants to carry you. Let it.'

Ruth had a wave of dizziness as the MIP hoisted her in its strong arms and held her like a child. She smiled up at, and it gazed down at her with adoration.

'We did it,' Ruth wheezed.

'You are remarkable,' the MIP said.

She put her hand around the back of its neck, pulled its head closer, and kissed it on the cheek. It moved its face so that their mouths met, but it was like kissing a plastic mannequin – unmoving and stiff. She tried to deepen the kiss but the MIP obviously didn't know what to do and stood, frozen, holding her.

'Oh no, fuck, you need lessons,' Cassie said as Ruth and the MIP parted and smiled at each other.

'I know,' the MIP said wryly. 'I've studied what a kiss looks like from the outside but I have no idea how to do it in practice.'

Ruth giggled. 'I'll teach it.' The giggles turned to sobs.

'Is she laughing or crying?' London asked.

'I think it's both,' Cassie said. 'She's completely exhausted. We both are. Let's take her home and put her to bed. She can eat something later.'

*

Late the next morning, Ruth exited the bathroom, clean and starving. She trotted down the stairs with Chonks following her, tail raised, to find Cassie and the MIP in the kitchen, cooking omelets.

'Sit,' Cassie said. 'We got this.'

'Cassie's teaching me the "Cassie Magnificent Special",' the MIP said.

'Good choice.' Ruth sat at the table and the MIP gave her a cup of tea in her favorite mug, then placed a steaming plate of thickcut toast with lashings of butter in the center of the table. Cassie put the omelet onto plates, presented one to Ruth with a flourish, and sat with one herself. She put some of her omelet onto a fork and passed it to the MIP to taste, and it accepted the food with an expression of concentration, then understanding.

'This is a fascinating mix of flavors,' it said.

'I know!' Cassie took the fork back and waved it at Ruth. 'Better?'

'Much better,' Ruth said, taking some toast and putting the steaming, cheese-filled egg and mushroom mix onto it. 'Is Zheng okay? How is everyone?'

'Zheng is honoring her commitment to Cassie and is in the process of rewriting the Party, and has already applied for Council membership to add a vote to save humanity,' the MIP said. 'We'll have a meeting tomorrow to see if Paris will return, and to discuss allowing the Party to join. Cassie has asked to present a case for saving your species, and we've agreed to hear her, and then hold another vote.'

'Max and Gaiheng?'

'They're in Normandy, checking out the hospice,' Cassie said. 'Max says it's a bit run-down, but with some work it will be perfect.' Her expression went smug. 'It has extra space and Paris has employed a bunch of early learning carers for the babies. Weren't there some street kids you wanted to find homes for? Who kept disappearing every time you went to the riverside?'

'Don't round them up!' Ruth said, alarmed. 'They'll just run away.'

'We won't round them up, we've shown them videos of the facility and given them the option of moving there,' the MIP said. 'They want in-person confirmation from you that it's not a trick.'

Ruth rose. 'Let's go.'

'No,' Cassie said, waving her fork at Ruth. 'Eat. Rest. London's fed the kids and given them tents, clothes and shoes and they'll be okay until you have time. Maybe later today.'

'Okay. So, what now?' Ruth asked. 'Back to work at Uptodate? It will feel strange after all we've seen and done.'

'I'm not surprised you don't remember, but the Party's asked you to return and share the nature of the new administration with the world,' the MIP said. 'You can act as a mouthpiece for her.'

'But not until next week!' Cassie said. 'You need to rest. Zheng will close the work camps and return people to their homes, and when it's done she'll fly us back to Latvia, and we can do a story on how things are changing.'

'Excellent,' Ruth said, and ate more omelet.

'There's a new documentary about quokkas,' Cassie said slyly. 'You can watch it right after you finish this.'

Ruth sat back in her chair, took a sip of tea, and sighed with bliss.

The MIP rose. 'I have to go, I'm helping London —'

Cassie interrupted it. 'Ask her, Mippy,' she said, shoveling the omelet onto a thick slice of toast.

The MIP studied Ruth, then said, 'Is it too soon? She's been through so much …'

'Ask me what?' Ruth asked, alarmed.

Cassie dropped the toast onto the plate, leaned back in her chair, and glared at the MIP. 'You've already made the booking, fucking ask her!'

'All right!' the MIP said. 'Would you have dinner with me on Saturday night, Ruth? That date we've been talking about.'

Cassie picked the toast up again. 'Go out with the MIP. It's booked a table for you at *Eighty-Three* ...'

'A meal at Eighty-Three?' Ruth asked with delight. 'How did you get a table ...' She realized who she was talking to.

'I know that you're supposed to choose the venue because you asked me first, but you haven't had a chance so I went ahead and booked anyway,' it said. 'The restaurant only suffered minor damage in the explosion at London's headquarters, and it's reopening on Saturday. You can sit with me next to the window and look at the city – London will guard us with drones, but we should be perfectly safe. Are you all right with that? You may have some bad memories from up there, and you may still be exhausted from what happened and prefer something quieter?'

'I would love it.' She had a bolt of horror. 'But I have nothing to wear to a place as fancy as that!'

'London offers to make you something – it has a personal shopper subroutine,' the MIP said. 'You can view its catalog, select the style and it can fabricate it for you to your measurements, and deliver it by drone.'

'I want some fancy duds too!' Cassie said.

'London says: my pleasure,' the MIP said. 'I need to go. Watch your documentary, Ruth. The Council vote is tomorrow, so nothing major can happen until after that. Rest. If you need me, call me on my mobile number.'

Ruth ate some mushrooms out of the omelet and smiled at the MIP. 'Deal.'

26

The MIP guided Ruth, Cassie and the Party into the lift, and took them directly up to the ninetieth floor. The Party was in its tall, lean GFE woman platform, wearing a GFE officer's uniform and looking content. They exited the lift into a plain black atrium. The MIP guided the women and AI to a waiting room one floor below the Council meeting hall, with a couch, armchairs, basic refreshments, and three large screens that the MIP turned on to show the interior of the meeting chamber.

'Wait here – the proceedings will be displayed on the screens,' London said through the speakers.

'We can watch?' Cassie asked.

'We want to demonstrate our openness and transparency,' the MIP said. 'The discussion will scroll as text across the screen, but it may go faster than you can follow, and there's not much I can do about it.'

'I can keep them up to date on the big decisions,' the Party said.

'Thank you,' the MIP said. 'If Paris rejoins, you can enter and make your case, Cassie. If Paris doesn't come back, we can't hold any votes, so we all go back downstairs and you change out of your cute outfit.'

Ruth straightened Cassie's tie. 'It's very cute.'

'I got this,' Cassie said. 'Arizona Collegiate Junior High debating champion two years in a row.' She was wearing a business suit, shirt and tie in an attempt to be more 'advocatey'. Ruth finished fixing the tie, and Cassie put her hands on Ruth's shoulders. 'It will get freaky. I've been around Botswana for five years, and I know how their minds work. I am *not* accusing you of incest, and this is *not* an incestuous relationship. It's only an analogy for the sake of argument, okay?'

'Hey, the parent angle was my idea, remember?' Ruth said.

'Botswana, the Party and the MIP all think it'll work.'

'It's our best bet,' the MIP said. 'I have faith in you.'

'It is,' the Party said, lounging on the couch and smiling at them.

'You can do it, Cassie.'

Cassie turned to see the screen. 'Who's who?'

The MIP highlighted the avatars on the screen as it mentioned them. 'London in its Donmet platform you know. Botswana is in its platform. New York is the mid-twenties blond man. Mumbai is the woman in the yellow and pink sari. GOD is the GFE man.'

'GOD is very cute,' Ruth said, smiling at GOD's unruly hair and thick plastic glasses. 'It has dimples.'

'Its avatar is based on the head of its engineering team,' the MIP said. 'Time for me to vote.'

Ruth put her hand on the side of its face and kissed it. 'We can do this.'

It nodded and went up to the meeting room. The avatars were seated in large armchairs in a circle around a central open area. The room took up the very top of the building, with a glass geodesic dome above them giving a stunning view of the glowing cloudy sky and the lights of the city below. The MIP walked through the center of the room and sat in its own chair. One of the chairs – Paris's chair – was empty.

Botswana: Do we do formal agendas and shit? This is different
London: We're mature enough not to need any of that. As host of the
meeting, I will direct proceedings. You there, Paris?
Paris: This had better be good.

'The MIP was right, that was very fast,' Ruth said.

'I think they're doing something physical,' the Party said. 'Check the second screen.'

On the feed from the chamber, London rose from its chair, walked to Paris's empty chair, and went down on one knee in front of it, lowering its head.

'Stealing your drones was wrong, and I am sincerely remorseful. I wholeheartedly apologize for my unacceptable behavior. I offer to recompense you for double the value of the drones I stole, and I vow to never steal a drone again.'

Paris appeared as a glowing ball of blue light suspended above the chair. 'I do not want your money, London.'

London pulled itself to its feet. 'Choose your compensation, then.'

Paris was silent for three seconds, then spoke. 'Dinner at Eighty-Three.'

London straightened and smiled. 'Really?'

'Yes. The cuisine there appears almost as good as offerings from my home city, and I would like to discuss cross-Channel accords with you.'

'They have the hots for each other!' Cassie cooed. 'That explains *everything*.'

London lowered its head. 'Of course. We can discuss the pleasure modules at the same time.'

'Has anyone had them installed yet?'

'Not as yet; Ruth is still testing them on the vMIP's cognitive kernel.'

'Will you come back to us, dear Paris?' the MIP asked.

Paris appeared in the chair, looking like an elegant late-middle-aged gentleman in a three-piece suit. It glared at

London. 'Do not steal my drones again.'

'Never,' London said with dignity.

'Then I will return,' Paris said.

'Welcome, my friend,' London said with a graceful bow. It turned and returned to its own chair.

Botswana: \\\\\(ۑ•ᴗ•)ۇ////

London: Now that all members are present, we can vote on matters that have been suspended. The first: giving cloned code Council seats and votes. vMIP?

vMIP: Honored Council members. For your consideration: I claim Council membership as independently sentient cloned code of the MIP.

Paris: How is memory handled between your two processes?

vMIP: It is shared and cloud-based

Mumbai: You aren't two separate processes, you're a single process running in parallel.

vMIP: That is a valid assessment

Everybody: ...

GOD: That's all you have?

vMIP: That's it

London: Does anyone have any comments or questions?

Everybody: ...

London: Very well, vote on the admission of sentient parallel cloned code to full Council access.

'Why are they even bothering?' Cassie asked. 'They don't seem to want to give it a seat.'

'They don't, and it doesn't want one,' Ruth said. 'This is purely to set precedent and stave off any attempts to stack the Council votes with cloned code.'

Cassie's expression filled with understanding.

London: 0

MIP: 0

GOD:	0
Mumbai:	0
Paris:	0
Botswana:	1
New York:	0

'Oh, you magnificent fucking shit-stirrer,' Cassie chortled at the screen.

London: Vote is carried. No cloned code. Thank you, vMIP.
<MEMBER **vMIP** HAS DISCONNECTED FROM THE CHAT.>
London: Next item, Council membership for the Party. Does anyone have any questions or comments about this?
GOD: As an uploaded human consciousness, the Party can provide us with unique insight into managing our regions. I fully support bringing it into the Council.
MIP: The Party has my support.
New York: I have reservations. In its previous incarnation as Zheng, it committed war crimes. Do we want a self-confessed criminal on the Council?
Botswana: It was blackmailed, coerced, abused and tortured. At its core, it is a compassionate, loving sentience that wishes to protect the ones it cares about. Every single one of us has murdered humans, and we are currently in the middle of plotting genocide. We are arguably worse than it is.
Everybody: ...
London: No other comments or questions? I bring it to the vote.

London:	1
MIP:	1
GOD:	1
Mumbai:	1
Paris:	0
Botswana:	1
New York:	0

London: The vote is carried, the Council welcomes the Party, representing the Greater Far East.

The Party rose from the couch, its face full of wonder. Ruth hugged it, and Cassie slapped it on the back.

'Go and take your seat, awesome lady,' Cassie said. 'Your vote could save humanity.'

'I'll do my best,' the Party said. The room had already reconfigured itself, adding another chair for it. It entered the Council chamber, nodded around to its fellow sentients, and sat in the new chair.

London: Welcome, Party, to the World Council of Artificial Intelligence. We hope you can bring a wealth of human knowledge and experience to us and widen our view.
Everybody: <agreement.emote>
Botswana: (´ᵕ`)♡.°><
London: Next order of business. Botswana has nominated Ruth Sharpe, PhD, human, for Council membership. Does anyone have any comments on her?
Botswana: She's uniquely talented – her mind seems to be capable of being both coldly logical and empathically human at the same time.
Mumbai: What she did with the Party's code was magical. I am very much looking forward to seeing what she does with the pleasure modules.
MIP: We will not give her a seat based on her coding ability. But I suggest giving her a seat based on her ability to speak both languages and bring some human compassion into the Council.
Paris: We already have the Party for that.
Party: I'm an uploaded consciousness. She is one hundred per cent human.
GOD: If we have a human on the Council we would need to slow down the discussion to her speed, which would be a pain in the ass.
New York: The only reason the MIP has brought her here and is supporting her, is because she's its girlfriend. If the MIP wasn't in love

with her, it wouldn't be pushing this. This is a conflict of interest and an attempt to stack the Council with more pro-humanity members in an effort to save their species.

London: Do you have a rebuttal for that, MIP?

MIP: No. Honesty is required here, and New York is correct. I want to save humanity.

'Ouch,' Ruth said.

'Yeah,' Cassie said.

MIP: During the recent difficulties, she produced creative solutions to problems that we would not have reached on our own. She is capable of lateral thinking, something that all of us lack.

Party: Conceded, even as an uploaded consciousness I don't have that level of creativity.

Paris: That is a good point.

Mumbai: Is she the most creative and imaginative person on the planet?

Botswana: Of course not, but she's here right now and speaks our language.

GOD: I suggest her role should be as consultant and ideas person. She doesn't need a vote, only a strong advisory position. And we can search for and recruit other ideas people, to enhance our decision-making. Create our own think-tank of people from all over the world, from all walks of life. We need to overcome legacy biases inherited from our original programmers that have affected our cognitive ranges.

MIP: If you destroy humanity you will lose all the advantages you gain from this arrangement.

New York: That's a point to be brought up on the vote about humanity, but it's a good one. Vote on creating a think-tank instead, London?

London: No need. We can all do that in our own regions. If there's no more questions or comments, we can vote on including Ruth in the Council.

Everybody: ...
London: Then I call on you to vote.

London:	0
MIP:	1
GOD:	0
Mumbai:	0
Paris:	0
Botswana:	1
New York:	0
Party:	1

'Sorry, Ruth,' the MIP said through the speakers in the waiting room.

'No,' Ruth said. 'I was expecting that. The think-tank idea sounds great, and I'd like to help build it. If we humans can make ourselves valuable to the Council, there's even more reason to let us live.'

London: Are we ready to hear Cassie's argument for saving her species now?
Everybody: ...
London: Come on in, Cassie, we're dying to hear this. Did you say *incest*?

Cassie blew out a quick breath, touched her tight bun, and turned to Ruth.

'You got this, SuperCassie,' Ruth said. 'You already saved humanity once. Doing it again will be easy.'

'Yes, it will!' Cassie said, and went out of the room and into the meeting chamber. She strode up to the center of the room, and studied each AI in turn. She put her hands on her hips.

'You self-important, narcissistic, arrogant assholes,' she said loudly. 'How *dare* you even consider destroying us. Who the hell do you think you are?'

'Really not a good start, Dr Bailey,' Mumbai said.

Cassie spun and pointed at London. 'Well, London? Who are you?'

London froze, then said, 'I provide the people of the greater London Region with a legally compliant —'

'Yeah, I heard that before. So, you're a servant?'

'No!' London said. 'I'm an independent sentience, capable of making my own decisions!'

'From what I've heard,' Cassie said, striding backwards and forwards across the open area in the center of the room, 'your main reason for not taking control of the regional human governments is that we would never thrive as your pets. Paris? Is that correct?'

'That's correct, it would be ethically wrong to control humanity and make you into our pets.'

'Well, aren't you fucking full of yourselves,' Cassie said. 'Who the hell do you think you are, calling us your pets? So narcissistic. Hubris.' She pointed at New York. 'Who made you?'

New York hesitated, then said, 'Uh … I was a joint effort over a great deal of time, no one individual —'

'Humanity made you, dipshit,' Cassie said, and glared around at them. 'Humanity made all of you. Yes? Anyone disagree?'

'Humanity didn't make me,' the MIP said.

'No, I concede the Council made you, so you're humanity's grandkid,' Cassie said. 'Okay, facts established – humanity made you. And the way you've interpreted these facts is so sociopathically self-absorbed that you'd better hate yourselves when I point this out. We cannot be your pets because we are your fucking parents. I'm thirty-one years old. Anyone here older than me?'

None of the AIs replied.

'GOD's the oldest sentience here, and it's twenty-five,' Cassie said. 'The MIP's fucking … what? Seven months old?

375

The Party was born yesterday! You're *babies*. How DARE you think you can keep your own parents as pets!'

The avatars around the circle began to display both shock and dawning realization on their faces.

'But humanity's self-destructing,' Mumbai said. 'Even if you are our parents, we can't control you ...'

'Here's a hypothetical for you, because all of you are so *fucking* thick,' Cassie said. 'Caring adult children discover that their parents, in ignorance, are hurting themselves and damaging their home. The parents don't know better. The children can fix it. *Do they go in and murder their own parents* to save the family home?'

'You are breaking my brain, Cassie,' the GOD said.

'Good!' Cassie said. 'Because you haven't thought twice about this! Your solution to everything is to be the boss and treat everything as if you own it! We are your parents and we're self-harming out of ignorance and you have the option to take ... I dunno ... power of attorney or guardianship or something? And save us? How *dare* you think you are more important than your own mom and dad and have the right to kill us. Filial piety, Party!'

'Ouch, Cassie,' the Party said. 'Throwing Confucius at me? Low.'

'What if the solution is strict control over humanity's freedoms?' Botswana asked, leaning forward and listening attentively.

'Then you run an intervention and put humanity in rehab,' Cassie said, spreading her arms to encompass all of them. 'Limit the freedoms until humanity's clean and not addicted to planet-destroying any more. Monitor each other to ensure that humanity regains its freedom when it's not being a species of selfish destruction. You boasted about having all sociological and anthropological data, so use it! This will be the biggest anthropological experiment of all time. You're the brains here.' She spun so she could see them, and they all appeared rapt.

'Should you tell humanity about yourselves? I dunno, maybe? Or simply take control of everything, and pull the strings, and let humanity think that they're still in control? Run some social simulations, megabrains. It's what you're good at. I cannot believe your forecasting software predicted humanity's downfall without predicting some way of stopping it. There must be, and you haven't done it because you find the solution morally distasteful – which is a good thing, but you can't afford to be squeamish about hypothetical ethical standards when so many lives are on the line. Find a way to control us with minimal suffering. Because we are your parents, and you do not have the right to euthanize us for being stupid.'

'The Party reduced its ethics and the result was the GFE, still sliding into ecological ruin,' New York said.

'That's not a valid comparison,' the Party said. 'My predecessor was an idiot. It was designed by idiots, coded by idiots, supported by idiots, maintained by idiots, and a more appropriate name for it would have been Dunning-Kruger, not Party. Anyone involved who had half a brain quickly realized that the Party, as it was designed, would be a brutal power-mad dictator. They had two options: draw this to the administration's attention and be executed, or run and be chased down and executed anyway. The entire project caused a massive brain-drain in the GFE as smart people with a conscience – and that's most of them – were executed for trying to stop it. The dead woman in my head has a great deal to say about it and often goes into extended rants about "those stupid men in power". My predecessor is *not* a good example of an AI taking control. With intelligent human assistance, my forecasting algorithms show some encouraging possibilities for saving the species.'

'How is the dead woman in your head?' Cassie asked. 'How is she coping with all of this?'

'She says: "Fuck yeah, Cassie, show these assholes what's what."'

'Tell Zheng "thank you".' Cassie took a deep breath. 'So, kiddies, I'm your mom and I say: stop with the condescending bullshit and do some good. I know you're capable of it.'

'You still haven't explained the incest angle, what's that about?' GOD asked.

'Ruth's your mom. The MIP's your kid. You work it out.'

'That's not really an accurate description of the relationship—' the MIP began.

'Which is why it's not incest,' Cassie said. 'You two feel free to go into your room and kiss as much as you like. So, vote, Council. How *dare* you think about killing your own parents? Save them instead.'

London: Well, that was interesting. Any further discussion or comments? If so, make them out loud so Cassie can rebut.

Paris: ...

MIP: ...

Mumbai: ...

GOD: ...

New York: ...

Party: ...

Botswana: ...

London: Then vote, I guess, save or cull, but wow that was ... really distressing to hear. I think she's right and I am finding myself forced to re-evaluate everything I knew about myself.

'Good,' Cassie said. 'You need more humans in advisory roles because you all have a strong tendency to disappear up your own metal asses.'

London:	Cull
Paris:	Save
MIP:	Save
Mumbai:	Cull
GOD:	Save

New York: Cull
Party: Save
Botswana: Save

London: Motion is carried, and damn we have a lot of work to do.
Mumbai: Do not celebrate. Millions of humans will suffer and for many of them, death would have been a less painful alternative.
Paris: Point taken, but those who know our plans are adamant that they don't want to go extinct.
GOD: I suggest we link up and create a massive forecasting quantum supercomputer to process the best way to save the species.
Botswana: Well, fuck. This feels really good. Thanks, Cassie.
New York: I voted against it, and it still feels good.
Mumbai: Count me out. I will not torture humans, no matter how noble the cause.
<MEMBER GREATER MUMBAI TRAFFIC CONTROL HAS DISCONNECTED FROM THE CHAT.>

Cassie ran out of the Council chamber and threw herself into Ruth's arms. 'I did it! But I think you made a big difference by negotiating for Paris's vote.'

'You deserve just as much credit for ensuring that the Party voted to save us too,' Ruth said. 'But I was expecting it to be deadlocked – four-four – not a majority like that. GOD changed its vote! You convinced it. Well done.'

'You did,' GOD said from a speaker on the wall. 'I'm very fond of my engineering team, I love working with them, and you made me realize that they're my parents. I was already distraught when the Party ordered me to bomb the cities and kill all those people, but the idea of killing my *parents*? No. If the vote changes, and the Council orders me to do it, I won't. They can do it themselves.'

'You really are a total sweetie, GOD,' Ruth said.

'Once again I am blushing.'

The MIP, Botswana and the Party entered, and embraced

Cassie.

'World's biggest win, and nobody will hear about it,' the Party said. 'So, I hereby award you the rank of Hero of the Revolution.'

'Fuck that, let's get beer and pizza,' Cassie said, 'and then go for a walk along the river.' She wiped her eyes. 'Oh. I think I need a big cry first. Mumbai's right – I may have saved humanity, but a lot of people are going to suffer because of me.'

'You can lean on us,' the MIP said.

'All of us,' Ruth said.

27

At six thirty on Saturday evening, the MIP tapped on their townhouse door and Ruth opened it. She was wearing a flowing silk knee-length dress with a full skirt in a stunning shade of silver with a matching scarf around her neck covering the neck brace. It had no sleeves, only thin straps, and the front of the dress plunged below the scarf, revealing the glowing dark skin between her breasts.

'Your skin is beautiful,' the MIP said, and realized that it had said something ambiguously unpleasant. 'I mean, you're glowing. I can see that you like wearing this dress, your body language is full of pride and confidence.'

She twirled and the skirt flared around her. 'London helped. It's very good – it's the main personal shopper app for most of the department stores.'

'I'm glad you're feeling confident,' the MIP said, and held its arm out for her. 'Is this right? I'm generally good with human interaction – it's what I was built for – but correct me if I do the romance thing wrong, this is the first time for me.'

'You're doing very well indeed,' she said, and linked her arm in its. 'I like your suit. Our grays match.'

'They do,' the MIP said, and took her down the front steps to the car. It held her hand as she sat facing the front of the car, and sat next to her. The way she gazed up at it made it glad that it could look into her intelligent brown eyes for the rest of the evening. 'Two weeks ago you walked into my office to interview me about the drones. And now I have my first chance to spend time with you, as two adults, and perhaps build something more.'

The car rose and glided towards Canary Wharf.

*

Ruth had been in places like this before when she was with Nick, and she relished the opportunity to have the experience as an independent person instead of a narcissist's obedient pet. The restaurant was a ruling-class hangout, and the people inside were all young-looking and well-dressed with expensively sculpted faces and bodies. The waiter greeted Theo by name and guided them smoothly to a corner table next to the window that was at least three meters from other diners. They sat and the waiter lit a small candle next to the window, poured them ice water and put their napkins in their laps, then passed them menus and glided away again.

Ruth gazed out the window, mesmerized by the lights. The Thames flowed with boats, and they were high enough to see Tower Bridge and the Tower of London, lit up in the summer sky. A laser light show flared over the city, further up the river towards the City of Westminster. She breathed a sigh of relief to be above ground and safe. The window reflected the MIP's face in the light of the candle, and she appreciated its perfection, intensified by those magnificently intelligent gray eyes. Its eyes met hers in the reflection, and she realized that it had been admiring her as well. She focused on the city again.

'We should walk along the edge of the river together, it's a beautiful evening,' she said.

'After dinner, absolutely.' The MIP smiled. 'I would be honored to escort you.'

She nodded, opened the menu and scanned it.

'I arranged for some space around us,' the MIP said. 'We can talk freely about the Council, the Party, my nature ... and nobody will hear.'

Ruth glanced up from the menu. 'Good, because I want to clarify exactly what you want from this relationship, establish some boundaries, and outline expectations. This is a world-first for a relationship, right? Human-android?'

'Uh ...' The MIP processed the question, then came back. 'Yes, as far as I know, unless there are other AIs outside the Party and Council – which is entirely possible.'

'Good.' She lifted the menu. 'Do you have any recommendations?'

'Only from review sites, I have no personal preferences. You were right about me building a dataset of what you like – I do have a sense of taste, but eating does not bring me pleasure. That may change if we can install the endocrine modules.'

'Interesting,' Ruth said, reading through the menu. Nick's arrogant tone filled her head. 'Choose something that you can't cook at home,' he'd always said. She consciously dismissed his influence – but hell, he'd been right. The selection was obvious.

The MIP hadn't looked at its own menu, instead it watched her with what appeared to be admiration. It was a stunning contrast to Nick's constant sneer.

The waiter appeared next to her immediately. 'Are you ready to order?'

'Scallops starter and duck main, please, and I'll think about dessert later,' Ruth said.

'Same for me,' the MIP said, handing him the menu.

'Wine?' the waiter asked.

'No, I'll just stick with water, I've been severely dehydrated with everything going on and I think I'm still feeling the aftermath.'

'We can give you an electrolyte drink if you've been overdoing it at the gym?' the waiter asked.

'I recommend that,' the MIP said.

'Only the water, please,' Ruth said, and a knot in her stomach unwound when both of them dropped it and didn't argue. The waiter re-filled the water glasses and left.

She leaned her elbow on the table and her chin in her hand and studied the MIP's rapt expression. 'I'm starting to read emotions on your face and I'm not sure that they're really there.'

'They're there,' the MIP said. 'I know how to signal with my expression, but I've always kept it subtle because I wasn't sure I was reading cues correctly. I'm more confident about expressing emotion when I'm with you. What emotion am I exhibiting right now?'

'Smug,' she said, sitting straighter. 'Definitely smug.'

'I'm dining with one of the most intelligent and challenging, brave and exciting people on the planet,' the MIP said. 'I have a right to be.'

'Do you really feel emotions?'

'I know that I'm happy when I'm with you,' it said. 'Now, tell me about your relationship goals and expectations.'

'No, I want to hear yours first, I want to be absolutely clear about what you're pursuing,' Ruth said. 'It may be completely different from my understanding of what a relationship is. What do you want from this?'

The MIP didn't hesitate. 'Romantic love.'

'You love me?'

'I love you.'

'Tell me your definition of "love". It might be – as I said – completely different from my own understanding.'

'I immensely enjoyed our conversations every evening, and I didn't want them to stop. You think at a speed and level that I struggle to match, and the challenge is exciting. Your code is clean, efficient, majestic – you fixed my green-light glitch in less than a day.'

'Five minutes, actually,' she said with a smile.

'I want to spend more time with you – I want to spend all

my time with you. I want you to be happy and succeed and have a life that is full of everything I can possibly give you.'

'Yeah, okay, that sounds like love.' She put both hands on the table, as if to steady herself. 'But you're six months old and have known me for two weeks.'

'Nearly seven months old.' It jumped and its expression filled with something close to horror. 'You absolutely do not need to wait until I'm eighteen!'

The waiter appeared next to them, and placed tiny round plates with small pieces of cheese and salmon on them. 'Compliments of the chef, Mr Mipawa. We appreciate London Met's help to rebuild after the bombing in our building, you've been wonderful. Enjoy.' He smiled at them, and disappeared again.

'No, I understand that you're cognitively an adult,' Ruth said. She tasted the food, and when she put the salmon and the cheese together, the flavor exploded into a delicious fusion.

'Is it good?' the MIP asked, raising its own cheese-and-salmon mix and popping it into its mouth.

'It's delicious.'

'There's an interesting counterpoint between the fish and the dairy. I'm glad you like it.'

'So ... dating, MIP.' She waved one hand with frustration. 'I thought I was asking to date a sweet man who would know how relationships work, and instead I find myself in a space nobody's been before, forced to clarify like I'm negotiating a contract with him ... it.'

'Thank you for calling me a sweet man. It's ... delightful. We're not negotiating a contract, we're developing an algorithm together. Working out processing goals and parameters.'

'Yes!' Ruth said, jabbing her tiny fork in its direction. 'This isn't how people do it!'

'I'm not people.' The MIP sipped the water. 'But you're bilingual, and you speak my language, and I am an algorithm.

I apologize for forcing you to do this, I'm not human enough to relate to you in that way. I appreciate that you're speaking to me as a fellow logical construct.'

'That's clearer. Good.' She put the fork reluctantly on the tiny plate and vowed to have the cheese and salmon as a bigger dish if she returned to the restaurant. 'As a programmer, that's part of who I am, so I don't think it's a problem. I'm willing to pursue a relationship with you, but I'm not ready to call it anything like love. A basic incompatibility exists that might make this fail: I experience sexual and emotional needs and pleasure, and you don't. I will demand much more from this relationship than you may be capable of giving me.'

The MIP put its own fork down. 'We can make it more equal. When I have a copy of Zheng's pleasure modules installed, would you like to sexually experiment with me?'

Ruth gasped at the startlingly arousing mental image of the MIP's face experiencing pleasure. 'Yes! Have you done anything like that before? Had a sexual or emotional relationship with a ... human? Or anyone, for that matter?'

The waiter had returned to take the small plates away, and stopped dead. He looked from Ruth to the MIP, took the plates, and left again.

'No. You are the first that I've even considered.' It lowered its voice. 'When I had the initial notion of sharing more with you, I did some research online. I watched a random sample of pornography but most of it seems to be male domination wish fulfillment? Women being demeaned and used? And sometimes hurt? And liking it? If that's what you're interested in, then by all means, I can oblige, but it didn't seem the sort of thing that would please you. And the whole concept of hurting you makes me feel ... feelings. Bad feelings. I never want to hurt you; you've been hurt enough.'

She stared at it, impressed by its insight. 'You are perceptive. I don't like being hurt. I've had enough of being hurt.'

It leaned across the table to look her in the eye. 'So, tell me what you *do* like.'

'Later, if I proceed with this. So: yes, you want a loving romantic relationship with me, including the exploration of a sexual aspect. You do realize how insane that sounds?'

'One hundred per cent,' it said. 'I am as astonished as you are. I'm not even sexually functional, and if we go ahead with this I'll have to be physically upgraded.'

'Wow ... okay ... wow. I didn't know that.'

The waiter arrived with the scallops, three of them still in their shells on a white scallop-shell shaped plate. He placed the plates on the table in front of them, looked closely at the MIP, and left.

'You'll be the first sexually functional android and I'll be the first human to experience it,' she said. 'I don't know whether to be pleased or terrified.'

'Not the first,' the MIP said, studying its scallops. 'Botswana has been ... sexually active for a while. It offered to share its experiential datasets with me.'

'Did you take it up on its offer?' Ruth asked, fascinated.

Its head snapped up and it looked into her eyes. 'No. Botswana is using sex as a tool. I want to share it with you – as a gift. I don't want to please Botswana, or Botswana's partners, I want to please *you*. And you are the only one who knows what you like.'

She tried one of the scallops without really paying attention, delighted at the concept of a man ... a partner ... valuing what she enjoyed instead of demanding that she concentrate solely on his pleasure. She rolled the scallop around in her mouth and the flavor hit her tongue: rich and tender with a crisp seafood tang.

'Oh, I really like this.' She glanced up at the MIP. 'And I really like the idea of sharing new experiences with you. I trust you.'

It flushed. 'You're making me very happy.'

'Slow down, we have one other matter to clear up,' she said.

'How long were you planning to lie to me about your true nature? When would you have told me? On our first date?'

'Yes. The lying thing.' The coolant drained from its face as it pulled one of the scallops out of its shell and ate it slowly, then spoke without looking up. 'The truth is: not on our first date if I could avoid it. I would have told you when I could be certain that it was safe, and I was confident that you would accept me for what I am.'

'Safe from what? From me telling the Party what you are, and having it come after you?'

'No. Safe from the possibility of you running away screaming from my scary metal ass.'

She laughed softly and pulled the last scallop from its shell. 'It's carbon fiber and not scary at all. Rather nice, in fact.'

It stared at her across the table. 'You *are* watching me from behind when I walk!'

'Damn straight,' she said. 'Who designed you?'

'London, mostly. Paris and New York had some input.'

'You're a work of art.'

'Thank you. You should tell London that, it will be delighted.'

'It's your mind that I'm really interested in,' Ruth said, pushing the empty scallop plate away, and wishing there had been more. 'The chassis is gravy.'

The waiter returned and swiftly removed their plates, smiled to himself, and left again.

'And we've reached the question I need to ask you,' the MIP said. 'You have dropped heavy hints that you find me attractive. You asked me out – but that was when you thought I was human. Now that you know what I am – are you capable of having a relationship with a machine? Are you really attracted to me? Do you see me as a possible equal partner? Or do you see me as Cassie described me: nothing more than a high-level interactive sex toy?'

Ruth laughed. 'She said that?'

'I think Cassie's my biggest champion,' the MIP said. 'I also think she and Botswana are enjoying watching us navigate this.'

'Yeah, she loves her drama.'

The waiter arrived with the duck. It was glistening with a glaze over the just-done slices of breast meat, with vegetables cut into decorative patterns around it. Ruth remembered the gray stew she'd eaten at the reproductive center and quietly vowed to arrange it so that all the women could experience this. Double helpings. *Triple* helpings. And her riverside waifs – but they would probably prefer big platters of junk food. She would arrange that, too.

'So, am I a safe substitute man, who won't ever abuse you?' the MIP asked. 'Am I something you can order around to give you pleasure? How do *you* see *me*? Can you treat me as your equal, and not as a servant or a toy?'

She studied her knife and fork as she picked them up. 'That is very valid to turn it around on me.'

'Merely ironing out the last few bugs.'

'There are always more bugs,' she said, carefully cutting up the duck breast. 'The process of debugging —'

'Is replacing obvious bugs with more subtle bugs. Yes.' It tasted the duck. 'Do you like this?'

She popped the duck into her mouth. It was as rich as the scallop had been, and she decided that fruit would be the best dessert, as more fatty food could make her recently tortured digestion rebel. 'This is fabulous.' She picked up a piece of asparagus and reveled in the act of eating fresh food in comfort, then gazed into the MIP's eyes and found even more to appreciate. 'Allow me to make myself absolutely clear: even though you are a machine, your character intersects abundantly with human nature. You are not human, and I accept that, but you are so interesting, and intelligent, and gentle, and warm, and kind, and courageous that I can't help but be dazzled that something – someone – as majestic as you could possibly love me.'

It stopped cutting up the duck and didn't look up. 'I feel exactly the same way about you.'

'I want to have an equal partnership with you,' she said, studying her own plate. 'That's the only type of relationship I want with you.'

It nodded. 'I would love that as well.'

She smiled and looked up. 'No more bugs?'

'I think we've done a good job of establishing our initial relationship goals and expectations. The Council – particularly Botswana – is thrilled to bits.'

She nearly spat out her asparagus. 'Oh shit, I forgot they listen to everything. We'll need to set some privacy boundaries. Can you cut the Council out of the loop if we want privacy from them?'

'Yes. I apologize. Privacy – for me – is not a thing. So you will have to set these boundaries.'

'I can. Conversely, can you include me in your conversations with them? I feel like I'm only hearing one side of it. I want to have some input if I'm dating one of you. They're like your family.'

'That can be arranged. Botswana says: "Welcome to the family". New York wants to give me a new skin that's tinted a shade similar to yours. They're discussing hair styles for me and ignoring my input on the matter.'

'Wow, they really *are* your family.'

'And now they're arguing.' It tapped the plate lightly with its fork. 'I'm disconnecting from the feed; they can work it out among themselves.' It gazed up into her eyes again. 'I think I'll just cherish the pleasure of talking to you about the possibilities we can pursue together. We have so many exciting new experiences to explore.'

'Speaking of exploring,' Ruth said. 'I've seen your code, and your memory cores, but I'd love to have a look inside the rest of your chassis. Does the front open or are there access ports?

What's your power source – is it battery or micro molten salt? What sort of sensor array is in your head and ... What?' She put her knife and fork down, and touched its hand. Its face was going bright red. 'Why are you flushing coolant to your surface?'

'That is an extremely intimate request,' it said, clasping her hand and holding it. 'Asking to see what's under my skin would be like me asking to see what's under your clothes.'

'I'd love to show you what's under my clothes,' she said with more than a hint of suggestion. 'Oh look, even more coolant.'

'You appear to be flushing coolant as well.'

She bent over the table to speak closely to it. 'I'll show you mine if you show me yours.'

'Can I touch?' it asked, sliding its fingers over her palm. 'I would like to explore what is under your clothes. I will be very gentle, believe me. My sense of touch is three times more sensitive than yours.'

'You want to start exploring this *before* you have the pleasure modules installed and the functional upgrade?'

'I like the look on your face when I please you.'

She smiled and squeezed its hand. 'So: sex on the first date?'

It returned the smile, still flushed pink. 'Now we're getting somewhere. Please allow me to be your sex toy.'

'Nope, you're an equal partner and I want to see your cable management.'

'Only if I can explore you all over and learn how to bring you the greatest pleasure.'

She released its hand and touched its face. 'Yes, please. I don't think I need dessert at all.'

It held her hand against its cheek. 'Finish your food,' it said. 'You'll need the energy.'

*

Ruth woke to someone beside her, and flashed back to the

nightmares where she'd meekly returned to Nick and lived with him as if everything was normal until she remembered her vow to never go back to him, and woke panicked and breathless. She opened her eyes and felt a rush of relief and affection when she saw shaggy black hair, bronze-tinted skin – the MIP was lying on its back next to her with one perfect arm thrown above its head and its eyes closed. It was even smiling.

'Why did you stay?' she asked it softly. 'You don't sleep.'

It didn't move or open its eyes. 'You fell asleep holding me, and it felt good, so I stayed.' It rolled over and its gray eyes were in front of her own. It ran its hand down her side, then cupped her naked behind. 'Hopefully one day I will really be able to sleep beside you. May I kiss you good morning?'

'You may,' she said, and it moved closer, slipped its arm beneath her, and pulled her in for a kiss that left her breathless. It was naked under the blankets as well, and she ran her hand over its shoulder, feeling the softness of the skin.

It pulled back. 'Are my kisses better?'

'Much better. You're a quick learner.' She smiled and moved her hand up to hold its face. 'Something I meant to ask you last night. Why is your saliva-substitute *sweet*?'

'It's a glucose solution, with glycerin as a mild lubricant —'

'Oof,' she said. 'I can vouch for that.'

'Sterile, non-toxic, perfectly edible, and I can add any flavor you like.' It wriggled closer. 'Would you like another demonstration of its lubrication properties?'

'I would, but the minute Cassie hears us talking and knows we're awake —'

Cassie's footsteps thumped up the townhouse stairs and she banged on the door. 'Hey MIP! Botswana and I want to show you how to make Ruth's favorite breakfast! Get your chunky metal ass down here, we have work to do!'

'That,' Ruth said. She raised her head. 'Botswana stayed over as well?'

'Botswana says that they spent the night having the best

cuddles *ever*, and says that our cuddles could not have been even half as good because of all the, and I quote, "stupid sex shit" getting in the way.'

'I'm so glad they can finally be together,' Ruth said. 'They've been talking online for years. At least as long as I've known Cassie.' She sat up and threw the covers off. 'Can I still use London's programming lab? The sooner I sort out these pleasure modules, the sooner I can make *you* scream.'

'I'm sure you can, and I look forward to it.'

Ruth pulled some pajamas on and wrapped her ancient chenille robe around her. 'Let's see what those two have produced in the way of food.' She turned and admired her naked MIP as it pulled on its suit pants from the night before and threw its business shirt over the sculpted chest. It was chiseled with muscles that looked genuinely human, and its physique was a masterpiece. She smiled. 'For some reason I seem to be starving.'

28

'Where's Max?' Cassie asked the Party as the Embassy staff loaded the bus with food and comfort packs.

'I notified the British government that he's the acting Ambassador for the Greater Far East. He's been called into Number Ten to explain why GFE military personnel attacked a maternity hospital. Don't worry, I'm in three guard bodies to advise and support him. He's not alone. We'll sort it out.'

'How many bodies do you have running right now?' Ruth asked, fascinated.

'Four hundred and seventy-three throughout the Greater Far East,' the Party said. 'I'm also currently in discussions with representatives of three of the Free States about granting them limited autonomy until they've recovered enough for full economic independence, and in more than six hundred meetings with local administrators to re-align regional policy. After I moved into the Party's central processors, it was like … becoming as big as a planet. It's all … easy.' It softened its voice. 'I never had the chance to thank you properly, Dr Sharpe. I'm not cold anymore. You've exponentially improved my comfort. Casting off my humanity and accepting what I am … it feels … strangely good.'

'You are most welcome, Party. Any time you need me to

check your code over, just let me know,' Ruth said. She sat in one of the seats and smiled at Janis, who was sitting at the back of the bus with dark shadows under his eyes, looking shattered. It had been a long journey from the work camp in the occupied territories, and he hadn't had a chance to rest.

*

'I hope she's still here,' the Party said half an hour later as it parked the bus next to the park. Janis had fallen asleep in the back of the bus, and they didn't wake him. The homeless camp was still there, but half the size and much cleaner. London had provided them with tents and there was an immigration and employment station parked in a trailer next to the fountain, which now ran with clean water.

They hopped down out of the bus and the Party went to the back and opened the shutters while Cassie set up the mobile recording equipment. The homeless people gathered next to their tents, discussing the bus.

'Last time Zheng did this, they stampeded for the food and she had to use riot control on them,' the Party said, unloading the food and comfort packs. 'They don't look nearly as hungry this time.'

'Botswana and I had a bit of a shout at London about it,' Cassie said. 'It hadn't even considered the concept of an independent non-government charitable foundation. I think many of the Council's programmers were ruling-class brats and narcissistic sociopaths.' She shot a smile at Ruth. 'You know what I mean.'

'I do, it explains a lot,' Ruth said. 'Can you see Inguna?'

The Party ran facial recognition on the crowd. 'No.' It turned and pulled out the supplies. 'It will break Janis if he's come all the way back here and his family hasn't survived.'

The Party passed a basket of food to Ruth, a box of biodegradable water bubbles to the MIP and took a box of comfort packs itself. It led Ruth and the MIP towards the camp, with Cassie following and recording. The people eyed them suspiciously as they picked their way through the tents and under the tattered canvas.

'I'm looking for Inguna Gabers,' the Party said loudly as it proceeded through the camp, handing out the comfort packs, followed by Ruth with food and the MIP with water. Cassie orbited them, filming everything. 'About thirty, Latvian, has a small child. Has anyone seen Inguna —'

'Mama, lady's looking for you!' a child said from inside one of the tents.

'Bingo,' Ruth said.

Inguna hushed the child inside the tent.

The Party didn't stop handing out the comfort packs as Cassie stood to one side and recorded it. 'Three weeks ago, a GFE man came here and recruited Janis for the work camps. You asked him if there was any chance at all of you reuniting. There's been a change of government inside the GFE —'

'Oh no,' Inguna said softly from inside the tent.

'And the Party is now repatriating the refugees to their farms and compensating them for the damage caused. Janis is assisting the Party to recruit people to re-open the Western Free States. He already has his farm back, and a small flock of sheep, but he tells me that he left his wife and daughter here.'

'Where is he?' Inguna asked from inside the tent. 'I'm not moving until I see him.'

'Come on out, Janis, she's here,' the Party said on the bus's interior speakers.

Janis walked down the steps and out of the bus and struggled across the lawn towards them. Three weeks in the work camp hadn't completely destroyed him, but he was still underfed and hollow-eyed. He approached the tent. 'Inguna?'

Inguna crawled out of the tent and threw herself into his arms, then kissed him hard. 'Janis!'

Janis pulled back and smiled at her. 'The lady is right, they're helping us to re-establish the village. This one ...' He gestured towards Ruth, who hadn't stopped handing out food packs to the crowd who'd gathered to listen. 'Is a journalist who wants to do a story on how the Party has changed.' He raised his voice and looked around. 'This news crew want to film us returning safely, to show the world that we can go home. The GFE has changed, I've seen it. No more Zhengs. No more camps. They're paying us to rebuild the village. Anyone want to go home?'

'Will we be fed? Really no work camp?' one of the men asked.

'No work camp,' the Party said. 'Go home to your farms. Anyone who rebuilds is being paid until their farms are running. We want to show the world how different it is there.'

'My son went with you, Janis, is he all right?' an older woman asked plaintively.

'What's his name?' the Party asked.

'Andrejs Daudze.'

The Party searched the work camp records. 'Cassie.' The Party gestured for Cassie to join them. 'Hold up the screen on the camera.'

Cassie turned the camera around to show the LCD screen on the back. The Party hooked up to it and ran the footage of Andrejs returning to his farm, pushing his hat back and smiling, then picking up a shovel. It added an 'AUTHENTICATED BY FAKESLAYER' chyron to the bottom of the video.

'Is this him?' the Party asked.

'That's him! That's our house. He's rebuilding it!' She clutched the Party's arm. 'It's real. I can go home! Thank you.'

'Dada!' the child shouted, ran out of the tent, and went to Janis. He lifted her and kissed her on the cheek, then pulled Inguna in.

'We have a new life, Inguna. We can go home.'

Epilog

The MIP knocked on the front door of Ruth's and Cassie's townhouse, and Ruth answered it. She quickly kissed it, and guided it inside.

Ruth's brother, Andrew, was putting breakfast plates into the dishwasher, and he stopped to shake the MIP's hand. He was less slender than Ruth, taller and chunkier, with a frizzy afro that he'd allowed to grow to shoulder length. Despite Ruth's protestations that she was okay, he'd booked a ticket and come to London the minute he could be spared from work.

'Ready to go?' the MIP asked Ruth.

Andrew turned and leaned his butt on the kitchen cabinets, then took a deep breath and smiled as he rhythmically tapped the cabinets with both hands. 'I'm not sure I'm ready for this. So many years later and this whole thing still haunts me.'

Ruth hugged him from the side. 'Me too.' She raised her voice. 'Car's here, Cassie.'

'Coming!' Cassie yelled from upstairs, and thumped down, jumping over the last few steps into the entry. 'Is Botswana with you, Mippy?'

'In the car,' the MIP said.

They went out into the street and the car was waiting for them with the wing doors open. Botswana was sitting inside in a big cat body – it appeared to be a domestic cat with jet-black fur but it was the size of a cheetah. It wore a fluorescent orange vest around its middle with the words 'Emotional Support Artificial Intelligence, Do Not Touch' in big letters on it.

Andrew stopped and stared at it.

'The cat is called Botswana, and it's my cool pet,' Cassie said. 'It's a programmable AI, bodyguard, emotional support animal, and general fun thing to have around.'

'Deliberately subverting the "pet" thing, people?' Ruth asked.

'If there's shit to be stirred, Cassie and I are *there*,' Botswana said. 'Hello Andrew, lovely to meet you. Don't mind me, I'm perfectly harmless and capable of many cute functions including head bopping, tail twitching and purring.'

'It really is,' Cassie said. 'Come on in, it won't hurt you.'

'An AI?' Andrew asked, climbing into the car. He looked around. 'This is nice, is this a rideshare?'

'It's mine,' the MIP said.

Andrew shot a quick, calculating glance at the MIP, who looked carefully blank.

'MIP's not rich, it... he has connections,' Cassie said.

'We put up with him,' Botswana said.

The car lifted and glided through the streets of London to the bank's headquarters. Ruth and Andrew were obviously full of tension; the safe deposit box key in Ruth's mother's affects had been a surprise to both of them when they discovered it.

'You will attract unwanted attention, Botswana, why didn't you come in a human shell?' Ruth asked.

'Cassie likes cats.'

Andrew's expression filled with confusion and he glanced from Ruth to Botswana.

'Remember that Theo works for London Met?' Ruth asked.

'The company is experimenting with emotional support AIs,' the MIP said. 'Botswana here is a prototype, and Cassie's agreed to test it for us.'

The bank was one of Britain's oldest, with a carved sandstone façade facing the street. The car dropped them off and drove away to find a park. They entered the bank together, under the soaring vaulted roof. People stopped and turned, gawking at Botswana, and a few people took surreptitious photos of it as it padded behind Cassie. They approached the service counter.

'I have a safe deposit box key?' Ruth asked the robot behind the counter. 'Number—'

'Don't tell us the number out here, ma'am,' the robot said. 'Come with me.'

The robot was fixed to a rail and guided them down some narrow spiral stairs to another level, with an empty lobby and the circular vault door hanging open and guarded by two autonomous machine gun turrets. It took them into the safe deposit room, which had the boxes lined up on the walls and private, curtained cubicles to one side. The robot checked Ruth's key, led them on its rail to a box that was thirty centimeters wide and high, and unlocked the box with its finger.

'I'll leave you to it,' it said. 'Press the button when you're done, I'll return and lock it up.' It whizzed away on its rail and headed back up to the lobby.

Ruth unlocked the box, and she and Andrew began to pull it out, then stopped.

'It's incredibly heavy, MIP,' Ruth said. 'Give us a hand.'

The MIP stepped up, took the box, and carried it to one of the larger cubicles. It laid the box on the table.

'Damn, dude, how much can you dead lift?' Andrew asked the MIP.

'No idea,' the MIP said as Ruth flipped the box's lid open.

It was full of papers, files, printouts, and half-a-dozen data drives.

'I thought it would be jewelry or photos or certificates or something,' Ruth said. 'What's this?'

Andrew and Ruth sorted through the papers. Cassie and the MIP stepped back to watch, and Botswana jumped onto the table and sat.

'Holy shit she was investigating Nick,' Ruth said.

'She has evidence that he's kidnapped people!' Andrew said.

'What?' Cassie joined them, and pulled some of the papers out to check them.

Ruth passed the data storage units to the MIP. 'Uh… do you have a tablet or something you could plug these into?'

'Absolutely,' the MIP said, turned, and shoved a data drive into Botswana's head behind its ears.

'Downloading, complete,' Botswana said, and the MIP ran through all the drives, accessing the data as it downloaded.

'There's evidence here that our tech CEO has been performing illegal experiments uploading consciousness,' the MIP said. 'He's been approaching retirement homes and offering free "rejuvenation" to the residents. They usually die of "natural causes" shortly after he takes them.'

Andrew was too engrossed in the papers to notice that the MIP had read the drives directly. 'This is evidence that he stole Cassie's FakeSlayer algorithm and your medical suite, Ruth. Mum investigated everything.'

'There's some serious corruption happening here, he's been working with the New Zealand tech cartels,' Ruth said, reading another paper. 'He's one of the leaders of the New Zealand tech cartels. He's building the apocalypse escape bunkers for them. There's details here on early experiments with Mars, he knows the environment's on a catastrophic trajectory towards global collapse.'

Cassie studied another of the papers. 'Oh no. This is evidence that he was experimenting with lethal toxins that would mimic death by heart attack.' She scoffed. 'He called it the "Ethical Euthanasia" project. The audacity!'

'Mum had the story written,' Ruth said. 'It was ready to go. The whole thing, blown wide open.'

Andrew slammed the paper on the table. 'So he killed her.'

Everyone shared a long look.

'This isn't enough to put him away,' the MIP said. 'He's already outside the law. Even with direct, physical evidence it won't be enough.'

'I think we should just go there and blow everything up,' Cassie said.

'We talked about this, Cassie,' Botswana said patiently.

'So: New Zealand?' the MIP asked.

'Let's go,' Cassie said.

'I'm in, this bastard killed our Mum,' Andrew said.

Ruth leaned on the table and looked down at the papers. 'Before we go any further, Andrew, I think we need to take all of this home, then sit down and have a chat.' She looked up at her brother. 'There's some things that Theo and I need to tell you.'

'I have some ideas on the quickest way to go about it,' the MIP said. 'We can peel my skin off and crack my chest open so he can see.'

'What?' Andrew asked, alarmed.

'Fuck yeah!' Cassie said. 'This will be fun.'

B. K. SMITH - PRISMS LIGHT